BAD
SAIN†

BAD
SAIN✝

VOLUME
ONE

A DARK ROMANCE

International Bestselling Author
MONICA JAMES

BAD SAINT

(All The Pretty Things Trilogy, Volume One)

Cover Design: Perfect Pear Creative Covers
Editing: Editing 4 Indies
Formatting: E.M. Tippetts Book Designs

E.M.
TIPPETTS
BOOK DESIGNS

Follow me on:
monicajamesbooks.blogspot.com.au

OTHER BOOKS BY
MONICA JAMES

THE I SURRENDER SERIES
I Surrender
Surrender to Me
Surrendered
White

SOMETHING LIKE NORMAL SERIES
Something like Normal
Something like Redemption
Something like Love

A HARD LOVE ROMANCE
Dirty Dix
Wicked Dix
The Hunt

MEMORIES FROM YESTERDAY
Forgetting You, Forgetting Me
Forgetting You, Remembering Me

SINS OF THE HEART
Absinthe of the Heart
Defiance of the Heart

ALL THE PRETTY THINGS TRILOGY

Bad Saint

STANDALONE

Mr. Write

AUTHOR'S NOTE

CONTENT WARNING: **BAD SAINT** is Volume One in a Trilogy. The following book in the series will release shortly after the first. This is a continuing story, therefore, not all questions will be answered in Volume One.

BAD SAINT is a DARK ROMANCE containing mature themes that might make some readers uncomfortable. It includes: kidnapping, captivity, strong violence, mild language, and some dark and disturbing scenes.

This twisted tale is not intended for the fainthearted. So, if you're game…welcome to the madness.

God save your soul.

CHAPTER ONE

I don't want to do this, but what choice do I have? She is relying on me to save her...and I won't fail her again. I can't.

Day 1

"Don't drop me."

"I wouldn't dream of it...wife."

"Say it again."

"Wife...wife...wife." Squealing like a love-struck teenager, I kick my legs high in the air as my husband of two days carries me over the threshold.

This ritual holds much significance, and to most, it's probably absurd, but to me, it's absolutely perfect because I just married the most wonderful man. Never in my wildest dreams did I ever think little ole me, Willow Shaw, would marry millionaire Drew Gibbs.

But the thing about Drew is that he doesn't flash his wealth. He doesn't drive an expensive car, nor does he deck himself out in designer threads and flashy gold. He is humble and kind, and when we first locked eyes across that runway, I knew I was done for.

"Welcome home, babe," he says with his boyish, playful charm. "Well, our home away from home for the next two weeks."

Still reeling from the fact I'm on my honeymoon, I gape around in awe at our secluded villa in one of the less populated areas of the Greek Islands. Our wedding at Los Angeles's City Hall was a quick affair, which seems to be the theme for my entire relationship with Drew.

Call me crazy because it's not like I haven't heard it before, but Drew and I met six weeks ago while I was modeling for a local designer in LA. When I stepped out onto that runway and saw Drew sitting in the front row, I just knew our paths had crossed for a reason.

After the show, all the girls were gossiping about a tall, dark, and handsome millionaire, but when that stranger came my way, they could see he only had eyes for me. He asked me out for a drink, and the rest is history.

We spent every waking minute together getting to know one another, and by week two, I was in love. I know what you're thinking, but with a past like mine, you come to learn that time is precious, and when the heavens present you with a gift, you take it.

I was born and bred in a small town in Texas. My father was the local Baptist pastor, and our family was well respected in our community. My parents were high school sweethearts, and together, they shined. But when fate intervened and took my dad away when I was twelve, my mother's light faded.

Dad died of a heart attack. There was nothing the hospital could do. But my mom saw my father's death as a betrayal from the big guy upstairs. She had put her faith in God her whole life, and in return, He took away the love of her life.

My mother changed, turning her back on the church and her friends. Liquor became her new salvation and so did seeking solace in the random men she would bring home late at night from whatever bar she frequented.

I had no one to talk to. I was an only child, and my grandparents lived out of state. The woman passed out on the recliner with a bottle of whiskey dangling from her limp fingers as she mumbled my father's name was someone I no longer recognized.

When I turned thirteen, I began to develop in ways I didn't understand, and things just got worse. As I came from a strict, religious family, my parents never explained what happened when your body changed. I grew tall, lost the baby fat, and my breasts doubled in size.

I hated it because I was no longer daddy's little girl.

Girls at school picked on me, calling me a slut, while the boys suddenly showed interest, wondering if my nickname of "Satan's Whore" was, in fact, true. All in all, I was miserable. And the only person I could talk to seemed to hate the sight of me.

I was the spitting image of my father, a fact my mom once loved, but now, it was a reminder of everything she had lost.

I kept to myself, hoping things would change, and they did when I was fifteen—when my mom moved her new boyfriend, Kenny, into our home. I didn't know what miserable was until I met Kenny Smith.

My mom and I barely spoke as she was too strung out to even notice I was there half the time, but when Kenny arrived, it was like she wanted to have the perfect family once again. But what she didn't know was that Kenny was a predator, a monster lurking in the dark.

At first, he was nice and attentive, showing a real interest in me. But my mother's nightly ritual of going to bed early drugged up on sleeping pills and liquor made his true colors shine. It started out as innocent touching— an accidental bump of my breasts or passing by me too close—but when he came into my bedroom late one night and sat at the foot of my bed, I now know those accidents weren't accidents at all. He was grooming me.

When he questioned if I'd ever kissed a boy before, I told him no. He then asked if I would like to kiss him. Kenny was forty-two. I was fifteen and a half. I didn't understand what he meant, so I leaned over and kissed his cheek. But when he turned his head, and I felt his thick, rubbery lips under mine, I soon realized he wanted more.

I begged him to leave, that I would tell my mom, but he simply laughed. I would never forget that haunting laughter. He said she'd never believe a cock tease like me. And deep down, I knew he was right. So I didn't say anything. I stayed as quiet as a mouse.

After that night when Kenny kissed me, I decided to get a job, working the graveyard shift at a local diner. The pay was good, and it also meant I didn't have to worry about Kenny coming into my room at night.

Working at Lea's Diner was one of the fondest memories I had as a kid. That, and of course my father, but he soon became a distant memory, slowly disappearing as I watched my mother deteriorate before my eyes.

Life was good, well, as good as life could be for a misfit like me. My mom seemed happy I was out of her hair as she had Kenny all to herself, but late one night, everything changed forever.

It was just after two a.m., and I'd finished work a little early. Lea, who I knew from church, usually let me crash for a few hours at her house, which was just behind the diner, until I went to school. But that night, she had to close up late, so I rode my bike home.

I remembered the feeling of tiptoeing through the back door and holding my breath just like it was yesterday, but it was in vain because sitting in my daddy's chair was Kenny. His round belly was poking out of his white tank, sporting a stain down the front from where the whiskey missed his mouth.

When we locked eyes, I knew it. I knew what he wanted. What I'd been avoiding since the night he came into my room. I ran, but he was faster, trapping me under him as he pinned me to the living room floor. His whiskey-soaked breath promised to make me feel real good.

I was so scared I couldn't move. My chest was pressed into the carpet with Kenny's heavy weight on top of me, and I couldn't breathe. And when I felt his disgusting erection dig into my back, I knew my nickname would soon come true.

One hand was down my pants, reaching around the front. The other hand was over my mouth so I wouldn't scream. He bit me on the side of the neck just how a predator would with its prey. He forced my cheek to the carpet, the rough fibers rubbing my skin raw. I squeezed my eyes shut.

I thought of Daddy. Of how he told me to pray when I was scared…so I did.

I prayed that this wasn't happening. That Kenny wasn't unzipping his pants and telling me to be a good little girl. I prayed that my mom would come back to me as the loving mother she once was. I prayed for a miracle and prayed that this vile man wasn't seconds away from raping me, but when I heard a guttural scream and my mother telling me what a dirty slut I was for seducing my stepfather, I knew I would never pray again.

My mom kicked me out—I was a harlot, a whore—and with nowhere else to go, I went to Lea's. My only friend. She never married and didn't have any kids, so she treated me like her own. When I told her what had happened, she insisted we go to the police, but I didn't want to. I just wanted to leave. The day my father died was the day this place did too.

Lea lent me some money, and I hopped on a flight to LA where my grandparents lived. They missed my father terribly and had tried to reach out, but my mother had forbidden them to contact me. I just thought they didn't care.

So I finished school and got a job waiting tables at a local restaurant, which was where I met Raffaella Mercino. She owned Models Inc., the hottest modeling agency in all of LA, and when she asked if I had ever modeled, I laughed in response.

Mom told me I used my looks for evil, but Raffaella showed me I could now use my looks for good.

I don't think I'm anything special, but to this day, Raffaella tells me I'm one of the prettiest girls she has working for her. She said that's because I have an innocent look about me, and all men want to break a good girl. Her analogy is disgusting and sexist, but hey, she seemed to be right because, in six short months, I was one of the most sought-after models.

I'm now twenty-five, but I suppose my looks haven't changed all that much. My long, golden brown hair is naturally wavy. The California sun has brought out the blonde tones, which complement the deep blue of my almond-shaped eyes.

My upturned nose gives my look an air of arrogance, and my lips are full and pouty. Many of the girls I work with are certain I've had a surgical date with Dr. Hollywood, but they're mistaken.

My boobs are bigger than most standard models, and so are my curves. I have an ass and muscular thighs and am proud of it. The yoga exercises I do religiously and the fact I run five miles a day keep my stomach toned. At five foot six, I'm short for a model, but I make up for that with the personality I bring to the runway. I suppose I'm not your "typical" model. I eat whatever I want, and I'm not afraid to speak my mind. I know that's awfully judgmental, but I've been ostracized for being different by my peers. They're the ones who told me I was weird for eating carbs without any regrets.

My childhood taught me you can be a victim or a fighter, and after what Kenny did to me, I refuse to be a victim again. I worked hard, made a name for myself, and focused solely on my career. So when I met Drew, you can imagine my surprise because now, it wasn't only me.

Because of what happened in my childhood, I am still a virgin, though I've kissed a couple of guys and fooled around. I no longer consider myself religious, but I wanted to abide by that one rule of no sex before marriage. It was one my father firmly believed in, so it's one thing from my childhood I'm happy to embrace in adulthood.

But tonight, everything changes because now, I'm a married woman.

Drew kisses the tip of my nose, carrying me through the villa. When we reach the master bedroom, he arches a golden brow. "Like it?" he whispers while I nod eagerly.

"I love it," I correct, my gaze drifting to the king-size bed draped in crisp white linens.

Drew knows I'm a virgin, but he's a gentleman, and he hasn't pushed me. He respects my beliefs to wait until marriage. I would even go so far as to say he embraces it. However, I'm not stupid, and I know he's not a saint. With his baby blues and golden hair, he doesn't lack female attention.

With money and good looks, he could have any woman he wanted, but he chose me. So it seems fitting I start this new chapter of my life with a man who chooses me—flaws and all. On the outside, people see me as beautiful, successful, and fierce, but on the inside, I'm still looking for my place to belong. Which is why I said yes when Drew proposed—I finally found my place.

My friends told me I was crazy because I barely knew anything about him, but when you know, you know, and life is short. I don't intend to waste a second of it.

"You can put me down." I giggle, not sure why he's still carrying me.

We left Los Angeles right after the wedding and flew to Greece. Drew was very secretive about where we were going, and now, I can see why. There is no way to describe this place.

It's isolated, away from prying eyes. When we rode our boat in, I didn't see a soul for miles. The beachfront is our private beach and isn't used by anyone. No one can hear me scream.

When Drew's bowed lips tip into a mischievous grin, it's evident that's exactly what he intended. "Okay." He feigns a sigh, placing my bare feet on the plush carpet. "But only because I'm going to take a shower. Can I get you anything?"

I shake my head, still reeling that this is my life.

"Okay, babe, love you. I won't be long. Why don't you go downstairs and wait for me on the terrace? The view is something else."

"That sounds amazing. I love you…husband."

Drew draws in a victorious breath. "And I love you, wife." I will never tire of that title.

We kiss gently, a promise of what's to come.

Drew grabs a few things and makes his way into the bathroom. When he shuts the door, I exhale because this is really happening. I can't believe I am here, on my honeymoon, with the man of my dreams.

Deciding to follow Drew's suggestion, I make my way downstairs, marveling at the high glass windows, which provide breathtaking 360-degree views of the full moon illuminating the rippling ocean. I've been lucky enough to go to Milan and Paris for fashion shows, but this is something else.

It's so quiet.

The carpet feels like heaven beneath my bare feet, and when I see my reflection in the double terrace doors, I stop and take a moment to absorb it all. My hair is down and windswept from the boat ride we took to get here. My cheeks are flushed, and that's not because I'm wearing makeup as I'm hardly wearing any at all.

I'm happy.

My eyes sparkle, and a permanent smile is affixed to my lips. I look giddy, but I suppose I am. My simple white cotton summer dress may not be glitz and glamour, but it's me. When I'm not modeling clothes, I'm usually in jeans or a casual dress. My face and body may be plastered on billboards and magazines, but at heart, I'm still the innocent Texas girl who likes to wear her cowboy boots and prefers the country to the city.

My beautiful diamond puts any star-kissed night to shame and shines brightly as I place my hand in front of me, wiggling my finger. This cements my commitment, and I don't ever intend to take it off.

Walking out onto the terrace, I inhale deeply and sigh. I

tilt my head back and peer into the star-filled heavens. I like to think my father is looking down on me and is proud of everything I've accomplished. Instinctively, I reach for the small silver cross around my neck. My father gave it to me as a gift many years ago, and I haven't removed it since.

I have no idea what happened to my mother or Kenny. I lost all contact when I moved.

Drew knows everything. The first thing I wanted to do was tell him about my not so perfect past. He wrapped me in his arms and told me he was my family now. The fact my childhood was so shitty seemed to encourage Drew to speed up the marriage. He knows he's the only family I have as my grandparents passed years ago.

I suppose you could say I'm a loner. I don't really have any close friends, merely acquaintances. If I were to disappear… the only person who would truly miss me is Drew—my husband and the man I trust with my life.

An electric charge suddenly fills the air. I don't hear it until I feel it, which, in most cases, is too late. "Don't move and you won't get hurt."

Those words out here in paradise sound so wrong, as nothing but tranquility surrounds us, but when I feel something cold and hard shoved into the small of my back, that serenity soon shatters.

"Wha—"

"I said *don't* move," says someone with a thick, cruel Russian accent. My fingers dig into the railing, afraid if I don't hold onto something, my knees will give out from under me.

Another voice sounds behind me. I can't understand

what they're saying, but they're definitely speaking Russian. They seem to be arguing.

My eyes dart from left to right as my fight or flight kicks into full swing. I can jump from this terrace and land on the sand. It's not high. Worst-case scenario—I'll end up with a sprained ankle. Better than the alternative of ending up dead.

I dare not look behind me as my hearing is all I need. Whoever is behind me is still arguing, which will give me the opportunity to jump from the terrace and call for help. Adrenaline soars through my veins, and I can taste it at the back of my throat. Just as I boost myself up, about to spring for safety, a warm hand grips my bicep, dragging me back.

"Now where do you think you're going?" His hoarse, honeyed breath bathes the back of my neck, and I know he's close. When his chest presses against my back, I'm hit with a combination of smells—spicy, sweet, and floral.

"Please let me go," I whimper, attempting to feign innocence. I hope he falls for it because then I'm going to fight with all my might.

He doesn't.

"You're coming with us. Move." He's American.

"My hu-husband is upstairs," I plead. Shrugging from his hold, I keep my gaze forward because if I don't see him, he won't have to kill me.

"That's nice for your husband," he quips while I feel the walls beginning to close in on me. "Now move." He tugs at my right arm without any real force, but another hand rips at my left, almost tearing my shoulder from my socket.

Tears of pain sting my eyes as I feel like I'm being torn

apart by a savage dog. "Put this on!" Russian number one shouts. "Bitch, I said put it on!"

My fight gives way to flight because I am suddenly scared.

"No, please, no," I beg, but when I'm spun around and forced to face all three of them, I know this isn't optional.

My brain can't seem to process what's going on because standing before me in paradise are three men in ski masks. This place is not meant for such a sight, but they don't seem to appreciate the beauty. One steps forward and slaps me so hard across the cheek, I taste blood. This can't be happening.

"Won't ask again," he snarls as he attempts to shove a gag into my mouth, and I know the thick black pillowcase hanging from his hand will be next.

Memories of Kenny shoving me into the carpet and my air being siphoned off by his large hand smash into me, and I sway, instantly gripping the first solid thing I can find, which just happens to be the hulking bicep of one of my captors.

The warmth through his long-sleeved T-shirt burns me. Slowly peering up, I lock eyes with him and am confronted with an unusual shade of green with swirls of warm amber. The color of his eyes are akin to a bottle of chartreuse. Out here in the pitch black, they glow...like a predator.

The thought has me quickly severing our connection.

The Russians are losing patience with me because when I don't bend to their demands, another attempt is made to shove a white cloth into my mouth.

"Please, don't gag me," I say. Holding my hands up in surrender, I hope they see reason. They don't.

Just as Russian number two rears back to pistol-whip me,

the American's arm shoots out in lightning-quick speed and grips his wrist in warning. I have no idea why he just saved me, but that doesn't matter because Drew suddenly appears.

"What the fuck?" he curses as he frantically attempts to make sense of what he's seeing. "Who are you?"

"Drew, run!" I scream, lunging forward, but the move is my last as I'm slapped once again. I stagger backward, gasping for air and cradling my cheek, but I still manage to slur, "Run."

Drew rushes forward, but he doesn't stand a chance when the American advances and slams his fist into Drew's jaw. Drew stumbles backward, dazed and confused. The American doesn't show him any mercy as he pushes him onto the floor and commences to beat the hell out of him.

He drops to one knee and pins Drew by his shoulder as he raises his fist over and over again. I scream, begging for mercy for my husband, but there is none. The American towers over Drew, and even though he's donned in head-to-toe black, it's evident he's in good shape.

Drew doesn't stand a chance.

Although tears cloud my vision, I still attempt to save Drew, but Russian number two is sick of my disobedience. He raises his gun, and this time, he pistol-whips me. The world spins on its axis before I hit the deck.

I'm floating in and out of consciousness, but I'm certain I see Drew's lips move. I can't make out what he's saying, though. The American punches him one last time before spitting on him. This seems personal. But what do I know because I'm suddenly losing consciousness.

My eyes flicker shut, but with what little strength I have

left, I extend my arm out to Drew. He's feet away, wheezing. "Dreeww." It comes out slurred, but I need him to know I'm here.

It's too late.

Although my lack of strength leaves me floppy like a rag doll, one of the Russians jerks me up and shoves the white gag into my mouth. When he attempts to shove the pillowcase onto my head, I kick out, squealing muted screams, but my body is limp.

You're going to be a good little girl, aren't you, Willow? Let me fuck that tight virgin pussy. You're gonna come for Daddy.

Tears leak from my eyes, mixing with the blood gushing from my temple as the horrible memory, one which I haven't allowed into my world, floods me, and I can't breathe. I gasp for air, but the harder I try, the more difficult it becomes, and soon, I'm hyperventilating.

I'm preparing myself for another strike, but I don't get one. Instead, the American brushes the bloody, matted hair from my cheeks. I try to fight, but my depleted body fails me.

"Trust me. Just put it on." Trust him? Is he fucking serious? He's asking me to trust him when I just witnessed him beat my husband into a bloody mess.

But what choice do I have? Clearly, this is happening whether I cooperate or not, so I surrender. Just as I did with Kenny, I grow lax and allow him to win.

"Good, ангел."

I have no idea what he just called me, but it didn't sound insulting. It sounded almost…thankful.

He nods, indicating he's putting the pillowcase on, and all

I can do is comply. However, when Drew moans, twisting and turning and still very much alert, I see something in his white bathrobe pocket, but I must be hallucinating as there is surely some mistake.

Before I can question myself, the world turns black, and I am engulfed in my own personal hell. The pillowcase and gag are certain to kill me soon, and if not, my racing heart will give out in next to no time. Arms link through mine from behind and help me stand. I know it's the American. His fragrance gives him away. I stand wearily, but I will stagger to my death before anyone carries me.

Drew is groaning, but when I hear those pained sounds floating farther and farther away, I know we're going to wherever my captors intend on taking me.

"Ten steps," the American whispers from behind me. I flinch at his muffled voice through the pillowcase. He stands at my back, ensuring I don't fall. I could mistake his actions for him giving half a shit, but it's clear that wherever I'm going, they need me alive. If not, they would have killed me already.

This isn't a robbery. It's a kidnapping.

Once I shakily descend the ten steps, my feet hit the sand, and in any other circumstance, I could appreciate the softness between my toes. But when I'm pushed and shoved as the American no longer seems to be near, all I can appreciate is that I'm not dead—well, not yet anyway.

Through the pillowcase, I can hear the gentle lapping of the ocean against the shore, but it's none the wiser that three criminals are about to use it to aid in changing my world forever. When my feet tread water, I jolt with the sudden fear that they're going to drown me. But that doesn't make any sense.

If I'm going to survive this, I have to keep my head clear.

"Boat. In," says someone, maybe Russian two or one. They all sound the same.

I'm yanked up—someone pulling on my floppy arms while the other lifts my legs—and I feel like a chew toy being ripped into two. Once I'm dragged onto the boat, I'm directed on where to go as someone shoves me in the back, screaming at me in a language I don't understand.

I'm then forced down some stairs where I lose my footing and fall flat onto my stomach. Grunting on impact, I instantly search around, hoping to distinguish where I am—I'm in the bottom of the boat. The galley.

"Stay," someone commands, ensuring I be the good dog they clearly see me as being.

Fuck them.

I rise slowly, using my hands as eyes as I feel my way around blindly. I need to find a weapon. One small enough to hide. Blood is seeping into my eyes from the wound on my temple, so I close them because I can't see through this thick pillowcase anyway.

My fingers come into contact with what feels like a small torch. Not the weapon I had in mind, but it'll have to do.

I'm interrupted when I hear someone tsk me before I'm being dragged by my long hair which falls down my back and hurled against what feels like a cushioned bench seat. The pain in my head just amplifies. "Arms behind. Hands together."

I shakily comply, sobbing around the gag.

He reaches around me, and when the unmistakable feel of metal snaps around my wrists, I know my freedom is dwindling by the second. He yanks at the handcuffs to ensure they are tight. They are.

My breathless panting reveals my fear, but when I feel the predatory touch at the back of my calves, I freeze. Two hands glide up and down my flesh, humming in satisfaction. He's on his knees before me.

Oh, god.

"You pretty." His English is broken, but I'm not lost in translation. I know what he wants.

*Your looks are used for evil…*my mom's words echo loudly within. Maybe she was right after all.

"We going to have fun, and it'll be our secret." Next, I feel a wet tongue lap its way up the side of my calf. The smell of cigarettes and sweat has my stomach roiling.

Adrenaline takes over, and I attempt to kick him, but he's too fast, chuckling as he pushes down on my ankles. He then begins to bind them with coarse rope. "You bad girl. Boss going to like you."

Who is this boss, and why does he want me?

Once he tugs at my restraints, it sounds like he stands. I try to kick my feet out, but they're tied to something hard beneath me. I'm bound. Hands and feet. And gagged. I'm not going anywhere.

"She tied up?" I almost sigh in relief when I hear the American. He was the only one who showed me an iota of mercy. The other two scare me. The American doesn't.

"Yes, like a present. You want to unwrap her?"

I suddenly feel so objectified and dirty and attempt to recoil, but I can't move. My heart is racing, and my breathing is uneven. The tears have long dried as I'm awaiting their next move.

"Shut the fuck up and let's go."

That was not the response I was expecting. The Russian laughs.

"Calm down, неудачник."

"Fuck you. Up on deck now." The American talks big and seems to be calling the shots. I wonder who he is?

My only clue to what's going on is what I hear, and before the hatch closes, I'm presented with clue number one. "Be in Turkey soon. I hope you don't get seasick, Saint." Then the hatch closes, leaving me with the sound of the muted voices above me.

Turkey? Why are we going there? But more importantly, I just uncovered the name of my American captor...Saint.

Ironic, isn't it, that someone who bears a name denoting nothing but holiness can deliver nothing but hell.

Bon voyage.

I awake from a nightmare so heinous, I can't believe my brain could conjure up such images.

Blood, violence, abduction. I really need to lay off the caffeine.

As I attempt to roll over and snuggle into the warmth of

my new husband, terror overcomes me because I can't move.

No.

My eyes snap open, only to be confronted by pure blackness. I try to scream, but it dies a muffled death when I realize I'm gagged. Panic overcomes me as I attempt to move, but I can't because I'm bound.

No.

Realization hits, and I shake my head helplessly. Passing out from shock and fatigue was a small mercy, but now that I'm awake, I have no other choice but to face this reality.

Three men kidnapped me while on my honeymoon. Two Russian. One American named Saint. I scoff at the notion. We're on a boat headed to Turkey to see someone they call Boss? Ugh, this is adding to the throbbing in my head.

I think back to what I remember, hoping it'll give me more clues. Flinching when I recall Saint beating Drew to a pulp has something materializing. In the pocket of his white bathrobe, I could have sworn…but I shrug it off. It's impossible that what I thought I saw buried deep in his pocket was a cell phone because if it was, why didn't he call the police?

Yes, he was struck down, but when I left, he was moving and moaning. He had every opportunity to dial for help, so why didn't he?

I scold the troublesome voice for even thinking such blasphemy and instead focus on getting the hell out of here. There is no way I'm doing that tied up, so I need to think outside the box. Saint was the only one who showed a lick of humanity, so he's the key to getting me off this boat.

Your looks are used for evil…

It's time I listened to Momma.

Even though it's a long shot, I can't sit here and wait for them to strike. So I take a deep breath and scream. It comes out as a wail, a muted whimpering, but I can only hope it'll draw the attention of the person I want. I continue yelling, tears leaking from my eyes as I thrash about, hoping to evoke some sort of a response.

Finally, it works.

The latch opens, and I'm hit with the crisp ocean breeze as well as a punch of spice. That masculine and refined smell seem to be his trademark fragrance. I listen as he descends the stairs slowly. My chest rises and falls swiftly, and my heart is in my throat.

"What's wrong?" he has the gall to ask.

I'm bound and gagged, you asshole. That's what's wrong, I silently reply, but I merely just whimper, hoping he understands what I want.

His footsteps advance toward me before they come to a stop. I have no idea what I look like, but I try my best to feign submission. "Please," I muffle from around the gag, shaking my head, implying I want him to take off the pillowcase.

Silence surrounds me, but his pensive thinking can be felt.

"I'll take out your gag, but you have to promise me you won't scream." His voice is deep, rough even.

I nod quickly, holding my breath.

A heavy sigh leaves him as he's clearly hoping I'm not lying. When his heavy footsteps hint that he's proceeding forward, I'm glad I'm a convincing liar even when gagged and bound. I hear a rustle, like he's putting something on.

I wait with bated breath, mentally crossing my fingers that he doesn't back out. He doesn't.

His scent is unique, and when he steps closer, I'm once again cloaked with a spicy, sweet cloud of promise. He's careful not to frighten me as he gently removes the pillowcase from my head. The cool air on my flushed cheeks feels like heaven, and I sigh. I keep my eyes squeezed shut, needing a moment to center myself.

With two deep breaths, I open them gradually, blinking rapidly to focus on where I am. My eyes are caked in dried tears and blood, causing everything to appear blurry. Peering around as best I can, I see that I'm in a small room below deck. There is hardly any lighting, but I can make out a small table and chair set, a kitchen sink with shelves stacked with canned goods above it, and a white leather bench seat in front of me. It matches the one I'm tied to. The décor is wooden and almost modern. I take a guess that we're on a yacht.

In the far corner, there is a door. I can only hope my plan works.

My panting is heavy, and the gag in my mouth isn't helping. I need it out. Now. Gradually peering upward under my lashes, I see him—Saint. He stands unbending a few feet away, the pillowcase hanging from his fingers.

His eyes are on fire, watching me closely. He's donned the ski mask, which is no surprise as it's clear he doesn't want me to see his face. I didn't realize how tall he was. But now that he's in front of me, I crane my neck up to take in his whole stature.

His shoulders are broad, and his muscles are bulging through his tight, long-sleeved top. He is in black cargo pants and black boots, but I still have no clue who he is. And the air of mystery around him has nothing to do with his mask. His eyes are the only thing I can really see, but they are the window to one's soul, so they say.

When he focuses on the cross around my neck, he seems remorseful, which has me wondering why he's doing this.

"Please," I mumble from around the gag, pleading he take it out.

He rocks back on his heels, wrestling with my demands. The only thing I have at my disposal are my eyes, which is ironic because so does he. I beg him for help, putting everything I can into my expression. He is my only hope at getting out of here.

A single tear trickles down my cheek and into my gag. This is useless. I'm bargaining with the devil. But when he exhales loudly and slowly bends forward, a new sense of hope overcomes me.

"I'm going to take this out, all right? Don't make me regret it." He pins me with a promise—if I disobey him, I will pay.

I dare not breathe.

The blood whooshes through my ears, and my heart races in a deafening staccato as he removes the gag from my mouth. He is poised by me, ready to put it back in if I go back on my word. I don't…for now.

The moment it's out, I gulp in mouthfuls of air to replenish my depleted lungs. I instantly get dizzy as it's too much, too fast. Steadying my breathing, I calm the storm within.

When I stop wheezing, I peer upward at Saint. "Th-thank you." My mouth is dry, and my voice hoarse, so it takes me three attempts to speak. He nods once, arms folded, but other than that, he makes no attempts to move or talk.

Visions of him dropping to one knee and punishing Drew with his fists overwhelm me, but I swallow down my fear. "I need to use the bathroom."

It's the oldest trick in the book, but I'm certain that door leads to a bathroom, a bathroom which will hopefully have a window. As far as plans go, it's weak and will probably get me killed, but I'd prefer that option to awaiting my doom.

Saint's chest rises before it depresses with a loud exhale. "Please, I know you're not like the others," I say in a rushed breath. "You tried to help me earlier."

"You know nothing," he growls, shaking his head firmly.

Recoiling, I quickly backtrack. "My name is Willow, Willow Shaw." By telling him my name, I'm hopefully allowing him to see that I'm a person and not a thing.

"Stop talking." He swoops forward, intent on gagging me again, but tears, ugly tears break past the floodgates.

"Please d-don't gag m-me." My lower lip quivers as the thought of it turns my stomach.

"You talk too much," he counters as though gagging me is the acceptable solution.

"I know. I'm s-sorry. But I'm sc-scared. What are you going to do with m-me?" I whisper, afraid of his reply but needing to hear it anyway.

Thankfully, he stops his advance and doesn't gag me for the time being. There is so much behind those vivid eyes. He is wrestling with his decision once again. "I'm going to untie you so you can use the bathroom. You go with the door open."

I nod eagerly.

Sighing, he yanks a thin silver chain from under his shirt, and I see a key dangling from the end. I have the sudden urge to draw back when he steps forward because his presence commands attention, but I remain utterly still as he bends low and reaches behind me.

My breathing is heavy, and being this close to him intensifies his fragrance. His fingers on my skin have me breaking out into goose bumps. He works deftly as he slips the key into the cuffs and unlocks them.

I instantly drop my hands by my side and roll my shoulders to get the feeling back into my arms. I clench and relax my hands until the circulation begins to flow.

He pulls away slowly, stopping when our faces are mere inches apart. An intake of breath gets trapped in my throat, but I peer up, challenging him to do his best.

Our pants fill the air as we examine each other carefully. My proximity appears to affect him, causing his pupils to dilate, and I gasp. His eyes dart to my heaving chest before they snap back up to meet my terrified ones.

He reaches behind him with an unhurried speed, and when the full moon peeking in from the window reflects off the silver from the blade he holds, I whimper, but I don't move. This is a test, and I pass with flying colors as he drops to his knees, eyes still locked with mine, and he cuts through the rope around my ankles.

He is feral and in command, but I don't feel threatened.

Lord knows I should, but I'm not because I know that using my looks for evil has bought me some time. He likes what he sees, which is maybe why he skims his finger over my silver anklet before he stands and pockets his switchblade. If I wasn't paying attention, I would have missed it or played it off as an accidental touch. But I know there is no such thing.

I'm free, but I suddenly have never felt more imprisoned than I do right now.

He's waiting for me to make my next move. Again, another test.

I rise cautiously as I have no doubt I will be lightheaded. The blood whooshes through my body, but I find my center of gravity and stay upright. Placing my arms out wide, I balance myself, inhaling and exhaling slowly.

The decking feels cold beneath my feet, but I commence a slow stagger toward the bathroom. My steps are sluggish with the pins and needles feeling in my legs, but I make sure not to touch Saint as I stumble past him. He inhales through his nose.

When the bathroom is within reach, I open the door, never feeling more relieved. However, seeing the small window above the toilet pleases me more. I do as he says and leave the door open as I shuffle into the tiny space. There is only enough room for a toilet, a tiny shower, and a sink, but it'll do.

I watch him, arching a brow, hinting for some privacy.

With arms folded, he turns slowly, showing me his back.

Not wanting to alert him to my plan, I shyly reach under my skirt to pull down my underwear and quickly sit onto the toilet. I have to go, but with him standing there, my bladder gets stage fright.

"What's taking so long?" he asks when there is silence.

My cheeks turn a beet red. "I can't…pee with you standing there."

"Either you go with me here, or you don't go at all. Take your pick."

Narrowing my eyes, I plot the ways to make him pay for being such an asshole, then decide to hum under my breath so I can pee under the cloak of music. It works. I don't even know what I'm humming to, but it doesn't matter because once I'm done, I'm going to slam this door shut and attempt to get the fuck off this boat.

Craning my neck, I see that the window has a latch. It's unlocked. It's small, but I'll be able to squeeze through. Once I'm done, I reach for some toilet paper, my gaze floating between Saint and the window.

I flush and decide to wash my hands as that'll give me more time for him to lower his guard. When I peer into the square mirror above the sink, I gasp as my reflection resembles something out of a horror movie.

Coagulated blood sticks to my matted hair in clumps. Crimson paints my cheeks, with rivets of dried tears cascading all the way down my chin. My mouth looks swollen and my eyes puffy. So much for using my looks because the only look I'm rocking right now is shit.

The reason that is zaps through my veins, and a surge of adrenaline overthrows me. It's now or never. Ensuring his back is still turned, I take a deep breath. And then another.

With the water still running, I lunge for the door and lock it, taking back my life. I only have seconds before he's breaking down the flimsy door. My heart is in my throat as I climb onto the toilet, and with fumbling fingers, I unlatch the window.

When it pops open, I don't have time to celebrate as I frantically boost myself up and wiggle my body through the hole. I can taste my freedom as I'm almost through, but it's the last time I will taste it on my tongue because before I know it, I hear an ear-splitting crash and am being hauled backward violently.

"No!" I scream, flailing like a madwoman as I kick my legs. But it's in vain. "Let me go!"

Saint jerks me back, wrapping his hands around my waist as I clutch onto the frame of the window, holding on for dear life. He is so strong, and eventually, I cave, afraid he'll rip me into two.

"No." I sob as he throws me over his shoulder like I weigh nothing at all. I pound on his back, thrashing to break free, but he only tightens his hold. When he twists, and I'm able to reach his side, I go on instinct and bite down—hard.

He grunts as my bite clearly stung, but when he rips free from my teeth, I know I've just made things so much worse. He is furious. His hulking body trembles in rage as he storms through the boat and slams me to my feet. I attempt to run, but he grabs me by the throat and shoves me backward. My back hits a support pole, and I gasp for breath.

"You want to act like a dog, I'll treat you like one."

"Please," I beg, tears and spittle running down my face.

But he doesn't listen.

With his fingers still clutched around my throat, he reaches for a length of rope and forces my hands behind my back. With the rope, he then viciously ties it around my arms, just under my breasts, so I'm bound to the pole.

"You don't have to do this," I plead, but he's so angry, he won't listen to a word I have to say.

When he drops to his knees and forces my legs shut so he can tie them to the pole also, my fight dies, and I begin to weep. By the time he's bound my ankles, tiny snivels wrack my body. I'm bound to the pole by my arms, legs, and feet. I'm not going anywhere.

Yet what scares me the most is how he won't look at me.

"Saint…" It's too late to take it back.

His head snaps up, and he launches off the floor, roaring into my face, "How do you know my name?"

"I-I…" I fumble over my words, his once smooth, chartreuse-colored eyes now a flaming amber.

"Tell me!" he yells, his breath fanning the hair from my cheeks.

"I h-heard one of the men call y-you th-that. I'm so-sorry." I am gasping for breath because my fear is robbing me of air.

"Don't mistake my kindness for weakness because I am far crueler than those two upstairs," he growls, cupping my throat once again. Swallowing hard, I bow backward in an attempt to escape, but I have nowhere to go. "I have a lot more to lose than they do, so don't force me to hurt you."

He releases me, and I sag forward, sobbing. I have never felt more defeated in my life.

When he reaches for a roll of duct tape, I whimper. "Pl-please do-don't gag m-me. I can't st-stand it. Pl-please."

My pleas go unheard as he stretches out a length and is about to fasten it to my lips. It's my last chance. "Please, Saint, d-don't…" I don't even care what he does to me for using his name. I'm dead anyway.

I brace for the suffocation, squeezing my eyes shut, but I don't get it. I get nothing.

"Fuck!" he roars before I hear something smash. He's going to kill me; I'm sure of it. But when I hear his heavy boots pound along the floor and up the stairs, slamming the hatch closed, it appears I'm not sure of anything at all.

My heavy eyelids open, and I take in my surroundings. He's gone. I'm still tied to a pole, but he's gone. The smash I heard was the duct tape being hurled against the wall, shattering a glass in the process.

I have no idea why he didn't gag me. The fact I used his name was enough of a reason to. But he didn't, and I need to know why.

But for now, I surrender to the exhaustion, anticipating what day two holds.

CHAPTER TWO

She isn't what I was expecting. She is strong-willed and stubborn. I have no other choice but to break her. It's for her own good.

Day 2

I've been awake since well before dawn.

The night wasn't kind to me. I had hoped to pass out from fatigue and the splitting pain in my head and not stir for hours, but that wasn't the case. I slipped in and out of reality, but I eventually stayed awake, counting the stars I could see through the small window to my left. It was my only glimpse of the outside world.

When the sun peaked across the horizon and the moon surrendered to her light, I waited for my punishment. My attempted escape made Saint so angry last night, I'm certain my retribution was coming. But I waited and waited to no avail.

I can hear them up on the deck. The boat has either stopped or is going at a very slow pace, but they are merely torturing me. In some ways, I wish they'd just get it over with because the waiting…that's half the torture.

I don't know where we are, why they kidnapped me, or how they knew where to find me. Our location was off the grid. I didn't see a soul for miles. If they want a ransom, knowing Drew is wealthy, then why are they taking me to Turkey?

None of this makes any sense.

The hatch opens, letting in the vibrant sunshine, but I feel anything but lively. When one of the Russians comes bouncing down the stairs, I don't know if I should be relieved or scared. Of course, the ski mask covers his face, so I will only be able to tell who he is when he speaks.

Holding my breath, I watch as he hunts through the shelves of canned food, grabbing two. "Eat?" he asks in very broken English. Russian number two. He is the one who speaks little English. He is also the bastard who pistol-whipped me.

"No, thank you," I spit. I'd rather starve than break bread with them. My throat is dry, and I'm thirsty as all get-out, but it'll be a cold day in hell when I tell him that. He shrugs, probably thankful there is more for him. He heads back up on the deck, slamming the hatch behind him.

Every part of my body aches, and I desperately need a shower. I am covered in blood, sweat, and tears. The thought of standing under a hot spray to wash away this filth has me slipping into a happy place…until the devil ruins it.

"You need to eat."

Inhaling, I turn my cheek, refusing to look at him. He responds with laughter.

He seems to have more pep in his step than when he left last night, and I begin to wonder why that is. The closer he gets to me, the more the memories of him foiling my escape incite my anger. "Eat," he repeats.

"No," I push out between clenched teeth, my face still facing away. I don't want to look at him. I won't be held responsible for my actions if I do.

"I made it myself," he quips, shoving a plate of baked beans under my nose. My stomach gurgles, and the urge to vomit overpowers me.

"Fuck you," I scowl, uncaring what the repercussions are.

Silence.

I'm testing his patience, but I won't roll over and die. I did that once, and I won't ever do it again. If he wanted a docile little hostage, then he kidnapped the wrong girl.

My insolence hasn't affected him in the slightest because I hear the wooden chair being dragged across the floor and then a loud thump onto the table. "So if you won't eat…what do you want?"

"For you to let me go," I counter in lightning-quick speed. Risking a glance his way, I scoff when I see him perched casually on the chair, boots resting on the table, ankles crossed. He has his hands linked behind his head. Just another day in paradise for this asshole.

When we lock eyes, I glare, hoping he knows how much I hate him.

"I can't do that," he says, shaking his head slowly. "So pick again."

"Is this a game to you?" I ask, enraged he seems to be enjoying himself. "My husband is going to find you and kill you." As far as threats go, it's pretty severe, but once again, Saint finds my offensiveness hilarious.

"Ooh…I'm shaking in my boots." He chuckles, waving his hands in the air and feigning horror.

I really fucking hate him.

"This is growing old fast, so you have one of three options." He raises a finger. "One—you eat." I curl my lip in response. He raises another finger. "Two—you shower." When I don't reply, he completes his counting with a third finger. "Or three—I gag you, and you don't have any other options until we dock this boat."

I pale at the thought. "So what will it be, ангел?" There's that name again. It's on the tip of my tongue to ask him what it means, but I won't give him the satisfaction of my curiosity. "I won't ask again."

"Two!" I shout when he kicks his legs off the table and slides his chair back. "Two."

He stands slowly, nodding. "Good pick because you fucking stink." My cheeks instantly redden as I'm mortified.

His eyes soften, but it's probably just the way the sunlight hits his strange eyes because nothing about the man standing in front of me is soft. "Now, the last time I untied you, we had issues. Is that going to happen again?"

"No," I reply because with him foiling my plans of slipping out the window, I need to find another escape route.

"Good." He paces toward me, causing me to shrink back.

Now that I'm standing, I can see that he is, in fact, well over six feet. At a guess, I would say six-three. I have no hopes of outrunning or outweighing him, so it looks like I'll have to outsmart him, and I will.

When he comes to a standstill behind me and begins untying the rope, I can't believe I'm actually thankful since he's the reason I'm tied up in the first place. When he frees my arms, I sigh as the relief is incredible. I rub my shoulders, hoping to get the feeling back.

He then unties my legs and lastly, my ankles.

I'm too relieved to be free to even attempt to run because where would I run to anyway? My jelly legs barely hold me up. That shower can't come soon enough. I turn in the direction of the bathroom, but Saint grabs me by my bicep and leads me toward the stairs.

I dig my heels in. "Where are we going? The shower is back there." I hook my thumb behind me, but he ignores me and continues to haul me up the stairs. With no other choice, I follow.

The hot sun blasts down around me, and I shield my eyes with my hand as it hurts my sensitive pupils. The Russians are mid bite of their breakfast when they see me behind Saint. It's clear this wasn't part of their plans.

They exchange words in Russian, and I am surprised when Saint replies back in their native tongue. I didn't know he spoke Russian, but I suppose I don't know a lot of things about him. They eventually cave as it's clearly not a fight worth having.

I take in my surroundings and see nothing but blue ocean for miles. The scene would be quite pretty if I wasn't here against my will.

I was right. We are on a mid-sized yacht. Nothing too fancy, but nothing too shabby to alert anyone of the illegal activities on board. Standing out here, I feel my skin begin to fry. I can't believe they are sitting out here in long sleeves and ski masks. They look ridiculous. I wouldn't be surprised if they sleep with the masks on.

Saint allows me to take it all in, which surprises me. His mood swings are sure to leave me with whiplash. I peer around, wondering if maybe a shower is located somewhere up here. But there doesn't seem to be. Just when I'm about to ask, he clarifies just why we're here.

"Strip."

My mouth gapes open, and I blink once. "Excuse me?"

"Strip," he repeats, releasing me.

I stumble backward, his command winding me. "I will not," I argue, folding my arms around me in protection. The two Russians watch on, our quarrel much more interesting than their food it seems.

"Suit yourself." He grips my forearm and drags me toward the front of the yacht. I squirm, attempting to break free, but it's useless. When we get to the edge, he gestures with his chin to the water. "You can just jump in wearing your clothes. See if I care."

"Jump?" I question, horrified. No way is he implying for

me to shower in the ocean. But when he stands rigid, I know that's exactly what he's proposing. "You're fucking insane! I'll drown."

He chuckles in response. "There are worse ways to die." Even though he's right, what's wrong with using the shower?

Curse my inability to mask my thoughts, because before I know what he's doing, he's taking off one boot, hopping on one leg as he then removes the other. When he begins to unbuckle his belt, I back up, gulping. "What are you doing?" I don't want to know, but I torture myself anyway.

"Preparing in case you drown."

Fuck him and his smugness.

When he threads his fingers into the waistband of his pants, clearly about to disrobe, I instantly turn my back, embarrassed. I feel stupid, but I don't want to see him get naked. I hate the man.

As I look out at the ocean, I wonder if maybe this isn't such a bad idea. This could be escape attempt number two. I literally have nothing to lose, which is why I shift to the right, hoping the high sail can provide some privacy. But the thought of taking off my dress in front of those two Russian perverts turns my stomach. And with them gone, I only have to outswim one captor instead of three.

Saint comes up behind me, startling me. "We haven't got all day. You have one minute."

"I…" I lick my lips, refusing to look at him. "Please make them go away. I don't want them to see." I know this is absurd as I model for a living, and most times, I don't wear much to those shoots, but that's different. That's work, and this is… something else.

"Don't be shy. They've seen plenty of ass and tits before, believe me."

I flush all over as his bluntness catches me unaware. "Well, congratulations to them, but they haven't seen mine, and I would prefer to keep it that way."

I'm expecting him to tell me to stop being so precious, but when he shouts, "Go," I almost fall over my feet.

They exchange words in Russian, a few expletives I believe, before I hear them rise and pound down the stairs. The hatch slams shut, leaving me alone with my captor.

"Your wish is my command. Now hurry up." He's running out of patience. Not wanting to push him more than I already have, I spin around, surprised to see his pants are still on.

But I soon recover. "You too."

"Me too what?" he asks, the vibrant yellow in his eyes challenging the golden sun.

"You leave as well."

"Nice try, but I don't think so." When he stands with his arms folded, legs apart, I know this is the best I'm going to get.

"Fine." Sighing, I pretend I'm just at a photo shoot as I turn my back and lift the hem of my soiled dress over my head. I toss it to the floor, standing in my white underwear and matching bra. Instantly, I wrap an arm around me to cover my breasts.

Saint is quiet. I nervously shuffle my feet.

"You done?" I'm surprised he's given me the option of keeping my undergarments on.

I nod quickly.

My hair whips in the wind, and the sun thaws the chill

from my skin. It's actually quite pleasant up here. Too bad I can't enjoy it, seeing as I'm a prisoner. Looking over the edge, I see that the jump isn't too far, but I'm not worried about that. I'm desperately seeking a way to escape.

Maybe luck will be on my side, and a passing ship will save me. Or a massive wave will sweep me toward shore. All unlikely scenarios, but I will take my chances because I will take drowning over getting back onto this boat.

I shuffle forward, stepping over the silver railing and standing on the tip of the boat. Luckily, I have no fear of the water, and fortunately, I'm a damn good swimmer. With a kick of adrenaline, I take my leap of faith to what was supposed to be my freedom. But when I hear a snap around my wrist and a heavy weight crashing into the water with me, I realize I've just jumped holding an anchor.

I submerge fast, the water sucking me under, and as I sink, I fight the urge to kick back up and break the surface. Drowning would be less painful than having to deal with Saint, who handcuffed himself to me right before I jumped. He's always two steps in front of me—so much for outsmarting him.

He wraps his arm around my waist as he swims us toward the surface. When we emerge, I take a deep breath. Saint does the same.

"You asshole! You could have killed us!" Those words are ridiculous in light of our current situation, but when I go, it'll be by my hand, and that hand will not be attached to his.

He laughs, and I notice his teeth are a sharp shade of white. The top ones are perfectly straight; however, the two bottom middle ones are slightly crooked. "Hardly. Besides, you said you'd drown. I wouldn't want that."

"Ugh!" I groan, attempting to swim away from him, but I can't, seeing as we're handcuffed to one another.

He digs around in his pocket with his non-cuffed hand and produces a bar of soap. "It's lavender."

I snatch it from his palm, scowling. When we make contact, however, I notice he flinches. It seems he doesn't like to be touched.

"This is the reason you want me to wash out here, isn't it? So you can watch me?" The bathroom is tiny, and there is no way we'd both fit in there. He clearly doesn't trust me, but he respects my privacy. So this is the happy medium.

Saint doesn't reply. Instead, he twirls his finger in the air, hinting I'm to hurry up.

Not interested in being tied to him for longer than I have to, I unwrap the soap and lather it up as best I can. I dip my head backward, relishing in washing the grime from my hair. Saint bobs beside me, surprising me as he turns his cheek to give me some privacy.

Everything about him is an oxymoron.

"You look ridiculous with your ski mask on," I state, passing the soap over my upper body.

"Lucky for me, I don't care what you think," he replies, head still turned away.

I take this opportunity to examine him for any clues that might give away his identity. He's still dressed in his usual attire, but now that we're surrounded by daylight, instead of cloaked in darkness, I can just make out wisps of dirty blond hair curling at his nape.

Thanks to the gentle sway of the ocean, his long-sleeved shirt has shifted slightly, allowing me to see a hint of ink just over the crease of his upper shoulder. I have no idea what it is, but I suppose it just adds to the mystery.

Even though I'm cuffed to a psychopath, feeling the water against my skin is wonderful. This is hardly what I thought when I agreed to a shower, but I suppose it's better than nothing. Peering around, I wonder if, by some miracle, an escape route will present itself. But it doesn't. I'm surrounded by absolutely nothing.

"Okay, time's up."

"What's in Turkey?" I respond to his suggestion.

He turns slowly, clearly not interested in having a heart to heart. "Let's go." He swims us toward the boat, but I pull back with all my might.

His eyes widen, clearly surprised by my rebellion.

"You don't scare me," I reveal, leaving out the word *much*.

He wades in the water, watching me closely. The air begins to grow thick, and I brace myself for my punishment. "Are you always this disobedient?"

I gulp as I was not expecting such a response, especially with a hint of wickedness wrapped around his words. Desperate to escape, I attempt to swim away, but Saint swings his arm inward so I'm forced to face him as he turns his body.

We're paddling together, eyes locked, wrists bound. "I asked you a question."

"So did I," I counter, thankful my legs are submerged so he can't see them trembling.

He snickers, shaking his head at my insolence. "We're not going to Turkey," he reveals while I cock a brow.

"But I heard—"

He abruptly talks over me. "Turkey is merely a means to an end…like you."

My lower lip quivers because that was just plain mean. Being out here in the open, with the sun shining and not a cloud in the blue sky, I have let my guard down because Saint has shown me a sliver of kindness. But as his words come back to haunt me, I won't make the same mistake again.

Don't mistake my kindness for weakness…

"I'm ready to go back," I say blankly as I refuse to allow him to see what his words have done.

He nods once without any argument; he's probably happy to shut me up. We swim toward the boat, and when I see a ladder hanging off the side, I allow him to ascend first. He is sopping wet as he climbs the steps, dragging me behind him.

There are a million things I want to say, but I decide the less I speak to him, the better. I need to save my energy to strategize how the fuck to get off this yacht.

I don't give him the respect of looking at him, but instead, I turn over my shoulder, refusing to make eye contact. When I feel the cuff snap open, I instantly rub my raw wrist. As he pushes me lightly, hinting I move, I shrug from his touch as I want no part of him near me.

If I were thinking straight, I would be covering myself as I am parading around in very transparent white underwear, but what do I care about modesty? It's clear he sees me as nothing but chattel.

We walk past the Russians who are sitting near the wooden wheel, watching us curiously. They are ogling me, and just as I'm about to cover my breasts, I see it—my escape. Sitting under the helm is a CB radio. If I can get to this, I can alert someone, anyone that I'm in trouble.

One of the Russians sits on a white chest, eyeing me. But he can gawk all he wants because I bet flares and a life vest are in there. I want to take a closer look, but Saint hurls me away, sensing his partner in crime appreciates my transparency a little too much.

But this is exactly what I need, God save my soul. One of them expressed interest in me when he tied me...if I can play on that, then maybe I have a fighting chance at getting off this boat. The longer he stares, the more certain I am that he is the one.

I need a distinguishing mark, something to tell them apart, and when he turns his head to whisper something to the other Russian, I see it—a small birthmark under his left eye. He returns his attention my way, and that's when I put my plan into motion.

As he's spooning canned sardines into his mouth, I wink—it's subtle, and I'm playing with fire, but this ship is only as strong as its weakest link, and I just found a hole in the design. His mouth hinges open.

Jackpot.

I don't have time to gloat because Saint moves me down the stairs, but I go willingly. When down in my dungeon, I'm surprised to see a change of clothes on the leather seat. It seems they have this all planned.

Not bothering to ask if they're for me, I walk toward the shorts and tank top. I really want to change my underwear, but they don't seem to be that prepared. As I reach for the jean shorts, I only then realize that Saint is still here, watching me.

I'm about to spit a sarcastic comment, but the look in his eyes steals the air from my lungs. He watches me closely, just how he always does, but something is different, something dangerously...predatory.

My heart begins a deafening rhythm, and my legs begin to tremble.

I quickly slip into the shorts and throw the tank over my head, thankful to be dressed even though I didn't dry off. My bravado soon dies, and I await his next move. His heavy breathing fills the small space while I toe over a flaw in the wooden floor design.

Finally, he breaks this tangible electricity and walks over to a small bar fridge to grab a bottle of water. I practically salivate at the sight because I am so thirsty, but I won't ask this asshole to do me any favors.

"Sit," he commands, gesturing to the bench seat, and I do.

If I could see his face, I imagine he would be arching a brow, surprised by my submission. But he doesn't know a lot about me. He thinks he can break me, but he can't. I will get off this hell on earth one way or another, and when I do, I will make him pay for all the horrible things he's done.

There is something different about him, the way he seems to be careful not to touch me for too long as if he can't stand to make contact. He removes the cuffs from his pocket and snaps one around my wrist, refusing to look at me. He then attaches it to the silver railing of the seat.

I'm expecting him to drop to his knees and tie my ankles, but he doesn't.

He simply places the bottle of water near me and exits up the stairs. When the hatch closes, leaving me alone, I exhale, releasing the breath I was holding. Frantically reaching for the bottle of water, I place it in my cuffed hand and uncap it with my other. Once it's opened, I gulp it down in one long swig.

The coolness has me gasping, but my body relishes in being replenished. The water dribbles down my chin, but I savor the feeling as I don't know when I'll experience it again. Once I've drained the bottle, I slouch back, but then sigh as I have a little room to move.

Tugging at the cuffs, I'm surprised Saint has bound me this way. My eyes grow heavy as the cushy leather beneath me and the sway of the ocean lulls me into a sleepy state. I rearrange myself to lie down, a comfort I will never take for granted again.

My arm is raised above my head, but I use it as a makeshift pillow, and here finally, I lose myself to the calm.

I wake to voices…a lot of them.

Rubbing the sleep from my eyes, I see the full moon slipping in from the window, revealing I finally succumbed to my exhaustion and slept for hours.

Shuffling up, I come to sit, my arm throbbing from the

odd angle it was bent in. But at least I was able to lie down. It's dark as there is no light on, but the moon is my beacon, allowing me to see that on the table lies a black, long-sleeved shirt and a shiny key—the key to my cuffs. My heart begins to pound.

Saint must have taken off the necklace, intent on changing, but the fact it's still down here has me guessing that whoever is upstairs was unexpected and Saint greeted them half dressed.

Is this stranger a friend or foe?

Steadying my breathing, I listen for any clue as to who they may be, but I can't make out anything specific, just a clutter of voices. It's now or never.

The table is a few feet away. Looking back and forth between it and the hatch, and ensuring the voices are still present, I tongue the corner of my mouth and slide my body off the seat, extending as far as I can go. My arm is jerked from its socket as I stretch out, willing my body to grow just a few more inches.

"Come on," I growl, craning my neck to see how far away I am. I kick my foot out, hoping I'll be able to loop it around the leg of the table, but I'm still too far away. Sweat gathers along my brow as I extend my leg, but it's not enough. "Shit."

I try to maneuver my arm to give me some more slack, but it's no use. Sighing, I study my escape, and the few measly feet separating me from it. I know what I have to do. Chewing the inside of my cheek, I rotate my arm backward, muting my whimpers as I reach out. Tears sting my eyes as I continue pushing my body until I hear a pop. My shoulder gives way, and I stretch those few extra inches to be able to loop my foot around the leg of the table and drag it toward me slowly, ensuring I don't make a sound.

My shoulder throbs, and I've chewed the inside of my cheek until I've drawn blood, but when that table is within reach, I slide the shirt toward me and grab the necklace with the tips of my fingers. Whimpering in relief, I don't waste a moment as I unlock myself.

The moment I do, I gnaw at my lip to stifle my pained breaths as I cup my elbow to support my shoulder. Inhaling slowly, I calm myself because I need to focus on popping my dislocated shoulder back into place.

I drop my injured arm by my side, flinching when it flops lifelessly. I then begin to rotate my shoulder backward as far as it can go before slowly bringing it forward. The pressure in the joint is unbearable, and I bite my fist to mute my screams. Closing my eyes and mentally counting to three, I jar it forward quickly, and it pops back into the socket with a snap.

I only know how to do this thanks to the first-aid skills Lea taught me.

My eyes flicker as I almost pass out from the pain. But I shake my head and breathe in and out heavily. Once the dizziness subsides, and I think I can walk without throwing up, I head for the small window near the sink and cautiously peer out of it.

I ensure to stay out of sight, shielding myself as I scope out what's going on outside. I can't see much, just a flurry of shadows. Cursing, I decide to use the window in the bathroom. Hobbling toward it, I brush the sweaty hair from my eyes and position myself so I can hopefully see what's going on outside.

I can hear the voices clearer. One belongs to Saint. And another deep, menacing voice belongs to a stranger. Craning my neck, I stand on tippy toes for a better look, but when my vision focuses on a figure, I almost fall from my perch.

Ensuring I'm not seeing things, I press my nose to the glass, and when I see the unmissable uniform of a police officer, adrenaline soars through me, and I run for the hatch. My breath is heavy, and my heart is in my throat because the police are here. In moments, I will be rescued. This must be because of Drew. I feel awful for doubting him for even a second.

Charging up the stairs, I throw open the hatch and almost fall flat onto the deck as my feet can't keep up. "Help me! Please!" However, what I see before me has me skidding to a sudden stop.

The full moon is high above me, a true spotlight for me to see my colossal fuckup. Before me stands eight men. Three I know. The rest I do not. And from the filthy look of them, I don't want to get to know them.

The man in uniform, my supposed savior, is indeed wearing a police outfit, but in no way is he here to protect me. His long dreadlocks fall limply around his dirty face. His toothless smile lifts when he sees me—I'm a lamb to slaughter.

The air is heavy with utter fury, and it takes my breath away. When I center on the reason, I forget everything and instead give way to the absolute beauty in front of me. A broad, golden back faces me, each sculptured muscle catching the moonlight, emphasizing the perfection to not only the canvas but also to the artwork which adorns it—Saint's creation.

Angel wings which glisten to life are tattooed across his back and shoulders, and then running down the length of his hulking arms. The delicate feathers sweep across his rippling biceps and curve downward, stopping halfway down his taunt forearms. His name is all the more intriguing now.

I know it's him because I'm intoxicated by those eyes as he glares wickedly at me over his shoulder. He is wearing his ski mask as he clearly doesn't want this band of nomads to know his identity either. But he is topless, and seeing him bare does something—it makes him human.

The man in uniform who lurks toward me, however, is not. "Oh, I'll help you," he says in an accent I can't quite place. Persian maybe? He is beyond tanned, his skin resembling leather from clearly being at sea for a while.

I don't know how he got that police uniform, and I have no interest in finding out because everything about this man screams danger. His fellow sailors, dressed in ripped and dirty rags, follow him, sneering. Are they pirates? I suddenly wish for the friendly Captain Jack Sparrow.

I instantly back up.

"Now aren't you a pretty thing. We haven't seen a girl like you for quite some time, have we, boys?" They nod and grunt in acknowledgment. "With all the pretty soft skin, I bet you taste like a cherry." He snaps whatever remaining teeth he has left together.

I stand tall, but the predatory behaviors of these men have me fearing for my life.

Saint turns slowly, watching to see how I handle myself. His chest and stomach are yet another creation adorned with more ink, but I don't have time to appreciate it or the silver bar piercing his left nipple.

"How much?" the man asks, and I pale.

"She's not for sale," Saint barks. I exhale in relief.

"Everyone has a price," he argues, continuing to advance. I am hit with his stench—stale piss, sweat, and rum.

"She doesn't," Saint replies, unbending. The two Russians stand by him, rubbing the back of their necks. They are clearly worried.

Saint, however, is as calm as can be.

The man runs a hand over his unkempt beard. His long fingernails have thick dirt caked underneath them. I swallow down my revulsion. "Okay, friend. How about I pay for an hour with her? A few bottles of wine and some precious jewels should do."

"I'm not a whore," I spit, storming forward. What century are they living in anyway? Who trades goods for sex?

However, setting sights on their wooden ship, which does resemble a pirate boat, I figure this is the law of the sea. These people are true nomads, sailing the seas and robbing and pillaging where they can.

"Good, I like them virtuous. They always seem to scream the loudest." I feel sick to my stomach as his slippery tongue licks his dry bottom lip.

Saint is our barrier, the point of no return. When the man gets closer and closer, I peer around for a weapon because I don't know if Saint will protect me or feed me to the wolves for my defiance.

"You smell like lavender," he groans, rearranging the front

of his pants. Just as he advances, I recoil swiftly, but Saint's arm snaps out and stops the man from taking another step. "I only need twenty minutes. I'll pay you two thousand dollars."

His friends gripe, clearly not seeing my value to match that of what their leader just offered. "Pipe," one of them says, but Pipe, the man in uniform, holds up his hand, signaling this isn't negotiable.

"Two thousand dollars?" Saint whistles, shaking his head. "That's a lot of money."

"It's worth every penny. As long as I have free rein."

Free rein? Excuse me?

He isn't actually considering this, is he? But when he looks at me, infuriated I defied him yet again, I know that he is.

"No…" I whisper, eyes wide. "Please, no." But it's too late. This is my punishment for once again mistaking him to be anything but a monster.

"Okay, she's yours."

"No!" I cry, backing up, but it's in vain.

Saint lowers his arm, allowing Pipe to prowl toward me, grinning. "Oh, yes, sweetheart." The two Russians shout at Saint, but he ignores them, his eyes never leaving mine.

Pipe grips my bicep and inhales deeply. I gag, his stench making my stomach turn. "Let's go." He drags me to the stairs, but I struggle, digging in my heels.

"Let me go! No!" I scream at the top of my lungs. "Saint! No! I'm sorry. I won't disobey you again." Saint is impassive to my pleas.

Pipe simply snickers. "Sweet surrender…music to my ears." I have clearly proven his point that us virtuous ones scream the loudest. But when he presses his blunt erection into my leg, I soon will no longer bear that title. "I'm going to split you into two."

Tears sting my eyes as I fight him, but he drags me down the stairs and pushes me to the floor. I frantically scramble to get to my feet, but he places his foot at the small of my back and kicks me back down. "Stay down, you bitch."

I slide on my stomach, desperately trying to stand to fight him off, but he's on top of me, licking the side of my neck. I buck wildly, flailing and screaming, but the harder I fight, the harder he becomes. "It's been a long time since I had a girl like you…I'll try to be gentle."

When he unzips his fly, sheer terror overcomes me as I'm transported back to being fifteen years old.

Let me fuck that tight virgin pussy. You're gonna come for Daddy.

Those words a forever manacle smash into me because this time, I won't surrender. "No!" I shriek. "Get off!" I thrash about, intent on killing him when he gets my shorts down my legs. "You bastard! Don't touch me! I'll kill you!"

Adrenaline overtakes me, and just as I'm about to fight with everything I have, there is a hollow gurgle, followed by vibration and a sharp jerking. Time stands still as I have no idea what's going on when I feel a warmth squirt all over my back and bare ass.

My heart is hammering, and every part of me is telling me to close my eyes and not look. But it's too late. As I turn over my shoulder slowly, I scream a guttural howl when I witness Pipe clutching his neck, blood gushing from a wound to his throat. Behind him stands Saint, knife in hand, his chest scattered in warpaint from the fatal gash he just delivered. It seems I didn't have to kill anyone after all.

He kicks Pipe from my body, who plummets with a wheezing thud, and reaches down, dragging him up the stairs by his dreadlocks. Each thud of his wounded body over the steps has me flinching. So does the trail of blood he leaves behind.

I lie sprawled out on the floor, certain I'm about to have a heart attack.

The Russians shout at Saint, and it's no surprise a fight erupts when I'm assuming Pipe's crew sees their leader's body. Breathing in deeply, I pull up my shorts before crawling on hands and knees to the stairs, my body fighting me to turn back around. But I can't.

In the stairwell, coated in Pipe's blood, I watch as Saint plows through them, the punches he receives a mere tickle as he shakes them off. Three are down and two to go when a Russian raises a gun in the air and fires. It has the desired effect, and the men, bar Saint, freeze.

"Get off my boat," Saint warns, spitting out a mouthful of blood. "And take that filth with you."

His threat is downright frightening, and the men do as he says, quickly pulling the wounded to safety as they walk the plank to their boat. By this point, Pipe has stopped writhing and gasping for air.

Once they're gone, the Russians' and Saint's eyes never waver, and they don't turn their backs until the pirates are sailing off into the bitter night.

"Why?" screams one of the Russians, shoving Saint's shoulder. He barely moves an inch. "You know what this means! We have to change route now. They'll want vengeance. This puts us off by days! Weeks! Boss…"

"You let me handle him," Saint cautions.

He is lathered in bright red blood, and the sight contrasts with his angelic wings. An angel of death, that's what he is.

"Why didn't you let him have his way? Boss wouldn't know…"

I shrink in on myself, horrified. But Saint slaps the back of his head. Hard. "She is for Boss, and Boss only…don't you forget that." It's evident he's seen the way they look at me.

My brain can't keep up, and my teeth chatter at his promise. I have no idea what it means. I should feel grateful he protected me and even killed a man for me, but if he hadn't offered me up on a silver platter in the first place, none of this would have happened.

So why did he?

When he turns slowly, privy to me eavesdropping, I suddenly know why. He did it to teach me a lesson…just how he's going to once again.

I scuttle down the stairs, attempting to run to safety, but it's too late. Saint charges after me, gripping my forearm to stop me from going anywhere. His golden flesh is now a bright red, his huge body dwarfing mine. His chest rises and falls, his heavy breathing deafening.

"You never fucking listen!" he roars, hurling me toward him.

"Let me go!" I shout, attempting to pry myself free.

"A thank you would be nice."

"Thank you?" I scoff, my temper exploding. "You sold me for two thousand dollars to some…pirate! There is no way I'm thanking you. Not to mention you kidnapped me! I hate you!" I stand on tippy toes, not intimated as I invade his personal space. "You better kill me now because that's the only way your *boss* will have me."

Oh, shit. In my moment of anger, I didn't consider the impact of my words. But it's too late.

"You will obey me."

"Fuck you. Obey this!" I raise my knee in an attempt to connect with his balls, but he's too fast, and suddenly, things turn ominous. At this moment, he scares me.

A menacing growl gets trapped in his throat before he tosses me onto the seat and comes charging over. The wind gets ripped from my sails, but I don't have time to get up because, before I know what's happening, he's dragged me over his lap and is yanking down my shorts.

My cheeks burst into flames as he exposes my bare ass, but what he does next puts my bashfulness to shame.

He spanks me.

It takes me a moment to register just what the hell he's doing, and when I do, that's when the pain kicks in.

"You bastard!" I scream, kicking and screaming. But he has a firm hold on me and strikes me once again.

My eyes bulge from my head as I shift upward from the force. I don't know what to think. I am furious, but more than anything, I'm mortified. I've never been spanked before. This is new territory because with the blood whizzing through my

ears and the adrenaline burning my tongue, it doesn't hurt…
it feels good.

I am ashamed and instantly shake such perverse thoughts
from my brain.

"You sick asshole. Is this getting you off?"

Smack.

"I hate you!"

Smack.

Each defiance results in my ass getting slapped, and each
strike stokes something primeval. Between each slap, Saint
rubs me gently, soothing the burn with a tender touch of his
strong, calloused hand.

"Enough?"

"Fuck you."

Smack.

"You will break, ангел."

"Never," I rebel, bracing myself for the onslaught, followed
by the softness.

Smack.

It should bother me that my ass is bared to Saint, but it
doesn't. And I need to figure out why.

"You will, soon enough." It's a promise, one filled with so
many questions…and I have a sneaking suspicion the answers
lie with Boss, whoever he is.

We will see, you asshole.

Smack.

He gently strokes my ass before pulling up my shorts,
which once again confounds me. Is that it?

I don't know what to do because now that the adrenaline

has subsided, embarrassment kicks in. I just let the angel of death spank me…and I liked it. Something is seriously wrong with me. Maybe the knocks to my head scrambled my brain.

He sits me up and stands casually like something weird didn't just transpire between us. It wasn't sexual as such, but it felt like Saint was training me, preparing me…but for what?

The cuffs sit by me, and he snaps one around my wrist. I don't bother fighting him. "Submit," he warns, folding his arms.

In response, I flip him off.

His broad shoulders rise in an inhale before he exhales in finality. "Have it your way then."

Playtime is over, and I instantly regret my words because Saint leaves me alone, wondering if Boss goes by another name…and that name is Master.

CHAPTER THREE

This is the only kindness I can show her because where she's headed, he will show her no mercy. She'll be expected to submit, and if she doesn't...he will kill her, regardless of how beautiful she is. And she is...beautiful.

Day 4

Twenty-six cans of tuna fish. Eight lemon pepper. Seven honey barbecue. Five herb and garlic. Six ranch.

Forty-eight ounce tin of classic roast ground coffee. A bottle of vodka.

There are three hundred and sixteen panes of wood decorating the ceiling and walls.

I know all this because I've been stuck down here for two

days. Forty-eight hours of utter hell. I ache. Mind. Body. And soul.

After that very strange evening when I was sold to a pirate for two thousand dollars before Saint slit his throat and then spanked me, all to teach me a lesson, he left me down here in hopes the solitude would break me—it didn't.

He visited every hour, proposing the same thing—*submit*. And each time, I replied the same way—*fuck you.*

The visits became less frequent, and before long, it seemed I was the only one who could stand my own company. But that suited me just fine as I needed the quiet to process everything that has happened.

I don't know much, but what I do know is that Saint intends to give me to someone named Boss. That's why he kidnapped me, it appears. But the thing is, I have no idea who Boss is, so I don't know how he knows me.

Yes, my face may be recognizable to some because of my modeling, but it's not like I'm in the league of Victoria's Secret models. Besides, my audience is more homegrown and not European, which is where we are clearly heading.

I also can't deny that talks of submission, breaking, obeying, and the spanking are very troubling. Whoever Boss is doesn't want a companion...he wants a slave, and apparently, I fit the bill.

Swallowing down my fear, I reach for the bottle of water left for me by the Russian with the birthmark, who I have named Mark. He also left a bucket and some food close by, cementing that I am indeed a prisoner.

Reality has set in, and my bravado is slipping every single

minute I am caged down here. The fight in me is slowly fading because each sunrise brings me closer to my doom. And that's why he's left me down here covered in my attacker's blood... to break me.

The hatch opens, and like a vampire confronting the breaking dawn, I shrink backward, protecting my eyes from the bright light. I know it's him, and a small part of me, a part I loathe, is relieved he's here.

When I see him, all dominating and commanding, I blush, thinking about the control he showed when he threw me over his knee. But I soon forget such ridiculous thoughts. "I've been too lenient with you. We need to set some ground rules," he states, ducking as he walks down the stairs to avoid hitting his head on the ceiling. I hate how refined he looks and smells.

I could ignore him, but I desperately want to take a shower and change my clothes, so I simply arch a brow, indicating I'm listening.

He pulls up a chair and spins it around, so he's straddling it. I can't believe that after four days, I still haven't seen his face. "Thanks to the shit you pulled, we'll now be spending a lot more time together."

I lick my dry lips. "What does that mean?"

"It means, everything has changed. So if you disobey me...I punish you."

My mouth parts, and I half laugh in disbelief. But when I see that he's serious, I blanch. "Excuse me?"

"You talk out of line...I punish you."

"Wha—"

"You try to escape again…I punish you," he says, interrupting me to prove my point. "We clear?"

"Where are we going?"

He inhales through his nose, clearly annoyed I'm not acknowledging his ground rules. "I said, are…we…clear?" His pause between each word is a warning.

"Very," I snarl, glaring at him.

"Good. You will no longer address me by my name. From now on, it's мастер."

I have no idea what that word means, but it's no doubt Russian as it rolls freely off Saint's tongue. He can't be serious. But when he taps his boot against the floor, awaiting my response, I cave. "Fine."

He clears his throat while it takes all my willpower to yield. "Yes…мастер." I don't know what I just called him since my pronunciation is horrible, but he nods once.

Victorious, he stands. I want to cut out my tongue. "Good. You behave; I reward you. You don't; I punish you."

But it's not that simple. "What happened to my husband?" I ask quickly, afraid he's going to leave me down here for another two days.

"Forget him," he snaps, surprising me.

The ring on my finger burns in defiance because I will do no such thing. "He will be looking for me."

"Don't hold your breath." I open my mouth, intent on arguing, but Saint hints this conversation is done. "I'm going to uncuff you, and then you're going to take a shower."

That sounds like heaven, but what's the catch?

He reads my suspicion instantly. "This is your reward for

listening. Would you like to take a shower?"

He waits patiently while I grind my teeth. "Yes." When he folds his arms across his chest, I add, "мастер."

I may as well have told him to go fuck himself, but he seems pleased.

He loops the chain out from under his shirt and eyes me closely as he bends low to unlock my cuff. We lock gazes, and I can't keep the contempt from mine while he can't mask the triumph in his. The moment I'm free, I rub my wrist, which is red and raw. The skin is grazed and swollen.

He walks over to a white waterproof box in the corner and opens it, revealing a stack of clothes inside. They are clearly for me. When I see a white bra and matching underwear on top of what looks like a yellow sundress, I sigh in relief.

He offers it to me while I purse my lips with my head tilted to the side. I can't help but feel this comes with strings attached. However, the need to shower wins out, and I stand wearily as I haven't used my legs for two days.

I stagger forward, the sting in my ass reminding me of what transpired between Saint and me. My cheeks flourish a deep crimson, but I snatch the clothes from his hand and await further instruction. He hums low, satisfied by my submission.

"Here." He opens the box once again, and I almost cry in happiness when he produces a toiletry bag filled with shampoo, conditioner, toothpaste, and everything else a girl who hasn't had a proper shower in four days would need.

"Thank you." It comes naturally, but Saint nods once.

Now the kicker.

There is no way I'm undressing with him in here. When I

stand firm, he knows it.

"Cut the innocent act. Undress now."

His judgment of me pisses me off, and I come apart. "It's not an act," I state defensively. When those green eyes widen, I arch a defying brow. "Where I'm from, saving yourself for marriage isn't a crime. Stop looking at me like that."

It's not like I haven't heard it before, but it still riles me up. It's no one's business but my own.

But what Saint says next has me gasping. "Where I'm from...it *is* a crime. A crime against you." He sighs, heavy with burden.

What the hell does that mean?

"Where exactly are you from?" I'm speaking out of line, but his reaction confuses me. He almost looks...saddened by the fact.

He steps forward, and I'm engulfed in his spice as he towers over me. "A world you don't belong in."

The air suddenly sizzles, and a palpable electricity has the hair on the back of my neck standing on end. I have so many more questions, but he makes it clear that question time is over as he cocks his head toward the shower.

"You have ten minutes."

I blink once, stunned he's going to let me shower alone.

I don't waste a second and quickly hobble toward the bathroom, sighing when I hear him march up the stairs and close the hatch behind him. With this newfound freedom, I don't know what to do first. I have a bad case of cotton mouth, so I decide to brush my teeth.

When I peer at my reflection in the mirror, I stagger back,

covering my mouth in horror. I barely recognize myself.

Caked in blood and my eyes wild, my soiled appearance scares me. Is this what I have become?

Unable to face the truth, I strip and toss my clothes into the corner of the room. The moment I step into the shower and turn the faucet to hot, I fold and relish in the feel of washing away my sins. The water runs red, but I coax it down the drain with my big toe.

My muscles uncoil from the warmth, and I melt into the feeling of being clean once more. The water feels wonderful, but when I turn, and the spray hits my ass, I flinch. Peering over my shoulder, I flush as bright as my ass cheeks when I see the red prints left by Saint's hands. I still can't believe he spanked me, but what's most disturbing is I can't believe my response.

Tears threaten to break past the floodgates, but I don't have time to grieve.

Saint said ten minutes, and I know he won't give me a second more, so I hurried to wash my hair and condition it as I lathered the vanilla soap over my body. I'm clean with two minutes to spare, so I turn off the water and dry hurriedly.

I've applied deodorant, some body lotion, and brushed my hair when I hear heavy footsteps up on the deck. He's coming.

Stepping into my underwear, which fit, I thread my arms through the bra, and although the cups are a size too small, I hook it and arrange my breasts so they don't pop out. Just as I reach for my dress, the hatch opens, and Saint appears.

I attempt to throw it on over my head, but he stops me.

"Wait."

With my arms raised in the air, I pause, my chest rising and falling quickly as I catch my breath.

"Come here."

There is no point in arguing with him, so I remove the dress and place it over the edge of the basin and walk toward him slowly. I stop when I am a few feet away.

Bashful to be standing in nothing but underwear, especially a bra that barely fits, I cast my eyes downward, unable to look at him. I bite my lip, unsure what he wants me to do.

"Kneel," he commands.

Although every fiber of my being is demanding I fight, I know this will be over a lot quicker if I just surrender...so I do.

Gradually, I drop to my knees, averting my gaze as I'm embarrassed to be seen this way. But something changes in Saint. His exhalations are deep as he takes his time before he reaches down and caresses the cross at my throat.

My skin breaks out into goose bumps, but I remain passive, unsure what comes next.

"You look...beautiful," he says painfully slow while I snap my chin upward, locking gazes with him. I was not expecting him to say that.

The feral look reflected in those green depths has me instantly dropping my chin. My cheeks blister. Using my hair as a veil, I hide behind it as I sit back on my heels, measuring my breaths and wringing my hands together.

Although this could be looked at as sexual, as Saint

dominating me, I don't feel objectified. I feel empowered as I'm the one in control. That doesn't make a lick of sense, but neither does any of this.

I stay this way, awaiting his next move, and when I hear the distinct shutter of a camera clicking, one on a phone, I realize I've just found another means of communication. Him slipping up is slim to none, but stranger things have happened—like him leaving his key for me to uncuff myself with or…calling me beautiful.

"Okay, you can get dressed now."

This is bizarre, to say the least, but I don't argue.

Standing, I flick back my damp hair, aware he's watching me, but I quickly make my way into the bathroom and slip the dress over my head. I don't know what happens next. So I make my way over to the seat and extend my hands, ready to be cuffed, but he shakes his head.

"You're coming up on deck."

"I am?" I ask, surprised.

"Yes," he replies firmly, peering down at my grazed wrist. "You need some sunshine. And you need to eat." The mere mention of food has my stomach growling.

It's on the tip of my tongue to mention I look anemic because he's locked me down here for four days, but I decide against it. The thought of feeling the sunshine on my Vitamin-D depleted skin is too good an opportunity to pass up.

In regards to food, I peer over at the poorly stocked shelves and frown. "Do you have anything that isn't canned?"

He sweeps his hand outward, gesturing I'm to look for myself.

This new sense of freedom is unsettling. Something which I took for granted has been snatched out from under me, and now that I've been given it back, I don't know what to do with it—like a bird being released from her cage but is too scared to spread her wings.

Not sure when I will be given this freedom again, I brush past him, his trademark scent smashing into me. It's not a bad sensation; it's just…familiar, which is absurd. I stop in front of the shelves, placing my hands on my hips and blowing the hair from my cheeks.

Tuna fish, a few cans of soup, a small bag of flour, dry milk, and what appears to be dried jerky—nothing looks remotely appetizing. However, when I see some potatoes, eggs, and a bag of rice in a drawer below the sink, things start looking up slightly.

Tapping my chin, I begin to channel my inner *MasterChef*.

"See anything acceptable?" Saint asks, and if I didn't know any better, I'd say his tone carried a touch of playfulness in it.

"It doesn't look completely hopeless," I reply, my back still turned. "Growing up in my household, you were forced to make do with whatever was lying around."

I realize this is the first piece of information I've shared about myself with Saint. How will he respond? Will he see me as a person and not merely a means to an end?

"Didn't your parents stick around?"

Surprised that he actually cares, I don't make a big deal about it and shrug. "My dad died when I was twelve. After that, my mom just sort of forgot I existed." When he's quiet, I turn over my shoulder, and add, "What? Not the story you were expecting? Expecting the life of a spoiled brat who turned to modeling after sleeping with every hotshot in LA?"

His predominant Adam's apple bobs as he swallows. I've caught him off guard. "I've come to learn not to expect anything when you're involved."

Well, damn. That's given me food for thought.

Clearing my throat, I go back to making sense of our menu, rather than analyzing what he means by that comment. "I can probably make some sort of a frittata or omelet." Forgetting he's here, I walk over to the small fridge and find some frozen vegetables in the tiny freezer. I can work with that.

Grabbing what I need, I dump everything onto the table, pointing at each item to catalog its purpose in my head. The potatoes can't go in whole. I need a knife. I switch my gaze from the small pile to Saint, who stands on the opposite side of the table watching me.

"I need utensils like a bowl, spoon. A knife," I add nonchalantly, trying my best to mask my nerves.

He sighs low as if deep in thought.

"Or you can always help?" I suggest as I need to play this off. I don't plan on using the knife, but I plan on gaining his trust with it.

A cloud of uncertainty lingers, but eventually, he reaches into his back pocket and produces his switchblade. My nose instantly screws up in revulsion. "I am *not* using that to prepare my meal."

That blade is the same one he severed my attacker's throat with. The sunshine catches the bright silver of the metal, and I shiver as memories crash into me. But I pull it together and extend my hand.

I wish I could see his face because right now, I'm just guessing his thoughts. Without any facial expressions, he is merely my captor, but that is exactly what he is, and I need to remember that. Just because he's showing a shred of decency doesn't excuse the despicable things he's done.

This is a test. I'm testing him, and he's testing me.

My gaze never wavers from his as I appear bored, waiting for him to give me the knife. But there is no doubt he's contemplating his next move. This is the first step to gaining his trust because all I need is a little leeway to get to the radio or to somehow steal his phone.

The air is thick with anticipation, but eventually, he caves.

When he places the switchblade into my palm, every part of me sings in victory, but I remain passive.

"Thank you…мастер."

A hiss escapes him as he takes a small step back, which is exactly the response I wanted. But I play it off and instead turn, hunting for a saucepan. When I find a small one, I place it on the stovetop and pour half a bottle of water into it.

I may have agreed to use the knife, but I won't be using it without boiling it first. As I wait for the water to boil, I hunt for a chopping board and some bowls. Once I decide on eggs and hash browns, my mouth waters at the thought of freshly baked biscuits.

As the water begins to boil, I dump the blade into the pot, hoping it'll be sanitized to the point of being able to use it without remembering it took someone's life. But I know it never will.

Needing a distraction, I reach for the flour and dry milk

and decide to attempt to make biscuits. It's my comfort food, and right now, I need all the comfort I can get. Once the knife has bubbled and boiled for a few minutes, I turn off the stove and reach into the water with tongs. Images of using this blade for my escape crash into me as I begin to wonder if Saint is now unarmed.

Peering at his statue—arms folded, eyes sharp, legs spread—I know there is no way I'd make it three steps. Besides, I have to pick my battles wisely, and doing this is for the greater good.

Curling my fingers around the cold handle, I detach myself from what it's capable of, of what I've seen it do, and focus on the good it can do, like make me breakfast. I begin to peel the potatoes, willing my shaky fingers to steady. It's a little hard to do, however, when Saint pulls up a chair, straddles it, and watches me intently.

My heart is racing, and I'm certain he can see my fear, but I continue working, fixated on making food because I'm suddenly famished. "Can I make some coffee?"

Saint nods.

For the next twenty minutes, I work like a madwoman, but it's nice to lose myself in normality seeing as I've been surrounded by anything but. Once I'm done, I stand back, smiling at my creation. With limited ingredients and supplies, I was able to whip up hash browns, eggs, and biscuits, which are a little flat, but regardless, they smell amazing. The coffee, however, is the crème de la crème because after living without it for four days, my body craves a caffeine hit.

Saint has watched me the entire time, which, of course,

is no surprise. I have to earn his trust before he leaves me unsupervised, which is why I give his knife a wash and slide it across the table. "Thank you."

He reaches for it and places it into his back pocket. "You're welcome, ангел."

"What does that mean?" It's out before I can stop myself.

Saint stiffens as if he's just been called out, which just intrigues me further. He comes to a slow stand, and I gulp when peering upward, examining his tall stature. "Let's eat." And that puts an end to a conversation Saint clearly has no interest in having.

Yet his evasiveness just intrigues me all the more.

I've made enough food to feed a small nation, so I reach for four plates and serve up breakfast. Once the coffee is poured, I wait for further instruction. Saint turns over his shoulder and shouts in Russian. Although the language is so foreign to me, I find it almost entrancing when spoken in Saint's hoarse tone.

When the two Russians pound down the stairs, all entrancement is long gone.

They look at the food on the table and then up at me. This is strange, to say the least, but clearly, their appetite is more important than dealing with this weirdness as they almost fight one another to snatch a plate for themselves.

Saint steps aside, allowing the scavengers to feed first.

I sip my coffee, relishing in the bitterness. I don't fancy eating down here as I'm tired of the dark. I want to feel the sunshine against my skin. I also need to scope out the radio, and I can't do that with Saint breathing down my throat.

"Let's go outside."

It's a touch scary he can read me so well, but I suppose he's at an advantage. He can see my face after all.

Mark stops shoveling the eggs into his mouth as I reach for my plate. His ravenous eyes instantly drop to the front of my dress as the scooped neckline reveals a little too much cleavage when bending low. I feel disgusting, like my mom's words are true when I play on his attraction and reach forward for my fork.

It's innocent enough, but I know it has the desired effect when Mark's tongue sweeps along his bottom lip. His smell alone has me wanting to gag, but I smile shyly, hoping to feign innocence and submission.

The other Russian just continues to inhale his food, not at all affected by me.

I wait for Saint to lead the way with my eyes cast downward. When I hear his heavy boots march up the stairs, I follow, ensuring to brush Mark gently with my shoulder on the way out. I know I'm playing with fire, but Saint will eventually have to sleep. I can only hope when that happens, Mark is awake. I will then make up some excuse as to why I need to go upstairs.

It's weak, but it's all I have.

The sun feels wonderful against my skin, and I pause for a moment, closing my eyes and tipping my chin upward to savor the feeling as I don't know when I will experience it again. My growling stomach interrupts my basking, so I open my eyes. Saint is sitting on the white chest near the helm. I try my best to remain unaffected, but it's difficult to when that radio is within reach.

Wanting to get as close as possible to the radio, I sit across from Saint on a small wooden bench seat. Sitting cross-legged, I place my plate on my lap and the coffee beside me. I reach for the biscuit and separate it into two pieces. Using my fork, I pile on the fluffy scrambled eggs onto one side before sealing it shut.

A perfect meal.

The moment I take a bite, a small moan leaves me as my taste buds sing in delight. It's the first real thing I've eaten in days. Uncaring I look like a caveman, I shove the entire biscuit into my mouth, stuffing my cheeks full.

Once I'm done gulping that down, I dig into the hash browns, scraping the plate clean. It takes me all of five minutes to finish my meal. Leaning back against the railing, I place my hands on my full stomach and sigh.

That was so unladylike, but lucky for me, I don't care. Saint only sees me as a means to an end anyway, so why bother with manners. However, I risk a glance his way, and if I didn't know any better, I could swear I see his lips twitch. But that's impossible.

As I sip my coffee, my mind wanders to Drew. It's been four days since I was kidnapped. He must be beside himself.

We didn't even get a chance to consummate our marriage. What a cruel fucking joke. The need to escape has never been more crucial.

"When will we arrive at wherever we're going?" I ask cautiously, unsure how he'll respond.

His fork pauses en route to his mouth.

I know I'm overstepping a boundary, but he did say if I

behaved, he'd reward me. And the fact I didn't stab him in the jugular *is* me behaving. I don't expect much, so when he replies, I almost fall from my seat.

"A week. Give or take. Then we go by car."

"Go where?" I ask in a small voice.

He finishes his eggs, appearing to need the time to prepare his response. "It's better if you don't know."

His ominous reply has tears welling in my eyes. "Will you let me go?"

"No, I can't," he replies, averting his eyes. It's the first sign he's expressed that reveals he's human.

"Where I'm going"— I pause, steadying my quaking voice —"will it hurt?"

"Yes," he simply yet remorsefully responds.

"Will I ever be able to go home?" I work my bottom lip, fearful, but better I know.

Silence.

The only sound is the gentle sway of the ocean. But in that silence is a riotous ruckus within me.

"…No."

A single tear scores my cheek as Saint locks eyes with me. I'm trying to be strong, but I've just been told that life as I know it has changed forever.

"Will you be there?" I ask, picking at my dusty pink nail polish. "Wherever there is."

I don't know why it matters, but a familiar face or, rather, a familiar swirl of chartreuse might ease the pain. But this is all a false sense of security because nothing ever will.

"No…Willow, I won't be."

I gasp. It's the first time he's used my name, and it sounds almost forbidden slipping past his lips. In some ways, I know that it is.

I sniff back my tears, attempting to be strong, but the quiver to my lower lip gives me away. "So you're just going to deliver me and then what? Get paid?"

He stands abruptly, passing a hand over his head. I presume this is an involuntary habit of his because if not for the ski mask, he'd be able to run his fingers through his hair. "I don't get paid how you think I do."

"What does that mean?"

"It means"—he interlaces his hands behind his nape—"that I don't get paid with money."

I cock my head to the side, utterly confused.

No matter which way I look at this, there is no doubt that once I arrive at my destination, the chance to escape will no longer be an option. Which means I need to escape now.

"Is Boss"—a sob gets trapped in my throat, but I pull it together—"a nice man?" I'm not stupid. From the small snippets he's fed me and the conversations I've heard in passing, I will soon have to obey Boss. I don't know who he is, or why he wants me, but he's the reason this happened, and he's the reason I will fight with my life to flee.

Sighing, Saint takes his time once again, grappling with how much he should disclose. But when he looks into my dogged eyes, he knows I won't settle for anything but the truth. "No, he is not."

I nod, biting my bottom lip as tears trickle down my cheeks. "Thank you for being ho-honest."

Saint nods once, but he's clearly not happy with what's headed my way. So the question is, why is he doing it? If not for money, then what else? What else can one be paid with that they would risk their lives for?

The Russians emerge, and I quickly wipe away my tears, refusing to show weakness. "I'd like to go back downstairs, please."

My request throws Saint for a loop, but he doesn't ask me why. He leads the way, and I follow like the good captive that I am because even though Saint has shown me a lick of kindness, I won't mistake him for anything other than what he is—and that's a monster.

He's leading a lamb to the slaughter, but the one thing he doesn't realize…is that I'm not a lamb. And I never will be.

CHAPTER FOUR

She won't break. No matter what I do, she will not submit. Each time I punish her, I feel whatever small shred of humanity I have left slip away. I know this is wrong but so is delivering her to that soulless asshole.

I don't have a choice. God save my soul.

Day 6

It's been six days since life as I know it changed forever. It's been six days since I was bound, gagged, and kidnapped. It's been six days, and all I've seen are the anonymous faces of three men who mean me harm. And during those six days, I'm still no closer to figuring out what the hell is going on.

It's been two days since I buckled and behaved like the good little girl Saint wanted me to be. I said yes, мастер, no мастер, three bags full, мастер, and in return, he only cuffed me at nighttime. During the day, I could roam "freely." I use the word sparingly because it was always under the watchful eye of one of my captors.

I haven't seen another soul for days, but after the last encounter I had, it's probably a blessing in disguise.

It's almost been one week since I last saw Drew. Each minute and each second erases a small part of him from my mind because the farther away we sail, the farther away I am from going home. There doesn't seem to be a light at the end of the tunnel because I'm still no closer to communicating with the outside world.

Mark is still his ogling disgusting self, which is exactly what I hoped for. What I didn't hope for, however, was Saint ensuring we're not alone together for too long. Saint also sees the lingering glances and the need for Mark to be close to me when he can.

The only saving grace is being able to feel the sunlight on my skin because sometimes, if I close my eyes really tight, I can pretend I'm sailing the seas on my honeymoon with Drew. In my make-believe world, I'm happy, but more importantly, I'm free.

The fantasy doesn't last long, and I'm soon transported back to reality. A bleak reality where I sit among my captors… waiting.

The afternoon is reasonably warm, and in the mystery box downstairs, it appears Saint has an array of items for me. I was thankful I was able to shower every day and change clothes, but whoever packed my kidnap kit was also thoughtful enough to include a bathing suit because apparently rocking a tan when enslaved is the new black.

If I wasn't so damn hot, I would tell Saint to wear the royal blue one-piece himself, but here I am, sitting at the front of the yacht, looking out into complete nothingness. Saint sits across from me, doing his damn sudoku puzzles. The man is obsessed.

I draw my knees into my chest, resting my cheek against my legs. The ocean is a tranquil blue, and on any other day, under any other circumstances, I would be eager to jump into the water and bask in its beauty. But not today. Because today, all I can think about is how if I did jump, I would never want to surface ever again.

Sighing, I hate that I think this way because I'm succumbing to Saint's wishes—I'm breaking. Yes, I may pretend to submit, but the longer I pretend, the harder it is to remember what the end goal is.

Turning my cheek subtly, I peer at the radio. Fifteen, twenty steps top, and I would be free. But how, how can I get to it without being caught? I'm running out of time.

When I hear a beep from Saint's pocket, I close my eyes, as it's just a reminder that he also has an escape route—some fancy phone that looks like something from the 80s, but I know it's a satellite phone. But getting to that is impossible as it's just as much a part of Saint as his arm.

I need a miracle.

Saint stands, speaking in a language I don't recognize,

which has me focusing my attention back on him. He waves to Mark who nods and takes the wheel.

What's going on?

"In about five minutes, we're going to have company." The sharpness to his tone has me sitting upright, wondering why he's suddenly so capricious. "I need you to do me a favor."

I scoff. Now I've heard it all.

His patience is wearing thin as he clearly wants to talk to the Russians about whoever we're about to intercept. "If you do what I say"—he takes a deep breath, clearly not pleased with what he's about to propose—"I'll tell you everything you want to know."

Is this yet another test? Either way, there is no way I'm going to pass up this opportunity. "Deal."

Saint's rigid stance is a warning—I'm to behave; otherwise, this will be the last choice I ever get.

He nods once before quickly marching toward the Russians. They are definitely rattled, which makes me think they've not dealt with these people before. Could they be the key?

Needing to occupy myself before I give myself away, I reach for Saint's tattered sudoku book and open it to a random page. I'm surprised to see that most of these puzzles are completed. I'm no sudoku expert, but what I see is pretty impressive. It appears beneath that ski mask lies quite an intelligent man.

The mystery just continues. A kidnapper who does sudoku…just who is this man?

But I can ponder that later because I see it, a white boat in the distance, the first sign of humanity in days. My heart races as the possibilities flood me. I don't exactly know what this favor is, but in a warped way, I trust Saint. I know what that says about me, but I can question my sanity later.

"On that boat," he says, walking toward me, one of the Russians in tow, "are the Coast Guards. Seeing as we're off course, this was not part of the plan. I need you to pretend that you and Kazimir are just out here holidaying. That's it."

"That might be a hard story to believe seeing as Kazimir here"—my eyes swing his way —"thinks the essential boating attire this season is a ski mask."

Saint exhales, annoyed by my stubbornness. But what he does next displays just how desperate he is. Before Kazimir can protest, Saint rips the ski mask from his head, unveiling just who my attacker is. Kazimir's hands fly up to cover his face, but it's too late. I've seen his dull brown eyes, his portly nose, and his bald, shiny head. I've also seen the birthmark. It appears Mark now has a name.

Kazimir, my admirer, is in his late 40s at a guess. He's also the vilest looking man I've ever seen. Not in the looks department, but rather, he appears as though he's seen and also done some evil in his lifetime. I instantly shudder.

Kazimir begins arguing with Saint, furious at him for revealing his identity. But Saint's response, whatever that may be as it's in Russian, shuts him right up.

"I will be downstairs. If they ask questions, let Kazimir talk. I just need you to nod and agree with whatever story he comes up with. If you don't…" Saint leans forward while I slouch back, but it's futile as the rail behind me prohibits me from moving any farther.

I'm barely breathing when he places his hands either side of my arms, gripping the rail and confining me in my own personal prison. His heated breath bathes my cheeks as we're so close. My pulse begins to spike, and my mouth goes dry. How is it he leaves me breathless without me even seeing his face?

"This means trouble for all of us," he continues, probing every inch of me. "Don't get any ideas. Got it?"

Peering over his shoulder, I see the speedboat getting closer, which means my time is running out.

"Ангел, do you understand?"

Kazimir's rubbery lips part as he turns slowly to look at Saint. Whatever name Saint just used is clearly not one Kazimir was expecting to hear. But I have other pressing issues to deal with, like Saint gripping my arm and rubbing his thumb over the crease of my elbow.

The touch is so unexpected, and my skin instantly breaks out into goose bumps. I don't understand, nor do I like my response to him, so I yank my arm away. His lips twitch in response.

"Yes, I understand." When he continues staring at me, uncaring he has mere moments to get away undetected, I know what he wants. And…I surrender. "Yes, мастер."

Kazimir steps back, interlacing his hands atop his bald head.

"Good." Saint leaves me speechless and frozen to the spot as he reaches forward and brushes a lock of hair from my cheek. I am suddenly drowning in chartreuse. Before I can question anything, he turns and sprints down the stairs like nothing happened. The other Russian follows, slamming the hatch shut.

The touch, just like the one seconds ago on my arm, was weighed down with… warmth, but that's ridiculous. I sound like a crazy person. But I can still feel the warmth his finger left behind. Shaking my head, I violently scrub at my cheek, horrified at myself for feeling…whatever this is.

Kazimir taking off his shirt is the reality check I need to snap the fuck out of this insanity. I recoil at the beads of sweat collecting in the thick hair on his chest. His rounded belly just adds to the monstrosity, but I gather my bearings and lean back, feigning leisure as I open the sudoku book, refusing to think about Saint's hands.

The motor of the boat gets louder and louder until eventually, it switches off, announcing its arrival. I risk a glance at Kazimir who is behind the wheel, but he almost looks friendly as he waves at the older man who walks around the side of his boat so he can address him.

"What are you doing out here?" the man asks in a thick accent.

"Just out with my lady," replies Kazimir, while I continue perusing the sudoku puzzles.

The silence reveals the man isn't convinced, which has me wondering just how far off course we are.

"I'm coming on board."

My heart begins to pound as this is my chance. This man speaks English. He's also the Coast Guard, which means he's probably a good guy. I know I promised Saint, but this is my out. However, when I focus on the hatch, my stomach drops. By saving myself, I am condemning Saint.

I grapple with what to do. This shouldn't be an issue…so why is it? My cheek burns, the same one he touched moments ago.

But shaking such thoughts from my head, I sit upright, watching the man attach some ramp thing onto the yacht so he can come across. My palms sweat, and I discreetly rub them together. When he's aboard, he makes eye contact with me.

"Hello, miss."

I wave limply, trying my best not to draw any attention to myself because I'm still wrestling with what to do.

The man looks around, his eagle eye examining for anything out of the ordinary. This is my chance. *Get the fuck up and scream for help.*

But I remain rooted to the spot. I continue watching him, unsure why I haven't made my move.

The hatch in the distance is the reason, which is ironic. It should be the reason I, in fact, plead with this man to take me off this yacht and to safety. He comes to a stop in front of me, shielding the harsh sun with his hand. "Everything okay?" he asks while I freeze akin to a deer in headlights.

Sweat collects along my brow. My voice gets trapped in my throat. I'm certain I'm moments away from having a heart attack. This entire moment depends on me and my response. It's evident this man doesn't believe Kazimir, and he's waiting for me to confirm his suspicions.

"Speak English?" he gently says as he has mistaken me

clamming up for me not understanding.

I nod quickly, my breathing accelerating as each second passes.

He waits patiently, his kindness giving me the confidence I need. I think about Drew and about Saint's admission that I will never see him again. Tears sting my eyes as I refuse to accept that as truth.

This is my chance, and I have no other choice but to take it.

Standing, I clear my throat, unsure what to say. The air is stagnated. "Miss, do you need help?"

"…Yes," I whisper, surprised that small, terrified voice is mine.

The man jumps into action. "What's the matter?"

My attention flickers back and forth between him and the hatch. Kazimir has backed up, realizing that I've turned rogue. But they've left me with no other option.

"I…I…" I'm suddenly filled with a mouth full of nothing, and I have no idea why. My subconscious screams at me, demanding I tell the truth, but when I see the hatch lift and the unmistakable shine to the barrel of a gun, I know that's the reason I can't speak.

There is no getting off this yacht. Saint will ensure that.

My gaze drops to his gold wedding band, and guilt smashes into me. I can't jeopardize his life because I would be robbing a family of their husband, father, grandfather. How can I live with that on my conscience?

I can't.

"Miss?" he presses.

The gun barrel catches the sunlight, and I swallow down my tears. "We're in dire need of food. All my husband packed was tuna fish. He knows how much I hate fish," I say, feigning annoyance. Inside, I'm dying as my lie is burning a hole straight through me.

The man arches a brow. He doesn't believe me. "Food?" he repeats, ensuring he's heard me correctly.

I nod with a strained smile.

"And you're here because you want to be?"

"Of course, I am." Holding up my hand, I flash my ring, certain I've just sold a piece of my soul. "We're on our honeymoon."

Kazimir exhales and saunters toward me now that I'm on his side. "Aren't I lucky man?" Before I have a chance to protest, he wraps an arm around my shoulders and kisses my cheek.

Bile rises, but I go along with the charade.

The man doesn't look convinced, but there is nothing he can do. Without me confessing, he's got nothing. "Okay then. Have a good day." He tips his hat my way, his intelligent eyes sizing me up.

It's his last attempt to help me, but I just can't. There is no point in both of us losing our lives. "Thank you."

Kazimir falls quite easily into the role of doting husband as his lips trail down my neck. My stomach roils, and I think I'm going to be sick.

As the man walks past the hatch, he looks down at it but doesn't bother probing further because I'm clearly a convincing actress. When he drags the ramp back onto his boat, he takes away my last chance at freedom.

"Good girl," Kazimir whispers into my ear, waving at the man who starts his boat and leaves me alone to deal with my lies. I watch with tears in my eyes as he sails off.

The moment he's out of sight, I shrug Kazimir off me and wipe my cheek and neck, wanting to erase his touch from my skin. He smirks in response. "I'll reward you later…when everyone is asleep." He accentuates his promise with a wink while I remain stoic, not wanting to clue him in on what I'm currently feeling inside.

Disgust. Hopelessness. Betrayal. That's just a start to how I feel. But I will ensure my efforts don't go unrewarded. "I can't wait," I reply, batting my eyelashes because I will make sure this bastard lowers his guard, allowing me to get to that radio.

That can wait because when Saint emerges, I have other matters to deal with. "Good, ангел."

"We had a deal," I reply, not interested in small talk. And neither is he.

"Yes, we did. Come on then." He gestures with his head for me to follow.

I do.

I leave the two Russians up top as I follow Saint down the stairs. He casually takes a seat, indicating the floor is mine.

Given the option of knowing it all is suddenly daunting, and I begin to pace. How much do I want to know? He's shared tiny scraps of information, all of which have left me with nightmares. But knowing he won't give me this opportunity again, I quash down my fears.

"Why me?"

Saint rocks back in his seat, the air thick with tension. "You were chosen because of your looks. Because of your background."

"Background?" I ask, confused.

He nods. "No one will miss you when you're gone," he explains while I stop pacing.

"My husband will!" I shout, annoyed that he believes he's privy to what my relationship entails.

"I wouldn't be so sure," he replies coolly, crossing his legs and resting his ankle against his knee.

"How dare you! You know nothing, nothing!" I shout, storming forward.

"Stop yelling and ask your questions." He remains unmoved by my emotion.

"Where are we going?"

"Russia."

Russia? I thought they smuggled people *out* of Russia, not in.

His sharpness is hard to digest, but I continue. "Why?"

"You've been sold to Aleksei Popov."

I blink once. There is so much wrong with that short sentence. "Sold?" I whisper because I've surely misheard him. But when he nods, I know that this is really happening. "Who is he?"

He takes his time, which scares me. "He's one of the most powerful, most feared men in Russia. His specialty is drugs, guns, and money." Now his nickname of Boss makes sense because it appears that's what he literally is.

"Why does he want me?"

"Because he likes to collect pretty things."

I flinch, turning my cheek, never feeling dirtier. "So I'm his...plaything?"

Saint's shoulders rise and fall. "Yes."

"I don't understand. Who sold me?" I cry, dropping to my knees in front of him, begging he end this turmoil once and for all. "Please, tell me."

Saint sighs, the first sign of emotion surfacing. He reaches forward and sweeps the hair from my brow. I hate myself because his touch, his kindness are what I crave, and I lean into him, wanting him to take away this pain. But what he says next just slashes at the already gaping wound. "Your husband."

"*What?*" His touch suddenly feels like acid because I've been burned. I immediately recoil. "No. *No*," I repeat, shaking my head wildly. "You lie."

"No, I don't. Your husband sold you to Popov because he's a worthless piece of shit. You were always a pawn, his get out of jail for free card," he presses, but I cover my ears, unable to listen to the deceit spilling from his lips.

"Willow—" When he attempts to touch me once again, I shrink back, falling onto my ass.

"Stop it!" I scream, my body shuddering. "I don't want to hear any more." Images of Saint beating Drew viciously assault me, and I remember thinking it seemed personal at the time. Could I have been right?

I'm drowning in tears as they flow freely with no end in sight. There must be some mistake. I know Drew. He would never do what Saint is proposing. He's my husband, for god's sake! What sort of monster would do that to his wife?

"Le-leave," I whimper, choking on my stilted breaths, thumping my fist against the floor. This can't be happening.

Saint comes to a slow stand, respecting my wishes. "I would never lie to you. Not about this."

"I hate you," I snarl, spit and tears running down my downturned chin. How dare he say such filth about Drew?

His trademark scent engulfs me, and I realize the only person I hate is myself. Dropping to a squat, he lifts my chin with a finger, pinning me with those eyes. "You wish that you did…but you don't."

"Fuck you," I spit, ripping from his hold. He doesn't know me.

I brace for punishment, but I receive a different sort of torture. Saint walks up the stairs, leaving me alone with this giant hole in my chest.

Only when I'm shrouded in darkness do I allow my guard to drop and weep ugly tears. I lie down on the cool floor and curl myself into a ball. There must be some mistake, a different sort of torture. Not physical, but emotional. Saint wanted to break me, but that doesn't make any sense.

I did what he wanted.

Nothing makes any sense anymore.

I squeeze my eyes shut, closing myself off from this anguish because if what Saint says is true…then I truly am alone in this world.

I wake to someone sucking my big toe. Surely, there must be some mistake.

My eyes snap open, and when I see a bald dome at my feet, I know there is no mistake. I lower my head to the floor, muting my voiceless screams by shoving my fist into my mouth.

I passed out after Saint delivered the worst news of my life. My mind clearly needed to shut off from reality. I still don't know what to believe. And now I wake to this—to Kazimir sucking my toe.

Gathering my courage, I peer around to see Saint passed out on his stomach on the lounge he once tied me to with a half-empty bottle of vodka hanging limply from his fingers. The other Russian sits slumped in a chair, snoring softly.

That just leaves me alone with Kazimir, who is clearly making good on his word to pay me back later when everyone is asleep. I focus on anything other than his lips kissing a trail from the top of my foot to over my ankle. He swirls his tongue along the bony ridge before licking his way upward.

I remain perfectly still because this is what I wanted—to exploit the weakest link—but with the way he's slithering up my body, I can't help but feel like I'm the one who's being exploited. My legs tremble, and my stomach roils, wanting to be sick.

When I feel his wet tongue slurp at my inner thigh, I can't

pretend any longer. I shoot up, cupping his cheeks. His beard is coarse beneath my fingers. "Upstairs," I whisper with doe eyes, hoping he falls for the innocent act.

His attention flicks back and forth between Saint and his other comrade, weighing the options, but he finally agrees. "Okay."

I release him as the need to flee is more than overwhelming. He comes to a stand, ensuring to be quiet. I do the same.

I take one final look at Saint because regardless if what he told me is true or not, I need to get the hell off this boat. I need to look Drew in the eyes and ask him if he did what Saint said he did. Tears sting, but I quickly wipe them away.

Kazimir opens the hatch slowly, waving me to follow. It's pitch black out, but the sliver of moon provides all the light I need. I ensure to close the hatch, desperate to place something on top of it so if one of my captors' wake, they can't follow.

But I don't have time to do anything because the moment we're alone, Kazimir is on me, his chest pressed to my back as he fondles my breasts and bites my neck. I fight my instinct to strike back and headbutt him, and instead, I go lax, eyes focused on the radio.

He speaks to me in Russian as I walk us deliberately toward the helm. He pinches my nipples as I'm still in my bathing suit and rubs his hard-on against my ass. I detach myself from my body as I continue leading us toward the radio.

"I want to fuck," he says into my ear, sucking the side of my neck. My mouth gapes open as I silently dry retch, but I just hum in response.

When I'm close enough, I know what I have to do.

Bending forward, I grab the railing and position my ass high in the air. The radio is within reach, but I can't make a reach for it until this asshole is knocked out cold.

"Fuck me," I purr, but the tremble to my tone gives away my nerves.

Kazimir either doesn't notice or care. His pants hit the deck before I hear him spit in what I'm guessing is his hand. I bite the inside of my cheek to stop my screams. When a distinctive friction noise is heard, it's evident he's working himself up and down, intent on fulfilling my request.

He cups my ass, grunting, his hand still moving frantically. I desperately search for a weapon, and when I see it, I don't hesitate. Kazimir violently forces my bottoms aside, exposing me to him. "Your pink pussy is heaven." He runs his rough finger along my entrance, hissing low.

I am horrified, but I use that to dive for the fire extinguisher, and in one smooth motion, I spin around and strike out, connecting with Kazimir's temple.

My heart is in my throat as I watch Kazimir's eyes widen in utter shock before he slumps to the deck with his disgusting dick still in hand. I hold the fire extinguisher high, as I'm expecting him to come back to life like some bad horror movie, but he doesn't move.

His cock soon deflates and flops lifelessly against his leg.

Gulping in mouthfuls of air, I drop the extinguisher and cry in relief, brushing back my hair. But I'm not done. Jumping over Kazimir's unmoving body, I sink to my knees and unhook the fist mic, fiddling frantically with the dials. "Hello? Hello? Can anybody hear me?" I hysterically say into the mic.

All I get is static in response.

I continue turning the dials, hoping for some kind of a response. "Come on!" I cry, squeezing the button on the mic, refusing to give up.

"Hello? Help me, please. I've been kidnapped." The radio frequency continues cackling at my expense. This is hopeless.

Peering into the heavens, I pray for a miracle. I beg that for once, the universe cuts me some slack. A tear scores my cheek because if this doesn't work, I have just signed my own death warrant.

Ripping open the white chest, I see that I was right as inside is a life vest and some flares. If this doesn't work, then this will have to be my Plan B. Just as I'm about to slip the vest over my head, I hear it…a sign from above.

"Hello?"

I sob in response as I dive for the fist mic. "Hello? Can you hear me?"

"Yes," the male voice says through the static. The connection isn't great, but all that matters is that I've made contact. "What are your coordinates?"

"I don't know," I say in a rushed breath. "I've been kidnapped. My name is Willow Shaw. I'm an American. Please help me."

I slump to the floor, tears streaming down my cheeks. I did it. I'm saved. Now that that realization hits, I begin to tremble uncontrollably. The past six days crash into me, and I struggle to breathe.

"What is the name of your vessel?"

"I-I d-don't kn-know," I stutter, measuring my breathing

so I can answer his questions. "All I know is that we're headed for Russia. Aleksei—" The line suddenly goes dead.

Fear overthrows me, and I desperately spring into action, turning the dials, but it's useless. "No!" I sob, searching the radio for signs of why it just died. "Hello?" The fist mic button echoes uselessly.

Just as I'm about to try again, a darkness shadows me, revealing the reason my communication to the outside world has just been severed.

I hastily shrink backward, hiding behind the helm because before me stands Saint, and he's holding the cables he tore from the radio in his hand. He is fucking furious. "You have no...*no* idea what you've just done."

There is a fraction of calm, but it's the calm before the storm.

He lunges forward, reaching for my legs, but I kick out hysterically, screaming at the top of my lungs as I attempt to curl myself into a small ball. "No!"

But it's useless as he drops to a squat and grips my ankle. I lash out, violently fighting, hoping the small space I'm hidden in will protect me, but nothing will protect me from the wrath of Saint. I kick my legs, writhing and attempting to escape, but Saint yanks me forward, uncaring he'll probably decapitate me in the process.

I search for anything to grab onto, but the wheel is out of my reach, and I fall onto my back, my head slamming onto the hard, wooden decking. He drags me out as I scramble to anchor myself, my fingernails bending backward as they claw uselessly at the floor. He simply shoves Kazimir aside with his boot and continues hauling me like a sack of potatoes.

"I'm sorry!" I sob, but it's too late. He doesn't want my apologies. He's out for blood.

I squirm madly, kicking and thrashing about, but Saint only tightens his hold around my ankle. I frantically search for a weapon, but the world is upside down—a perfect analogy for my life right now.

When we reach the stairs, he doesn't stop, and each bump of the step causes my head to bang against the hard wood. I twist onto my stomach, attempting to reach out to grab the railing, but Saint pulls me roughly, and I let go, afraid he'll tear me into two.

When I'm at the bottom of the stairs, he lets me go, roaring loudly and punching what sounds like the wall. I immediately scamper for the lounge, curling my knees toward my chest as I sob hysterically, rocking. Saint slams the first-aid kit into the Russian's chest, screaming in Russian.

I assume he's just told him what I've done.

The Russian snarls, advancing forward with his fist raised. I cower, whimpering, awaiting the blow. But it never comes.

"Don't you fucking touch her!" Saint bellows. I'm too lost to even digest why that is.

Footsteps dart up the stairs, and all I can think is what comes next.

My body is vibrating violently, and my sobs are robbing me of breath. This is it. He's finally going to kill me. For a split second, I believed I had actually done it. That I was free.

"I have tried to be nice, ангел, so why do you force my hand? Do you want me to chain you up like a dog? Is that it?"

I just weep in response.

I can hear him pacing, clearly grappling with what to do next. "Kneel," he finally commands.

I'm too broken to object, so I unfold myself and quickly obey.

My eyes are cast downward as I can't look at him. I'm afraid. His staggered breathing reveals his rage.

"Why won't you listen? Why won't you break?" he screams, infuriated. "Don't you understand…this cruelness is the only kindness I can show you. I can't deliver you to him with you behaving this way. He will…" He abruptly stops speaking.

It seems he wants to apologize, but I don't know what he's seeking absolution for until I hear him unbuckling his belt. I squeeze my eyes shut, shivering, awaiting my punishment.

A hiss slicing through the air is what I hear before I feel him whip me. It still doesn't prepare me for the agony which has my mouth bursting open, but my scream has gone into hiding, and all that leaves me is a pained grunt.

He strikes me once again, and as the belt comes down across my ass, the impact has my body whiplashing forward. Tears leak from my eyes. "I'm sorry!" I sob, but it's too late for apologies.

Whack.

Each crack rattles my core.

Spittle and tears coat my face as I choke on my raspy breaths. When he hits me again, it's across my lower back. "Please stop." The pain is sharp. The sting is punishing. But I know this is a tickle compared to what Saint could do to me.

"You have to learn."

Whack.

"You will listen."

Whack.

He continues whipping me until I can no longer feel my body as I've detached myself from this plane. When he hits me across my ass, I slump forward, begging he stops.

"Get up," he pants, his tone filled with irritation.

But I can't.

My entire body is broken. "No…more. I'll be-behave," I whisper, weeping.

"I wish I could believe you."

Whack.

It doesn't matter what position I'm in, Saint won't stop until he's satisfied I've learned my lesson.

"I'm so-sorry," I stutter, suppressing my absolute suffering as this is the only way to make him stop.

"Who do you belong to?" he asks, breathless and manic.

"You." And the air fills with victory.

I want to cut out my own tongue for surrendering, but I can't take anymore.

He uses his foot to part my legs slightly as he coaxes my ankles apart. I wonder why. My question is answered soon enough. When he hits me across the ass, with a lot less force this time, it's quite low and skims my sex. It vibrates all the way to my core. I shudder involuntarily, and my nipples instantly pearl. When he does it again, the flick is somehow able to strike me in a way that it feels like he's just hit me against my center. I whimper, biting my lip.

What in the actual fuck?

My cheeks burst into flames because in some perverse way, just how when he spanked me, this feels good. I am disgusting. I deserve every blow he gives me. But this is so taboo; the immorality of it has me wanting more.

My body has suffered countless strikes. Each time he's brought down his belt, a whoosh of air leaves him, and he's left breathless. I'd like to think he's not getting off on punishing me, but history proves otherwise.

I am hot all over, and my flesh feels raw. Tears are streaming down my cheek, and I can't breathe. But underneath that lies this…craving. I need it to stop.

"Please. No more. I'm sorry."

The belt drops to the floor with a thud.

I am aching all over as my body feels as tight as a bow. A bundle of nerves scratches down low, and I discreetly rub my legs together, desperate to douse the flames.

"You can shower," Saint says before he staggers up the stairs, leaving me alone with this deep-rooted shame…which is exactly what he wanted.

Once he's gone, I only then allow myself to feel and collapse onto my side, sobbing. Drawing my knees to my chest, I hug them tightly, confused and scared. Through the pain is utmost confusion because I don't understand why I responded the way I did.

Yes, it hurt, as he fucking hit me with his belt, but each blow masqueraded a luscious sensation, hovering between pleasure and pain. What is wrong with me?

Closing my eyes, I succumb to sleep as it's the only place where my demons don't judge me for the wicked creature I've become.

CHAPTER FIVE

She is worming her way into my soul, and each time she cries, I want to console her. But then I remember I'm not the good guy in this story. I am her captor.
And she is my slave.

Day 7

I wake in the same position I fell asleep in—curled in a ball, hoping this blanket of confusion will go away. It hasn't.

It's right at dawn, and usually, one can look into the heavens and be thankful a new day is upon them. But today, I don't feel thankful. How can I be when I'm covered in red welts with an electric energy thrumming through my veins?

The hatch opens, but I don't stir. I simply lie on my side, broken.

If my father were alive, he would be so ashamed of me. He would wonder when the exact moment his baby girl turned into some wanton fiend.

I know Saint is close by because his fragrance drifts down the stairs. I wonder what he sees. I wonder if he feels victorious.

"This cruelness is the only kindness I can show you."

What does that mean?

Nothing makes sense anymore.

"Kazimir will live," he says. I remain silent in response, staring at a smudge mark on the wall.

This is nothing short of awkward, but I can't stop thinking about my response to him last night. I was...aroused. Closing my eyes, I shake my head, sickened.

"Ангел..."

"Don't," I whisper, shifting away when he crouches down behind me. I can hear every single taut muscle bend and move with his lithe actions. "Don't call me that. My name is Willow." I need to say it for my sake as well as his.

He sighs, clearly frustrated. But that's all he's getting out of me because I just want to be left alone. He reads the silent "fuck you" and stands. When the hatch closes, I exhale, thankful for the solitude.

Escaping now seems impossible, which leaves me with dire thoughts. I don't want to be sold to someone named Aleksei Popov, but according to Saint, the deal is already done. So what options do I have left?

The fact Drew was the one who apparently orchestrated this hurts more than I can explain. But how can I believe

Saint? How can I believe Drew would do that to me?

What a mess, and to make matters worse, I have formed some sort of…attachment to my kidnapper.

I don't know what it is. I don't even like him, but I can't deny whenever he's near, my body responds in ways it shouldn't. I know some say it's normal to respond sexually in extremely anxious or stressful situations, but it feels wrong. I feel dirty, just how I once did.

My heart is heavy, but I've run out of tears. I have never felt more imprisoned than I do right now. Thoughts which scare me cross my mind because I can't, I won't be held captive anymore. Saint has made it clear where I'm going won't be sunshine and flowers. I will never be able to go home. I will forever be a prisoner.

So the choice seems simple as my hands are tied.

Clutching the cross around my neck, I apologize to my father. "Sorry, Daddy, but I won't live like this. I hope you can forgive me."

Coming to a slow rise, I ignore the throbbing in every part of my body and mind and focus on looking for something to end the pain. My eyes instantly seek out a length of rope and then scan the wooden rafter above me.

It's an out. A bleak end, but at least I'll decide my fate.

Climbing to my feet sluggishly, I flinch, breathing steadily through my nose to push past the pain. I put one foot in front of the other and commence my stagger toward the rope. I've been in a dark place before, but this time, it feels different.

I work in a robotic manner as I reach for the rope and tie a noose. Once it's tight, I drag a chair along the floor and stand on it, looping the rope around the rafter and tying it tight. With the noose in hand, I go to place it over my head but stop, holding it in front of me and peering through the simple loop with the ability to take away life.

They say when faced with death, your life flashes before your eyes. That doesn't happen to me. All I see is my hopelessness. With a deep breath, I loop the noose around my neck and tighten it. A single tear falls because I wanted to achieve so much, but it'll never be.

Peering down at the floor, I wonder what Saint will do with my body. A sea burial makes the most sense, and besides, who would mourn me? If I had a gravestone, marking my existence to the world, who would visit?

My father is dead. My mother may as well be too. And my husband is apparently the reason I stand here with a noose around my neck.

"No one will miss you when you're gone." And Saint is right. No one will.

I don't have any last words. My soul is broken. So taking a deep breath, I step forward, ready to take the plunge, but it seems God isn't done with me yet. The noose tightens, and I gasp for air, but after only hanging for a split second, the rope comes undone, and I plummet to the floor with a thud.

Wheezing, I yank at the rope, tearing it from my neck and tossing it across the room with rage. I can't even do this right. "Fuck you," I curse at no one in particular, thumping my fist against the floor.

I'm half expecting Saint to come charging down here to cuff me until we arrive in Russia. But he doesn't.

Helplessness overcomes me once again, so I surrender. I could lie down on the lounge, but I much rather prefer the coldness to the hard floor. Besides, I should get used to such lodgings because where I'm headed, I doubt I'll be given any comforts. I was sold, remember? Like some animal at market.

Drawing my knees to my chest as I lie on my side, I close my eyes and wonder why I was saved…when I didn't want to be.

"Come on, you need to eat."

The urge to inhale deeply and bask in a delectable scent has my eyes popping open, but when I realize I'm still in hell, I quickly squeeze them tight.

Saint crouches behind me, attempting to lift me from my half-sitting position. I don't know why he's helping me, but I refuse to talk to him. I may be his prisoner, but I'll be damned if I speak to him again.

I'm floppy from lethargy and a broken spirit, and it doesn't take him long to coax me to my feet. I'm unstable, but he uses the chair I stood on hours ago to set me down. How ironic. It now offers me support, when once upon a time, it offered me death.

I don't focus on anything. I just stare into thin air. This irritates Saint as he crouches down in front of me, forcing me to look at him as he grips my chin and offers me some jerky. But he can go to hell. "Eat."

I turn my cheek in response.

"So you're not talking to me anymore, is that it?"

We never talked. He's delusional if he thought we ever did.

An infuriated sigh leaves him. I internally high-five myself. "You can either eat, or you can sit here gagged and cuffed. The choice is yours."

Silly lamb. I never had a choice. He took away all my choices when he kidnapped me and put me on this fucking boat.

I remain unmoving.

"Fine then," he states, digging into his back pocket to produce the cuffs. He doesn't even need to tell me to put my hands behind my back. I do it automatically. I know the drill.

He pauses, surprised, but soon recovers as he snaps the cuffs around my wrists. Next, however, the surprise is on me because he does something which rips the air from my lungs. Standing in front of me, he reaches behind him and yanks off the shirt from the back of his collar. His scent is absolutely potent, and I gnaw at the inside of my cheek until I taste blood.

He's topless before me, and I want to claw out my eyeballs because they scan upward on their own accord, completely under his spell. I saw him out in the darkness, but now, the sunshine streaming in from the windows seems to only showcase him in all his glory.

His waist is tapered, his rock-solid abs golden and firm. The well-defined V muscle which peeks out from the low waistband of his black cargos is deliciously sinful, as is the light dusting of dirty blond hair which paints his navel and licks downward along his flesh.

I notice a tattoo on his flank. It's a cursive font. A single word.

Sinner.

Seems appropriate.

I continue my examination, focusing on the silver barbell in his left nipple. The shine to it seems to emphasize his muscled, broad chest. He has some dark hair between his pecs, but it isn't thick enough to cover the deep scars he has scattered all over him. They look like knife wounds.

Across his upper chest, he has more ink. It seems to work in with his wing tattoo as he has a thick scroll spread across his collar with two large red roses, the only color on his design, sitting just under each collarbone. Around the scroll looks like more feathers. The design is spectacular, but what has me transfixed is what is written inside the scroll.

Only God Can Judge Me.

I don't know why, but those words resonate with me because I can relate…I can relate to that right now.

He has a thick black armband tattoo below his elbow. The feathers painted down over his bulging biceps ripple as he tenses, sensing me studying him. When I finally meet his eyes, they are smoldering beneath that mask he wears. He is utterly hypnotic.

He has just revealed a small part of himself to me, and I need to know why.

Rounding the chair, he ties his shirt around my mouth, forcing me to inhale his fragrance as I'm swimming in it. *This* is torture.

Without a word, he leaves me gagged and cuffed, the

vision of his wings the last thing I see as he walks up onto the deck. The moment he's gone, I sag, breathing heavily around the…gag. I'm gagged, and I didn't freak out. Not once did I think about Kenny's hands on me because I was too busy sniffing the delectable material in my mouth.

I don't know what comes next because I am so lost. And the only comfort is inhaling his scent, which is somehow able to soothe the tempest within.

My thoughts once again drift to Drew. I need to know the truth. I don't want to believe Saint, but how did they know where to find me? Why did Drew choose such a remote place to honeymoon? Shaking my head, I push those thoughts from my mind because I know my husband. He would never do what Saint said he did.

My body aches. Not only from the welts on my ass, back, and legs, but my neck is starting to chafe as well. Peering upward, I close my eyes and allow the tears to fall. After everything I've been through, I thought I was strong, but I'm not. I'm breaking, which is exactly what Saint wants.

I'm trying to be strong, but each day chips away at my resolve, and I feel the person I once was slip away. Before long, she'll be gone for good.

Fatigue overtakes me, and I slump forward, happy to lose myself in the darkness once more.

I wake because someone is watching me. I can feel their

astute eyes dissecting every inch of my flesh. No guessing who it is.

I'm still not talking to him, so I feign sleep. But he calls bullshit.

"Thanks to the shit you pulled…again, we now have to hang low for a couple of days. We also have to change boats. It's too risky to continue sailing this thing."

If Saint is expecting an apology, he'll be waiting a long time.

"We're going to dock in about an hour and stay there until shit blows over. I also have some business to take care of."

My head is downturned, my hair shrouding my face so I'm hidden, and I intend on staying this way since I have absolutely nothing to say to him. However, this piece of information changes things. It buys me time. A couple of days is more days than I had moments ago. And docking means dry land.

But I remain passive as I don't want Saint privy to my thoughts.

"You probably want a shower? Use the bathroom?"

My full bladder rejoices, but I squash down the happiness as I don't want to owe this asshole anything. I remain silent.

I'm expecting him to storm out, leaving me tied up, but he walks around the chair and uncuffs me. His fingers against my skin have me flinching as his touch is a reminder of what he did to me last night. He waits for me to move, but I don't. I remain slumped forward, my arms hanging by my sides. The relief from being uncuffed is wonderful, but I remain unresponsive.

His heavy breathing indicates my silent act is pissing him off, but he can go to hell. "Fine, have it your way then."

He marches up the stairs coolly, closing the hatch. The moment it seals shut, I fumble with the gag as my fingers are trembling, but when I eventually get it off, I throw it across the room. I gulp in mouthfuls of air and rub my aching arms. Gradually, I stand, as my legs are shaky and my body throbs. I waddle to the bathroom, thankful to use the toilet. Once I'm done, I shimmy out of the swimsuit.

I kick it out of sight as I never want to see the infernal thing ever again.

As I turn on the water and wait for it to run warm, I turn over my shoulder and glimpse the red lashes across my back, ass, and legs. They aren't as bad as I thought, which means Saint went easy on me. But I already knew that.

In spite of that, I feel nauseous and jump into the shower, desperate to wash away the evidence as best I can. The water stings, but it's an appreciated pain. After five minutes, I begin to feel and smell like me again.

Turning off the water, I dry myself and hobble over to the sink. Wiping down the glass, I gasp when I see my appearance. Who is this stranger staring back at me with lifeless eyes? I arch my neck and sigh. The inflamed rope burn has feelings of shame crushing me.

If it wasn't for my shitty knot tying, I wouldn't be standing here right now. Clutching the cross at my neck, I like to think it's my father's presence watching over me, lending me the strength I so need. "I promise you, I will never do that again," I whisper to my mirror image, hopeful my dad can hear.

And I never will.

There is always another way. I can only hope that way is when we dock and get the hell off this boat.

Deciding to dress, I hunt through the chest, digging out a pair of white underwear from the bulk pack of ten and a green cotton summer dress. I can't stand to wear anything tight or restricting as my skin hurts.

It's still hard to believe they've packed me clothes and in my size, no less.

"Your husband sold you to Popov…"

Saint's words echo loudly, but I shake my head, refusing to entertain that notion.

Once I'm dressed, I look around the room in vain, on the prowl for a weapon. There is no way Saint would leave me down here if there were. But I humor myself anyway. The only thing I find is a non-stick saucepan. I could linger in the shadows and strike whoever walks down those stairs unaware.

But then what?

If I come out swinging, I'll be knocked to my ass before I can make it up one step.

Sighing, I give up my vigilante plans for now and make my way over to the window. Kneeling onto the bench seat, I peer out and attempt to gather my bearings and figure out where we are.

Seven days ago, I was in the Greek Islands. Then I believe we were on our way to Turkey. Thanks to me ruining that plan, however, we are now off course. If our destination is Russia, that means we must be somewhere in between.

The scenery doesn't hold any distinguishing landmarks.

Just deep blue seas. But Saint did say we would be docking in an hour, so we have to be approaching land soon. I wait patiently because time is all I have of late, and after ten minutes, I see it…a rocky landscape in the distance.

I press my nose to the glass, my eyes scanning from left to right. There isn't a hint of green. Just a sandy texture to the scenery. It looks dry and hot. I instantly think we're in the Middle East.

As we drift farther, it becomes apparent by the old-world feel that we aren't sailing into a big city. A few small fishing boats contain fisherman standing on the edge holding outdated fishing rods as they eye our fancy yacht.

The landscape is still sandy, and other than enormous hills, there is nothing to see. I try to distinguish anything that will give me a clue to where we are, but we could be anywhere. Though it's obvious that wherever we are, we are certainly off the grid.

Defeat overtakes me because I was hoping we would at least dock in a major city, but the closer we get to the weatherworn, wooden port, it's apparent that is not the case. I can see fish markets and other food stalls set up along the marina. Everything is simple. No fancy flashing lights or franchise brands in sight. The stalls are run by men in white robes, which seems to be the general attire for the populace.

Women wearing long gowns with head scarves carry local produce. This is clearly a fresh food market as such. The closer we get, the more attention we seem to attract as a lavish yacht such as this seems like an eyesore compared to the modest boats surrounding us.

Our speed slows, and the boat turns slightly to the left, finding a spot to dock. I continue watching, desperately seeking any hints as to where we are. When I see a woman on a cell, however, I don't care because wherever we are has cell service.

I'm lost in the foreign sights when the hatch opens. Peering toward it, I instantly shrink back when I see Kazimir walk down the stairs. The moment he sees me, his eyes narrow, and the hair at the back of my neck stands on end.

He isn't wearing his ski mask, so I can see the angry, egg-sized lump on the side of his temple—the one I put there. "We docking now. You stay here."

I open my mouth, about to protest, but he stalks forward.

"Just in case you get any ideas."

I have no idea what he means until he makes his intentions crystal clear. He stops in front of me, sizing me up. The waves of fury can be felt rolling off him, and just when I'm about to back away, he slaps my cheek—hard. I instantly taste blood.

Cupping my cheek as I turn my face away from him, stunned pants leave me as my brain tries to come to terms with this asshole laying his hands on me. "Stay," he spits, addressing me like a dog.

Every fiber of my body is demanding I retaliate, but I don't. This is his payback.

When he reaches out and violently grips my hair, yanking my head back, I cry out because he's hurting me. He leans forward and runs his nose along the column of my neck, sniffing. "We not done, you fucking bitch."

His promise scares me, but he eventually lets me go.

I scamper away from him, drawing my knees to my chest, tears welling. My fear is like an aphrodisiac because he reaches down and rubs over the bulge in his pants. I feel sick.

"See you and that sweet pink pussy soon." He licks his fat bottom lip while I whimper softly. He leaves me cowering, only breathing again when the hatch closes, and it sounds like it's bolted shut.

The need to flee is even more imperative because Kazimir is out for blood.

I jolt forward as the boat hits the port, taking my mind off his ominous promise. This is the first time in seven days I've seen land, and I'm stuck in here. I watch as Kazimir jumps from the yacht and ties it to a large white cleat.

Saint surely would have removed his ski mask, but he remains out of sight as he no doubt knows I will be watching. I wait for him to come to get me, but after ten minutes, it's clear that isn't the case.

Groaning, I lift my hair from the back of my neck and hold it atop my head as it's awfully stuffy and I'm annoyed. Sweat trickles down the length of my spine, but I focus on my surroundings, mesmerized by this foreign sight. They're speaking in Arabic, I think, but it sounds different.

Placing my hand on the window, I try to tune in to the vibrations offered by this new world as a contagious buzz fills the air. The vendors hold up gigantic fish as they try to convince potential customers to take a closer look at their goods.

Kids run along the dock eating round golden dough balls, the syrup sticking to their fingers as they lick them clean. I have no idea what they are, but my stomach instantly growls.

Their laughter and the cheerful calls of the merchants are a nice thing to see, considering I've been surrounded by nothing but despair for so long.

When a street vendor with a portable cart stops in front of me, I crane my neck to see what he sells. It seems he has sunglasses, umbrellas, souvenirs. A one-stop shop. And when he unravels a blue linen scarf, he reveals just how versatile he truly is. We're in Egypt, according to the shawl, and the gimmicky pyramid keepsakes and mummy mementos confirm this.

Holy shit.

Saint said he has business here. I wonder of what nature? I doubt he's here to sample the local produce.

The young vendor sets up a small radio, playing some 80s pop song as he drinks a bottle of Coke. If he's here, surely that means he's expecting tourists to arrive soon. The locals aren't interested, but the gullible vacationers would be.

A surge of excitement overcomes me, and I bang on the window, screaming hysterically at the top of my lungs. "Help!" I shout, thumping my open palm against the glass. But he doesn't hear me, thanks to Madonna blaring over the speakers.

Jumping down from the bench seat, I run up the stairs and attempt to open the hatch, but I almost smash my head into the hard wood because it doesn't move an inch. It's locked, which is no surprise.

"No!" I scream, forcing it with my shoulder as I work the handle frantically. It's useless. It doesn't budge.

Running down the stairs, I search the room, desperate to find something I can pry the lock open with. Or something I can use to smash through the hatch. When my search comes up empty, I sprint to the bathroom window, attempting to open the latch. But it's locked as well.

I push at it with all my might, banging on it and working the handle desperately, but it doesn't budge. "Goddammit!"

Refusing to give up, my feet slide along the flooring as I grab the saucepan and don't think twice as I throw it at the window, bracing for it to break as I turn my back. When I don't hear a shatter, I look over my shoulder, only to see the saucepan sitting in a sad heap on the floor. It bounced off the glass—the shatterproof glass it appears.

Breathless, I slide down the wall, tears welling. No wonder Saint had no qualms leaving me down here, unbound. The freedom is more of an imprisonment than being cuffed because I can look out at something that is just out of reach.

"Help," I whimper in barely a whisper, defeated.

I religiously watch the hands on the clock, and when a half an hour ticks over, I hear the unmissable voices of enthusiastic tourists, speaking English. The street vendor's music loudens as he calls for the visitors to come look at his goods.

Beaten, I commence a slow crawl toward the window, clambering onto the seat and peering out the window. The mixture of T-shirts and hats reveals these travelers are from all over the globe. There are only about twelve people, as this part of Egypt is clearly not as popular as other parts, but it still draws the curious explorer or two.

I place my open palm to the window, begging someone

sees me, begging to be rescued, but it never happens. All I can do is watch them laugh happily, sampling the local foods, oblivious to my situation because down here, I'm hidden, forgotten to the world.

An hour passes, and the street vendor begins to pack up his loot. He's done for the day. The tourists are long gone, but sadly, I'm not. Here I kneel, peering out into a world I was once a part of. When the air turns still and the 80s pop vanishes, I sink down and crumple into a heap.

That was a wasted opportunity, and I don't know how many more I'll get. Saint said we would be here for a few days. That we're going to dock to change boats. But I can only imagine that will be done under the veil of night because here, I stand out like dog's balls.

I'm trying not to be disheartened, but that is impossible. And when the hatch clicks and opens, and I hear heavy footsteps, I realize I'm about to face the epitome of impossible.

I turn on my side, refusing to look at him. That doesn't deter him, however.

"I got you something to eat." I hear a thud onto the table.

His heavy sigh is my victory, but I remain unmoving. A static crackles, hinting shit is about to get real.

Before I know what's happening, the seat suddenly depresses, the air is ripped from my lungs, and I'm flipped onto my stomach as Saint throws me over his lap. I'm lying stretched out with him under me. He's so damn smooth, I don't even know how he maneuvers me this way like I weigh nothing at all.

I don't bother fighting him, but instead, I turn my cheek, looking away.

"You know," he starts, two simple words filled with such wicked promised, "I can make you talk."

A shudder passes through me because I have no doubt he can. I'm clueless to what he's about to do because the last time we were this way, he spanked me. The memory smashes into me, and I bite my tongue to prevent any verbal response.

When the material of my dress slowly glides up my legs, I measure my breaths, but my heart begins to race. He stops just at the small of my back. I exhale, but it's in vain because what he does next has my cheeks bursting into flames.

He leisurely lowers my innocent white underwear to expose my ass. I close my eyes, humiliated, which is exactly the response he wants.

He hums low while I remain unresponsive. However, when I hear what sounds like a jar being opened and feel a cool cream being applied to my ass cheeks, I jolt, dismayed. I'm about to tell him what a sick, perverted creep he is until the soothing scents of myrrh, lavender, and tea tree catch the air. Then a cooling sensation against my tender flesh follows.

Helpless to resist and also a tad confused, I instantly relax and allow Saint to surprisingly tend to my wounds. It feels absolutely wonderful as the burn to my skin fades. He gently massages my ass, applying just the right pressure to make what he's doing feel so good.

He lifts the hem of my dress and exposes my back, where he applies more ointment. By the time he gets to my shoulder blades, I'm almost drooling. His strong fingers dig into my tender muscles, kneading out the stiffness. Over the past seven days, my poor shoulders have suffered such abuse.

My breasts are still covered, but being this way is so intimate. I've never had a man touch me like this. Not even Drew. But with Saint, it almost is effortless.

Once he finishes massaging my back, he detours to my ass once again, gripping my cheeks in both hands and squeezing softly to ensure every inch is slathered in cream. A contented sigh betrays my pleasure, but I'm too relaxed to care or question why he's being so nice.

His heavy breaths are hypnotic and lull me into a sleepy bubble. I must look ridiculous with my ass poised high, covered in whatever balm he's applying. It doesn't even seem like having me half-naked on his lap has affected him, which is a good thing, I remind myself. This is all methodical for him, seeing as he can't deliver damaged goods.

He scoops more cream into his hands and pays attention to my legs. He works my inner thighs, never drifting too close to my sex, which I'm thankful for. Once I'm slathered in the ointment, he puts the lid back onto the container and gently pulls my underwear back up.

When he lowers my dress, a small, insolent part of me is disappointed. But I'm quick to dispel such thoughts. I'm so relaxed, I feel like an overcooked piece of spaghetti.

"You see, it doesn't have to be all unpleasant between us. I can be kind too." His honeyed voice is smooth, and I hate myself because I want to hear it again.

My wish is granted, but what he says next confirms his kindness comes with strings. "Will you behave?"

His thoughtfulness is because he wants something from me. It wasn't done out of the kindness of his heart, which is my error, forgetting he doesn't have one. But this act proves otherwise. Doesn't it?

"Ангел?" He waits for me to reply, but he'll be waiting for a long time to come.

A string of profanity severs the serenity as he slides out from under me. I lounge on my stomach with no intention of moving or replying.

"I promise...you will talk."

He leaves me with that oath as he marches up the stairs and slams the hatch shut. A smile spreads from cheek to cheek because for once, Saint knows how it feels to be used.

Once Saint left, I fell into a deep slumber, exhaustion creeping up on me. For once, my body didn't ache, thanks to Saint, which is ironic, considering he's the reason I was sore in the first place.

I was too drained to even try to comprehend why he helped me. His hot and cold behavior leaves me confused because I don't know which version of Saint I'll get whenever he walks down those stairs.

Kazimir frightens me because, without a doubt, he will ensure I pay for what I did to him, but Saint scares me in a different way. I'm not fearful for my life when I'm with him. I'm fearful for my soul. I hate myself because each time he's near, I crave more—more of his voice, his touches, more of him. I want to know the man beneath the mask.

My body's response to him is…curiosity. I've never met a man like him before. He takes what he wants and commands control. In no way am I attracted to him, I mean, I've never even seen his face, and there is a little thing that he kidnapped me, but I can't deny he makes me feel something…I just don't know what that something is.

However, when the hatch opens, and the unmistakable sound of a woman's moans travels down the stairs, I'm soon to identify what that something is.

It's pitch black down here as the moon has gone into hiding, and there are no lights close by, but I see and hear enough to understand what is currently taking place before my eyes. My immediate reaction is to turn away, but there's a reason he's down here, parading his new prize. And I intend to find out what it is.

I shrink into the shadows, but Saint knows I'm awake, watching him as he comes tumbling down the stairs with some strange woman. I know it's him by the broad width of his shoulders and his menacing height. A strangled gasp gets caught in my throat, and I strain my eyes. There must be some mistake. But as I perch on the end of the seat and dig my fists into my eyes to ensure I'm not seeing things, I see it…he's not wearing his ski mask.

I can't make out any distinguishing features, but when the moon peeks its head out from behind the darkness, it highlights strands of messy dark hair. It looks wild and untamed, just long enough to tie back. The long tresses are thick and full of volume. He looks like he just tumbled from bed.

When he slams his eager lover against the wall, I flinch, wishing I'd chosen another analogy.

Once again, the moon takes cover, but her impassioned moans fill in the blanks. His back faces me while she writhes against the wall, speaking to him in Arabic. I'm taken aback when he replies in her native tongue.

I feel obscene bearing witness to something so personal, but this is just so...foreign. Sure, I've watched the occasional porn clip, who hasn't, but seeing this in real life is utterly captivating. Drew went down on me, and I returned the favor, but this is something else. The way her moans intensify like she's about to explode has me inching forward, desperate for a closer look.

All I can make out are shadows, so I rely on my ears to fill in the blanks. When I hear a garment being shred, it's apparent things are about to get messy. Her bracelets jingle as I presume she undoes his pants because a second later, I hear a zipper being unfastened and the crinkle of a wrapper.

"Fuck me," she hums.

I grip the leather beneath me, my fingernails almost tearing through the material. I don't know what's come over me, but I suddenly want to rip out her tongue. My heart begins to race, and I'm covered in a light sheen of perspiration. What's wrong with me?

Her impatient sighs deepen, and the sound does something to me which it should not. I feel myself growing wet between the legs because I feel like a secret voyager, privy to the most intimate act between two people. I am ashamed and disgusted, but I can deal with that later because when a guttural cry penetrates the air, I know Saint has hit home.

The rough slapping of flesh soon follows as the woman howls in delight, mumbling words in a language I don't understand. What I do understand however is Saint hissing as I see a sharp tug of his head. "No kissing."

Relief swarms me because to me, a kiss is more sacred, and in some sick way, it pleases me that he won't kiss her. But he certainly has no qualms fucking her. I hate referring to the act in such a way, but the untamed sounds of flesh sliding together and the banging against the wall hints that this is exactly that.

Fucking. And fucking hard.

Even though I can't see a whole lot, tears sting my eyes because I suddenly feel so dirty. Why did he bring her down here? Her honeysuckle perfume will forever mar these walls as will the cry of her coming loudly as Saint drives into her violently.

Once again, so many emotions flood me, but this time, I can't help the jealousy that rises. I don't even know why I'm jealous. I suppose I miss the connection with another human being. But deep down, in a secret place, the truth floats just below the surface.

I'm jealous because I want to know what it feels like. If what Saint says is true, then I will be losing my virginity to a monster. If I've been sold, there is only one reason. Is that why Saint brought her down here? To show me what's headed my way?

God only knows what perverse things that man will subject me to. Is Saint once again showing me kindness by being cruel?

I can't stand to hear anymore, so I lower myself onto the lounge and lie on my side, covering my ears. When the vibrations stop, I know he's done.

My cheeks are damp with tears as I suddenly feel so betrayed. After he tended so kindly to me today, I thought that maybe he wasn't all bad. But here he is, lying post-coitus with some random woman.

This room may be my prison, but it's mine.

"I promise...you will talk."

His parting words today echo loudly, and I succumb, just as I always do, which is exactly why he did what he did. This is once again a lesson.

"Make her leave," I whisper, heavy with despair. I can't stand to have her here.

I'm not even sure if he heard me, but when I hear him utter something in Arabic, I know that he did.

"You're not serious?" she wails, clearly horror-struck there won't be any snuggling.

"Get out," Saint replies, in case she is lost in translation.

The woman turns banshee as she shrieks in Arabic, but I tune it out. Before the hatch closes, however, what I hear confuses me even more so. "You could only come when you looked at her...so fuck her next time!"

I tremble violently, curling myself into a ball, afraid and so perturbed. What does she mean? He could only come when he looked at me? Why? He doesn't even like me as every chance he gets, he's hurting me...like right now.

"Good night, Ангел."

And I reply the only way I can.

"Good night...мастер."

CHAPTER SIX

This fearless creature utterly fascinates me. She is far braver than anyone I've ever met, and I find myself wanting to know more about her. My methods have never failed me in the past. I am Popov's best. So why can't I break her the way I want to? And why can I only find satisfaction when she's near? This obsession of mine must end.

It will only lead to trouble.

Day 8

Memories of last night assault me, and when I smell Saint's cologne, it only brings home the truth that I witnessed him having sex with some woman, and then he threw her out at my request. But her admission still plays over and over in my mind.

What does it mean?

I've been staring at the ceiling for hours, refusing to look elsewhere because Saint sleeps on the opposite sofa. He obviously passed out last night.

I have so many questions, and they all begin with why.

Even though I didn't see much, it seems to somehow make what I witnessed so much worse. I've been speculating all morning, and my mind has had no issues adding lib. I saw him without his ski mask, and even though I couldn't get a clear picture of what he looks like, what I did see has me spellbound.

I don't understand him or his motives. I want nothing more than to ask him why, but I have a feeling he's doing this to prepare me for a world I'm not accustomed to. In no way am I making excuses for his actions, but no matter how hard I try to hate him, I can't shake the feeling he's just as trapped as I am.

"Hey." His raspy voice snaps me from my thoughts.

The silent treatment now seems obsolete, considering everything I saw. "Hi."

An awkwardness lingers like one would expect for the morning-after talk. Even though we didn't have sex, I did witness him screwing someone else, so I guess in a way, the awkwardness is warranted.

I have no idea what comes next. I can only hope we get a new means of transport because this one has been tainted by the shrill screams of last night.

"I'm going to shower."

As I jump up, Saint does too. He must have put his ski mask back on during the night, which angers me that some random bimbo can see his face, but I can't. I cast my gaze downward, unsure of what he wants. I also don't want to look at him after last night.

"Are you hungry?"

I shake my head, hiding behind my hair.

"You have to eat," he says, walking forward. When he's within reach, he places his finger under my chin, coaxing me to look at him.

I eventually do.

The green to his eyes is so bright, I gasp as the color is stunning. However, they soon flicker a furious black. I don't know what's wrong, and on instinct, I drop to my knees, kneeling. It was an automatic response, and I shock myself at how quickly I was to obey.

"What did you do to yourself?" he asks, taking a step back.

I don't understand what he means.

Fear assails me, and my lower lip quivers. "I didn't do anything," I reply, puzzled. But he soon proves me to be a liar.

He marches forward and cups my chin, arching my head back to expose my neck. When he strokes over my throat, I know he's seen the rope mark. I was careless not to be more careful. "That's the coward's way out, and you're not a coward."

"How do you know?" I challenge, but my bravado soon dies when he tightens his hold around my chin.

"Because I've known you for eight days. And every single one of those eight days, you've disobeyed me, defied me, and attempted to escape, regardless of the consequences. If that doesn't take courage, then I don't know what does."

I gasp, stunned by his candor.

"Let me go," I whimper. Even though I know the answer, I still have to try. "Please."

The air is crackling with a live current, and when Saint rubs his thumb over my lower lip, everything around us detonates. My heart is thrashing wildly. I'm on my knees, peering up at my captor, unsure what this gentle touch means.

"Don't ask things you know the answer to," he softly replies.

"I'll never stop asking that, regardless if I know the answer."

I'm toeing a very dangerous line, but something is different in the way his thumb seems mesmerized by my lip. His eyes focus on my mouth as he caresses up and down. This is new. Up until now, his touch has never been filled with… hunger.

Another hunger smashes into me then—the one of the woman who Saint was buried in—and I instantly turn my cheek, averting my gaze. I don't want him touching me after his hands and other parts have stroked her.

"Tonight, we board a new boat," he reveals while I hold my breath. "I have a few things to take care of today, but I'll be back when it's dark."

"Can I go upstairs?" I ask even though it's in vain.

Saint sighs. "No, you can't. It's too risky."

"Risky for whom?" I challenge.

He takes his time to reply. "For the both of us."

There is no point in arguing.

The air is thick as I await his next move. "Behave, Ангел. I'll be back later."

I refrain from saluting him and simply nod.

I'm expecting him to leave, but he surprises me once again when he brushes the hair from my cheeks so he can see me. My eyes are still lowered, but I can feel him examine every inch of my face. He runs his thumb over the apple of my cheek while I dare not breathe.

Eventually, he retreats and leaves me alone to question what the hell is going on. Once the hatch closes, I bow forward and take three calming breaths, though it does nothing to settle my frantic heart.

I feel like I'm on a merry-go-round as the world is spinning, but I want to get off. I want to forget Saint's gentle touches because each act of kindness shakes everything up beyond repair.

I don't know what's worse—Saint's punishment or Saint's rewards. His bipolar behavior leaves me constantly questioning which version I'll get, and honestly, I don't know which I like best.

When the room stops turning, I slowly come to a stand. I have all day to kill as I'm once again confined to my cage. I decide to shower and then sit by the window and watch the world pass me by.

As I undress, my gaze floats to the wall in which Saint used as his makeshift fucking post. I cringe as I hate the term as well as what he did. I know he did it to teach me a lesson, to display that my fate is in his hands, and in the end, he will always win.

He broke me, didn't he? I ended up speaking.

He tried to be "nice," but when that didn't work, he resorted to measures he knew were out of my comfort zone. He's aware that I'm a virgin, and seeing him screw someone else was a sure way for me to break.

The sound of his flesh pressed against hers assaults me, and I instantly shake my head to dispel such wickedness. I need to focus on other matters—like escaping, and this time…nothing and no one will stand in my way.

It's dark out—a sight I've craved all day.

I spent my time devising ways I can make a run for it tonight, but sadly, I don't even know what I'm walking into. I will have to use my smarts and think on my toes because I know my window of opportunity will be small.

Most of the vendors have gone for the day, but a few fishermen are still working on their boats. I don't speak their language, so I can only hope me running for my life while screaming for help is understood universally.

When the hatch opens, I know it's now or never.

I watch as Saint descends the stairs, arching a brow when I notice a brown robe in his hand. "Here, put this on," he orders, offering me the garment. The material feels soft and light. When I unravel it, I see that it will cover me from head to toe.

I feel awful putting this on, as I'm probably offending many by wearing something which is sacred to certain religions, but I knew Saint wouldn't allow me to roam the streets exposed. I'm wearing shorts and a tank, so I quickly slip into the oversized robe and place the niqab over my head. I adjust it so the only part of me showing is my eyes.

Saint watches me, nodding when I'm dressed.

The temperature down here is already stifling, so being covered this way has me instantly breaking out into a sweat. It's quite disconcerting to view the world this way— a sliver at a time. But I suppose both Saint and I now have the same viewpoint.

"Our new boat is a few yards away. Kazimir will bring your clothes and other supplies. You are not to move from my side. Are we clear?" he cautions.

When I remain quiet, he steps forward. His presence is suffocating. "I asked you a question."

We're on equal ground seeing as he can't read me as well as he once could. The only clue he has to what I'm thinking is my eyes, which is the only thing I've had for the past eight days. "Yes, we're clear," I finally reply, crossing my fingers beneath my robe.

The apprehension rolls off his broad shoulders as he watches me carefully, but he has no other choice but to trust me. He gestures with his head to head upstairs. The moment of truth has arrived.

Taking one last look at what was my prison for the past eight days, I march up the stairs but suddenly come to a standstill on the top step, wishing I wasn't covered. I'd give anything to feel the fresh air on my skin. I tilt my chin upward, peering into the starless sky, and beg the universe shows me mercy.

Please give me the strength to do this.

But Saint clearly doesn't have any time for sentiments as he nudges me from behind, hinting I'm to keep moving.

When I'm up on the deck, I see Kazimir and the other Russian. The hair on the back of my neck instantly prickles as I get a foreboding sense that something awful lingers around the corner. "Kazimir, go downstairs and get everything."

Kazimir's glower is directed my way, and I immediately avert my gaze, terrified. "Luka called. There's been a mix-up with the boat."

"What?" Saint spits, as this clearly wasn't part of the plans. "That's impossible. I just spoke to him."

"He just called. Two minutes ago. Go see Mohammed now."

"Fuck," Saint curses under his breath. "Stay here. I'll be back soon."

My heart begins to race. "Take me with you," I plead, not wanting to be left alone with Kazimir. I latch onto his arm, hoping he sees reason, but then quickly shrink back when he makes it clear that touching him is forbidden.

Saint appears stunned by my request as his gaze flicks back and forth between Kazimir and me. "I won't be long," he promises, affirming I'm staying put. There is no point in arguing, so I can only hope he's right.

He expresses something to both men in Russian, and if I didn't know any better, I'd say he was giving them a warning.

He gives me one last look, before jumping from the yacht and hurrying down the dock.

When he's no longer in sight, the need to flee overcomes me because I know my life is in danger. But it's too late. Kazimir storms forward, gripping my bicep firmly and drawing my face to his. There is fire behind his soulless eyes. "Now's your chance to run," he says, which was not what I was expecting.

"What?" I question, licking my dry lips.

He responds by sweeping his hand outward, hinting I'm free to go. But I'm not stupid. Nothing in this world is free. "No." I shake my head. "He told me to stay here."

"Well, I tell you to go."

Before I know what's happening, the other Russian steps forward and punches Kazimir in the face— once, twice. I almost sigh in relief, but it's too good to be true to believe he's come to my rescue. They're both in on whatever scheme they're plotting when they laugh and exchange animated words in Russian.

Just as I'm about to question what the hell is going on, Kazimir yanks me forward and drags me toward the dock. My shoulder pops, and I yelp. "Let me go!" I shriek, attempting to pry myself free, but that isn't an option. "Help!"

My screams are useless when he slaps his hand violently over my mouth to muffle them.

I dig in my heels, but my flip-flops are almost ripped from my feet as he tugs me forward. "No!" I yell, over and over, but it's a muted mess as he continues to muzzle me. I can't believe this is happening again.

I'm finally getting off this boat, and all I want to do is stay.

When I see a disgusting brute standing by the yacht with his arms open, ready to catch me, it's apparent being here is far safer than wherever this man wants to take me. He snaps his head from left to right, ensuring the coast is clear as he snarls something in Russian to Kazimir.

"See you soon," Kazimir says into my ear before pushing me between my shoulder blades. I trip over the edge and into the arms of yet another captor. I squirm madly, but his hold on me is tight.

His stench of rotten fish and piss assaults me as he laughs at my pathetic attempts to get free. "No!" I scream, but he pays no attention to my cries for help as he runs down the dock with me thrown over his shoulder.

I have no idea where we're going, but it's clear Kazimir set Saint up. There never was a call. It was just a ruse to send Saint away. When I see two men wave us over to their tattered blue fishing boat, I know why.

It appears Aleksei Popov has been outbid.

They yell in a language I don't understand, but what I do know is that wherever I'm going, it will make where I was look like the Ritz. There is no compassion or goodness about these men. They see me as nothing but property—to do with as they please.

Tears stream down my cheeks as I sob violently, thumping on my attacker's back. But he snorts in humor, slapping my ass and making me feel like nothing but a piece of meat. He steps over the boat's edge as the other men help him aboard, hollering in celebration.

He leads me into a small galley where he throws me onto

a small bench seat. I spring up, attempting to run, but he soon puts an end to that escape plan when slaps my cheek. I see stars and slide onto my back, gasping for air. The boat comes to life with a splutter as two men stand over me, their lips almost smacking in delight.

I'm suddenly thankful I'm covered.

As I frantically scan my surroundings, searching for a weapon, the man who carried me steps forward and brutally yanks me up into a sitting position by my wrists. I flop forward like a rag doll, still winded from the slap. His yellowed teeth gnash together as his eyes scan over me. When they stop at my breasts, he reaches out and cups my left one.

Groaning low, he runs his meaty thumb over my nipple, tugging hard when he doesn't feel it pearl. He laughs when I cry out in pain. The other man joins him, cupping my other breast, palming and squeezing hard.

This is it this time. There is no one to save me. I never thought Saint was a knight in shining armor, but at least I never felt such fear like I do right now. These men are going to rape me and probably kill me, and not necessarily in that order.

They frantically claw their hands under my robe which has bunched up under me, but they don't let that stop them. I thrash around wildly, but it's two against one, and when one of them pushes me onto my back, cutting off my air supply by placing his forearm against my windpipe, I know it's only a matter of time before I pass out.

"No," I wheeze. "Please...no." But my pleas are a trigger for them, and they turn savage.

The man on top of me yanks up my robe until my shorts are exposed. He doesn't waste a second and shoves his hand inside them. I attempt to scream and claw at his arm, but he presses harder down on my throat, laughing when I gasp for air.

My eyes feel like they're about to bulge from my head from the pressure, but I kick my legs with the last shred of strength I have left. The other man grips my feet, however, pinning me still.

My innocent white underwear are no more when they are bypassed, and a rough finger skims along my sex. I slap the man's forearm wildly, but it's a mere tickle as my air supply is being siphoned. I go to a different plane, one where I'm not being held down by two men who are seconds away from raping me.

I await the darkness…but it never comes.

In a whoosh, the air returns to my lungs, and I take in large mouthfuls, starved for oxygen. I'm not even aware of the fact I'm no longer held down until I hear grunts and pained howls. Adrenaline soars through me as I shoot upward and witness a flurry of bodies being thrown around the room.

Everything happens in slow motion, and my small window of sight allows me to see a man, no, a warrior, annihilate three men who don't stand a chance. The warrior punches, kicks, chokes them, and each time they come back for more, he puts them down again and again.

The man who held my feet charges toward the warrior with a roar, but the warrior turns and delivers an uppercut, snapping the man's head backward with a sickening crack. He drops to the floor, twitching.

The man who was at the wheel of the boat has a knife and rushes toward the warrior, but he doesn't stand a chance as the warrior disarms him in some martial arts move before punching him in the throat. The man gasps for air, clawing at his throat, but soon slumps to the floor, joining his partner in crime.

Just who is this ninja warrior?

The last man, the one who carried me, the one who pinned me down and touched me, is the vilest of the three. He spits something in Russian as blood splutters down his chin, pointing at me before storming forward, poised on killing me.

He gets within two feet. I draw my knees to my chest, bracing for a blow, but it never comes. I hear a snap before a body drops. There is no mistaking that hollow sound. He's dead.

Everything happened so quickly, so I take my time to slowly raise my head and take in the carnage around me.

Three men lie in crumpled piles while a warrior stands triumphantly in the middle. His chest rises and falls as he inhales deeply, catching his breath, fists clenched by his sides. I am in awe as he just saved my life, but when he lifts those eyes, those chartreuse swirls, I know my life hangs in the balance because my warrior is…Saint.

"No," I whimper, but it's too late. I attempt to scramble back, but he jerks me up by the arms and drags me through the boat.

I step over the dead men, tears clouding my vision, as I am in so much trouble. "Let me explain," I plead, but there is no time for reasoning.

Saint grips the crease of my elbow and leads me off the boat, hauling me down the dock. I don't even bother fighting him because I've run out of fight. When I see a bloody Kazimir, he tries to mask his anger, but I can see it. He's furious Saint came to my rescue.

However, I use the term rescue lightly because when he continues jerking me roughly, I'm afraid of where he's taking me.

Kazimir and the other Russian follow, keeping their distance as Saint's anger is explosive. I choke on my raspy sobs, but Saint shows no mercy. We continue hustling until we reach a smaller sailing yacht than the one we arrived in. Saint all but pushes me onto it, never letting me go.

He screams in Russian, barking what I assume are orders, and when Kazimir gets behind the wheel and starts the boat, I know my punishment has only just begun. He glares at me, and I'm left breathless because an epiphany hits.

The other Russian punched him because...this was a setup. He said he would see me soon, meaning, he was planning on joining me on that boat. He would tell Saint I hit him, which wasn't the first time, and that I escaped.

But what he wasn't expecting was for Saint to come back quicker than he'd hoped.

He was hoping my captors would flee, where he would surely meet them at a designated spot. The only way he would get away from Saint would be by killing him. This tangled web just doesn't end.

And I'm about to uncover that in its truest form.

Saint drags me down the stairs and slams the door, revealing a small galley even more claustrophobic than the one I was in earlier.

A single light bulb hangs from the ceiling. The floor was once upon a time a polished wood. There are a small stove and a sink but no tables or chairs. A shabby double mattress covered in faded purple flowers rests on the floor. An archway at the back reveals a toilet and shower. A single silver pole sits dead center.

I gulp.

Saint releases me, pushing me forward as he begins to pace. I don't know what to do, so I instantly make a beeline for the mattress, but Saint stops me.

"Kneel," he commands. By the harshness to his tone, I know defying him isn't an option. So I quickly drop. He continues pacing, while I remain motionless, unsure what he's going to do.

Beneath the robe, I am sweating profusely, and I want nothing more than to take it off. Our heavy breaths are crashing into one another like two tidal waves, and before long, I'm sure to drown.

"Why?" he questions as he stops pacing, back turned to me. "Why do you continually disobey me?"

"I-I…" I stutter over my words, afraid. "I didn't want to g-go. I was forced. Kazimir—"

He scoffs in response, refusing to allow me to finish. "Forced?" he mocks, arms folded. "You have no idea what being forced feels like."

I bite my tongue to stop myself from retaliating because it

won't achieve a thing.

"You know"—he turns slowly—"tonight was the first time I ever saw you scared. No matter what I've done, I haven't been able to trigger that response from you."

"Why would you want to?" I whisper, not understanding.

"Because…it's my job to."

My heart begins to kick against my rib cage as he walks toward me, dangerously slow. He runs his hand over my masked head, examining me. Something between us is about to change.

"Strip."

He's asked this of me before, but this time feels different.

After what just happened, shedding myself of this getup is a welcomed comfort, so I slowly remove the niqab, exhaling when the fresh air brushes against my heated flesh. I shake out my hair, freeing it from sticking to the back of my neck. The security of hiding behind a mask is no longer, and I suddenly feel exposed. But Saint waits for me to continue.

I gather up the robe in my hands and slip it off over my head. Another exhale follows. I will never take a breeze pressed up against my body for granted ever again.

My skin instantly breaks out into goose bumps when the light air comes into contact with the sweat beads dotting my flesh. It's heavenly. I wait for further instruction, but it appears I already have the manual.

"I said strip," Saint says, while my eyes widen.

"What? No," I reply, shaking my head firmly. But this isn't optional. When Saint stands rigid, I sniff, holding back my humiliated tears.

My fingers tremble as I draw the tank over my head and toss it aside. I quickly cover my breasts with my arm. I'm wearing a bra, but regardless, my ample breasts spill over the tops of the cups as the size is too small.

"Ангел, you're not done."

My lower lip quivers as I look up at him, pleading. "Why?"

"I won't ask again," he warns, inhaling heavily.

The cross against my throat burns, announcing my sins, but what choice do I have?

With an arm still locked around me, I reach around with the other and unclasp the bra. With great difficulty, as I refuse to remove my arm, I finally maneuver myself out of it, and it drops to the floor with a victorious thud.

I'm kneeling before my captor topless, but this is only the beginning because when his wicked gaze drops to my shorts, I know I'm only halfway done. "Don't be like them," I beg softly. "You're not like them. You're different."

"You're right," he affirms with a nod. "I am different. Unlike everyone else, I don't want to fuck you." My cheeks blister as I chew my bottom lip. "I want to break you. But it appears the two are clearly linked. So I ask you again…strip."

"No, please, don't," I beseech. His detachment begins to scare me, which is exactly why he's doing this.

This is a different form of torture, and it's working.

"You have three seconds," he warns, stepping forward, and I instantly leap to my feet. "One."

"No!" I cry, backing away, but he only advances forward. "Two."

"Don't do this, please."

But Saint is way past my pleading.

"Three."

He lunges forward, intent on stripping me himself, but I refuse him the honor. If he wants me naked, then so be it, but it'll be my own hand.

"Fine!" I scream, baring my breasts to him as I spread my arms out wide. "Is this what you want, you sick bastard! To see me humiliated? Fuck you."

I tug my shorts down my legs, kicking them aside, anger overtaking me. My underwear are still on. For now.

Saint hisses and takes a small step back, but his retreat only spurs me on as I hastily advance. "At least I'm not the one hiding behind a mask! Look at you," I mock, a fierceness spurring me on. "You're pathetic! All you are is someone's dog...jumping to command."

I'm walking a very dangerous line, but I have nothing left to lose.

"You think you're big and strong, but you're not." I saunter toward him, my near nakedness suddenly making me feel like a goddess, dancing under a full moon. "You're a fucking coward."

Saint rushes forward, gripping my wrists, stopping me from moving an inch. "You have no idea what you're talking about." His grave tone reveals I've struck a nerve, and it inspires me to continue.

"You can't even show me your face." I laugh, mocking him. "If that doesn't spell coward, then I don't know what does." Standing on tippy toes, I level him with pure hatred. "Maybe you're afraid of what I'll see. It's easy to hide behind a mask…but being honest, that's what a real man does. He doesn't hide."

We are caught in a deadlock as Saint's heavy breathing and heaving chest reveals I'm moments away from being gagged forever. But so be it. "So it's safe to say, you're not a real man…Saint."

Oh…shit.

The already small room grows impossibly small as Saint shoves me backward and does something which rips the air from my lungs. He claws at the bottom of his ski mask and tears it from his face, throwing it across the room.

Time stands still.

My brain is unable to process the sight before me because for eight days, I've only been given a glimpse into those hypnotic eyes, but now that I'm faced with the entire picture, I don't know where to look first.

I start with his hair; the long, wild, dirty blond locks that frame his chiseled face. I instantly think of the surfers down at Venice Beach because his thick waves appear sun kissed and windswept, embodying the perfect mussed style.

His eyebrows are thick and dark, giving shape to those unusual green eyes and also emphasizing those angular cheekbones. His upturned nose only adds to his arrogance. His mouth is a succulent pink. His top lip is not overly thick, but it is slightly bowed in shape. However, his bottom lip is plump and undeniably fierce.

His sharp jawline complements his cleft chin. He has thick, unkempt stubble, but it only adds to his hardness.

I stagger backward, as Saint is entirely wayward and

rebellious, but more than anything…he is absolutely epic. A bad boy every mom warns their daughters about.

Unable to help myself, my gaze drifts down his hardened body as I know what lies beneath that long-sleeved shirt. Now that I have a face to go with his body, I am utterly speechless. I never thought he would look like a freaking…supermodel—a bad boy, no, scrap that, a bad *Saint*, as he isn't groomed or pretty. He is rough, hard, and totally sinful—a perfect look for everything he encompasses.

He allows me to eat him up, clearly knowing the effect he has on people. But that only lasts a second before he swoops forward and drags me toward him. It's the first time we've been this close unmasked, and it seems unfair that his good looks are only emphasized, up close.

Without the ski mask, he seems taller, and his shoulders broader somehow. "I'm not afraid…" he whispers in response to my claims. His wicked lips are in full view for me to see when they twitch, a lopsided smirk leaving me winded. "But you should be."

His warning should scare me, but it doesn't. It excites me.

When he yanks me forward, pressing us chest to chest, I whimper, my bashfulness of being this close to him slowly vanishing. I don't know what happens now, but I dare not breathe when his eyes drop to my chest, savoring the sight.

He takes his time, in no real hurry, while I'm certain my skin is about to burst into flames.

"Kneel, Ангел."

A small mewl, that betraying bitch, slips past my lips, hinting what hearing him say that to me, unmasked, does.

I'm basking in his fragrance, his touch, his entire makeup, and I'm helpless to stop it as I drop to my knees.

He nods once, clearly pleased.

My body is hypersensitive as everything is suddenly too much, too fast. Saint takes his time, walking around me, and I suddenly feel like prey as my predator circles me. When he comes to a stop behind me, I hold my breath.

He brushes the hair from my shoulder with a deliriously slow flick before running the back of two fingers down the side of my neck. A shiver surpasses me, and my nipples instantly pearl. "You're very responsive. Are you sure you're a virgin?" he says, insulting me.

"Go fuck yourself," I say. Saint chuckles deeply.

"Choose your words wisely, Ангел."

It's a warning, but it still doesn't prepare me for what he does next. Saint drops to his knees behind me and leaves mere inches between us. I can feel his hot breath bathing the back of my neck. My bravado stands tall, refusing to buckle, but when he places his hands, or more specifically, a single finger on me, I know it's only a matter of time until I concede.

He traces a line from under my ear, down the column of my neck. He comes to a stop at my racing pulse. "Are you scared?"

"N-no." My falter divulges my lie.

He hums low, then continues his exploration of me. My collarbone feels his touch next. Who knew a simple collarbone was able to experience such pleasure? I gnaw on my cheek to mute my whimpers, but Saint is in tune with my inner turmoil.

He runs the tip of his finger along the bony ridge before coming to rest at the cross at my throat. He traces it, clearly intrigued as to why I never take it off. "Do you think your God will save you?"

"He isn't my God anymore," I reply in a whisper. "He died the day my father did. If a Baptist pastor couldn't be shown any mercy, then there isn't any hope for me."

My confession has caught him off guard as his finger hovers over the cross. I think back to his tattoo and wonder if he feels the same way.

"I think He might make an exception"—he begins to trace downward, between the valley of my breasts—"for you."

My legs tremble as he detours his slow touch to my left breast. He takes his time, outlining the shape with his finger, skimming back and forth along the outer side. He's familiarizing himself with my body. I remain utterly still as I'm too afraid to move.

My cheeks blister, and I'm rendered speechless when he leisurely slithers across and circles my areola. My nipples are already erect, but when he comes within inches of them, they tingle and seem to grow heavy.

My chest rises and falls intermittently as weighty breaths leave me. I shamefully press my thighs together, but it doesn't stop the burn. "I hate you," I cry, quivering, desperate for more.

Saint gives into my silent pleas when he flicks over my nipple lazily. "Your mind may tell you that..." He begins a torturous rhythm, circling the swollen bud with his finger. I clench my teeth together. "But your body is telling me something else."

Before I have a chance to prove him wrong, his large, warm hand cups my entire breast and squeezes slowly. My eyes roll to the back of my head because goddamn him...it feels so good. I'm helpless to stop this because deep down...I don't want to. This is the first form of pleasure I've felt in days.

He continues sampling me, humming low when he pinches my nipple.

I whimper as I feel like a million volts of electricity have zapped me. Everything throbs. Wetness gathers between my legs, and no matter how hard I press my thighs together, it doesn't stop my arousal from coating my sex.

I know this is wrong, so very wrong, but I'm detached from my body, and the line between right and wrong begins to blur. The line blurred the moment Saint told me my husband sold me to some Russian mobster.

My breast is hot and heavy, and each squeeze and pinch transports me closer to hell. I'm trying to remain unaffected, but it's laughable. His touch mingling with the fierce breath on the back my neck is too much.

He tweaks my nipple one last time before he continues his journey. He uses his hand this time and slides down my stomach slowly. Peering down, I gasp as the sight is so foreign. I've seen those hands do some callous things, but pressed against my skin, I soon forget them because his touch is nothing but tenderness.

He circles my belly button before skimming along the waistband of my underwear. My stomach ripples and goose bumps butter my flesh when he dips low and traces over my sex. It's the wake-up call I needed, and I instantly buck my hips back, reality hitting hard.

What the fuck have I done?

"Don't touch me!"

"Shh, shh," he hushes calmly, wrapping his arm around my waist to stop me from moving. But I wriggle wildly as I can't believe I allowed this to get so far.

I just allowed my kidnapper to fondle me, and I liked it…I liked it a lot. I'm ashamed and humiliated, but more than anything, I am so turned on. Guilt overcomes me, and I hang my head in shame.

"Still hate me?" Saint huskily asks.

And the answer is no because I hate myself more.

I remain silent, unsure what to say or do, but when Saint presses his chest to my back and slithers his hand over my hip, it's evident I'm no longer in control. I should fight him, but I don't. I don't have the strength to.

He cups my heat, undoubtedly feeling my arousal. Air gets trapped in my throat, and I gasp, tears stinging my eyes. I am angry with myself for being such a fucking weakling, but when he slips his warm hand into my underwear, those feelings soon turn to yearning.

I disengage from everything and simply…surrender.

He runs a finger along my heat, hissing when he feels how wet I am. My sex pulses, wanting more. So I disgracefully part my legs slightly. He traces along my entrance, using my arousal as lubrication to slide along my feverish flesh with ease.

"Stop," I whimper, but it's weak as my actions are not reflecting my demands. My plea is met with Saint sinking a finger into my sex.

I slump forward with a winded cry, a thousand emotions overtaking me, but Saint ensures I stay upright when he drapes an arm around my middle and holds me prisoner in every sense of the word. He works his finger in and out deliriously slow while every part of me blushes.

"No," I moan, attempting to dance out of his hold, but the fight just has Saint nudging in deeper.

"Stop fighting me. You won't win...because you don't want to."

The sound of my ripe flesh sucking him into my warmth embarrasses me because it confirms my body is a traitorous whore. This man has caused me nothing but anguish, but when he increases his rhythm, I forget everything because the pleasure suddenly overrides the pain.

I am helpless, a gluttonous fiend because when he flicks over my swollen clit, I want so much more. I part my legs wider, allowing him deeper access, and he takes what I give. He works me sluggishly, exploring every part of me while I yield, allowing him to be my puppeteer.

I am no longer the same Willow because my body rules me. After feeling nothing but misery, I just want to feel good for a small fraction of time. I know this is wrong, but fighting him is pointless. He always wins. And this time, I want him to.

When he senses I've surrendered to his touch, he inserts another finger. My eyes bulge from my head as I'm stuffed full. "Oh, Ангел." He sighs low, sinking in deeper. "You really are a virgin."

I'm too lost to argue for my virtue because he slowly

plunges his fingers in and out…in and out, and before long, I'm arching back, leaning into him to deepen the angle. He is composed and completely in control as I come undone in his hand.

With two fingers, he begins to pumps in and out of me wildly as his thumb rubs over my inflamed core. The combination is a delicious evil, and I bite down on my lip to stop myself from asking for more.

After tonight, you'd think I'd shy away from being touched this way, but those advances weren't welcome. Saint's touches aren't either…so why do they feel so damn good?

A burning simmers low, and I know it will only take a few more strokes before I cross the line of no return. His skill is unmeasured because I don't remember ever feeling this way. He knows where to touch me to make this feel so good. I lose myself to the cadence of Saint thrusting those long fingers into me as he ensures I take everything he gives by pinning me between his chest and arm. I am engulfed in his signature fragrance, and I moan.

"Feel good, Ангел?"

His hoarse voice adds to the sensation, and I cry out. But I'll be damned if I express that to him. "No," I manage to choke out, bucking my hips and riding his fingers.

He chuckles in response and plunges in deeply while I scream, making a liar out of me.

I am disgusted with myself, but I want to see. I want to see what he's doing to me. With my heart in my throat, I peer downward, but nothing can prepare me for the sight before me. Saint's fingers sink deep into my swollen, ripe sex, controlling me and bending me to how he pleases. But when he strokes over my clit, I know this is for my pleasure. He wants me to come.

I'm transfixed and lax, rocking and bouncing, chasing my release which burns every part of me.

"I told you," Saint says with hunger, his speed almost punishing. "You behave; I reward you."

"Oh, god…" I groan, unable to tear my eyes away from him fingering me. "Please…" I need to come. Now. I am so close. I can taste the sweet surrender. I'm racing toward the pinnacle, and I just know my release will be explosive.

He uses the arm around my waist to pin me still, reminding me this is his show. "But you don't…"

His words are lost to my cries and breathless panting. Shame on me. "I punish you."

I don't understand what he means because when he pinches my clit, I see stars. But instead of continuing his assault, he withdraws his fingers and lets me go. I droop forward with a winded yelp, not understanding what just happened.

"No…please." I was almost there.

My heart is thrashing wildly, and my breaths are jerky as I gasp for air. But I turn over my shoulder to see a nonchalant Saint place the fingers that were just inside me into his mouth. He suckles them, his gaze never leaving mine. I instantly flush the brightest crimson.

His eyes flicker briefly when he licks his fingers clean. It appears he's just tasted the most delicious dessert. But his delight soon turns when he removes his fingers. "So this is your punishment," he concludes while I blink.

I suddenly feel like nothing but a whore. I cover my breasts, tears stinging my eyes. "You as-asshole," I stutter, my high soon fading.

The happy endorphins soon turn to nothing but shame.

"Yes," he affirms with a stiff nod. "I am." His words are contradictory to what I see, but I shove that aside.

A tear scores my cheek, but I let it fall as it's my scarlet letter, my mark that shows the world what an idiot I am. I allowed him to defile me, but worse still, I liked it—I wanted it. I wanted to come, and once again, Saint demonstrated that I don't do anything unless he allows it.

I feel cheap as if I've just sold a small piece of my soul.

Turning back around, I lower my chin, permitting the tears to fall freely. I am nearly naked, my body flushed from Saint's touch, but he's denied me any pleasure as yet another lesson—Saint is my master, and I am his slave. And no matter how smart I think I am, he's always ten steps ahead.

He leaves me alone, arms shielding my nakedness as I sob helpless tears. My body doesn't know what to do as I want to come. And I want to cry.

I crawl over to the mattress, curling into the fetal position as the heat simmers. What I just did crashes into me, and the ring on my finger weighs heavy like a manacle around my heart. I just cheated on my husband...and I did so without a second thought.

Saint humiliated me, which is what this little exercise was all about. Yet I know he doesn't remain unaffected...I saw the proof, the monster bulge in the front of his pants. But that doesn't matter. I need to stop seeing him as my savior because he's not.

I am merely a means to an end—he told me so himself. There is no happily ever after for me. And after what I just did…I don't deserve one. Clutching the cross around my neck, I remember Saint's words.

"I think He might make an exception for you."

But he's wrong. There aren't enough Hail Marys to save my soul.

CHAPTER SEVEN

She has every right to hate me. I hate me. But touching her that way...I am in way over my head.

Day 9

His smell.

His touch.

His entire being.

It still lingers in the air. On my body. Which is why I'm huddled in the tiny shower, scrubbing my skin raw. I want to eliminate every trace of him from me, and although the water can wash away his physical touch, nothing can eradicate the damage done to my soul.

I haven't slept a wink as I'm too afraid of dreaming. I lie on the filthy mattress, numb to everything. Kazimir brought down some things, including my change of clothes and some toiletries. Even though my back was turned, I could feel him eyeball me, as his lust has turned to hatred. If I make it off this boat alive, it'll be a miracle. But once I arrive in Russia, I have a feeling I'll have wished he killed me.

Saint hasn't been down here, which is a blessing, as I can't look at him without memories of what I did crashing into me. I don't understand why my body responded the way it did. I can deny it all I want, but his actions aroused me. When he plunged his fingers into my body, I wanted nothing more than to come and come by his hand.

Screaming, the water mutes my pain as I slam my fist against the wall, sobbing. I have never felt more helpless than I do right now. There is no getting off this boat. Saint has ensured that. So all I can do is wait until we reach our final destination.

Switching off the water, I dry myself and slip into a blue summer dress. I have about five days' worth of clean clothes. I wonder if that means I'll be in Russia before then. My stomach growls, reminding me of other pressing matters—I need to eat.

Kazimir also brought down some food. Most of it is non-perishable, seeing as we don't have a fridge. Hunting through the boxes, I decide on having some canned fruit as it's the only thing I can stomach. I don't want to go outside, but staying down here is beginning to give me cabin fever. So I suck it up and open the door.

The sun is bright and warm, and my skin instantly basks in the rays, desperate to thaw the chill from my bones. That feeling soon submerges, however, when I see Saint. He's sitting on the edge of the boat, writing in what looks to be a leather-bound journal. I arch a brow as I've never seen him writing in a journal.

He senses my arrival and slowly lifts his chin.

He isn't wearing his ski mask as it seems futile now. The sunshine just seems to highlight his good looks. Last night, it appears, the darkness revealed a sliver of what he's packing because the daylight exposes just how handsome he truly is. I suddenly hate the daytime and wish I was once again shrouded by darkness.

Ignoring him, I walk up the stairs and sit as far away as possible from him. My pleasured moans echo loudly around me, reminding me of when I was putty in his hands. Turning my back to all three of my captors, I open my can of fruit and fish for a piece of pineapple with my fingers. The moment the sweetness hits my tongue, I moan low as I didn't realize how hungry I was.

As I'm digging out a slice of peach, I'm hit with a delectable fragrance that has nothing to do with my fruit salad. I close my eyes and take three calming breaths, refusing to entertain the memories of last night as they collide into me. There is no point ignoring him as he's proven that doesn't work, but I refuse to be civil.

"Please go away...I'm trying to eat, and you being here is spoiling my appetite." He has the gall to laugh. I'm thankful my back is to him as I don't want to look at him.

"You look nice," he says, which has me inhaling my peach. I thump on my chest, hoping to dislodge it, but nothing can extricate this heaviness he makes me feel.

"Really? I'll be sure to never wear this again then." My bravado is big and tall, but I'm trembling on the inside.

"Well, I do prefer you with nothing on, but this is also good." Damn him and his smugness, and damn him for knowing what I look like without clothes.

My cheeks heat, and I instantly lose my appetite. As I attempt to stand, he places his hand around my hip, stopping me. His touch is electric, and goose bumps paint my skin. "Don't be shy. I know you liked it," he whispers into my ear while I hold my breath. "If you behaved...I would have allowed you to finish. But you know the rules."

"You know nothing," I spit, referring to many topics. "And rules? These were set without my consent. I don't want to play your game; therefore, these rules are not ones I will ever abide by. Your boss will never make a submissive out of me because that's what I am, right? To be his sex slave? Concubine? Whore?"

It's the first time I've expressed aloud what I fear my future holds. Saint doesn't need to reply because I know the answer. The answer I still do not know, however, is why is Saint here? What's in it for him?

"I'm beginning to see that," he replies, his soft scruff tickling my skin as he leans in closer over my shoulder. "But we all break, sooner or later."

There are promise and knowledge behind his words. "You may have, but I'm a lot stronger than you think I am," I reveal, unbending as his tepid breath bathes my flesh. "I learned that from when my mom's boyfriend pinned me down and tried to rape me when I was fifteen."

A sharp intake of breath escapes him, giving away his surprise as his fingers tighten around my waist.

"So you can do whatever you want to me…nothing can ever compare to my own flesh and blood turning her back on me when I needed her the most." I have no idea why I feel the need to share my deepest, darkest secrets with him. I suppose, after last night, he destroyed a piece of me. So this is me, taking it back.

His silence is my victory.

"You can break my body. It's only a shell. But my spirit, you will never touch. That will always belong to me. So I'm ready. Do your best. Take me to Russia and deliver me to your boss, but know that I will never stop fighting for my freedom. I will never stop trying to break free."

I have nothing left to lose.

"Now, please let me enjoy whatever freedom I have left alone. That's the least you can do." This sudden bravery has left us both stunned it appears.

His hold around me loosens, and he stands. "I'm sorry that happened to you," he says, leaving me winded as his heavy footsteps announce his retreat.

Only when his fragrance fades do I breathe normally again.

I wasn't expecting that response from Saint. I never wanted his pity. So what do I want from him? That's the million-dollar question.

I continue eating my fruit, not really tasting it as I lose myself in the vastness of the deep blue sea. Being out here confirms my problems are merely a drop in the ocean as I feel so insignificant, so small. No matter my problems, the world will continue to turn.

My thoughts as always drift to Drew. Is he okay? Even though he's the apparent reason I'm here, bound for Russia, I still want to know how he is. He made me happy once, and I can't help but care.

A phone ringing snaps me from my thoughts, especially when Saint's deep voice answers the call. He's speaking in Russian, and I get the sudden sense he's talking to someone important. My shoulders instantly sag as I guess it's Aleksei Popov.

Lost in Saint's voice, I don't notice Kazimir sneak up on me until his stench hits me. "You owe me, bitch. I was supposed to be off this boat a rich man, but I'm still here."

"Why did you do it?" I ask, leaving crescent moons into my palms as I clench my fists.

"Because your ass is worth a lot of money."

I was right. "So you sold me to some other asshole?"

His callous chuckle has my hair standing on end. "Yes. I did. But now I look like an idiot. Luckily, I have plan B."

"*What?*" My stomach drops. Plan B? I don't know what frightens me more—Russia or plan B.

My speech now seems obsolete because it appears I don't know my enemy at all. The unknown is all the more daunting.

"You will never see Russia, so don't you worry. I'll do you a favor. Boss will destroy you, just as he did Saint's…"

But Kazimir never gets to finish his sentence as Saint's sharp voice cracks through the air. "Kazimir, enough talking!"

I dare not turn over my shoulder. Saint's furious tone scares me. Kazimir grumbles under his breath, clearly annoyed with constantly being told what to do. He and Saint are fighting for top dog position, which means if plan B is in motion, Saint is in danger. And I am certain this time, Kazimir will ensure he doesn't fail.

Better the devil you know is the saying that seems fitting in my circumstances. Although Saint intends to deliver me to Popov, I know in some sense what's headed my way. But the men who worked with Kazimir, they were inhuman, and if they are an indication of what my future entails, I would rather die right now.

Saint and Kazimir exchange harsh words in Russian before I hear Kazimir slowly rise. I'm waiting for a war of words, but Kazimir knows his time will come and soon. The fruit I just ate threatens to come back up, so I quickly bend forward, poised to throw up over the edge of the boat.

My raw stomach refuses to give up the small meal I consumed, however, and eventually, the sickness subsides.

"Boss will destroy you, just as he did Saint's..." Just as he did Saint's what?

"Go back downstairs." Saint's command jolts me. Just as I'm about to protest, he reveals this isn't up for discussion. "There's a storm coming."

I'm about to scoff, but as I shield my eyes from the sun with my hand, I see that on the horizon, the sky looks punishing. I don't fancy being up here when that happens, so I stand and turn around. Saint is a few feet away, and when we lock eyes, the yearning I felt last night hits.

The sunlight draws out the lighter blond strands of his hair, contrasting the darker shade. It's kicked to the high heavens, and the reason that it is, is revealed when he runs his fingers through it. The bright sun highlights the golden swirls in his eyes and somehow seems to emphasize the pinkness to his supple lips.

I'm quick to snap myself from staring for too long and hurriedly push past him, muting my whimpers when I accidentally brush too close to him. What has me almost tripping over my own feet, however, is that I could swear a similar sound slips past his lips.

I don't allow it to come to fruition because that's just ridiculous.

The moment I'm in the galley, I inhale deeply as my heart races wildly. I instantly slump onto the mattress, drawing my knees to my chest as I bow my head and cradle my brow. Ironic that a storm is coming because I can't help but feel a tempest is brewing within.

A thunderclap pierces the punishing sky, the sharp flash of lightning illuminating my small haven below. We sailed into rough waters about two hours ago. I thought it would get better, but it hasn't. As the boat rocks from side to side, I press my back to the wall and take three deep breaths.

The howl from the punishing wind wails loudly, adding to the already unsettled vibe. Saint wasn't kidding when he said a storm was coming. But this kind of feels like a monster storm as the mammoth waves can be heard smashing against our small boat. I yelp and curl myself into a smaller ball when the crack of a thunderbolt sounds like the whip of God.

The door suddenly heaves opens, and a gust of wind yowls down the stairs. Turning my cheek, I see a sopping wet Saint fighting with the door to close it. He's wrestling with the wind and the rain, but he finally wins.

He bounces down the stairs, shaking the raindrops from his snarled hair. It's futile, however, because he is drenched. When he sees me huddled on the mattress, he stops in his tracks. It seems like he wants to ask me if I'm okay, but that would be a ridiculous and pointless question to ask.

I watch as he crosses the room in three large steps and heads into the bathroom. A small brown towel hangs from a hook, and he reaches for it, running it over his hair, face, and back of his neck. His long-sleeved shirt is soaked and clings to him like a second skin. It's difficult not to notice his rippling muscles and well-defined physique.

However, when he grips the edge of his shirt and tears it over his head, it's impossible not to admire that hard body in the flesh. His skin is slick and bronzed, and when he rubs the towel over his chest and abs, I'm transfixed by the way his hypnotic six-pack undulates. His obliques are firm and toned, adding to the muscled ecstasy.

I instantly turn my cheek, though, as I hate this response I have to him.

There is no mistaking him stepping out of his soggy boots, and when I hear his belt buckle and pants hit the floor, a shiver passes over me. Curiosity wins out in the end, and I sneak a peek, gasping when I see him standing in nothing but black boxer briefs.

He is drying himself off, and a simple chore shouldn't be able to elicit this response from me, but it does. I suddenly get hot. His legs are lean, muscled, but it's the impressive bulge which has me biting my lip to stifle my approval.

Once he's dry, he enters the room, and I quickly turn away, not wanting to give him the satisfaction of seeing me look at him without disgust. I almost breathe a sigh of relief when I hear him unfasten a bag and the rustle of clothes alerts me to him hunting for something to wear.

When I hear a zipper being pulled up, my heart begins to slow down.

When I think it's safe, I gingerly look his way, only to see he's still topless. He has no shoes on either. Just pants. They sit low on his narrow hips which just seems to accentuate his hardened V muscle. His wet hair hangs around his face and appears longer, and I really wish he'd put on a shirt because his tattoo and nipple piercing and entire nakedness are distracting.

I welcome a deafening thunderclap because it jolts me from my gawking.

"It'll pass," Saint comforts me, which is strange as his assurance feels foreign.

I nod in response, hugging my knees to my chest. "Are we safe in this thing?"

He cocks his head to the side, a grin shaping those sinful lips. "I didn't think you'd care if we capsized." He's right, I wouldn't, especially after what Kazimir revealed today. But regardless, it feels strange seeing him smile. I don't see it often, but it suits him.

There is a sudden silence. The air is heavy with unspoken, forbidden words. I know why that is a moment later. "I spoke to Popov earlier." My hunch was right, but it doesn't feel good to be right. "We will be in Russia in about seven days. There are a few stops along the way, but we will be there in a week or so."

I don't know why he's telling me this.

He walks toward the mattress, standing in front of me, waiting for me to speak. But I have nothing to say.

"He asked about you," he reveals. I lower my eyes, not wanting him to see me cry. "I told him he wouldn't be disappointed. I sent him your picture." No doubt the one he took of me as a submissive little lamb.

If this is some sort of pep talk, then Saint shouldn't give up his day job.

Unable to stomach any more, I lower myself to the mattress and lie on my side, my back turned to Saint. I weep silent tears. They slip into my parted lips, and I taste salty sadness. It's a flavor I should be accustomed to.

The storm is now a welcomed disturbance as the wild wind and ferocious waves drown out my weeping. In seven days, life as I know it will forever be changed. And there isn't a damn thing I can do about it.

Using my hands as a pillow, I prop them under my head, wishing sleep would finally save me from the horrifying images swirling around my mind. However, when the mattress dips minutes later, and I feel a comforting warmth at my back, those images soon settle and are replaced with silence.

My heart begins to race, and my breathing is shallow because there must be some mistake, but when a comforting fragrance floats through the air, I know that there is no mistake. Saint has laid down behind me.

He doesn't touch me, but the heat from his body instantly thaws the chill, and I melt. My world calms. I don't know why he's lying with me, but I don't question it because I need this human connection. I know this is crazy, but honestly, I'm forever questioning my sanity, especially when I languidly shuffle backward so I can feel his breath on the back of my neck.

We're still inches apart, but knowing he's beside me has a warmth spreading from head to toe. And the action within itself…I don't understand. Why is he offering me this comfort? I want to ask him. But I don't. I'm afraid he'll pull away, and I need this.

I need him.

I decide to tell him about what Kazimir said when I wake because now, the sluggish tempo of his inhales and exhales lulls me into a sleepy bubble, and I surrender, sleeping beside my captor.

When I was a child, I used to suffer terrible night terrors, so much so, my father gave up his own bed so I could sleep by my mother. The comfort of knowing she was there beside me gave me a false sense of security, but even so, my dreams weren't as real when I wasn't alone.

When I woke up screaming, she would comfort me and tell me it was all right. That is was only a bad dream. Hearing her voice and smelling her perfume caused the terror to fade, and I would realize it was just a nightmare.

I would give anything for her to tell me that again because when I feel something cold and hard press against my forehead, I know this isn't a bad dream. This is real.

"Wake up, bitch."

My eyes snap open.

Before me are two men or, rather, two monsters. The biggest monster of all, Kazimir, crouches down beside me with the barrel of a gun pressed to my brow. Instantly, I jerk back, but his hand snaps out and grips me by the bicep. "And where do you think you're going?"

I squirm against his hold, but it's useless.

"I told you, you owe me. It's time to pay up." He yanks me up violently while I writhe with all my might against his hold. However, when I see a bloodied Saint slouched in front of me with two men on either side of him, holding him back, my fight dies a quick death.

The one to his left grins, and I immediately remember him. He was one of Pipe's men. He seems to have taken on the role of captain, which has me believing Pipe is dead. Saint struggles wildly, but he doesn't stand a chance as he's clearly wounded.

His face is a bloodied mess, but that seems secondary as the deep gash to his side gushing bright red blood has my utmost attention. Those pained grunts and winded exhalations, I believed them to be just a bad dream, but seeing Saint, bloodied and wounded, I know they ambushed him when he was asleep…beside me.

He let his guard down for a split second, but he will pay for that moment dearly. I instantly feel guilty for being so needy because if I hadn't, we wouldn't be in this dire position. Without a doubt, they will kill him, and as for me, it looks like I'm about to finally pay my dues.

"Meet your new master, Gringo," Kazimir cockily says, waving the gun in the direction of the dirty, destitute looking man. He wears black pants with holes torn in the knees and a faded NIKE T-shirt. A red bandana holds back his long and matted hair.

When he sneers, I see he's missing a few teeth. The remaining ones are yellowed, like someone who has smoked too much tobacco. "Hello, peach. We're going to have some fun. Payback for what you did to Pipe. And once we're through, I have someone else who is very interested in seeing if you taste as sweet as you look."

Saint thrashes about madly, but when his other captor punches his wound, he screams in utter torment. I lock eyes with him, wondering what it feels like for my captor to now be a captive, but seeing him bound doesn't give me any satisfaction. The need to help him overcomes me, but I stay put.

Kazimir sold me out to god knows how many people. But this is personal for Gringo. I was inadvertently the reason for his friend's demise. He will ensure I pay. And pay dearly.

A bolt of lightning sparks to life, alerting me to the ferocious storm outside. It also kicks Kazimir's plan into motion. "Now, before I give you to Gringo, you owe me and Adal a taste."

When Adal steps forward, I know that the identity of my last captor has finally been revealed. I only have to look into those beady, cruel eyes to know he's the asshole who pistol-whipped me. He and Kazimir are here for their pound of flesh.

I flail frantically, but when Kazimir shoves the gun into my lower back, I freeze, a breath hitching in my throat. "No," I plead, but Adal advances toward me, running a hand over his rubbery lips.

Kazimir cackles cruelly, his grip on my arm punishing. "You were always the favorite," he snaps at Saint who is breathing heavily through clenched teeth. "Could never do no wrong by Boss. You arrogant bastard. This will teach you for telling me what to do. You can watch us fuck your precious ангел until she's begging us to kill her."

Saint struggles violently, grunting and gnashing his teeth, but it's no use. This is happening, and this time, there is no one here to save me.

"And when we're done fucking this tight cunt"—he grips my hair and yanks my head backward—"we will kill you. The last thing you see will be all of us breaking her in two."

Tears stream down my face.

"You won't get away with this," Saint spits, eyes narrowed, blood dripping from his lips. "Boss will know what you did. He will find you and make you wish I'd killed you."

Kazimir bursts into a sarcastic chuckle. "Good luck to

him. I'm sick of being his dog. I was the one who should have been his right-hand man, not you!" There is anger behind his words, but I focus on who Saint is to Popov.

His right-hand man. His most trusted friend. But what does Popov have that Saint wants in return? It's evident he didn't just fall into this lifestyle, which has me believing he was forced…but why?

However, those questions will forever remain unanswered because when Adal shoves me backward and my back slams into the wall, it's apparent question time is over. He paws at me eagerly—over my breasts and down between my thighs.

He slams his mouth to mine, and I'm instantly hit with the taste of whiskey. I gag, the liquor reminding me of Kenny, and I attempt to push him off, but Kazimir presses the gun to my temple. I am helpless to move.

Adal lifts the hem of my dress, thrusting his hips into me, so I'm able to feel his erection. He forcefully touches me over my sex, laughing in utter amusement when I try to close my legs. Kazimir joins in with the assault, licking and sucking along my neck while he fondles my breasts. When he pinches my nipples, I whimper in pain.

Saint is pushing against his captors, desperate to break free, but they hold him tight, transfixed on the sight of these two disgusting monsters molesting me. I don't know why, but keeping my eyes locked with Saint's is the only way I can survive this.

His chartreuse orbs blister in rage as he screams in fury. When Adal rips off my underwear and unzips his pants, Saint closes his eyes for a mere second, shaking his head. "I'm sorry, ангел." His words are filled with defeat.

I cry out, my body convulsing with fear because how do I brace myself for what's ahead? Kazimir tears the strap of my dress and forces down one shoulder to expose my bra. He yanks down the cup, baring my breast. Adal latches onto my nipple, biting me hard.

Gringo and the other man holding Saint holler loudly, speaking in a foreign language. The scene of rape and torture seems to get them off. Kazimir suckles my other breast as he forces aside my bra. He still has the gun pressed to my temple, so I remain still, too afraid to move.

Kazimir and Adal are latched onto my breasts while I silently beg to die.

"I have money. You can have it. Just let her go," Saint says, bargaining for my life. I hold my breath.

Why is he doing this?

The mention of money piques Kazimir's interest, and he detaches himself from me. With his gun still trained on me, he turns to look at Saint. "You'd give up everything for this whore? Zoey would be very disappointed to know that. I guess I can see the resemblance between the two."

"Leave her out of this!" Saint bellows as a hit of adrenaline courses through him. His two captors are barely able to hold him back. "You don't speak her name!"

Who is Zoey? And why is Saint bargaining for my freedom? He was the one who took it away in the first place.

"Things just got interesting," Kazimir says. "Maybe keeping you alive is worthwhile."

The suggestion has Adal soon forgetting his chore, and he

violently lets my breast go. I sag in relief, but my legs are still trembling uncontrollably. I cover my nakedness with my arm as best I can.

Adal and Kazimir argue in Russian, but Adal clearly doesn't agree with Kazimir's thoughts. He knows that as long as Saint is alive, their lives are in danger. But the prospect of money is far more important to Kazimir.

The conversation soon turns from sex to money.

"How much?" he asks while Adal shouts, shaking his head, livid.

Saint remains utterly composed. "Twenty million. Give or take."

My unstable legs buckle.

I remember Saint revealing he wasn't doing this for money. He wasn't lying, it appears.

Kazimir whistles, clearly interested. "Being Popov's number one…hitman sure does have its perks."

My eyes widen, and a gasp escapes me. *Hitman?* Saint is a *hitman?*

He lowers his chin, his blood-soaked hair shielding his face, but the guilt riddling him confirms my question and bile rises. Those hands that touched me, which had me whimpering and begging for a release, have taken away how many lives? They've destroyed how many?

I've been given small pieces to this puzzle, but I'm still no closer to uncovering what Saint's end game is. He's a hitman who works for the man who bought me. He's not doing it for the money, which makes me think…he's doing it for Zoey.

"We got a deal?" Saint barks, eyes murderous as he slowly

lifts his head.

The air is thick with tension as Kazimir ponders his proposal. "What do you think, Gringo? Want to trade this little slut's ass for a few million?"

Gringo weighs over his options. I don't know what he paid for me, but I am certain it's not even a fraction of what Kazimir is offering. He did say once he was done with me, I was going to the next contender in line, but passing up that sort of money seems too good an offer.

"No pussy is worth that much money. We got a deal."

Kazimir inhales victoriously while Saint's jaw is clenched. It seems I've been sold yet again. "We have a deal. Ангел," he mocks, "will be spared. But if you go back on your word, she's dead. You both are."

Why do I feel like Saint just made a deal with the devil?

It's revealed a moment later.

"But that doesn't mean we can't have some fun with her."

"No." I whimper, shaking my head.

"Oh, yes," Gringo counters. "Once we were all through with you, we were going to kill you, but now that we have a deal…"

"That wasn't part of the deal!" Saint roars, lunging forward, but he's restrained.

"It's as good as it gets," Kazimir states. "We promise not to kill her as long as we get our money. We have about two days until the next port. You get our money, and we let you both go. But in the meantime…"

"Make that bitch drop to her knees," suggests Gringo, eyes wide with excitement while tiny whimpers slip past my lips.

"Good idea." Kazimir nods, unbuttoning his pants. "Besides, we got unfinished business." I know he's talking about when I knocked him out cold. "Kneel."

My back is still pressed to the wall, but Kazimir turns me around wildly so my back faces Saint. He's done this so Saint has a clear view of Kazimir degrading me. He slips the tip of the gun past my quivering lips and into my mouth, sliding it in and out as an innuendo of what he wants me to do to him.

Tears leak from my eyes at this terrifying experience. I have a loaded weapon in my mouth with a sociopath holding the trigger. He adjusts the angle of the barrel, forcing me to drop to my knees.

When I do, he slides the gun farther down my throat, making me gag. "Just giving you a taste of what's to come." He laughs while I sob loudly around the metal, frightened he'll change his mind and blow a hole straight through me.

When he's done amusing himself, he removes the gun from my mouth. I take in a handful of breaths, breathing past my tears. But those inhalations are in vain because when Kazimir lowers his pants and his disgusting dick springs up happily, my lungs are robbed of air.

"It's not gonna suck itself," he taunts, gripping the back of my head and forcing me to his crotch. I recoil, reaching backward with one arm to pry his hand off me, but when he presses the barrel of the gun into my cheek, I stiffen.

With my body slack, he's able to coerce me forward and force me to open my mouth. When I do, he attempts to thrust into me roughly. I don't care if he shoots me; there is no way I am pleasuring him. I turn my cheek, refusing to comply.

"Wanna play rough?" Kazimir teases, the prospect making his dick twitch.

He holds my hair so tight, tears of pain sting my eyes as I slap his upper thighs, fighting him as he tries to force himself into my mouth. My heart is thrashing wildly, and I think I'm close to passing out. Adrenaline soars through me, but through the chaos, I hear something which anchors me.

"You want to act like a dog, they'll treat you like one."

Saint's hoarse voice cuts through my harsh breathing, and I have no idea why he would say that. Why does he want me to recall the time when he first said it? What happened?

I tried to escape; that's what happened. It was when I attempted to creep through the bathroom window. I, of course, failed, and as a result, Saint threw me over his shoulder and then tied me to a pole.

How is this supposed to help me?

Think, Willow.

My attempted escape led to Saint tying me up. What happened between?

Kazimir hollers in delight, amused Saint would say that, but he doesn't understand that Saint has said this to me for a reason. And when Kazimir's dick lunges at me, I know what that reason is.

Saint said that to me because I bit him—hard. And now, he wants me to do it again.

"Yes, be a good bitch, and suck it."

There is no way around this. Kazimir won't let me go until he gets what he wants, so I close my eyes, swallow down my revulsion, and surrender. The moment I do, he thrusts his dick into my mouth, and I fight the instinct to recoil.

He groans loudly, encouraging me to take him in deeper, then moans when I do. He still has the gun pressed to my cheek, but the pressure slackens as his guard lowers. He may have only been in my mouth for mere seconds, but it's mere seconds too long.

The grip on my hair loosens, and when he unthreads his fingers, I brace myself for what I have to do. Kazimir moans in Russian while his friends holler in encouragement, voicing it's their turn next. The blood whooshes through my veins, and I count down. I need something to prepare me for what I'm about to do.

Three…

Two…

One…

I pull back, ensuring I have a firm grip, and when I do…I bite down. There is silence before an explosion erupts. Kazimir's shrieks are bloodcurdling, and in some sick, perverse way, they're music to my ears.

He frantically shoves at my forehead, trying to pry me off, but I only bite down harder, shaking my head from side to side. He called me a bitch, so I intend to act like one. Rage overtakes me, and all I want to do is hurt him just how he did to me.

The moment the gun drops from his hand and tumbles to the floor, I hear an ear-splitting roar. The room then explodes into pandemonium.

I use my ears as I'm still on my knees with a locked jaw, gnawing off this bastard's dick. When I taste blood, it only has me biting down harder. Fighting erupts around me, and I can only hope Saint is the one delivering those punishing punches.

Kazimir begins twitching, and I assume he's on the cusp of passing out from the pain. I should feel remorse, but I don't. Blood and spittle trickle down my chin.

I jolt violently when I hear gunshots pop around the small room, but when I feel a comforting touch at the back of my neck, I sag in relief. "Ангел, let him go."

The thought of letting this bastard go after what he's done to me feels almost blasphemous, causing me to snarl. But when Saint strokes along my cheek, I eventually comply. My jaw aches as I slowly release him, and Kazimir drops to the floor, twitching as blood spurts from the gaping wound I inflicted at the base of his dick.

I wipe my mouth with the back of my hand, transfixed as it comes away with blood. But when what I did smashes into me, my stomach roils, and I feel bile rising. I lunge forward on all fours and throw up violently. My body shudders, and my head grows light.

"Go upstairs," Saint gently orders, arranging my bra and dress as best he can so I'm no longer bare.

The wind still howls around us, rocking the boat from side to side. So if Saint believes being up there in the storm is safer than being down here, I'm afraid to know what he's about to do.

When I think I can breathe again, I lift my head gradually and peer up at Saint. My bloody warrior is slathered in war paint while his victims lay in broken, lifeless heaps around the room.

"Being Popov's number one…hitman."

This is just another day in the office for Saint. Being around blood, gore, and murder is nothing new for a hitman.

Saint crouches before me, carefully reaching out as if he doesn't want to spook me. But I remain perfectly still. He grips my chin between his thumb and forefinger, sweeping his thumb under my lip as if wiping it clean. I realize I'm still coated in blood when his thumb comes away with a smear of red. "Go," he commands softly, his eyes combing over every inch of my face.

There is so much I want to say, but it will have to wait.

On hands and knees, I feel almost feral, but I suppose what I did to Kazimir can classify as being animalistic. I've crossed a line, and I have a feeling it's just the beginning. Slowly rising, I step over the unmoving bodies, pulling it together.

As I open the door, I almost tumble over from the force of the wind. The weather is punishing, but I persevere and slam the door shut behind me. The heavy rain pelts down around me, making it hard to see and hear. Brushing the hair from my face, I peer around from left to right, squinting to see if I can find a life vest. The boat thrashes to the side, but I hold the railing to keep my balance. The waves crash down around me, and a bolt of lightning illuminates just how rough the waters really are.

My body shivers, though it's not from the cold or being soaking wet; it's from the adrenaline coursing through my veins. I focus on the small glass window on the door. When I see consecutive booms of light, I shudder, knowing what they are.

Gunshots.

Kazimir has paid the ultimate price for betraying Saint. They all have. Everything suddenly crashes into me, and I feel faint. My legs are as firm as overcooked spaghetti, and I slump to the floor. Tears merge with the rain, and soon, I can't tell the difference between the two.

Who have I become? Just a few minutes ago, I was intent on gnawing off a man's penis. If Saint hadn't stopped me, I would be sitting here picking the flesh from my teeth. Opening my mouth, I tip my face to the heavens, needing to be baptized and wash away my sins.

I scrub at my face, mouth, and chest, but my immoralities have marred my soul forever.

"It's okay, ангел." It's Saint. I don't even know how long he's been here.

"No, it's really not," I cry, shaking my head from side to side. "Are they dead?"

His silence is all the answer I need.

"So what now?" I risk a look at Saint, who is clutching his side. Blood trickles through his fingers, reminding me just how serious his wound is. "Oh my god. Let me look."

He doesn't fight me when I hesitantly reach up and gently remove his warm fingers, the hands which saved my life. When I see blood oozing from the deep gash, I gasp at his stab wound. "You need stitches," I shout to be heard over the roar of the rain.

"I'm fine."

"Stop being a jackass and let me help you!" I yell, uncaring if he punishes me for my disobedience. At this rate, he'll bleed out anyway.

A ghost of a smile plays at his lips. "There's a first-aid kit over there." He gestures with his chin to a box near the wheel. As he takes a step toward it, he stumbles to the right and pales. I worry he's about to pass out.

Instantly springing up, I wrap my arm around his middle to support him. It was pure instinct to save him. Timidly peering up at him from under my lashes, I realize my body is pressed quite close to his. It feels good to have him near. I feel safe.

His wet hair flicks forward as he stares down at me, ripping the air from my lungs. A bead of water backflips from a strand of his hair and lands directly on my lips. Again, impulse takes over, and my tongue shoots out to sample the offering. It tastes how he smells—spicy and sweet.

His eyes widen, and his lips part. Most of the blood has washed off him, but he still appears wild. He slouches against me, his heavy breathing warming my dowsed cheeks. My heart begins a pitter-patter, and the uncontrollable urge to… kiss him overwhelms me.

My mouth waters as the small taste I had was just a tease. I want more.

Absolutely horrified at my thoughts, I slowly untangle myself, ensuring he's steady on his feet. He nods once, indicating he's fine as he slouches onto the railing so he can sit. Needing to put some distance between us, I make a mad dash for the kit.

I'm silently berating myself, wondering what is wrong with me. Even though Saint saved me, that doesn't excuse the fact he's the reason I'm out here in the first place. Nor does it change his occupation. I need to focus on what comes next instead of romanticizing about how his lips would feel against mine.

The rain, if possible, begins to get denser, so much so, I can barely see two feet in front of me. I grab the kit, and when I see two life vests, I have the sense to snare them as well. A thunderclap rumbles, and I scream, my already frayed nerves not needing the extra tension.

Just as I'm about to turn around, I feel it. The crackle of something sinister lurking. I should have known this wasn't over.

Spinning swiftly, I brush the rain from my face and squint, but what I see—there must be some mistake. But there isn't. Standing a few feet away is Saint, and he's surrounded by four filthy men. They are no doubt part of Gringo's crew.

Where did they come from?

The moon comes out of hiding, showcasing the fishing boat swaying in the distance. They were no doubt awaiting Gringo's cue, and when they didn't get one, they knew trouble lingered, and they've come armed to the teeth.

There is no way Saint and I will get out of this alive, especially when they see their friends butchered downstairs. I watch as they yank Saint up brutally, shoving him and screaming. Through the rain, I lock eyes with him, desperate to save him just how he did for me.

"I have money. You can have it. Just let her go."

This isn't the end. I need answers, and I'll be damned if I die without them.

Searching frantically for an escape route, I ignore the man charging toward me with his gun raised. When I hear Saint grunt in pain, I look down at the first-aid kit, and then at where it came from. The wheel.

Grabbing the first-aid kit, I frantically throw the life vest over my head. I try my best to toss one Saint's way before I run to the helm, peer into the heavens, and spin it like it's a wheel of fortune.

"I didn't think you'd care if we capsized."

Saint is right yet again.

The boat tips violently to the left, sending me off balance, but I grip the wheel and continue to turn it. The monster waves aid my ploy as it tips us further over until before long, the boat begins to take on water.

It seems like something out of a movie as torrents of water wrap around us and drag us toward a watery grave. Screams sound around me as our boat begins to submerge, and an enormous wave swallows us whole. I've probably killed us all, but it looks like I got what I've always wanted—I've gotten off this fucking boat.

CHAPTER EIGHT

She saved my fucking life. This strong, brave, courageous woman saved my life. She had every right to let me drown, but she didn't. She threw me a life vest, took the wheel, and showed us all who had the bigger balls.

But the problem is...where the fuck are we?

Day 10

I can't breathe.

Water fills my lungs, and no matter how hard I try to break the surface, I continue sinking. My muscles ache. I kick my legs and use my arms, but it's useless, and eventually,

I surrender to the darkness. Everything falls quiet, and I await the tender embrace of death. It's a relief, in a sense, because what do I have waiting for me? My husband is possibly not the man I thought him to be, and after everything I've seen and done these past ten days, how can I go home and pretend none of it happened?

My heart begins to slow, and I don't fight it. Once upon a time when I believed in God, I would expect my father to be waiting for me in front of those pearly white gates, welcoming me home. But after everything I've been through, it's safe to say I'm on my own.

I close my eyes, surrounded by peace...finally. There is no more pain. No more tears. But more importantly, no more shame for wanting a man who I shouldn't. "It'll be okay. I've got you." His words shouldn't hold such comfort, but they do. "We're almost there."

But I push them aside and focus on floating away.

Abruptly, however, the silence shatters as those chartreuse swirls come to life before me, and those sinful lips utter a name.

Ангел.

My body constricts, and everything warms as a spicy sweet taste lingers on my tongue. "Breathe, ангел."

Those two simple words are like an electric shock to my heart. The darkness soon becomes light as the air in my lungs is from the lifeforce Saint breathes into me. He's bringing me back to life.

"That's it." I follow his voice and wade through the stagnation before I surface and free myself from the manacles weighing me down.

My first sense of awareness comes when I gag on the saltiness from coughing up water to free my airways so I can breathe. The second thing that hits me is that I'm lying on rocks and sand. And lastly, I'm here with Saint. But the question is, where is here?

Electrocuted back to life, I spring up, coughing madly as I wheeze for air. It's sensory overload as I attempt to uncover where I am. My head snaps from left to right to gauge my surroundings, but I have no idea where we are.

From looks alone, it appears we're on an island and a deserted one at that. Dense greenery surrounds us. There are no hotels. No jetties. No people. Nothing.

It's dark out, but dawn is lingering. A new beginning is close by. When I clear the fog, I immediately search for Saint. I don't have far to look. He's crouched by my side, running a hand through his wet hair.

A life vest and a first-aid kit sit a few feet away—the one I tossed his way before I…oh, god.

The last thing I remember was sinking our boat. I didn't think it would work, but clearly, it did because here I am, surrounded by…nothing.

"Wh"—I clear my raspy throat—"where are we?" It hurts to speak. Actually, I ache all over. On instinct, I rub the back of my head. When I feel the grapefruit-sized lump, I groan.

Saint leaves his hand atop his head, clutching the strands. "I don't know," he replies, stumped. "I don't know how long I was asleep before…" He doesn't need to elaborate. "When we capsized, you hit your head. Your life vest came off, so you were sinking.

"I pulled you to safety. You were out cold, so I swam." Swam? If I was out cold, that means he was my arms, legs, my heart. "I don't know how long for, but after what felt like half an hour or so, I saw land. But the waters turned rough again. We got swept up in a wave and were separated, but when I finally found you, you were drowning. You had stopped breathing."

Thinking back to feeling weightless, I now know it was because I was drowning, but the fact that I'm here now confirms I was saved—by Saint.

"Thankfully, the wave pushed us toward land and well"—he sweeps his hand outward—"here we are."

"What about the rest of the men?"

Saint raises his shoulders in an untroubled shrug. "They all got what was owed to them."

The thought of our attackers has me remembering Saint's wound. Without thought, I reach out and attempt to shift his soggy shirt aside so I can see his wound. On instinct, however, his hand shoots out and grips my wrist to stop me.

Peering up at him, I question, "It's okay for you to touch me, but it's not okay for me to touch you?" It's no secret that Saint shies away from being touched, but considering we almost died, I thought things would be different.

I don't pull out of his hold, but instead, I deadpan him. The dynamics have changed. We are both prisoners, prisoners to this forsaken island. Saint clenches his jaw, but he eventually loosens his grip. I don't make a fuss because even though it feels good to take back a small piece of my independence, I don't want to push my luck.

Our situation may have changed, but that doesn't mean Saint will have turned into a soft, cuddly teddy bear. I only have to think about what he did to those men to remember, stranded or not, he's still a hitman, and I'm still here against my will.

His shirt is torn, so I move it aside gently to see the gaping, weeping wound is still very much there. "How are you still alive?" I say more to myself than to him.

"It's just a scratch." He plays it off, but the hiss that escapes him when I gently prod around the gash reveals he's in pain.

"Let me see what's in the first-aid kit." Even though I was out cold, I'm glad I had the good sense to clutch onto the kit because it'll come in handy as god knows what lurks in the thick jungle.

My legs are shaky, but I come to a slow stand and hobble to the kit. I should be thankful I'm walking at all, seeing as I would be dead if it wasn't for Saint. The fact I was out cold means he swam me to safety even though he was injured. It would have been easier for him to let me drown as I can imagine he could barely swim for one person, let alone two.

So helping him is the least I can do.

"Take off your shirt," I instruct, walking back over to where he sits. He doesn't argue and slips it over his head.

Even under the veil of darkness, his ripped body comes to life. But I focus on what's inside the kit as I open it up. Tylenol, alcohol wipes, bandages, gauze, and some sort of ointment. When I see a sewing kit, a knife, and a gun, my stomach drops.

This isn't your standard first-aid kit. It's the essential go-to for every hitman.

Dropping to my knees, I place the kit on the sand beside me and tear open the packet of wipes. I don't bother with a countdown and begin to clean the area gently. The jagged flesh will no doubt leave a scar, but what's one more as his body is covered in them.

I silently wipe the wound, using a new wipe to disinfect the area as best I can. His eyes watch my every move; I can feel them. The scrutiny has my fingers shaking, but I pull it together because for what I propose next, I will need a steady hand.

"I need to close it up. A simple Band-Aid won't fix this."

Gazing up at him from under my lashes, I wait for him to reply. The air is charged as I'm asking him to trust me to sew him back up. Beads of water coat his golden skin, collecting in the dark hair on his chest. My eyes leisurely drift to the barbell in his nipple. I've never really been a fan of ink or piercings, but having both within inches of me, I am suddenly a convert.

"Okay," he finally says, his low voice adding to my nerves.

"Can you lean back a little? I need to get the skin as tight as possible." He does as I ask, leaning back on his arms. The expanse of his torso has me wetting my lips because everything undulates as he shifts to get comfortable.

"I've never done this before," I confess, unwrapping the sewing kit. When I see the needle and thread, my hands begin to sweat. "I don't want to make a mess."

"I'm already ruined, so what's one more scar?" he confesses, surprising me. I wouldn't refer to the sight before me as ruined. Each scar tells a story, showing the world you were stronger than whatever tried to beat you.

I don't voice that aloud, though, as I attempt to thread the black yarn through the eye of the needle. My trembling fingers display my nerves, but Saint doesn't move. He simply sits back and waits. After countless attempts, I finally get it through.

Now the hard part. I can't imagine this will feel good. No matter how I go about it, it's going to hurt like a bitch. Swallowing down my fear, I wipe down the needle with the disinfectant and exhale loudly.

"If you need me to stop, just tell me." I meet his eyes, unable to read what flickers behind his.

"I won't," he replies firmly. He isn't trying to be tough. It's clear he's done this before so a breather won't be necessary.

With that as my green light, I position myself as best I can, count to three in my head, then pierce his skin with the needle and thread. I cringe at the absolutely disgusting sight, but I continue threading the thread through.

When I come back down and pierce his skin again, my stomach begins to turn. He flinches as my hand is unsteady, and I accidentally tug hard. "Sorry," I say, easing the pressure. "I haven't done this before. Am I doing it right?"

"You're doing fine," Saint replies coolly. I'm in awe of his composure.

With his assurance, I continue sewing him up, ensuring each stitch is close together. The gash is a decent size, so I want to close it up properly. His breathing is heavy, his chest rising and falling irregularly. He's in pain, but he stays true to his word and doesn't ask me to stop.

When I'm halfway done, my nerves begin to settle as the

wound has stopped bleeding. "Who did this to you?"

I need to fill the silence because the sound of sewing Saint's flesh together has my stomach turning once again.

"Kazimir," he replies, a hitch to his breath as I jerk when I hear his name.

"How do, did"—I correct—"you know him?"

I don't expect him to answer, but maybe talking takes his mind off what I'm doing as well. "He has worked for Popov for years."

"And you haven't?" I risk asking, unsure how or if he'll reply.

But he surprises me. "No."

"How long have you been Popov's…hitman?" Curiosity overrides common sense, and I chance a glance at Saint. I want him to know I haven't forgotten their conversation before the shit hit the fan.

He slouches back, impassive to my question. "Why do you want to know this?"

I pause from sewing him up, startled he asked me this. "Because I don't understand why you're doing this. I don't understand anything."

"I'm doing this because that's what someone like me does. I'm not a good man, so don't try to find redeeming qualities about me. There are none," he spits. But I don't believe him. I wouldn't be here if what he says is true.

I continue stitching him up, my mind racing. I know it's my funeral, but I need to know. "Who…who is Zoey?" I whisper, biting my lip as I know how this will end.

Her name is the only thing with the ability to make him

grunt out in pain. He grips my fingers tightly. "We're done." I don't know if he's referring to the stitches or the conversation. Either way, he recoils from my hand and ties a knot in the thread himself. It appears I'm finished playing nurse.

Thankfully, I am done sewing him up.

He snares a gauze pad from the first-aid kit and rips it open. He is clearly angry with me for asking him what I did, which just makes me all the more curious. He slaps the gauze over his wound, sticking it down so it's covered.

Even though he's unsteady on his feet, he stands, gathering his balance before he walks away.

Sighing, I'm disappointed in his response. We very well may be the only people on this island, which means we'll have to work together to figure out a way to get off.

Packing up the first-aid kit, I take a quick look around to see if anything else survived. I don't see anything, but I'm hoping some of our stuff may eventually wash up on shore. Saint is nowhere to be seen, so I decide to gather whatever I can to make an SOS signal.

Dawn is approaching, and now that the adrenaline has worn off, I realize I'm shivering. My dress hangs off one shoulder, thanks to Kazimir's rough hands. I also don't have on any underwear. Thankfully, my bra remains unscathed, but overall, I look like I belong on this island—a perfect castaway.

Reaching for Saint's long-sleeved shirt, I slip it over my head, ignoring the scent clinging to the soft material. It stops mid-thigh, which is perfect as I don't feel as exposed. Blowing out a breath, I gather some rocks from along the shoreline. This is going to take me all day, so I decide to venture uphill and into the thick jungle.

The towering trees and dense foliage mean I don't stray too far as I'm afraid I'll get lost. I gather whatever I can and return to the shoreline half a dozen times. I am nowhere near collecting enough supplies, but I refuse to give up.

The sun slowly rises over the horizon, the vibrant beams skimming the tranquil blue water. The crystal clear water allows me to see the schools of fish swimming through the colorful coral even from this distance. It really is a sight. Too bad I'm stranded out here with someone who probably won't ever speak to me again.

"What are you doing?" Saint asks, proving me wrong.

Turning over my shoulder, I refuse to appease my curiosity of watching his skin glisten under the rising sun and look into his eyes and nothing else. "I'm making an SOS," I reply as though it's a no-brainer. "Maybe we should start a fire?"

"Don't bother," he says, raining on my parade.

Spinning around, I place my hands on my hips, unappreciative of his negativity. "How will a passing plane know we're in trouble?"

He does a quick appraisal of my new attire but doesn't address the fact I'm wearing his clothes. "There will be no passing planes. Or ships for that matter. This place is off the grid. No one has been here for years."

I'm suddenly filled with dread. "You don't know that," I argue, but a small part of me agrees with him.

"No, I don't know for certain, but after a quick look around, it's safe to assume we're the only people here. I found a small hut, but it's been empty for a long time. There are some things in there, but judging by the appearance, it was left behind years ago."

"Years?" I gasp, shaking my head, unbelieving. "Where are we?"

Saint's cheeks billow as he exhales. "My guess is we're somewhere near Malta. We left Egypt roughly two days ago. There is no way Kazimir was headed back to Russia, so I think we've turned off course. The fish and coral are a sure sign that we're still in the Mediterranean Sea. Originally, we were headed to Cyprus, and from there, we were going to navigate around Turkey and sail the Black Sea. Once we hit Ukraine, we weren't far from a port in Russia."

My mouth gapes open because this is the most information he's given me since this nightmare began.

"Seven days, that was how long this journey was originally supposed to take." The frustration is clear in his tone. "But now, I have no fucking idea."

He doesn't need to say it. I know what he's probably thinking. If I had just been obedient, none of this would have happened. But I don't regret a thing. If I didn't do what I did, I would be in Russia right now as the personal slave of some mobster.

We may not know where we are, but at least I'm free.

"So what do we do now?" I ask, refusing to just give up.

"Let's hope some of our stuff washes up. I don't think we capsized too far away, so I hope the current works in our favor."

"And until then?"

"We scope out our surroundings. We need water. Food. Shelter."

"You said there was a hut? Let's start there. If someone was here, surely there is water nearby?"

Saint doesn't look too convinced since we're surrounded by salt water. But he humors me anyway. "Okay."

I forget my SOS idea for the moment and follow Saint as he hikes up a small hill and passes through a small alcove between two trees. I crane my neck to peer at the soaring greenery. Nothing distinguishes one way from another, which scares me because one could easily lose their way in here.

Saint seems to know where he's going, so I stick close. But the ground is littered with rocks and fallen branches, making walking with bare feet very uncomfortable. Before long, I'm hobbling from foot to foot to avoid hazards, but it's impossible.

"Wait," I breathlessly say, placing my hand on a tree trunk and balancing on one leg as I clean the sole of my foot and dig out a small twig embedded between my toes.

Saint turns to look at me, only just realizing that I'm walking barefoot. Sighing, he marches over while I instinctively back up. It doesn't stop him, however. "Here." He offers his back to me while I cock my head to the side, confused. "Get up."

"Get up?" I repeat, so lost in translation.

He turns over his shoulder, grips my wrist and drags me forward until I hit his back. "I'll carry you," he explains while I'm certain I've just inhaled a swarm of mosquitos as my mouth hinges open.

"It's fine," I argue. I don't want to owe him anything else.

I already owe him my life. But he clucks his tongue, annoyed.

"Stop arguing with me, and do what you're told for once."

It's on the tip of my tongue to tell him he should know by now that I don't follow the rules, but my aching feet are begging for mercy. I don't know how far away this hut is, and as I look farther ahead, all I see is dense forest. At this rate, I'll get there by nightfall.

I hate that this is the better option, but I eventually cave. Climbing him is going to be an issue because he's a freaking giant, but I wrap my arms around his shoulders and boost myself up. He grips the back of my knees and helps me get into a comfortable position.

Being pressed up this close to him is awkward, but I loop my arms around him, ensuring not to choke him as I position my legs on either side of his trunk. The fact he's topless does nothing to soothe my embarrassment as I'm not wearing any underwear, but I try my best to use his shirt and my dress as a barrier.

Saint doesn't seem to care either way.

He takes off quickly while I yelp and tighten my hold around him. I swear I feel his shoulders vibrate with a muted chuckle, but I ignore such nonsense and focus on the marvelous sights around me.

This place is truly another world, and I think Saint is right—I think we really are the only people here. Apart from the gentle rustle of leaves and the occasional bird squawking in the distance, there is absolute silence. I can't remember the last time such stillness surrounded me.

It's daunting, but also, in some ways, after the past ten

days, this peace is exactly what I need.

Saint's skin is scorching hot and slippery with sweat as the sunrise carries some warmth. I can only imagine how hot it'll get at its full peak. I feel bad that he's carrying me since he's wounded, but we are covering a lot more ground as he's like the wind.

His muscles ripple against me, and I gnaw the inside of my cheek to stop a mewl from escaping. Being this close to him just intensifies his scent, but it's mixed with a hit of pure masculinity. Being out here in the open has somehow upped his wildness.

A low fire begins to simmer, but we've reached the hut, putting an end to any inappropriate thoughts. When Saint said it was small, he was actually being generous.

The circular structure fashioned from sawed-off tree trunks looks weatherworn and unstable. I didn't think these sorts of things existed, but I've been proven wrong. It's not that far off the ground, but a tattered rope hangs over the edge of the logs, which seems to be the only way to enter and exit. There are no ladders. Just whatever this punishing forestry can provide.

The roof consists of giant palm leaves. The foundation is tree trunks or, more accurately, what looks like the trunks of coconut trees. I didn't think coconuts grew in the Mediterranean, but I hope I'm wrong because that would solve our water issue.

"Want to take a look?"

"Sure." I scale down his body, dismounting very ungracefully as I attempt to cover my modesty. He turns over his shoulder, his lips twitching.

I arch a brow, indicating I don't have all day, which technically, I do, but I'll be damned if I allow him to be clued in on my response to him. His grin soon disappears, and he reaches for the rope. His tattooed wings come to life, and he soars to the top with ease. I ignore the way his back muscles ripple with his sheer strength.

When he swings his legs over the edge and stands inside the hut, he cocks his own brow, indicating *he* doesn't have all day.

Screw him.

Peering up, I shield the sun from my eyes with my hand, wondering the best way to climb this weathered rope without falling on my ass or, worse yet, flashing Saint. I never excelled in gym class, and I'm not going to lie, I'm not a fan of heights.

But I suck it up, grab the rope, and pull myself up. It's a lot harder than I thought it would be, but I manage to climb it without chafing my lady parts. I'm sure I look ridiculous as I feel like a sloth, lazing around on a sunny day, so when Saint offers me his hand, I accept gratefully.

An electric current courses through me the moment we touch, but I disregard it and focus on climbing over and keeping my important parts covered. When my feet hit solid ground, a relieved breath leaves me.

My hand is still nestled in Saint's. He meets my eyes, the perfect poker face, while a blush overtakes me. "Thanks," I say, gently severing our connection.

He nods in response.

As I focus on my surroundings, my high soon fades

because there isn't much inside. Old food wrappers. A dirty sleeping bag. Some bottled water in a six-pack. That's it. "Is that water still sealed?"

"It seems to be," he replies, which has a bubble of hope surfacing.

"That's good, right? That means whoever was here had to be rescued. If they weren't, surely all their water would be gone."

Saint and I are clearly worlds apart on whatever happened to this lodger. "Not unless something happened to him," he suggests calmly.

"Happened to him?" I'm almost too afraid to ask.

Saint nods, not giving much away.

"What would happen to him? He had food, water, shelter."

I wait for Saint to argue, thinking my argument is pretty solid until he places his hands on my shoulders and turns me around. I'm too engrossed with his hands on me once again to take note of what he's implying, until he says, "That would happen to him."

I have no idea what he's talking about. "I don't see anything," I reply, wondering what I'm missing.

He reveals what a moment later. "Exactly. Who knows what's out there. The foliage is thick, so it's easy for one to take a wrong turn. Not to mention the animals that remain hidden, awaiting unsuspecting victims to stumble past their lairs. Here, we are the prey…"

I shiver at his ominous words because I know what that feels like firsthand.

"What sort of animals?"

His thumbs rub over my shoulder blades pensively, and it takes all my willpower not to buckle. "I don't know exactly. But I'm going to take a walk, and I'll let you know if I see any."

"What?" All pleasant feelings soon take a nose dive as I spin around, eyes wide.

"I need to figure out where we are. I also need to familiarize myself with this island. You stay up here. I won't be long."

"I'm coming with you," I argue. I'm not his prisoner anymore. He can't tell me what to do.

Saint shrugs as he snares a bottle of water. He slides it into his pocket before reaching for the rope and stepping over the wood edge. "Suit yourself. But don't expect me to piggyback you this time."

My bare feet scream at me, refusing to be subjected to the harsh terrain again.

He reads my thoughts and smirks. "I didn't think so. Besides, you have a bird's-eye view from up here. You can warn me if anything with fangs or claws is coming my way."

I fold my arms across my chest, arching a challenging brow.

"Well, you have a perfect view when it tears me apart then. I'm sure you wouldn't want to miss that." Is he making jokes now?

No matter what he's done to me, the thought of his death doesn't please me in the slightest. But I don't let him know that.

As he begins to shimmy down the rope, I quickly step forward. "Here. You need this more than I do." I go to take off his shirt, as he is the one traipsing through a jungle, but he makes use of his upper body strength and hangs from the rope, effortlessly.

"Keep it. It looks better on you." He scans my body from head to toe, before meeting my wide eyes. He smirks, continuing his climb down, while I'm unsure if I heard him correctly.

When his boots hit the hard ground with a thud, I peer over the edge, holding my breath. He doesn't look back and ventures off into the wilderness. My trapped breath escapes me. I don't know what has come over me, but it needs to stop. Just because he's no longer my captor doesn't mean he's changed into a good guy.

Once he's lost in the thick backwoods, I decide to strip his shirt off anyway because it's gotten quite hot. My dress hangs off me, and I feel utterly exposed with no underwear on. I can only hope some of our stuff washes ashore because parading around in this outfit is hardly practical in a place such as this.

Leaves and dust cover the faded blue sleeping bag, so while I wait for Saint, I decide to air it out because it may be our only source of warmth. As I shake it out at arm's length, fearful a posse of spiders will emerge and eat my face off, something shiny clutters to the floor. When I see what it is, I instantly peer from left to right, afraid Saint will spring out of nowhere and punish me for such insolent thoughts.

But he's not here. We're no longer on that boat. We're out here, wherever here is, and I need to fend for myself. So the pocketknife at my feet seems like a blessing from above. Dropping to a crouch, I hesitantly pick it up.

My fingers tremble as I open it and see that the blade isn't rusty. It's a Swiss Army knife, so I know these things are made to last. My reflection stares back at me from the knife's edge as I grapple with what to do.

Feelings of helplessness overwhelm me, and I refuse to be a victim again. With that as my mindset, I quickly place it in my bra as I have no other place to store it. If Saint finds this on me, god knows what he'll do.

A false sense of security blinds me, but it feels good to know I can protect myself if I need to.

The smelly sleeping bag needs a wash, so I decide to rinse it off in the ocean. The thought of all that water surrounding us suddenly sends my bladder wild. Saint told me to stay here, but as I hop from foot to foot, I realize that isn't an option.

Tossing the sleeping bag over the edge, I watch as it sails to the ground gracefully. I can only hope my plummet is just as elegant. However, when I step over the edge and try to reach for the rope without face planting, I know this won't end pretty.

After three attempts, I manage to grab the rope. But now that I have it, the thought of scaling down it leaves me with sweaty palms. I have no idea how the right way to do this is, but I count to five, breathe in and out, then wrap one leg around the rope. My other foot is still perched against the small platform of the hut, but I slowly push off, yelping as I attempt to climb down.

"Don't look down," I chant over and over, but it's hard not to because I need to know how many feet separate me and death.

I hang, suspended in midair as I shimmy down the rope,

inch by inch. My sweaty hands provide no grip, and I begin to slip. That is the kick in the ass I need to hurry my pace and scramble down until I'm low enough to jump to the ground.

I drop like a sack of potatoes, grunting on impact as the twigs and rocks roughly break my fall. I commando roll and end up slamming into a tree. Brushing myself off, I look from left to right, unsure exactly which way we came from.

When I see a purple flowering bush, I remember passing it on the way, so I hobble toward it, ignoring the small rocks biting into the soles of my feet. Although I am almost certain we came this way, I decide to leave a trail, like Hansel and Gretel for Saint.

My dress is ruined anyway, so I tear the neckline, ripping the fabric into small shreds to use as my breadcrumbs. I tie what's left of the ruined dress at the waist in a tight bow. My bra is all that's covering my top half. If this was Milan, I could parade this on the runway, but here, it only confirms my desperate need to find some clothes.

I secure a piece of my dress to a stem of the flowering bush and continue on my way, stopping every so often to tie some fabric onto a tree branch or trunk, leaving a clear path for Saint so he's able to trace my steps.

After a few minutes, I hear the crashing of waves, and a sense of accomplishment overcomes me. I'm proud of myself for being able to navigate through this maze. But I can pat myself on the back later because when I push through the dense foliage and see the water, I half run, half waddle toward it. The crispness feels incredible as I wade in the water, and when I'm about knee deep, I squat and relieve my bladder.

This is not ideal, but it's the best I'm going to get seeing as there are no bathrooms. I sigh in relief, but that's soon replaced by a yelp when something nudges my back. Images of being ripped apart by Jaws has me screaming like a banshee and running for the shore faster than the wind.

Breathless and thankful I'm not floating in a pool of blood, I turn around to ensure whatever touched me hasn't followed, but what I see has me rubbing my eyes to confirm I'm not seeing things. I'm not. Floating feet away is the waterproof box that contained my clothes and toiletries. Saint was right. I wonder what else will wash up on shore.

Running toward it, I drag it out of the water, relieved I will be able to change clothes, but more importantly, brush my teeth. Once it's far away from the shoreline, I drop to my knees and throw open the lid. I cry out when I see my clothes and toiletries are inside. A black backpack which I assume contains Saint's clothes is also inside.

Saint's sudoku book and the leather-bound journal I saw him writing in sits in the open bag. Curiosity has me running my fingers over the leather because this innocent book may be privy to Saint's most protected thoughts. I should respect his privacy, but in the end, my snooping wins out.

Just as I open it to the first page, however, all prying comes to a screeching halt.

"I heard you scream," Saint pants as he emerges from the trees. I quickly slam the journal shut, peering up at him. He's covered in sweat and dirt.

"I'm fine," I reply, wondering if he ran to find me. His sticky appearance certainly hints that. "I was going to the bathroom in the water when I felt something nudge me. I thought it was a shark, but it wasn't. It was this."

Saint's attention drops to the box in front of me. I'm about to reveal the good news that his beloved sudoku book survived, but it's clear that doesn't matter. He is furious. "I told you to stay put."

"Excuse me?" I gasp, coming to a slow stand. "I left you a trail on where to find me."

"And what if I was going another way?"

"You can't tell me what to do."

"Like hell, I can't," he rebukes, storming forward.

Fuck him and his arrogance. I've had enough. "I'm no longer your prisoner. We're both stranded here."

"Thanks to you," he spits, coming to a sudden stop a few feet away from me. His nostrils flare, and his chest rises and falls rapidly.

"So, what? You'd rather I just submitted to you? Is that it?"

"It would have been a lot easier," he counters, running his fingers through his snarled hair.

"Easier for you maybe, but I told you I don't give up. I would rather die than be someone's plaything." I deadpan him.

He returns the glower. "If you had just listened, none of this would have happened."

He has some nerve. "Well, if you hadn't kidnapped me, we wouldn't be here, shipwrecked, god knows where!" I refuse to shoulder the blame. "But now, we're both stuck with one another!"

He rushes forward, gripping my bicep and dragging me

inches from his face. I fight to break free, but his anger is toxic and potent. "That may be true," he snarls, his eyes pinning me to the spot I stand, "but make no mistake, you will do what I tell you. Nothing has changed."

"Everything has changed," I bark, ripping free from his hold. "You can't stand not being in control, can you?" The truth slaps me in the face because that's what this is about. Saint needs control. And he's never had that over me. I infuriate him because I won't buckle. But more importantly, he doesn't scare me. And he hates it.

"I refuse to die on this fucking island with you! So stop being such a stubborn jackass and let's work together so we can figure out a way to get off it. You can go back to whatever life you led and forget the day we met. And I plan on doing the same."

I hope he sees reason. But that's just wishful thinking.

"If you really believe that, then you're more naïve than I thought."

"Fuck you," I spit, shoving him in the chest. "You know nothing about me."

He stumbles backward as I've caught him off guard but soon recovers. "I know that no matter what you say, you believe me."

"You're hardly credible," I reply, but my wavering tone hints at my nerves. He's referring to Drew. But I refuse to show weakness. "So you can say whatever you want, but I plan on returning to my life, to my husband. And you can go back to kidnapping and murdering for fun."

That comment was supposed to hurt him, but when he

laughs, it seems to have had the opposite effect. "Your life of what? Changing the world, parading around in ridiculous clothes as you shake your ass on the catwalk? That sounds very fulfilling."

I blink once. "Are you seriously judging me? At least I don't kill people for a living!"

Saint inhales sharply. "You have no idea what you're talking about. Things aren't always black and white, but I don't expect someone like you to understand that."

"What's that supposed to mean?" I place my hands on my hips, furious. How dare he judge me.

"It means you have no idea what's really going on here. It means your *husband*," he snarls, and a phrase has never sounded dirtier, "is the reason you're here. With me. You wish to return to your perfect life. Go ahead." He spreads his arms out wide. "But know that the man you lie beside is the man who…"

He pauses as if regretting his words.

"Go on then! Who what?" I scream, calling his bluff. I wish I hadn't. And I wish I'd used a different phrase.

"Who sold you in a game of poker!" he exclaims. I'm unable to digest what he just said without wanting to be sick. "That's right. Your precious husband lost a game of poker to Popov, and when he couldn't pay his dues because he lost his fortune to hookers, gambling, and bad investments, he had to pay up in another way."

"You lie." I stumble backward, shaking my head firmly. Drew never flaunted his money, and that was one of the many things I liked about him. Could it be because he never had any money to flaunt?

But it seems now that Saint has started, he can't stop. "I was there. I saw it all. I am Popov's right-hand man, remember?" he spits, eyes narrowed as he knows I've judged him based on that fact. I now know why watching Saint beat Drew felt personal—it was. "Your husband promised Popov an American girl in exchange for his debt to be cleared. He owed a quarter of a million dollars. It was the only way he could leave Russia with his life intact."

"Stop it," I whimper, covering my ears. But Saint storms over, refusing me mercy as he rips my hands free. I wrestle with him, trying to break free, but he holds my wrists tight.

"Popov wanted a docile, pretty girl. Someone obedient. Someone he could dominate. Your husband clearly didn't do his homework. But I suppose he got one thing right." I dare not ask what that thing is.

"He was the one who organized the hit. Think about it," he says, tightening his hold as I writhe like a caged animal. I want to murder him with my bare hands. "How did we know where to find you? At that precise time? Standing on that terrace?"

"Why don't you go downstairs and wait for me on the terrace? The view is something else."

Drew's words play on repeat because that's why I was standing out there when I was kidnapped. He told me to wait for him there.

Nausea rises, and tears sting my eyes.

"Don't you think your fairy-tale meeting was a little too convenient?" he poses, but no, I refuse to allow him to taint my love.

"Nice story," I say, feigning courage. "But why did he marry me? He could have just organized for you to kidnap me anywhere. Why go through the effort of marrying me?" I am confident Saint's lies will unravel, but I should know by now that Saint is always two steps ahead.

"He took out a life insurance policy on you," he states without pause. "With you kidnapped and presumed dead, he would get a lot of money. You cleared his debt with Popov, but you've also made him a rich man again. He used you… and you fell for it." He seems disgusted with me. That makes two of us.

The fight in me dies, and I doubt it will return ever again.

"So don't *you* dare judge me because at least I can admit what I am," he says, releasing me. I instantly sag forward, afraid my legs won't hold me up. "As for you, you can live in your fantasy world, but sooner or later, reality will catch up to you. It always does." Regret swarms him, but I disregard it because this man is incapable of such a human emotion.

A tear rolls down my cheek as I am broken. My heart, spirit, everything I thought I was is now shattered forever. I watch as he marches away from me and rips open the first-aid kit. Shrinking back, I automatically assume he's going to shoot me dead. But he doesn't.

He pockets the knife and goes to turn. "I'm going to find us some food," he explains, exhausted, while I hold back my ugly tears. "There's a pond filled with rainwater just past the hut if you want to bathe."

I watch as he ventures the way he came, leaving me alone with a secret so heavy, I don't know how to deal with it by myself. He just destroyed me in one breath, and in another, he offered me kindness. This man is my tormentor, but by the same token, he's also the only person who can give me the answers I so desperately seek.

But I have them now. The truth to why I was kidnapped. To why I'm here. The truth should set you free. But it hasn't. All it's done is leave me wishing Saint had left me to drown.

CHAPTER NINE

She now knows the truth, the truth I was trying so hard to keep from her because the look in her eyes will haunt me forever. I can only offer her pain, but I'm a sick bastard who gets off on her tears because they mean I'm one step closer to breaking her, to getting Zoey back...

Day 11

can't sleep, and that's not because I'm not tired. I'm utterly exhausted, but I'm way past being able to slip into a comatose state and forget the past eleven days.

Yesterday, after Saint revealed the truth, I staggered to the hut, needing time to process everything he revealed. Even though it seems so farfetched, I can't deny the logic. I hate that it makes sense because it means I married a lying asshole who never loved me at all. All I was to him was a pawn, his get out of jail for free card.

I was thankful Saint didn't come find me because I needed time alone. So I laid on the rough, wooden floor and stared up at the leafy ceiling, wondering what to do now. When the sun set and gave way to the full moon, I was thankful for the darkness as it seemed easier to accept the deceit.

My stomach growled, and my throat was parched, but the thought of consuming anything made my belly turn.

Well into the early hours of the morning, the bugs and mosquitos buzz around me, having a field day biting me any chance they get. Slapping my arm, I sit upright, brushing back my hair with a sigh.

I'm restless, hungry, tired, and nothing I do alleviates my agitation. I feel like hitting something because each time I think about what Saint said, my temper seems to surge. He showed no remorse and even made me feel like some pathetic airhead for not seeing through Drew's lies.

The knife against my breast burns as if it's a sign of what I can do to claim back a small piece of my soul. If it wasn't for Saint, I wouldn't be here. Yes, Drew may have orchestrated this entire thing, but Saint didn't have to agree to it. He could have told Popov what a lowlife psychopath he was and gotten a new job.

But he has no qualms about being a hitman. Kidnapping and murdering come naturally to him, it seems. Drew isn't here, but Saint is. And I have every intention of making him pay for what he did.

I spring up before I chicken out, adrenaline coursing through me as I leap over the edge of the hut and reach for the rope. The fact I can't see makes my descent a little easier, but I don't take as long this time because I am amped on revenge.

Strips of my dress catch in the light breeze, signaling the direction of the shore. I have no idea if Saint is here, but I work on pure instinct. Reaching for the Swiss blade in my bra, I charge through the foliage, ignoring the excruciating pain in my feet because that can't compare to the agony within.

I know he will probably disarm me before I get within five feet of him, but being in control drives me forward. Just as I storm out from between the trees, ready to tackle Saint where he hopefully sleeps, a sight I was not expecting to see flashes before me.

I freeze because seeing Saint waist deep in water, the full moon illuminating his stature, simmers my fury. Standing still with his face tipped toward the heavens, he skims the water with the tips of his fingers. Something about him appears so pensive.

His angel wings come alive under the moonlight, reminding me of the first time I saw them. I was as mesmerized then as I am now. Someone who delivers such punishment to people bearing something so angelic seems so wrong.

But it adds to the mystery of who Saint is. I may know why Drew did what he did, but I'm still no closer to figuring out what's in it for Saint. He's not doing it for the money. But I think it's safe to say he's doing it for Zoey.

So my next question is, who is Zoey?

Sneaking up on him while he's unarmed suddenly feels so wrong, so I decide to bench my vengeance for the moment and try to get some sleep. However, what I see next is confirmation I may not move from this spot ever again.

Even though what I'm witnessing is crystal clear, it's still hard to believe. But there is no mistaking the sight of Saint's left hand dipping into the water as he strokes himself. It's slow at first, like he's testing the waters, so to speak, but his tempo soon increases.

Through the still night, I can hear his husky inhalations and the sloshing of water as he pleasures himself. I am transfixed, hooked on the utterly intoxicating and completely taboo sight. I should turn around because that's what any respectable woman would do.

But my morality was questioned the first moment Saint laid his hands on me, and I liked it…a lot.

I'm shrouded by the shadow of the trees, so I remain hidden, unable to look away as Saint continues to stroke his shaft, his muscles rippling as his rhythm builds. Not being able to see is a potent wickedness as my curious mind begins to conjure up images of what Saint would look like.

The thought of his cock has a wetness gathering between my legs, and I instantly squeeze my thighs together, ashamed, but the friction only makes it worse. Watching with bated breath, I'm hypnotized by the sway of his back as he rocks with the rhythm of his hand.

The sound of his strokes intensifies, only adding to the fire burning within me. I imagine the slickness of his skin combined with the hardness of his shaft. I am certainly no expert on the matter as I can count on one hand how many cocks I've seen in the flesh, but the thought of Saint's has a whimper escaping.

A groan slips past his lips as he arches his head farther back, the slapping of his flesh combined with the spattering of water indicating he's close. This rugged beast takes what he wants. His arm works frantically, and I lean forward, desperate for a closer look.

It seems to go on for minutes, and my mind wanders to this man's stamina. I've seen him kill a roomful of men without breaking a sweat. He is commanding, strong, and in control. And watching him jerk himself off is no different.

The moon is my beacon, highlighting Saint in all his glory as his body tightens before a low moan fills the air and his back bows. The moan soon turns into a hoarse growl as he curses in Russian. The sound has me biting the inside of my cheek, my knees buckling at the sight of him coming.

That was the most erotic thing I've ever seen, and I didn't even see the whole thing. But the mystery is what turned me on and has my arousal trickling down the inside of my thigh.

His head hangs low as his raspy breaths evoke my body to swell, frantic for a release too. But once again, shame overcomes me, because I shouldn't respond to him this way, but I do…time and time again.

Memories of when his fingers were on me, in me, only stoke this fire, and the temptation to soothe this ache between my legs overwhelms me, but then I remember his cruelness. I remember everything he's done to me—the humiliation he makes me feel—and my high soon fades.

I came out here to teach him a lesson, but once again, it seems he's taught me something. Whatever I feel for him seems to be strengthening and evolving, no matter how badly I don't want it to.

Once Saint's breathing returns to normal, he cups some water and passes it over his body and through his hair. He sweeps his wet locks back, and the sight is too much. Placing the knife back into my bra, I turn the way I came and creep through the jungle and away from the image of Saint exploding with a guttural moan.

My flesh is warm and ripe, but the farther away I walk, the need soon simmers. When I get to the hut, without delay, I reach the rope and climb it, desperate to get away from what I just saw. Memories of why I went there fade because Drew seems to be the furthest thing from my mind.

What is wrong with me?

Curling into a fetal position on the hard floor, I close my eyes and promise not to think about what I just saw. But through the darkness, no matter how hard I try to lock them away, I see Saint's angel wings and hear his ardent moans when he came; it's the lullaby which lulls me to sleep.

I wake to my stomach growling.

Propping open an eye, I see that it's daylight, which means I slept for a few hours. Rising slowly, my body screams in protest. Everything hurts. My mouth is drier than the Sahara

Desert.

Reaching for a bottle of water, I crack open the lid and take a small sip, testing to see if it's any good. Apart from being hot, it tastes like heaven, and I throw back the entire contents. Once water fills my belly, it gurgles, hinting it needs to be filled with food.

Unsure where Saint is, I decide to head down to the beach to grab a change of clothes. He mentioned a pond filled with rainwater, which is screaming my name. I'll bathe and then think about what to eat.

The descent down the rope is a little easier, but I will be glad when I'm in underwear and a pair of shorts. Not to mention shoes. I stagger through the rocky terrain, flinching as the soles of my feet are raw.

Following the trail I left yesterday, I find the shoreline easily enough. Memories of what I saw early this morning crash into me, but I put them out of my mind and focus on bathing and finding food. The box with my clothes sits where I left it, so I open it up and grab the toiletry pack, underwear, denim shorts, a white tank, and some tennis shoes.

Saint's bag with his journal and sudoku book is nowhere to be seen.

Just as I close the lid, a rustle from the trees has my head snapping up. Saint emerges with his hands filled with coconuts. When we lock eyes, he pauses but soon recovers.

He's ripped his pants into shorts, and the jagged edges cover his knees, but he's still topless. He looks rugged and rough as his beard has grown and an elastic band ties his hair back. The shorter strands have slipped free from the tie, and it seems the saltwater has given him edgy beach waves.

His body rivals Michelangelo, and all the ink just adds to the appeal. I really wish he'd put on a shirt because seeing him this way just cements my attraction to him.

I don't know where we stand, seeing as the last time we spoke was when he exposed the ugly truth. My heart feels heavy when I remember Saint's confession. *"Sold you in a game of poker!"*

Frowning, I avert my gaze, not wanting him to see my eyes grow wet with tears.

"I found some coconuts," he says, breaking the silence. "With the bottled water, I'll bring it down here and keep it in the water so it stays cool."

Good idea.

Nodding, I stand, gathering my clothes to my chest. "Where is the pond?" I ask, my voice small.

"I'll show you," he replies, walking over and dumping the coconuts near the box.

Up close, it's difficult not to replay what I saw him do, but I nod, hoping my inner thoughts don't give me away.

He leads the way, and I follow. However, when we get to the edge of the jungle, I slip on my tennis shoes. A small piece of independence returns when I'm able to walk over the rocky ground without Saint helping me.

We walk the journey in silence, both at a loss for words. I don't know what I feel. I'm a mixed bag of emotions, but at the forefront is betrayal. No matter how cruel Saint's words were, I know they were the truth. Drew never loved me; I was merely a pawn in his sick, twisted game.

Not only did he sell me like chattel, but he also took out a life insurance policy, making me feel like nothing but a means to an end—which is what Saint once told me I was. How could I have been such a fool?

However, I focus on where we're going because I need to know how to get here on my own. When we pass the purple flowering bush, I decide to leave markers so I know where to go in the future. The terrain becomes more compact, so I stop when I can and rip the hem of my dress, tying the material to branches and plants. By the time I'm done, the short hemline exposes much of my legs.

I should be shy, but I'm not. It's nothing Saint hasn't seen before. He allows me to do my thing, watching closely as I leave my trail of breadcrumbs. We turn left and venture between two towering trees arching over the other and a large, clear pond beyond that.

Rocks cover the ground, and a bent tree trunk protruding from the water's edge gives me the perfect place to hang my clothes. The flourishing leaves from the towering trees provide a perfect screen for privacy.

Walking to the edge, I stand on one foot and take off my shoe, balancing it on the tree trunk. I do the same with the other. Saint is still here, watching me.

"There is a cave just beyond those trees," he says, pointing straight ahead. "I'll look inside and see if I can find anything."

"Okay," I reply, not really sure why he's being so informative, seeing as he's been anything but in the past.

He rocks back on his heels, appearing to want to say something, but he doesn't. He nods once before walking back the way we came, leaving me alone.

When I can no longer hear his footsteps, I untie the bow from around my waist and kick my ruined dress aside. Unhooking my bra, I toss it and my knife on the trunk, then rub over my shoulders where the tight straps have left deep indentions. It feels liberating to be naked.

I stroll into the water, gasping when it cools my heated skin. I will never take fresh water for granted again because this feels amazing. My muscles unwind as I bob up and down, wetting my body before flopping onto my back. I'm a water angel as I float, skimming the water with my fingertips.

The sun beams down on me, and I close my eyes, allowing the stillness to take over. Even though I'm lost to the world, this is the first time in days I've felt at peace. Drew's treachery never leaves my mind, but I allow myself this small reprieve of just being in the moment.

I don't know what the future holds, but I'm proud of myself for coming this far. It's only been eleven days, but it feels like eleven years as each minute, each second has tested me in ways I never imagined.

If I was back home, would I have allowed someone like Saint to treat me or to touch me in the way he has? The answer is no. But not many people will ever have to face these circumstances in their lifetime. I don't understand my attraction to Saint. He's not someone I would usually find myself attracted to.

I wonder if maybe I'm suffering from some form of Stockholm Syndrome. I am certainly not in love with Saint, but I'm not repulsed by him either even though I should be.

He is not a good man, and he guards so many secrets, but instead of that being a deterrent, I find myself wanting to know more.

He has been cruel, physically and emotionally, but he's also been kind. Anyone looking in would scoff at my thoughts, but I can't help how I feel. Maybe I'm truly broken after all?

Deciding I won't solve this mystery anytime soon, I stand and walk over to my toiletries. As I unwrap the soap, the smell of lavender hits me, evoking memories of being handcuffed to Saint. I walk into the deeper water, then dip the bar of soap into the water and lather up a soapy handful.

I pass it over my body, sighing in bliss as I wash away the filth. Not wanting to waste too much, I toss it onto the dry land and begin to wash my hair with the shampoo and conditioner. The knots are terrible, so I run my fingers through it, eventually able to brush out the snags.

When I feel clean and more like myself, I brush my teeth and rinse off and make my way to my clothes. I don't have a towel, but with the blistering sun, I will be dry in a few minutes.

A thought suddenly hits me. What happens if I get my period while here?

Thanks to my IUD, I haven't had a period in months, but I have to prepare myself just in case. However, all thoughts are put on hold because as I wring out my hair, I hear something rustling in the bushes. I pause, head tilted to the side, to ensure I'm not hearing things.

When it sounds again, I yelp, afraid Saint has returned. I quickly slip into my clothes, beyond thankful to be in underwear and shorts. Pocketing my knife, I wait for Saint to emerge, but he doesn't. The air suddenly falls silent, and I begin to question my sanity.

Shaking my head, I tie my hair into a topknot, twisting the strands of hair to secure it into place. I feel a million times better. Deciding on heading back to the beach, I gather my things and follow my trail. This place is truly a labyrinth. If not for the pieces of cloth, I would be lost. Saint's ability to navigate is impressive, but I suppose in his line of work, he needs to know his surroundings like the back of his hand.

The purple flowers are ahead, so I make my way toward them; however, there is no mistaking the rustling of leaves this time. Spinning quickly, I reach for my knife, but what I see has me pausing, unsure what to think.

A white chicken appears, pecking at the ground, none the wiser she almost gave me a heart attack.

I stare at her for seconds, certain I am hallucinating, but when she ambles over and squawks, I know that I haven't lost my mind—yet.

Dropping to a squat, I offer my hand. I'm familiar with chickens as I grew up with many animals on the ranch I lived on. She waddles over unafraid and pecks my palm, clearly disappointed when I'm empty-handed. I can't help but laugh. "Hi," I coo. "What are you doing out here?"

She clucks in response.

Peering from left to right, I wonder if she's on her own. She appears to be. I don't know how she got here, but she's proof someone else was here. I don't know how long ago, but the fact is, this island may not be as remote as I once thought it to be.

Maybe someone sailed here, stopped for a few nights, then went on their way. Another ship will surely pass by soon. I'm sure of it. My new friend is a confirmation of it.

"Come on," I say to the chicken, coming to a stand. She tilts her head from side to side, then follows me.

I have always loved animals, but finding this chicken feels like a miracle. In absolute nothingness, I found hope, something which I haven't felt in days. When we reach the shore, I dump my things into the box and decide to walk along the beach to see if I can find anything to eat.

The chicken clucks, and I smile. "Don't worry, I won't eat you. Besides, my rule is, if you name something, you can't eat it, and I name you…"

"A chicken?" Saint's surprised voice booms from out of nowhere, scaring the chicken as she runs behind me.

I can practically see Saint's tongue hit the ground as he visualizes roasting my friend over an open fire. Not on my watch.

I notice he has a brown wooden drum thrown over his shoulder. "What's that?" I ask, pointing at it.

"Rum," he replies, eyes still fixated on the chicken.

"Rum?" I repeat. "You found that in the cave?"

He nods, dropping the keg onto the sand. "Yes. Where did you find the chicken?"

"I didn't. She found me." I step to the side when he advances forward.

He arches a brow. "What are you doing?"

"What are *you* doing?"

He purses his lips. "I'm going to make us lunch."

When he continues marching toward me, I stand my ground, blocking his path. "I don't think so." When his nose scrunches up in confusion, I explain, "I named her. Therefore, she is my pet, and the rules are, you can't eat a pet."

"Rules?" he queries, confused. "Whose rules? That's fucking ridiculous."

"No, actually, it's not." I fold my arms firmly. "You can't eat her."

"What's her name then?" he challenges.

Shit.

"Harriet," I blurt out, unsure where the name came from, but it'll do.

Saint places his hands on his hips, his cheeks billowing as he exhales. This is an argument he will not win. "I have a name for her." I wait for him to enlighten me. "Pot pie."

My lips twitch, but I refuse to laugh because he's not eating my chicken. "Well, it looks like she has two names, so we definitely can't eat her now."

Harriet Pot Pie squawks in agreement.

"I can't believe you're going to keep her as a pet." He shakes his head, but there is no ammunition.

"She'll be a lot more useful to us alive." He waits for me to explain how. "Yes, we could eat her." It feels sacrilegious even uttering those words. "But that will last us one maybe two meals. But I'm pretty sure having a constant supply of eggs will be more beneficial in the long run."

He opens his mouth, ready to argue, but he closes it soon after. He knows I'm right. "Fine. But if she doesn't lay any eggs, name or no name, she better watch out."

I bite my lip to smother my smile.

"So we have coconuts and rum?"

Saint nods, rubbing the back of his neck. We're both roasting under the sun. "I can't find anything to eat other than fish. There are a few berry bushes growing up near the cave. They look like blackberries, but I can't be sure. Mushrooms are growing everywhere, but I don't fancy an acid trip or dying, so they're out.

"I'll gather what I can and test it out."

"Test it how?"

He walks over to the coconuts and picks one up. "There a few ways," he explains, walking toward me. "Place the plant against your wrist to see if it irritates the skin. Or touch it to your lips. Or tongue."

I watch on in awe. How does he know all this?

He reaches for the knife in his back pocket and stabs the coconut in its three holes. When he finds the one he's most happy with, he inserts his knife, making a small hole. "If you develop a rash or feel a tingle, it's usually a sign the food is poisonous or not suitable to eat." He passes me the coconut. "Drink."

"How do you know all this?" I ask, accepting his offering. When I place the coconut to my lips and drink, a rush of endorphins swarms me as my body sings in delight. I had every intention of sharing, but I can't stop drinking. Once I'm done, I shyly wipe my mouth with the back of my hand.

Saint smiles, gesturing I'm to give the coconut back to him. I do.

"It's common knowledge," he replies, walking over to a

tree. When he smashes the coconut against the thick trunk, and it splits open, he cements his point.

But I scoff in humor. "Common knowledge for you maybe."

He removes the meat of the coconut with his knife, offering me a piece of the white flesh. I practically lunge for it, stuffing it into my mouth. My ravenous stomach demands more.

"There are plenty of fish, so we shouldn't starve." He pries the meat off the coconut, popping a piece into his mouth. I am suddenly envious of that sliver.

"I can help fish."

Saint pauses from chewing, not looking too convinced. "In fear of you naming every fish we find, I think it's best you stay here."

"I'm pretty sure we discussed this," I argue. "You can't tell me what to do."

I'm expecting World War III to erupt, but it doesn't. "Suit yourself," he says with a languid shrug. A bubble of disappointment stirs as I was prepared to go head to head.

A squawk breaks the silence.

"Actually, I better make some sort of coop for Harriet Pot Pie. I wouldn't want her running away."

Saint nods coolly, not at all amused by her name.

His aloofness is pissing me off. I am so used to us arguing that I don't know what to do with this apathetic Saint. "Her being here means this island isn't as remote as we believed it to be."

He chews his coconut, mulling over my claims. "Yes,

that's true. Though the fact there is rum has me believing this is a route for outcasts."

"Why?" I question.

"Because rum is a common currency of the seas. If someone was sailing on a yacht, you wouldn't think they'd leave something like that behind."

He's right.

"So we wait until a ship passes?" I don't know what the next step is.

"No, we just wait and see what happens." He offers me the last of the coconut, which I thankfully accept.

I don't know what his comment means, but it's clear this conversation is over when he places the coconut shells on the box and brushes past me. Both Harriet Pot Pie and I watch as he walks along the shoreline, picking up a thin branch which he no doubt will sharpen into a spear and use to catch our dinner with.

Well, that was awfully unsatisfying.

This meek version of Saint confuses me. Yes, I've wanted him to allow me freedom, but now that I have it, I don't know what to do with it. Seeing so many sides to him leaves me constantly questioning which is the real him.

Sighing, I decide to focus on finding material to build Harriet Pot Pie's coop. I need to keep busy before I say or do something I'll regret.

I'm laying some leaves down for Harriet Pot Pie when Saint returns. He's been gone all day. Not having an idea of time is horrible because the guessing is far worse than knowing the truth. The sun set hours ago. With no other choice, I was forced to make a fire. It took me hours, but I was impressed when the sparks came alive. My Girl Scout leader would be so proud.

I occupied my day by collecting branches, leaves—anything I could use to construct a coop. It took me all day, but when I placed all the pieces together, I was certain Harriet Pot Pie would love her new home.

She disagreed when she flapped her wings and flew over the wooden perimeter. Regardless, I decided to lay some leaves down and give her the option of returning if she ever changed her mind.

Saint carries a spear he's carved from a tree branch over his shoulder. It seems he's a good fisherman as he's caught a few fish. When he sees the fire, he arches a brow. I wait for him to acknowledge it, but I get nothing.

The restlessness I've felt all day gets amped up.

Saint stands by the fire, peering around for what I assume are smaller sticks to roast our dinner on. I pass him two from Harriet Pot Pie's coop, seeing as she isn't using it. He accepts them with a nod.

This silence is killing me. I would even settle for him barking orders or telling me to kneel. I then realize he hasn't called me ahren lately. It bugs me. It shouldn't, but it does.

"Do you want something to drink?" I ask, needing to fill the static. "I brought the bottled water down from the hut and stored it in the water like you said." Oh, my god. I sound pathetic. Seeking praise.

Saint peers at the bottled water, which I've secured by his shirt to a tree stump protruding from the sand so it doesn't float away. "I'll have some rum." When he stops stabbing the fishes onto the branches and makes a move for the drum, I dance to the left.

"I'll get it."

The tiny jerk to his brow is the only sign he gives that he's impressed with my submission. But he continues spearing the fish onto the sticks and places them over the fire.

I make my way to the barrel, unsure why I have this desperate need to seek his approval. It hasn't mattered in the past, but here, the dynamics have changed. Thankfully, there is a nozzle I can use to pour our drinks. Using the coconut shells as our cups, I carefully turn the tap, not wanting to waste a drop.

The strong smell of alcohol hits my nose, and my queasy stomach turns. I'm not a big drinker—how can I be when it's done nothing but cause me pain—but for tonight, I decide to forget my reservations. Saint's share is a lot more generous than mine, which is fine. I feel drunk from the smell alone.

Once I'm done, I make my way over to the fire where he's cooking our dinner. "Here."

He accepts the drink, pulling a face when he smells the strong liquor. "Thanks."

Feeling ridiculous standing around, I sit down near the fire and sip my drink. The moment the bitterness hits my throat, I cough madly, thumping my chest to help swallow down the poison.

Saint peers at me over the fire. "There's a lagoon a mile or so up the beach."

Once I think I can talk without wheezing, I reply, "Did you see anything else?"

"No. Tomorrow I'll venture farther inland to see if I can find anything. There might be more caves. I don't know. It's worth a try." The terrain farther inland is rocky and dangerous. The hills are steep, and without proper supplies, Saint could end up hurt or, worse still, dead.

Once upon a time, that prospect wouldn't bother me as much as it does now. If something happens to him, I will be stuck here, alone. My palms begin to sweat. "Okay. Maybe you can show me where the lagoon is, and I can catch some fish. Or rummage for crabs."

He looks skeptical of my skills, which tips me over the edge.

"I know you think I'm some bimbo who can only make a living using my looks, but I'll have you know I'm a lot more than that. I grew up on a ranch in Texas, and I'm not afraid to get my hands dirty. I used to get up with my father every morning at sunup and help him tend to the animals. I also rode a quad bike instead of a horse," I add smartly, my Texan accent coming through, just as it does anytime I get mad. I don't know why I told him this. I guess I somehow need to prove my badassness.

Once my rant is over, I feel better until a lopsided smirk tugs at Saint's lips. "I don't think you're a bimbo."

"Oh?" My cheeks turn a beet red. Well, this isn't at all

awkward.

"A pain in the ass, yes"—my mouth hinges open—"but a bimbo, no."

This is the first time Saint has openly shared his feelings about me, and they weren't as insulting as I thought they would be.

"So you grew up on a ranch?"

I don't question his inquisitiveness as it feels nice to discuss everyday normal things when we are living anything but. "Yes. In a small town where everyone knew everyone else's business. You can just imagine how my mom and I were the talk of the town when the wife of a Baptist minister was seen in the next town over, consorting with *ungodly characters*," I mock with a deep Southern drawl.

"Thanks to my mom's indiscretions, the town began to believe the apple didn't fall from the tree. I was suddenly the most popular girl…but for all the wrong reasons. It sucked, and I was happy to get the fuck out of that town when I was almost sixteen."

I don't feel the need to share any more about Kenny or my mom because they don't deserve a second of my time. Besides, I've already shared what happened with Kenny.

"Where did you grow up?" It's out before I can stop myself.

I know absolutely nothing about Saint. Our circumstances bound us together unconventionally, but the fact we're stuck here, with no idea if or when we will ever get off this island, means all we have is time. And what better way to kill time than by playing twenty questions.

His poker face is in play as he draws the fish toward him

so he can take a closer look. Satisfied it's cooked, he passes me the stick, freshly roasted fish attached. "Thank you."

I'm disappointed he still won't share anything with me, but I guess we're not here on vacation. We're here against our will.

Reaching for a palm leaf behind me, I place the fish on it, careful not to burn my hands. It smells delicious, but honestly, anything smells appetizing when you're starving. Fanning it with my hand, I wait for it to cool down.

Saint sits across from me, the fire crackling between us.

I can hardly wait, and I dig into the flesh of the fish, blowing on my fingers because it's damn hot. However, when I place a piece of the soft meat into my mouth, I forget about third-degree burns and shovel the chunks into my mouth.

It tastes unlike anything I've ever eaten before.

"This is good," I say around a mouthful of food. Saint nods, sipping his drink with an indifferent expression. Uncaring I look like a caveman, I finish my dinner in minutes, thankful to be eating as it gives me something to do besides ask Saint questions he doesn't want to answer.

My full belly sighs in happiness as I lean back on my hands. I didn't realize how hungry I was because when I look up, I see that Saint's fish is still partially intact. "Do you want more?" he asks, offering me his dinner.

"No, thank you. I'm full." I drink my rum, cringing every time I swallow down a foul-tasting mouthful.

There isn't a star in sight, and I wonder what that means for all the dreamers out there. Where do they send their wishes to? If I had a wish, what would it be? My question is soon answered.

"I grew up in Syracuse, New York."

In what feels like slow motion, I lower my face from the heavens, meeting Saint's gaze. He waits for my reaction. Waits for me to fire a million and one questions. But I don't because, for now, this is enough.

"Oh, no...please don't tell me you're a Yankees fan. I can't be stranded with someone who thinks tiny white pants on a guy is a good thing."

He blinks once as I've clearly caught him off guard. Then he bursts into husky laughter, shocking me. "I suppose you're more of a rodeo girl then?"

This time, it's my turn to laugh. "Please, I may be from Texas, but I live in LA now. The only sport I like is catfights on the runway."

Saint raises his coconut in salute. "Looks like we have more in common than I thought."

I raise my coconut and feign clinking glasses. "Cheers." The ghastly rum now tastes like honey on my tongue because it's a victory drink, and victory has never tasted this good.

CHAPTER TEN

As each day turns into night, my tie to reality seems to slip. Being here, it's easy to forget that the outside world exists. I can close my eyes at night and forget what I am...and that's thanks to her. But I can't forget—it's too dangerous if I do.

No matter how much I want to touch her, I need to remember she doesn't belong to me...no matter how badly I want her to. I see the way she looks at me, but I have to be strong. Yet with each day, it's getting harder and harder not to own her... mind, body, and soul.

Day 15

We've been stuck on this island for five days, and during those five days, we've fallen into a routine. When I wake at sunrise, I stretch out my sore muscles. The hard floor of the hut isn't any softer, no matter how many leaves I use as a buffer.

Scaling down the rope, I'm still a little shaky but getting more confident every day. I venture through the terrain confidently as I'm familiar with the twists and turns. I barely need the markers anymore, and I know it'll only be a few more days until I know the route like the back of my hand.

When I reach the shore, I smile. Harriet Pot Pie eventually got used to her coop. She is usually waiting for me with an egg as my good morning greeting. Saint sleeps by the fire, refusing to sleep in the hut with me, which is sensible. It would be weird to snuggle up to him, I suppose, but I do get lonely at night.

He's awake before me, ensuring a breakfast of coconuts and fish by the time I arrive. He asks how I slept, and I always reply with fine. I ask how his wound is. He mimics my response. Once we're done, he takes off into the rocky terrain, looking for a way off this island. So far, he's had no luck.

I bathe, and sometimes, I clean out the hut. I talk to Harriet Pot Pie a lot. I gather supplies in case Saint changes his mind, and we end up making an SOS sign. But as the days turn into nights, it's clear that even if someone rescues us, where does that leave me?

Overall, the monotony of everything leaves me restless and desperate for change.

When night falls, Saint returns with fish and coconut,

and sometimes berries. We eat and talk a little but nothing personal. It seems when he opened up about where he lived, that was a one night only sort of deal. We drink some rum before I go back to the hut. In a sense, I feel like a prisoner once again. I offer to hunt for food, but he warns me to stay away from the waters near the lagoon. I don't know why.

This morning, I wake, hoping by some miracle that something will change. I make my way down the rope, walking on autopilot as I trek through the familiar terrain. Harriet Pot Pie is in her coop, clucking happily when she sees me.

I gather the egg before picking her up and carrying her to the beach with me. Saint sits by the fire with his legs stretched out in front of him as he does a sudoku puzzle. He must have bathed already as his hair is wet and he's changed into his makeshift cargo shorts and a black shirt that he's ripped the sleeves off.

He peers up at me when I arrive. "Morning. How'd you sleep?"

"Fine," I reply, passing him the egg. I place Harriet Pot Pie onto the beach, allowing her to peck around while I sit on the sand, drawing my knees toward my chest.

I watch as he cracks the egg into the shell of a coconut and scrambles it with a stick over the fire. "I was thinking," he starts, eyes focused on our breakfast. "I want to try to make a raft."

"Out of what?" I ask, curious.

"Whoever was here before us built that hut. I'm pretty sure I can construct something that will keep us afloat until we find a ship or mainland."

"And then what?" When he is silent, I shake my head, not liking this plan at all. "And then you call Popov?"

"I don't have a choice. You know that," he replies, finally meeting my eyes.

I was stupid to think that by some miracle he would change his mind. There is no happily ever after for me. The truth is, I'm safer here, shipwrecked on this island, than being rescued. How ironic is that?

I'm hurt. I don't want to be, but after five days together, I thought he'd show some humanity. Clearly, I was wrong.

Standing abruptly, I wipe the sand from my legs. I need some space as I feel like I'm about to burst into tears.

"Where are you going?" He pauses from scrambling the egg.

"To get some fresh air," I snap, furious at myself for thinking these past five days made a difference.

"What about breakfast?"

"I've suddenly lost my appetite," I spit, turning on my heel.

"Don't be childish," he has the nerve to say. "You can be angry with me on a full stomach."

"Fuck you and your food, Saint." I storm off, infuriated beyond belief. I can't believe nothing has changed. I feel betrayed and am angry with myself for thinking he transformed into a civil human being.

As I walk along the shore, I peer into the distance, wishing an answer would appear and solve my problem. Nothing does. I'm on my own—but that's no different. I walk for what feels like forever, and when I reach the lagoon, which I've seen in passing when looking for Saint, his words of warning echo loudly.

"Stay away from the waters near the lagoon."

I never really questioned it because I thought this was where Saint came when he needed some downtime. The hut was my hideaway, so I respected his request. But I've been stupid to show this man any respect because he sure as shit hasn't shown the same to me.

I continue walking, anger fueling my every step. I can see why he likes it here. The bright coral comes to life underwater, a gateway into another world. The sun is already blistering, so I decide to take a swim and disobey everything he told me about staying away.

Stripping off my shorts and tank, I venture into the water, gasping as it's a few degrees cooler than the water down the beach. Regardless, it feels incredible against my heated skin. I continue walking into deeper water, my anger fading, submerging with each step I take.

I want to believe that his small acts of kindness are his way of expressing he cares, but I'm an idiot. I dive into the water, swimming away from my stupidness because he doesn't care. He never did. All I am, all I've ever been is a means to an end…my bad for forgetting that.

I don't know how far I've swum, but it feels good to let go. I come up for air, bobbing in the water as I peer around me. I'm surrounded by nothing. As I'm treading water, a faint echo sounds. Disregarding it, I float on my back, peering up at the sun.

It's beautiful out here. I wish I could enjoy it without this constant heaviness weighing me down. I close my eyes, sighing. However, a moment later, I am certain I can hear someone shouting. But that's impossible.

I try to block it out, but it's soon apparent that I'm not hearing things.

Saint is no doubt shooing me out of his sacred place as he evidently doesn't want to share his special place with me. Springing up, I shield the sun from my eyes, ready to tell him what I think of his demands, but I must be seeing things because I'm certain I see Saint ripping off his shirt, then diving into the water.

He's shouting something. I don't know what. However, when he comes up for air and cups his mouth, screaming, "Swim...shark!" I realize I'm not seeing or hearing anything because when I turn over my shoulder, I see a gray fin in the distance.

Time stands still.

My entire body goes into hyperdrive, and I frantically swim to the shore. I'm a strong swimmer, but I'm a long way out, and there is no way I can outswim a shark. My muscles burn as I kick my legs. I tell myself not to look back and continue forward, but the shore is barely a speck in the distance.

Saint swims toward me, but we're still miles apart. I'm waiting to be dragged under as a meal for yet another predator. That's all I seem to be. But I won't give up.

The adrenaline whooshes through my ears, my breathing heavy as I desperately attempt to fill my lungs with enough oxygen to save my life. I'm certain I'm on the verge of having a heart attack from punishing my body this way and from the fear of being eaten alive.

I focus on Saint and how he looks like an athlete as he closes the distance between us. But surely, he's too late. Any moment now, it's my time…but my time never comes.

"Swim, ангел!"

That name sparks a fire in my belly, and I push with all my might. It gives me the strength to swim faster than I've ever swum before. Within moments, I reach Saint, who quickly turns to swim back to shore. He stays close to me, guarding me until we reach land. When I can touch the ocean floor, I breathlessly stand and run frantically toward safety.

Saint does the same.

The moment my feet touch sand, I flop to the ground, sobbing and breathing uncontrollably. Saint drops to his knees, brushing the wet hair from my cheeks, his eyes searching over every inch of me. "You're okay," he reassures me and also himself.

I'm too far gone to have any control over my emotions, and I throw my arms around his neck and bury my face in the crook of his neck. Being pressed this close brings home the fact I almost died, and I burst into fresh tears.

Saint surprises me when he wraps his arms around me cautiously before crushing me into his chest. "I told you to stay out of these waters. Why don't you listen?"

"Wh-why didn't y-you tell m-me?" I choke on my raspy breaths.

"Because I didn't want to worry you," he replies, pressing his lips to the top of my head as he drags me onto his lap.

"You've be-been fishing these waters?" I ask, but he doesn't need to answer. He's been risking his life so I could eat. Why? None of this makes any sense.

His heart pounds against me, rivaling mine. But I soon don't know if my racing heart is from the adrenaline coursing through me or the fact I'm pressed against Saint so intimately. He smells incredible, and on instinct, I inhale deeply. I've wanted to do this since I first smelled his unique scent.

A groan escapes me, and everything tightens. I want him so badly, and even though I can pretend it's because I almost died, it's not. I've wanted him since the first moment he touched me. And I want him to touch me again.

"You're letting me touch you," I whisper. He usually steers clear of being touched.

"I like…you touching me," he confesses, which rips a gasp from my lungs. "You will not go into these waters again, okay?"

"Okay. But neither will you," I add. I won't have him risking his life so I can eat. We will find somewhere else to fish.

The moment settles, and my heart rate eventually returns to normal.

When I realize I'm still clinging to him, I regrettably peel my arms from him. When he releases me, I bite my lip to mute the saddened cry. "You called me ангел."

He pulls back, surprised.

"You haven't called me that for days."

He clears his throat, shuffling back a fraction, but I'm still perched on his lap. "You told me not to call you that."

"What does it mean?"

A wall suddenly erects between us, and anything beautiful

we just shared fades to the wind. "Come on, let's go." He gently shifts me off his lap and stands.

I, however, stay seated, unbelieving that after everything, this bullshit still exists between us. "No, I'm not going anywhere until you tell me what it means."

"Why does it matter?" he questions, running a hand through his wet hair.

"I need to know because maybe it'll give me a clue into how you feel about me!"

Saint takes a step back, clearly stunned.

But I'm done. My close call with death has obliterated the filter on my mouth.

Launching up, I cry, "Am I just collateral to you? Do you even care what happens to me when we arrive in Russia?"

He turns his cheek, his jaw clenched. "You know what this is," he grits out. But I don't believe him.

"You lie," I spit, but he is fierce as he springs forward, gripping my bicep, yanking me toward him.

"I am not your knight in shining armor. Stop trying to see something that isn't there!" He is furious, which just encourages me to poke the bear.

"I know you don't want to hurt me." Contrary to his death grip on my arm. "You've always shown me kindness. Even when you've punished me…you've ensured not to hurt me too bad."

His nostrils flare. He's angered I'm privy to his secret.

"I saw what you did to Drew." I swallow past the lump in my throat as I can barely speak his name without wanting to be sick. "It looked personal because it was, wasn't it? You were there when he made the deal. I was dragged into this just like you were. Why? Tell me why you're doing this!"

"Stop talking," he snarls, shaking me like a rag doll. But I will not. This is the first emotion I've elicited from him, and I'm not about to stop now.

"Help me understand. You're the only person who can fix this. Please."

"This can't be fixed! Don't you understand? We're both dead if I don't do this. And I can't fail he—"

"You can't fail who?" I press, begging him to tell me what's going on. "I don't want to believe you're the villain. I know that you're not."

"You know nothing about me!" he screams, his wrath propelling the hair from my face. "You have no idea what I've done!"

"Tell me! I want to understand you."

"No, ангел, you don't," he counters sadly, releasing me. His touch has left bruises, but I don't care. They are not reflective of who he is. I refuse to believe they are.

"No one is perfect. My mother made me believe I was nothing but a whore, and that I deserved her boyfriend pinning me to the floor and telling me how hard he was going to fuck me."

Saint closes his eyes for a split second, appearing pained.

"And for a long time, I believed her. She told me my looks were used for nothing but evil, but I proved her wrong. You can do the same. Show Popov you're not the man he believes you to be."

"I can't," he exclaims, eyes wild. "No matter how badly I

want to."

"What has he got over you?" I inquire, shaking my head in confusion.

"You wouldn't understand."

"Try me," I rebuke, standing my ground.

"We are not having this conversation." A fire thrums through his veins. I can see it. He is about to explode.

With a match in hand, I declare, "It's Zoey, isn't it?"

I have snatched the air from his lungs.

"Don't," he warns, pointing his finger in caution.

It falls on deaf ears. "Why not? She's the only person who can stir any sort of human response from you. Is she—" The words are trapped forever when his arm shoots out, and he cups my throat.

I gasp, struggling to breathe, but I don't fight him. "She is the most important person to me, and I will do anything, *anything* to protect her. And if that means handing you over to Popov, I will gladly do so because you mean nothing to me!"

My lower lip begins to quiver.

I wasn't expecting him to recite a love poem in my honor, but I thought we were at least friends.

"You are insignificant to me, and quite frankly, the only reason you're still alive is because I need you." And he doesn't mean that in the warm and fuzzy sense.

"I *will* deliver you to Popov. So get used to that idea. There is nothing between us! Nothing! You're just a pretty face to jerk off to." He tightens the hold around my neck while I arch back. "Understood?"

I nod slowly, a tear scoring my cheek. I am defeated as this is the first time in fifteen days he's shown me true cruelness. My momma's words come back to haunt me.

He releases me, and I sag forward, gasping for air as I rub my neck.

"Good. Now get out of my sight. I have work to do."

He brushes past me, anger rolling off his broad shoulders, while I gather my pride from the ground, get dressed, and turn back to return to the hut. The entire walk back, I weep, never feeling cheaper than I do right now. Saint has just proven me to be a fool. I thought he felt something for me, no matter how small, but I was right all along—he's a monster.

The pocketknife sits heavily in my pocket, hinting what I need to do.

I pace the hut like a caged animal. Harriet Pot Pie sits in the corner, leaving me to my madness.

I am furious. Actually, now, I am fucking murderous.

The entire day, I've kept my distance from Saint because I don't trust myself in his presence. Once I got over the fact I was nearly eaten alive by a shark, I returned to the hut, but my fear was soon replaced by this blistering rage.

His hot and cold behavior leaves me beyond confused. I would prefer he be the cruel bastard he is because that would make hating him a lot easier. The small snippets of kindness, like today when I felt protected in his arms, mess with my head, and I can't take it anymore.

It's dark out, and even though I don't know what time it is, I know it's late. I haven't bothered to go down for dinner because I cannot sit around the fire and break bread like nothing happened. Saint made his feelings for me very clear, and I would be an even bigger idiot if I just forgot everything he said.

He hurt me today, and a small part of me reasons that he was able to do this because I care. If I didn't, his words wouldn't have affected me the way they have.

Groaning, I lace my hands behind my neck and continue to pace.

I need a plan. All options are bleak, but I need to get off this island, and I will have to divulge to my rescuers what Saint did to save myself. He isn't my safety net. He never was. The thought of ratting him out turns my stomach, but I quash down this nonsense because I need to remember what he is.

The wind howls around me, hinting a storm may be headed our way. The tense and restless atmosphere forewarns of something life changing lingering around the corner. And when I see the rope swinging wildly, like someone is climbing it, I know I'm moments away from uncovering what that is.

Instantly, I back up, feeling adrenaline course through me. My knife is burning a hole straight through my pocket, but Saint appears before I have a chance to reach for it. When our eyes lock, I know things are about to explode.

He swings his leg over the wooden ledge and steps into the hut. His chest heaves, but that has nothing to do with the climb. The air is thick with static. My skin prickles with goose bumps.

How dare he come here. This is my sanctuary, my haven, and him being here has just shit all over that safety. "Get out," I spit, folding my arms, but Saint does the total opposite when he steps forward. He comes to a stop a few feet away, his winded exhalations brushing the hair from my face.

I don't waver.

With his fists bunched by his sides, he looks to be barely holding on. I have no idea why *he's* angry as I was the one he insulted. "Can I help you?" I sarcastically quip when he remains mute. "For someone who had a hell of a lot to say, you sure are quiet."

His jaw clenches, which just spurs me on.

"You need to leave. Now. I may be stranded with you, but that doesn't mean I have to look at you. And besides, you made your feelings perfectly clear. I mean, I'm just a pretty face to jerk off to, right? Are you here for some bedtime material?" I jab, eyes narrowed.

Saint still doesn't speak, which pisses me off further. This morning was just a starter.

Closing the distance between us, I storm forward, craning my neck to peer up at him. "I hate you. I would rather die on this island than be a slave. So *you* get used to that idea," I snarl in reference to his comment about my fate of being Popov's plaything set in stone. "I belong to no one."

He shows no emotion, but the twitch beneath his eye is my victory dance. My bravado soars, and I run with it. "You are a gutless bastard, and whoever Zoey is"—his nostrils flare—"I feel sorry for her."

I am baiting him because I know Zoey is his weakness.

She is the only collateral I have against him.

"She's probably sick of you. I know I am. You think you're protecting her?" I challenge, standing on tippy toes to deadpan him. "Odds are, she needs protecting from you."

His eyes are alight, and he's barely holding it together, revealing I'm onto something.

Drawing my face to his, I smirk, sinisterly. "Looks like Zoey and I have a lot in common."

Saint's resolve finally snaps as he latches onto my bicep, pressing over the bruises he left earlier. I attempt to jerk from his hold, but he only tightens his grip. "Kneel," he commands in a low, menacing voice.

My heart begins to pound as in a sick, twisted way, it's exactly the response I was hoping to provoke from him. But I'll be damned if I allow him to see that.

"Fuck you." I rip free from his hold and make a run for the rope, but he lunges forward and wraps an arm around my waist, drawing me backward.

He presses my back to his chest, trapping me, his panting shooting a current straight through my center. He is shaking in rage. "Get off me!" I wriggle madly, kicking and flailing, but I'm not going anywhere.

"I said kneel…ангел."

"You tell me what that means, and I will," I counter, ignoring the way my skin tingles with his touch. Being faced away from him makes it easier for me to fight him. But when he presses his warm, supple lips to the side of my neck, my fight soon dies with a low moan.

I grow limp, not because his kiss feels so good, but because

I'm astounded by his actions. "Kneel," he repeats, hovering over my racing pulse. When he bites over it, I whimper and buckle, which allows Saint to force me to my knees with ease.

My body is hypersensitive. I await his next move.

With a slow pace, he stands in front of me. My breathless pants are indicative of how I'm feeling, and when Saint sweeps a strand of hair from my cheek, his fingers lingering, they only grow more profound.

"I should punish you," he declares, dangerously low.

"You being here is punishment enough." My words may seem big and strong, but I'm trembling.

A hoarse laugh escapes him.

He stands still while I concentrate on not squirming. I feel like a bug under a microscope. My eyes focus on the floor as I'm afraid to see what his gaze reflects. He cups my chin, coaxing me to look at him.

I do.

I arch my head back, locking eyes with him. He is feral, the chartreuse fire burning me alive. "You like when I punish you, don't you?"

My flushed cheeks speak volumes.

"What about when I slapped that perfect ass of yours? Did you like that?" He drags his thumb over my lower lip, focusing on our connection. "Or how about when your needy pussy gripped me so tight, I thought I was going to explode? I know you liked that. Your breathless moans still haunt my dreams."

The line between pleasure and pain once again begins to fade.

He gently parts my mouth with his thumb and strokes just inside my bottom lip, fixated on what he's doing to me. I try to remain impassive, but my efforts are laughable. He sighs before he removes his thumb and slides his palm down my chest. When he splays it over my pounding heart, I gasp.

The gesture is almost tender.

He seems hypnotized by my rising breasts, and when he cups my right one, he hums low. "You tell me you don't belong to anyone, but you're wrong, ангел. You belong to me," he whispers, an arrogant grin tugging at his lips. "And you hate yourself for it."

I refuse to allow my tears to fall because this is just another torture technique. He wants to break me emotionally. Psychologically. Physically. And when he rubs his thumb over my erect nipple, he knows he's slowly worming his way into my soul.

"But don't," he continues, kneading my breast as he runs his tongue along his bottom lip. "Because I hate myself, too." When he lets me go, I cry out in desperation or relief. I don't know. "I hate that you're able to stir this...this hunger in me. You defy me, and I allow it because I like it. I like the control I have over you because I know how"—he pauses, inhaling deeply—"wet it makes you. How your body begs for a release...because of me."

I bite my lip, needing to stifle my moan as my arousal coats my underwear.

Maybe I am a whore. Just like my mom said I was because what Saint says is...true.

He gently places his hand on the front of my shoulder

and pushes, hinting he wants me to lie down. God strike me down—I do.

I look up at him, my winded breaths leaving me lightheaded. He remains poised and in total control. "These hands"—he holds up both palms—"have done some unspeakable things. But when I touch you...I forget about all the horrible things I've done. You should fear me, but you don't. I want you to," he says, lowering himself onto me slowly.

He places his hands on either side of me and crawls up my body. My arms are rigid by my side because I don't know what to do. His heavy weight crushes me, yet we're still not close enough. He nuzzles under my ear before inhaling deeply along my throat. When he comes to the dip between my collarbones, he gazes up at me, savage and unrestrained.

"Fear always tastes sweeter," he reveals, closing his eyes as if savoring a sweetness. "But I bet your taste is unlike"— the tip of his pink tongue darts out to wet his lips—"anything else." When he reopens his eyes, I ignite in a way I never have before. "Do you taste as sweet as you look?"

I whimper, afraid...afraid of my response to him. My body tightens, and my sex clenches. I can't believe I am yielding to him yet again. His scent, his warmth, and the touch of his skin leave me with a heady, sinking feeling, and I am helpless to fight it.

He hovers over me, the moment charged, but my good sense shines when I remember him making me feel like nothing at all. His attention shifts to my swelling breasts, which are mere inches from his face. It's a rookie move on his behalf.

With lightning-quick speed, I lunge for my knife, and in one smooth motion, I flick it open and jab the pointed blade against the skin on the side of Saint's neck. His eyes widen as I've caught him off guard.

Kudos to me.

My hand trembles, but I pin him with a glower. "I belong to no one," I repeat even though it's a lie because right now, I want to let go and surrender to him.

"I'm proud of you, ангел. Not many can say they've caught me unaware and lived to tell the tale. It's my fault for not being more careful. So the question is, what are you going to do now?" He doesn't seem frightened that he has a blade pressed to his throat.

"Don't test me. I'll use it. I swear I will," I cry, digging in a fraction. The pliability of his flesh exposes how easily I could press a little deeper and draw blood.

"I don't doubt that for a second," he says, suspended over me calmly. "After what I've done to you, I deserve it. So, come on. Do it."

"What?" I gasp, the shake to my hand escalating.

"Do it," he repeats. When I freeze, he leans into the knife, causing a trickle of blood to seep from the small cut I've made. I attempt to pull back, horrified, but his hand shoots out and clutches tightly over mine. He forces my hand forward, cutting deeper into his flesh.

"No!" I cry, recoiling, but his grip is firm.

"Do me a favor and end my miserable life. At least I'll die by the hand of someone I respect."

"Saint, no!" I exclaim, my stomach turning when he forces

me to sink the tip of the knife deeper into his neck. But it falls on deaf ears. It cuts his skin like a hot knife through butter. I scream, bile rising because the blood begins to trickle faster.

"Ангел, this ensures your safety. With me dead, I won't be forced to hand you over to the man I despise most in this world. The man who destroyed my life. The man who made me into the monster I am today," he acknowledges with a bittersweet tone. "Nothing means anything to me anymore. I'm dead inside."

His admission and seeing him bleed have something in me relinquishing, and I whisper, "You're r-right. I do…" We're caught in a deadlock. It takes my breath away. And so does my confession because it changes everything. "I do…belong to you. And I hate it. So I can't hurt you. No matter how badly I want to, I can't, and that makes me pathetic. A coward. No wonder Drew chose me. I am a fucking weakling."

Tears of anger sting because all along, I've blamed Saint for my situation. But, in reality, it's my own fault for not seeing through Drew's lies sooner. I never should have married a stranger I barely knew, but I was desperately chasing my happily ever after and ignored the signs.

I should have known someone like me doesn't deserve a fairy-tale ending, no matter how badly I wanted it. No matter what I've accomplished, deep down, I'm still that young girl pinned beneath Kenny, trying to break free.

"No, ангел," Saint says, snapping me from the darkness. His sentiment touches me in a way I could never imagine. "That makes you human."

It happens in the blink of an eye.

Saint releases his grip on me, and I cry out in relief, my arm growing limp. He seizes the knife and tosses it across the hut. I don't have a chance to ask if he's all right because he's on me, pressing kisses down my throat, over my breasts, and down along my stomach.

This is happening so quickly, I don't have time to think. But when he lifts the hem of my tank and circles my navel with his tongue, I forget about everything and just feel. His heavy stubble is soft against my skin, and I arch backward, parting my legs to accommodate him.

This is wrong, so very wrong, but I quash down my good sense and lose myself in his touch. His fingers are frantic as they unsnap the top button of my shorts, then unfasten the zipper. When he yanks my shorts down and grips the top of my underwear to pull them down too, what he's about to do has me shutting my legs quickly.

His arm snaps out as he holds my upper thigh in place. "Open your legs, ангел."

My cheeks blister. "I, it's okay, you don't have to." I stumble over my words because I'm embarrassed.

He lifts his head unhurriedly from between my legs. His long hair hangs mussed around his face, his lips red and succulent. He is a commanding beast, and the sight has everything tingling. "I know I don't *have* to. I want to."

When he tugs at my underwear again, I push lightly at the front of his shoulder. He peers down at my hand, one brow raised higher than the other. "I don't like that," I confess softly, a complete buzzkill.

"Don't like what?"

Cringing, I'd rather pull out my fingernails than tell him, but my self-respect is long gone. Taking a breath, I avert my eyes and admit, "Oral sex. I don't like it." I never have, and being stranded on an island without a shower and proper toiletries has me disliking it even more.

When he's silent, I risk a glance his way. He seems to be mulling over my revelation.

"Don't take it personally," I quickly add, not wanting to ruin the moment. "It's just, in the past, I haven't enjoyed it. The guys who were down there made me feel like they were trying to eat me alive."

I'm expecting him to respect my wishes, but this is Saint we're talking about. "Oh, I promise, you'll enjoy it this time."

Before I can protest, he's sliding my shorts down my legs and tossing them aside. He sinks back on his heels, examining every inch of my body. He reaches forward and slowly removes my underwear. Even though I have an overpowering urge to cover my modesty, I allow him to strip me because it's clear this is happening.

Every part of me blushes as he runs a hand over his mouth, his eyes fixed on my sex. I really wish I had running water as the dip in the pond today barely allowed me to wash as well as I wanted. "I—"

But my objection never sees the light of day because he leans down and kisses the inside of my ankle. I'm highly strung, but I try my best to relax when he begins to kiss his way up my calf, gently spreading my legs apart as his lips slither up my inner thigh.

He takes his time, using his mouth and tongue, but when

he edges toward my sex, I clam up. His hands are either side of my hips, stroking softly. I tense, expecting a tongue to prod my heat, but instead, he settles between my thighs, using the tip of his tongue to draw what feels like the alphabet up and down my leg.

This is different and new, and goddamn, when he squeezes my hip and sweeps his tongue from my knee to inches from my sex, I groan. He's teasing me, and I like it. I know he doesn't like to be touched, so I clench my fists by my sides, squashing down the urge to thread my fingers through his long hair.

He continues to take unhurried licks, and the slow tempo suddenly drives me insane. I want more.

The coarseness of his facial hair adds to my heightened response, and I open my legs wider. But he doesn't take the bait. Instead, he switches from inner thigh to inner thigh, worshiping every inch of my skin. Before long, I grow even wetter than I already am and burn to feel his lips on my heat.

I arch my back off the ground as his touch sets me on fire. He holds me firmly in place, and his dominance just adds to my craving. "Please..." I whimper, peering down at him, mesmerized by the way he looks between my legs.

He inhales, a low hum escaping him before he lifts his head and reality smashes into me. We lock eyes, and it's evident that he knows we've just crossed a line. But that line was bound to be crossed because this spark between us has always been there.

He slips two fingers into his mouth, eyes never leaving mine as he sinks them into me. I bow my hips and arch my neck, a sated moan filling the air. He moves them in and out of my sex leisurely, sighing in approval.

I am a wanton fiend as I rock into his rhythm, my body undulating with each stroke. The noises coming from me express what he's doing to me, and I'm helpless to stop. He circles his thumb over my clit while I cry out, my needy body flooding.

It was never this way with Drew, or anyone else for that matter, but I suppose these circumstances aren't normal, so my body's response seems appropriate, considering where we are. He increases the tempo, plunging in deep and fast while I buck my hips.

I am lost to him, the feel of his fingers inside me almost too much, but I want more. Though I'm afraid to ask because the last time this happened, he left me dry. "Oh, god," I pant, clenching and unclenching my fists.

I'm slick and ripe and ready, but when Saint withdraws, I'm overwhelmed by panic. No, not again. Before I can protest, he slides down my body and comes to rest between my legs. He hooks one of my legs over his shoulder, while he bends the other out, opening me up to him, and lowers his mouth to my sex. The moment I feel his hot lips on me, I instantly arch into him, making a liar out of me because I want more.

He groans against me, the vibration rocking my core.

He uses his tongue, sampling in and around me, and hums when I cry out softly. He uses his index and middle finger to part my flesh, opening me up in a way that has my cheeks flushing a bright crimson.

He delves in deep, flicking his tongue, and I whimper because I'm certain my heart is about to burst from my chest.

He suckles, licking up and down my entrance, then tugs on my clit. I rocket off the floor, grinding deeper into his mouth.

He explores me completely, leaving no part of me untouched. He bites, sucks, and licks. He does everything to make this feel good for me. And it does. His stubble adds to the heightened touch because the wetness of his tongue and the coarseness of his beard are a perfect combination, and before long, I am rocking against his face, begging him to give me more.

"You're melting in my mouth," he groans against my sex, slipping his middle finger into my heat as he continues to lick me.

His words combined with his actions are a dangerous combination because it's sensory overload. Stimulating both my mind and body, he moves his head from side to side. His lips caress my heated flesh, and I moan, undulating with his touch.

I never liked oral sex, but this is something else entirely because this…I like. I like a lot. My body is coming alive.

He drags me toward him roughly, his hands resting on my hips as he controls the rhythm. I'm powerless to stop it and flop like a rag doll, using the leg over his shoulder to draw him closer. He is ravenous, eating me with a ferocious need. He leaves indents on my leg when he grips my thigh, spreading me farther.

My hands are still bunched by my side, but Saint does something that changes the course of everything. As he buries himself deeper, he slowly reaches for my clenched fist. The touch is hesitant at first, but when I unfurl my hand, he gently and cautiously interlaces his fingers through mine.

The touch is virgin as it feels like this is a first for us both.

He may know his way around a woman's most treasured part, but when it comes to affection, Saint is treading uncharted waters. He attempts to sever the connection, but I squeeze his hand, moaning loudly as the genuine sentiment has sped up my orgasm.

It comes out of nowhere and tackles me low. "Oh, god," I whimper, bouncing on his face and his tongue.

We suddenly grow desperate, both our movements echoing the other as we fight for domination. I want to come, and he wants to make me come. But a small part of him is holding out, drawing out the gratification so I explode in messy tears.

His fingers, tongue, and lips all work in unison as they stroke me deeply. I want to touch him, feel his golden, muscled flesh under my fingers, but I know, for now, this is all he can offer me. And that's okay.

My breaths are winded and his are hoarse as he guides me toward the finish line. The slapping of my flesh is music to my ears, but what he says next…I don't stand a chance.

Squeezing my hand, he confesses, "It means…angel." He exhales against my sex, slapping my swollen clit with his tongue.

I scream, stunned by his words and his actions, and come so hard, tears leak from my eyes. My body bows off the floor, and I writhe wildly, certain I'm about to burst into flames. My heart races, the blood whooshes through my ears, and my eyes squeeze shut. I have never come this hard before. When he lets go of my hand, I instantly miss the connection.

He takes every last tremor from my body, and when I grow lax, he kisses my sensitive flesh before untangling himself from me. I'm Jell-O, and I doubt my legs will work anytime soon.

I catch my breath, uncaring that I'm spread open to him because I need a minute to return to earth. I hear a rustle and then something warm being placed over me. Cracking open an eye, I see that he's placed his T-shirt over me to cover my modesty.

My mind is mush.

When he attempts to rise, panic overwhelms me, and my high soon fades. "Stay." My voice is hoarse from screaming. He appears surprised as I don't think he expected to stay and cuddle.

He is truly a dark beauty. His hair is wild, his lips are swollen, and his chest is glistening with perspiration. I know I'm being greedy, but I don't want to be alone. Not after what we just shared.

He wrestles with what to do. I don't want to force him, so I turn on my side and arrange his shirt as a blanket. I get comfortable within seconds, my eyes slipping shut. I haven't felt this relaxed in weeks.

On the cusp of sleep, I vaguely hear Saint lying down beside me, sure to keep his distance, but that's okay. His sated breathing is the sound I fall into a deep sleep to, and so are his monumental words...

"It means...angel."

I asked, and he delivered, so the question is, what happens now?

CHAPTER ELEVEN

I fucked up. I never should have touched her, but I couldn't help it. She is poison, a toxic combination to my body. I haven't touched a woman like that for over two years, but it was never like that with anyone else. When I was "normal," I never wanted someone as much as I want her. I don't know what to do because each day, the thought of letting her go evokes a possession I thought long dead. I'm so fucking screwed.

Day 16

I wake sore, but I hurt so good.

I have no idea of the time, but as I crack open my eyes, I see that it's well past dawn. I slept in, which is a first. Stretching, I see Harriet Pot Pie sitting quietly on her makeshift bed, an egg awaiting me. What I don't see, however, is Saint.

He no doubt left early, not wanting to have the awkward morning-after talk.

I don't know what last night means. It escalated so quickly, and before I knew it, I was giving in to my desires. It wasn't just a physical connection for me. When Saint reached for my hand, uncertain and afraid, it did something to me. And the name he's been calling me is a term of endearment. Why?

I don't expect us to ride off into the sunset together. Saint has a darkness. He confessed as much to me last night. He clearly hates Popov as it seems he is the man who robbed Saint of his humanity. Saint thinks he's dead inside, but I disagree.

I'm left with so many questions, but at the forefront is why.

Deciding to find him, I stand slowly, my legs complete Jell-O. I reach for my shoes, underwear, and shorts, and slip into them. Reaching for his shirt, I draw it up to my nose and inhale deeply. It smells like pure sin.

With Harriet Pot Pie in hand, I scale down the rope, my balance better as I'm getting used to my home being in a tree. We trek through the terrain, and when I hear a fire crackling on the beach, my heart begins to beat quicker.

Pushing through the trees, I make my way onto the sand. There are coconuts and fresh fish, but no Saint. Shielding the sun from my eyes with my hand, I scan the shoreline, but he's nowhere to be found.

"Hey."

"Sweet baby Jesus!" I yelp, clutching my chest. Saint's deep laughter floats through the air.

Craning my neck, I see that he's indeed not on the shoreline because he's perched in a tree. A thick, low hanging branch offers the perfect place to sit and write in his journal, which is what he's doing right now.

Sitting with his back pressed against the trunk, he has the journal resting in his lap. When we lock eyes, my cheeks immediately flush. Memories of last night crash into me, and I gnaw the inside of my cheek to mute my moan.

"I think a storm is coming," he says, thankfully breaking the silence.

Now that I'm semi-coherent, I look at the heavens and see that he's right. The sky is laden with swirls of gray, and the sun has decided to sleep in as well. Overall, an energy pulsates through the atmosphere.

Closing the journal, he jumps from the tree branch with ease. I instantly back up while he ignores my insanity. "Are you hungry?"

I nod, passing him the egg.

He pockets the journal before walking over to the fire to prepare our breakfast. "I think we should find higher ground for tonight. Maybe the cave? Let's grab whatever food and water we can and wait out the storm. I have a feeling it's going to get rough."

"Okay, if you think that's a good idea," I say, wringing my hands behind my back. The prospect of being caught in another monster storm makes me nervous. But so does seeking shelter in a cave with Saint. There is nowhere to go.

No escape. This could end ugly.

We are silent, both mulling over what's headed our way.

As Saint cooks the fish, I grab a coconut and attempt to crack it open like I've seen Saint do. I've tried countless times in private but failed miserably. I had the good sense to grab the pocketknife, so I reach for it and stab the three holes in the coconut. When I feel one give way, I make a small hole and bring it to my lips.

The juice of the coconut quenches my thirst, and I offer some to Saint, but he shakes his head. My knife rivets his attention, and when the green to his eyes spark to life, I know he recalls when I pressed it to his throat last night and the events that followed.

The memories slam into me also.

Needing to distract myself, I make my way over to a tree, count to three, and smash the coconut against the trunk. Examining it, I sigh when it didn't even make a dent. Saint makes it look so easy. I try again, each strike helping me forget the way my body undulated under his touch.

"Here, give it to me."

I jolt, startled as I didn't hear him approach me. Gingerly, I pass it to him and step aside. His muscles bulge when he slams the coconut against the tree, the unmissable sound of it splitting into two following. I notice him flinch slightly as if he's in pain, but he extends his hand, indicating he wants to use my knife.

I pass it to him without hesitation.

A small cut where I pressed the blade into his throat is red and a little puffy. I wonder if he should put some ointment on it so he doesn't get an infection. I'll suggest it after we eat.

He severs the coconut into two, using the knife to dig out the flesh. He passes me a piece, and I thankfully accept. When he places a portion into his mouth, a trickle of juice slides down his lip. He instantly laps at it with his tongue while I stop mid chew, transfixed by the sight.

Saint is aware of my gawking, but I can't help it. I attempt to distract myself by looking elsewhere. But it's no help as I take in the inked feathers running down his arms. And then the blood red roses on his chest. "I like your tattoos."

He smiles. I wish he'd stop doing that because it just adds to the appeal. "You don't have any?"

I shake my head.

He has seen me naked to know that I don't, but I guess we both need this small talk. The fact he's seen me naked has my cheeks heating yet again.

He offers me the remaining flesh of the coconut. I accept as it'll give me something to stuff my mouth with other than gibberish.

We sit by the fire, eating our fish in silence. There is an unspoken current between us because it seems neither of us knows what to say. I want to ask him about last night, but ask him what exactly? He got me off, is that all it was?

My appetite is suddenly shot because I want it to have meant something to him. It meant something to me. "I'm going to check out some plants I found early this morning," he says, hinting there will be no morning-after talk. "There has to be something on this island we can use."

So far, Saint and I have both searched for anything green

to eat with little success. I tested his theory, and he was right. Everything I pressed to my wrist or lips tingled or gave me a rash, so I knew consuming them wasn't an option.

I'm getting sick of fish and coconuts, so the prospect of finding something else to eat has me offering to help. "After I bathe, I'll come with you. The water is becoming stagnate so the rain will be welcomed," I say. "Maybe we can find something to collect the rainwater in?"

He finishes chewing and nods. "Good idea."

We're being awfully polite with one another, but the tension lingers. I can't stand it any longer. "Saint, about—" But I never get to finish.

He stands up quickly, grabbing his spear. "I'll meet you near the cave."

He doesn't give me a chance to get a word in edgewise as he disappears through the trees, leaving me and Harriet Pot Pie alone.

I understand this is awkward, but I need to acknowledge it happened. It appears, however, that Saint doesn't feel the same.

The dismal afternoon corroborates Saint's prediction. A storm is coming. The temperature has dropped and turned quite cold.

Saint fishes and transports our things to the cave while I hunt for food. So far, I've found nothing that looks edible. This is really Saint's forte as he's proven to be quite the outdoorsman with his knowledge, but the fact he doesn't want to get within a hundred feet of me has me rummaging on my own.

I don't know how I feel. Pissed off. Hurt. Overall, nothing has changed as these emotions have rocked me since this ordeal began. Even though it's only been sixteen days, it feels like a lifetime. I don't feel like the same person I once was.

Under normal circumstances, doing what I've done with someone like Saint would have never happened. Yes, my whirlwind romance with Drew happened in six short weeks, but during that time, I never allowed him to invade my soul like I have with Saint. Nor did I engage in such perverse acts.

Everything has changed, and the only person I have to talk to has suddenly gone silent.

Sighing, I focus on finding something to eat because I don't know how long this storm will last. When I pass a low growing plant that looks like spinach, I drop to a crouch and decide to investigate. When it passes Saint's tests, I'm elated to have finally found something useful. I may not know what it is, but it hasn't set my skin on fire, so it's okay with me.

"Harriet Pot Pie, did you see what I found?" I'm expecting her to cluck, just how she always does, but I don't hear a sound.

Standing, I turn around to see that she's not here. She was moments ago.

The sky begins to rumble as the white clouds give way to gray. "Harriet Pot Pie!" I call out, cupping my hands around my mouth. "Here, girl."

It's frightening how quickly the weather turns. The wind howls, and I grip a branch to stop from blowing over. Panic grips me. "Harriet Pot Pie!" I shout loudly, but a sudden crack of thunder drowns out my voice.

Just as I'm about to go searching for her, Saint emerges and grips my forearm. "We have to go. The storm is coming."

"I can't. Harriet Pot Pie is missing," I exclaim, shrugging from his hold.

"Ангел," he warns, but I shake my head stubbornly.

"I can't leave her out here."

Saint pinches the bridge of his nose and sighs. "When did you see her last?"

Shrugging, I hunt our surroundings. "About ten minutes ago, maybe. I found this and got distracted." I quickly pass Saint the green leafy plant and continue my search.

He smells it and touches it to the tip of his tongue. "It's Molokhia. It's rich in anti-inflammatory properties and speeds up the healing process. Good job." He yanks out a few handfuls, placing them into his backpack. "But we really have to go."

The thought of leaving Harriet Pot Pie out here has tears stinging my eyes.

Saint reads my distress and steps forward, placing his palm to my cheek with a wavering touch. I instantly turn into his palm. "She'll be okay. Animals are resilient. She survived on this island before you. She probably sensed the storm is coming and went to find shelter."

He's probably right.

"Okay," I agree, reluctantly. He runs his thumb over the apple of my cheek before severing our connection.

"Let's go." He gestures with his head that I'm to follow.

We race through the wilderness, a thunderclap or

lightning bolt following each step. The cave was Saint's thing, and I didn't want to intrude on his sanctuary, so I have no idea what I'm walking into. I am slightly claustrophobic, so I can only hope it isn't too small.

I follow Saint as he sprints up a rocky slope. "It's just up here," he shouts over his shoulder, heading toward the right.

Just as we're a few yards away, the heavens open, and a downpour drenches us. The ground soon becomes muddy and slippery, and I almost lose my footing. Thankfully, Saint reaches for my hand and helps me into the cave.

The mouth is quite large which helps put my claustrophobic mind at ease. The ground is rocky, so I watch my step as Saint leads me deeper into the cave. His grip has not loosened on my hand, so I have no other choice but to follow.

The farther we venture, the darker and colder it becomes. I'm thankful when I see our things a few feet away. Saint lets go of my hand and drops to a squat. I have no idea what he's doing until he begins to build a circle of large rocks. When he places twigs and leaves into the center, I realize he's making a fire.

I am so cold, my teeth chatter, so I walk over to my dry pile of clothes. I reach for a yellow sundress, wishing I had a pair of jeans and a warm sweater. Saint's back is turned, though it wouldn't matter after everything that happened last night, and I strip, slipping into the dress.

I feel remotely better, but a chill still rocks me. Rubbing my arms, I watch as Saint gets the fire going by skillfully only using sticks. He builds it up, and before long, it's blistering brightly. I don't realize I'm still shivering until he stands and reaches into his backpack.

"Here." He offers me his only remaining long-sleeved shirt. When I hesitate, knowing he's probably cold too, he unfolds my arms and gently slips it over my head. I help him by lifting my arms and allowing him to dress me.

I'm swimming in it, but it instantly thaws the chill to my bones. "Thank you."

He nods before stripping out of his T-shirt and standing in front of the fire to dry off. "I've left the empty bottles of water and the waterproof box outside to gather as much rainwater as we can."

The wind rattles around us, and my thoughts instantly drift to Harriet Pot Pie. I hope she's okay. I sit down on the sleeping bag which Saint has laid out and lean up against the rocky wall. I have no idea how long we're supposed to wait it out, but being locked away with Saint in such a confined space already has me feeling nervous.

Saint puts on a T-shirt once he's dry and takes a seat around the fire. I notice him flinch like he did earlier today as he tries to get comfortable, but I don't have time to question it because the tension between us is suffocating. "How long do you think the storm will last?" I ask, breaking the silence.

Saint shrugs. "I don't know. The last time we were caught in one, it went on for hours."

I gulp.

Hours? What are we supposed to do for hours? Saint hardly looks like an I Spy kind of guy.

Drawing my legs toward my chest, I hug my knees, thankful Saint's shirt is long enough to drag over my legs. I watch him closely, unable to hide my smile when he digs out his tattered sudoku book.

"What?" he asks, cocking his head to the side.

"Nothing," I reply, biting back my laughter.

"You have something against sudoku?"

"No." I raise my hands in mock surrender. "You just don't look like a math kind of guy."

"What do I look like then?" he counters quickly. Shame on me for not seeing that coming. I'm not sure if this is a trick question, so I decide to answer honestly.

"You look...pissed off most of the time?" I offer, phrasing it as a question.

His lips twitch. "Fair enough. I suppose that's because I am," he confesses coolly.

The air settles.

He sweeps his hand down his body. "You know, I wasn't always this."

"This?" I question, unsure what he means.

"The bad guy," he clarifies. My eyes widen. I was *not* expecting him to say that. "Before all of this, I was a...college professor."

I choke on my utter surprise, thumping on my chest to kickstart my heart. I don't want to make a big deal about it but oh, my god. A professor? Wow, the plot thickens.

"I taught mathematics at Columbia University," he continues, lost in what seems like another era. "I suppose you could call me a nerd."

I scoff. Saint and nerd are two words I would never associate together.

"Now I understand the sudoku fascination," I say evenly, desperate for him to share more.

He stares into the fire. "As mundane as it is, it's the one thing that anchors me to that life even though it feels like a lifetime ago."

"How long ago was that?" I ask softly, not wanting to press too hard.

"Two and a half years ago," he replies blankly; his gaze fixated on the smoldering flames.

I blink once.

For two and a half years, Saint has been confined to this miserable life, one he clearly didn't choose. He had a good job he obviously enjoyed, but he gave it up to be a hitman. What am I missing?

"Where do you live now?" I'm assuming he no longer lives in America.

"Russia, but that's not my home," he replies quickly.

I hug my knees tighter. "Then why do you stay there?"

I'm treading dangerous waters, but this is the most he's shared with me, and I want to know everything there is about him. "We all have to do things we don't want to do." That's not really an answer, but it confirms my suspicions that he's doing this because he believes he has no other choice.

"I suppose in some way then, we're both prisoners," I say sadly. "So will you go back to America? After your...job is done?" There is no point waiting around in hopes that Saint changes his mind. The job is me as my imprisonment ensures his freedom. No human would forfeit their freedom for the life of a stranger.

He meets my eyes. "I haven't thought that far ahead." I remember Saint confessing he won't stay when he hands me over to Popov. I'm the key to him getting his life back. At least my captivity will benefit someone.

"Maybe you could go back to teaching?" I suggest, but he scoffs.

"There isn't much that scares me, but going back to being 'normal' is one of the only things that terrifies me."

"I don't understand. Isn't that why you're doing this?"

He reaches for a twig and begins to draw circles absentmindedly in the dirt. "I can't go back to working nine to five, living in the suburbs, and having barbecues on the weekends."

"Why not? It sounds like a great life to me."

Just when I think we've reached our quota for talking, he reveals, "Sooner or later, this...darkness within me"—he places a fist over his heart—"will need more. I've seen and done so much, I can't go back to being normal because late at night, when everyone is safe and sound in their beds, everything I've done will come back and haunt me, reminding me that there isn't a 'normal' for someone like me. I need the darkness to survive. It's the only way I can live with what I've done." He lowers his head, his hair shielding his face.

A shiver passes over me at the torment lacing his confession. Just what has he done?

"Only God can judge me," I murmur aloud. Saint's head snaps up when I unintentionally recite his tattoo. It seems more than fitting. "No matter your past, there is always time to repent."

"I'm way past salvation." He's given me much to think about, and a realization suddenly hits.

"That's why you don't like to be touched, isn't it? You don't think you're…worthy of human affection?" I offer, hoping he sheds some light.

He appears haunted by my observation. "No, ангел, you're wrong. No one has *wanted* to touch me in two and a half years because who would want to touch a…hitman?"

A winded inhalation escapes me because this is the first time he's admitted what he is. "You weren't always a-a hitman." The word tastes like poison on my tongue, but nonetheless, it feels good, to be honest. "That doesn't define who you are."

"Stop it," he exclaims, tossing the twig into the fire. "Stop seeing me for something that I'm not. I had no qualms about kidnapping you, defiling you"—my cheeks redden—"all because I know that I could. Pain gets me off. It's the only thing that makes me feel alive."

This comes as no surprise when Saint clearly enjoyed punishing me. But I suppose for two and a half years, he's only known pain. "That may be true," I whisper, averting my eyes, "but you've also shown me kindness. I refuse to believe you're all bad."

"Believe what you want," he spits defensively. "But when I hand you over to Popov, you'll soon see how very wrong you are."

I've just seen a new side to Saint. Through his cruelness is a vulnerability that makes me want to comfort him. Yesterday, he allowed me to touch him, confessing that he liked it, so his claims are false. Whatever wall he's erected was to protect himself from feeling. The only way he can live with what he's done is to disconnect, which is a sure sign that beneath the darkness is the man he once was. He's not lost. Not yet.

I rub my arms when a sudden gust of wind rattles the cave walls. The storm is coming, but it can't compare to the squall within.

We sit in silence, a million thoughts running around my head, and soon, I zone out the punishing weather and focus on everything Saint shared. His existence sounds so lonely. A once well-respected professor turned hitman. It's as ridiculous as it sounds.

I wonder what he was like all those years ago. Sharing his knowledge with impressionable students and shaping their futures with his teachings. But he threw it all away for this wretched life.

The dots just don't join.

I begin to hypothesize Zoey's role in Saint's life. Is she his girlfriend? Wife? Friend? He did say she was the most important person to him. For him to do what he's doing, their love must be something incredible as he would do anything to protect her.

My belly begins to twist in knots.

I wonder what it feels like to give and receive that sort of love. I thought what I had with Drew was love, but would I give up everything and sell my soul like Saint has done for him? The answer is no. Maybe that says something about my character, but I have never wanted to end my life to save another.

And that speaks volumes for Saint's character.

Resting my cheek against my knee, I turn my head to peer at the rocky wall because I suddenly can't look at him. He wants me to hate him, but I can't. I should, but I don't. What does that say about me?

Just when I think things can't get any bleaker, a terrified clucking catches on the howling wind. Slowly, I raise my head, unsure if I heard the noise or not. When it sounds again, I know that I'm not imagining things.

"Harriet Pot Pie!" I shoot up, making a mad dash for the exit.

I grip the rocks along the sloped wall as the wind is rough, pushing me back as I advance. When I get to the mouth of the cave, I shield my eyes from the heavy downpour, desperate to find Harriet Pot Pie. I see her stuck halfway down the hill, drenched and squawking loudly.

"No!" I cry. Lunging forward, I'm intent on rescuing her, weather be damned. But I'm jarred backward as Saint grips my elbow.

"You can't go out there!" He has to shout to be heard over the thunder.

"I can't leave her out there. She'll die." I rip free from his hold, determined to do this.

But Saint stops me. "*You'll* die if you attempt to go out there."

And suddenly, it doesn't matter. What do I have to go back to? "I can't let her die." Turning over my shoulder, I allow my tears to shine. "I protect the things I love."

It's a double-edged sword because he can relate to this. And if he stops me from saving her, he's a fucking hypocrite.

Harriet Pot Pie may just be a chicken, but she represents so much more. I'm sick of cowering in the face of danger.

"Fuck!" Saint sighs. He's irritated I'm once again arguing with him, but he shouldn't expect anything less. "Stay here," he commands firmly.

Before I can tell him to go to hell, he pushes past me and runs into the brutal storm. My mouth hinges open as I was not expecting that.

"Saint, no!" This is my battle, not his. But it's too late. I watch as he runs down the hill, using his forearm to protect his face from the ruthless weather. The rain has obscured his form, so I lean forward to get a better look.

I can barely see a thing, but after what feels like minutes, when a lightning bolt sparks the atmosphere to life, I sag against the rocks in relief. Saint has reached Harriet Pot Pie. He tucks her under his arm and makes a mad dash up the hill.

My heart is in my throat as the terrain is slick with mud, and it's obvious he's having difficulty climbing it when he loses his footing and slips. Without thought, I run into the rain, intent on offering him my hand, but he screams at me to stay where I am.

I quickly retreat, using the rocky ledge above me as shelter. I shift from foot to foot, anxiously awaiting Saint to finish the climb. The heavens have really opened up, and it seems to take him twice as long getting back up.

When he's yards away, I exhale because, within moments, he'll be safe. But it appears fate doesn't like that outcome. From out of nowhere, a lightning bolt rocks the entire island. I feel the electricity all the way to my toes.

"Hurry up!" I shout because suddenly, every hair on my body stands on end.

I don't have time to question it because before I know it, a fierce cracking and an ominous shadow have me screaming and stabbing the air with my finger. "Watch out!" Saint turns over his shoulder, but it's too late.

Everything happens in slow motion.

He throws Harriet Pot Pie to safety, and in turn, he sacrifices his own because an enormous branch has snapped from a towering tree and strikes him down. The noise is sickening, but the sight of him trapped under the branch has me kicking up mud as I run toward him.

"Saint!" But he doesn't move.

I slip and slide as my tennis shoes have no grip, but I'm working on pure adrenaline and get to him within seconds. He's on his stomach. The thick branch crushing him into the soggy terrain. When I see blood on the back of his head, I know I only have minutes to set him free because he's unconscious.

Lightning and thunder work in unison, hinting I could be lying beside Saint if I don't hurry up. The branch fell across his back, and I try to move it off him, but it's heavy and doesn't budge. "Come on!" I yell as failing isn't an option.

I yank with all my might, but the waterlogged ground causes me to lose my footing. The rain continues to fall, sinking Saint into the saturated soil. I drop to my knees to check his pulse. When I feel the faint rhythm, I sob in relief.

"I'm sorry!" I cry to his still form because he wouldn't be out here if it wasn't for me. That thought causes a surge of energy to course through me. I bend my knees, engage my core, and use all my strength to lift. A guttural scream leaves me.

It's amazing what the human body is capable of because, before I know it, I've moved the branch a fraction. It's still not enough to free Saint, so I repeat my actions, tapping into strength I didn't even know I had. A roar slashes through the air as I deplete whatever energy I have, but it's well worth it when I'm able to move the branch and set Saint free.

I did it!

But I can celebrate later.

Saint is out cold, so just as he did for me when he swam me to safety, I now have to do the same for him. I have no idea what I'm doing, but I drop to my knees and roll him onto his back. Mud cakes his face, and the sight kicks me in the solar plexus, winding me.

Pulling it together, I look over my shoulder at the cave. It's not too far away, and the path is relatively clear, so without a choice, I grip his wrists and begin hauling him toward safety. He weighs more than the branch, but I continue to drag him, trying my best to avoid boulders and the rough ground.

I'm breathless, and my arms and legs are aching, and I lose my footing a handful of times, but I finally maneuver Saint into the cave. Tugging him toward the fire is going to be a lot harder in here with all the rocks, so I drag him as far as I can.

I sprint toward the sleeping bag and first-aid kit and am back at Saint's side in seconds. I drop to my knees and place a hand in front of his mouth. He's still breathing. I work frantically, rolling up the sleeping bag to place under his head gently as I roll him into the recovery position. When my hands come away with blood, I know the gash on his head is still bleeding.

I work madly, using whatever I can find in the first-aid kit to help clean the wound. When it stops bleeding after a few minutes, I sag in relief. All I can do is monitor him and hope he wakes soon, seeing as calling 911 isn't an option.

I sit beside him, brushing away the matted hair from his forehead and cleaning the dirt from his face. Each stroke wipes away the filth, and I wish it was that easy to wash away the sins on his soul. This is the first time I've touched his face, and being this close to him, I can't help but admire his strength.

My fingers linger over his cheeks and down through the soft stubble on his jaw. Touching him this way has something softening inside me. I can't believe he risked his safety for Harriet Pot Pie and...me.

He knew I would have gone down there to save her, but instead, he did, and now he lies here, unconscious and hurt. "I'm sorry," I whisper, running my fingers through his soft hair. "Please wake up."

The idea of being stuck here alone sends my blood cold, but that's not the issue invading my every thought. If Saint dies...I shake my head violently, needing to dispel such nonsense. What would it say for my self-respect if I confessed Saint's death would hurt...a lot?

A tear slides down my cheek.

"Ангел?" I yelp but cry out in relief when I see his eyes flickering.

"I'm here. Let me help you." He doesn't argue, and I slowly

help him turn onto his back, adjusting the sleeping bag. "You've hit your head," I explain. His eyes are still sealed shut.

"Tired," he pushes out breathlessly.

"Can you open your eyes?" He has a head injury, and even though he's tired, I don't think he should sleep.

"Will in a minute," he sleepily says.

"Saint..."

"Sleep," he interrupts. It appears his bossiness knows no bounds—conscious or unconscious. The fact he's talking and knows who I am are good signs. I will just watch him like a hawk.

I attempt to move, but he leaves me speechless when he reaches for my hand and links his fingers through mine. With my mouth agape, I peer down at our union. It looks so foreign, yet it doesn't.

"The chicken?" he drowsily asks. Harriet Pot Pies clucks.

"She's, she's okay," I reply, my words slow as I can't believe he reached for me.

Saint's heavy breathing indicates he's fallen asleep, but his grip never wavers from mine.

Saint has slept for what feels like hours. I've watched him the entire time, ensuring he's warm and comfortable.

I got as snug as I could, but the fact he wouldn't let my hand go had me contorting my body so I could lean against the wall. I sat watching him, studying this mysterious man like I'd just stumbled across a new species.

I don't understand him. I never have. But I can't deny that his actions tonight have done something to me. I have always felt some inexplicable connection to him, but now, it feels different. It feels like something has changed.

I have never met anyone like him before. He is dark and brooding and most definitely not one of the good guys, so why does he continue doing virtuous things? Yes, he's a downright asshole most of the time, but when he's not, he's something… else.

I want to know him, all of him because I don't understand the feelings he evokes in me. I am losing myself, piece by piece, to Saint, and I don't even care.

Sighing, I stretch my neck from side to side as my entire body aches. I don't want to wake him, but the fact he's been out cold for so long worries me. Running my thumb over the back of his knuckles lightly, I whisper, "Saint, wake up."

No response.

"Saint," I say, a little louder this time, but still, nothing.

Panic seizes me, and I gently brush the hair from his brow. When I do, however, I yank my hand back because he's burning up. "Saint! Can you hear me?"

Oh, god. *Nothing.*

I feel for a pulse and find a shallow and weak one. His skin almost burns mine when I touch his cheeks. He has a fever. I don't understand how that's possible. I didn't see any cuts on his body which were infected. Maybe it's a virus? He didn't complain about feeling unwell.

Hunting through the first-aid kit, I reach for some Tylenol

and a bottle of water. He is out cold, so I have no idea how I'm going to administer this. I decide to crush it up and mix it in with the water. "Saint, I need you to open your eyes."

His unresponsiveness has my heart racing.

When he doesn't move, I position myself behind him and prop him up so he's half sitting. He's floppy, so I'm sure to be quick as I settle in behind him and cradle his dead weight against my chest. Reaching over his shoulder, I press the bottle to his lips.

"Drink. Please."

His T-shirt is stuck to him, and I wonder if it's the rain or sweat because the heat coming from his body is almost unbearable. When the water trickles down his lips, I know this is useless. I can't force it down his throat in fear he'll choke to death.

I can't believe this is happening.

I manage to maneuver him onto his back and take vigil by his side. "Please don't die," I whisper, reaching for his hand.

"Zoey…"

I freeze, unsure what to say or do. In his delirious state, he is calling for her.

I quash down these feelings which resemble jealousy because they have no right to be there.

"Shh," I coo, squeezing his hand. "It's okay." He stops talking and drifts back off into his delirium. Harriet Pot Pie sits near me, and we both guard our savior.

The storm continues to rumble around us, and all I can do is sit and wait—both for the storm and Saint.

CHAPTER TWELVE

I'm lost to the silence...

Day 19

When absolute silence envelops you, you realize just how quickly we adjust to the constant noise that clutters our lives. Most say they want to get away from the hustle; that they want to spend a week on a deserted island and forget the world exists. Well, I've been there, done that, and let me tell you, the silence is overrated.

For three days, I've been lost in the silence, and I have never felt lonelier than I do right now.

Saint has faded in and out of consciousness. He doesn't talk or open his eyes. Sometimes, he mumbles incoherently, but most times, he screams in his sleep. I have tried everything to wake him up, but it's no use.

He needs a doctor because his condition seems to be getting worse. But that isn't an option, so all I can do is keep him comfortable and hydrated. I'm beyond exhausted because when I'm not constructing an SOS signal on the beach, I've been watching him like a hawk. I'm too scared to close my eyes in fear of when I open them, Saint may have succumbed to whatever illness plagues him.

This has nothing to do with the knock on his head. That may have contributed to his weakened state, but something else is at work here. I just don't know what.

The thought of doing this alone terrifies me, but I can't deny that the thought of losing Saint scares me more. He wouldn't be in this position if he hadn't been out to rescue Harriet Pot Pie, which I still don't understand why he did so.

He's a walking conundrum.

I still want to know so much more about him, but as I touch his forehead and it comes away wet with fever, I know that may never happen. I wipe away my tears with the back of my hand. I'm defeated—in every sense of the word.

The storm has thankfully passed. It was brutal. I have ventured out, and the terrain barely looks recognizable. I've had to mark a new path with shreds of old clothing as everything has washed away.

Beginning my day the same as I have these past three days, I shoulder Saint's backpack in order to collect more twigs and rocks to finish the SOS. It's the only hope we have of getting off this island.

Harriet Pot Pie is grazing outside. She never leaves. It seems she too realizes the sacrifice Saint made to save her life.

I bid her farewell and make my way down the hill.

The sun shines brightly without a cloud in the sky. Once I'm done with the SOS, I'll pick some coconuts and hunt for food. The water Saint collected thanks to the heavy downpour is still in excess, but after a few days of sitting around, it's beginning to taste a little stale.

I'm so sick of fish. I'm hoping I'll strike it lucky and find a crab or something else. I've steered clear of the waters near the lagoon in fear the shark will return and finish what he started. Without Saint, I feel vulnerable, which is ironic in every sense of the word.

I work on the SOS until my arms and legs ache. I'm almost finished with the O. I'm determined to have it completed by tomorrow. I try digging in the sand for crabs, but I come up empty and have no choice but to fish.

It takes me a little while, but I'm able to spear a couple of fish. Once I've collected a few coconuts that have fallen from the tree, I stagger back toward the cave. I have no idea of the time, but the sun is dipping, so I know it's almost dusk. Time passes me by on a loop because this has been my routine for the past three days. It's Groundhog Day, and I want out. But this is my life now, and I don't know how long for.

Feeling more than sorry for myself, I drag my feet, eyes peeled to the ground. When something green and bushy comes into view, I do a double take, and a winded gasp leaves me.

"It's molokhia. It's rich in anti-inflammatory properties and speeds up the healing process."

The first bubble of hope I've had in three days rises,

and I can't drop to my knees fast enough as I yank out more handfuls of the stuff. I already have some from when Saint picked it before the storm, but I want to ensure I have enough. I can't believe I didn't think of this sooner. Stuffing it into the backpack, I run through the thick terrain and up the hill.

My sides hurt, and I'm panting by the time I run into the cave and squat by Saint's sleeping form. I hope by some miracle his fever has broken, but when I touch his cheeks and forehead, I pull my hand away.

He's even hotter, and his skin is slick with sweat.

"No," I cry, quickly slipping my arms through the straps of the backpack.

His T-shirt is wet with perspiration, so without thought, I sit him up and take it off. His body is lax, which just adds to my nerves. As carefully as I can, I lay him back down and run over to his change of clothes. I grab a new shirt and the first-aid kit.

When I return, I drop to my knees, ignoring the shake to my hands as I open the kit. I will try the Tylenol again, and maybe this time, I'll add some of the molokhia with the water. As I'm about to dress him, my attention falls to the tattered gauze pad over his stab wound.

I had completely forgotten about his injury. When I asked him how it was, and he replied with fine, I just assumed it was. I didn't press because it was clear he didn't need me tending to his wounds anymore. But a light bulb suddenly appears out of nowhere. All this time, I assumed Saint had a virus or maybe even something similar to Dengue Fever thanks to all the mosquitos buzzing around us, but I'll bet my left arm he has an infection, thanks to this wound. I suddenly remember him flinching when he moved, like he was in pain.

I gently peel back the gauze inch by inch, and what I see has me gasping. The jagged cut I sewed together is red and raw. It's also inflamed and smells horrible. Peering up at Saint, I gently prod the area and watch for any signs. When he flinches and groans sluggishly, I know this is the reason he's been so sick.

He has a nasty infection. The pus oozing from the wound only confirms that fact.

I am livid at myself for not putting two and two together. But I can berate myself later because now, I have to tend to Saint's injury. I work on autopilot, boiling some water and preparing everything I need.

I sterilize the area with the boiling water, washing the weeping mess. I then use the antiseptic wipes to ensure the wound is as germ-free as I can get it. Hoping I'm right, I place some of the molokhia leaves in the boiling water and place them over the cut.

Saint did say they helped speed up the healing process. I don't know if he meant ingesting them or applying them directly to the source, so I'm going to do both. Once the wound is lathered with the juices of the molokhia, I dry it gently, place some ointment on there and then apply a fresh bandage.

I don't know if any of this will help, but I'll try anything.

I really wish I could force more than a trickle of water down his throat because the Tylenol would help. But the boiled molokhia juice will do just fine.

Placing Saint's head against my thigh, I blow on the concoction, ensuring it's not too hot. When it's cool enough, I gently cradle his head, lifting it slightly and pressing the coconut shell with the juice to his lips. I feed it to him in small doses. Most of it runs down his lips, but surely, he's swallowed some.

Not wanting to go too fast, too soon, I position myself so I can lean against the wall and still have his head on my lap. His chest rises and falls lethargically, but when I place my hand over his heart, I sigh in relief because it beats strong.

I didn't think to ask him how his wound was or even offer to dress it because Saint is so...Saint. He is so strong and independent, and I never thought about him getting sick or being vulnerable, but being stuck here, I've now seen both.

Instantly, the urge to comfort him overcomes me, and I run my fingers through his hair. He would never allow me to touch him this way if the circumstances were different. Or would he?

My exhausted mind demands sleep, so I close my eyes for a few seconds and welcome the quietness once more.

"Zoey..."

My eyes snap open as my groggy mind takes a second to adjust to where I am. I'm still stuck on this island.

Peering down, I see that Saint's head still rests on my lap. I touch his forehead, and even though he's still hot, he's not burning up. A small bubble of hope rises. Maybe he'll pull through.

I have no idea of the time and being cooped up in this dark cave doesn't help. I decide to try to feed Saint more of the molokhia concoction as I'm hoping this has helped with his fever. Without moving him from my lap, I reach for the remaining juice in the coconut shell and swish it around. Drawing the shell to his lips, I gently prop his floppy head forward.

"Saint, you need to drink this." I can only hope he can hear me. Most trickles down his chin but when I see the slow swallow of his throat, I cry in relief. "That's it. Drink." I don't want to force too much down, so once he's had a few small mouthfuls, I pull the shell away.

He sighs and nestles against my leg.

"Can you hear me?" I ask gently, brushing the hair back from his face. He looks so weak and vulnerable.

His shallow breaths are a welcomed sound because a few days ago, I didn't even know if I'd hear them again.

"Zoey?" he mumbles; his eyes are still squeezed shut.

"No, it's me. Willow," I whisper, continuing to stroke his hair.

"I'm sorry I didn't protect you," he says sluggishly.

"Shh, it's okay." I don't want him thinking like that. I just want him to focus on getting better.

"I should have come sooner. I'm sorry, Zoey."

My stomach drops because he thinks he's talking to Zoey and not me. I can't hide my disappointment, but I disregard it quickly.

"But I'll fix it," he slurs while I hold my breath. What is he about to confess? "I'm going to make it right, and then you can come back home, and everything will go back to normal."

Fix what?

"I've got what Popov wants."

My stomach drops. Is he, is he talking about me?

Saint has succumbed to sleep, but I'm wide-awake, stunned by his admission. I don't want to believe I'm involved in Saint's plans, but deep down, I know that I am. My attention drifts to his journal. The answers I seek are no doubt buried within those pages, but the question is, when I uncover what he has planned for me, will I turn into him? A murderer? Because if I'm proven wrong, and he *is* the bad guy, then I have no other choice but to fight.

It's survival of the fittest, and right now, Saint's survival depends on me.

Sighing, I lean my head back against the rocky wall and close my eyes. He is my foe, so why do I keep treating him like my friend?

Day 21

Three weeks have passed since I was kidnapped. How my life has changed since that day. I'm beginning to forget the small comforts like TV, toilet paper, and running water because being out here in the wilderness is slowly becoming my norm.

Saint seems to be getting better, but his constant cries for Zoey cement that once he wakes, we will go back to the way things were. His journal still lays untouched because I'm frightened to know what's inside.

I don't want to believe that he's the monster he claims to be because if it's so, what does that say about me? I allowed him to touch me, and I...liked it. And even now, I know nursing him back to health will ultimately lead to my demise. But I can't let him die.

I know that makes me a fool, but I couldn't live with myself if I took someone else's life. My subconscious never fails to remind me that Saint has no issues whatsoever doing so.

Shaking my head, I continue gathering coconuts because after working all day, I'm tired and hungry.

The SOS is finished. I was expecting to feel some sense of accomplishment, but the moment I laid the last stone, it hit home that for the past eleven days, I haven't seen a single soul. No passing planes or ships. It's like we were forgotten.

But I can't sit around, twiddling my thumbs. I need to at least try. In the back of my mind, I wonder what would happen if we were rescued. I would have to tell my rescuers everything, which would lead to Saint getting into serious trouble.

What would that mean for him? And Zoey?

My mind has been stuck on a loop these past two days because no matter how badly I want to get off this island, going back home will prove to be harder than being stuck here. Being lost seems simple compared to the shitstorm of being rescued.

How messed up is that?

Trudging back up to the cave, I look forward to passing out for a few hours because I am beyond exhausted. Harriet Pot Pie is grazing near the entrance. She's really proven to be good company because, without her, I would be talking to myself.

The fire crackles, illuminating Saint. He hasn't moved from when I left him this morning. I changed his dressing, and I was happy to see his wound looked less infected.

Dropping to a squat, I gather the coconuts and the molokhia, which has been his diet for the past couple of days. I go to work, breaking up the molokhia and mixing it with the coconut juice. I grind up some Tylenol and add it to the mix.

Just like always, I settle his head onto my thigh after I sit down. "Okay, are you going to make this easy for me today? Or will you continue to be a giant pain in my ass?" Placing the coconut shell to his lips, I slowly feed him the concoction.

I've learned to do it gradually as it allows more of it down his throat. "You need to shave," I say to his comatose form, brushing my fingers through his thick beard. "You also need a bath." I've tried my best to wash what parts of him I can, but I draw the line at a sponge bath.

Yawning, I feel my eyes grow heavy, but I continue feeding him. "I'd give my right arm for a pepperoni pizza right now." My stomach grumbles at the thought of eating anything but fish. "If we ever get off this island, I am going to eat for a week. I'll start at Dot's, where they make the best homemade butter pecan ice cream in all of LA." My mouth practically waters at the thought.

I'm lost in visions of velvety ice cream and completely unaware of my surroundings. So when I hear a winded, "I'm…more of a rocky road fan," I scream, as it sounds alien to hear another voice other than my own.

"S-Saint?" I gasp, blinking quickly to ensure I'm not seeing things. But when those chartreuse eyes focus on mine, I know that I haven't slipped into a food coma. "Oh, my god, you're awake!"

I know I'm stating the obvious, but I didn't know if I'd ever look into those eyes ever again.

I immediately remove the coconut shell from his lips and help him into a half sitting position because he can't do it on his own. He blinks once as if attempting to gather his bearings. "How long was I out?" he asks, his voice hoarse.

"Five days," I reply, while his mouth hinges open.

"You're fucking with me, right?"

I shake my head slowly, pulling a face.

"How is that possible?" He grips his side, wincing as he shuffles backward to lean against the wall.

"The night of the storm, a tree fell and knocked you out cold. I dragged you up here and thought you'd be okay once you woke up, but you had a fever. I didn't know why, but your stab wound, it was infected, hence the fever," I explain, biting my lip.

He nods slowly, appearing to process everything I've just said.

"I fed you the molokhia and bathed your wound in it. You

said it helped speed up the healing process." When he cocks a brow, I smile. "I do listen every so often."

"It appears so," he replies, flinching. He's still in a lot of pain. "You must be hungry. Let me catch my breath, and I'll find us something to eat."

When he attempts to push off the wall, I place my arm over his chest to stop him. He peers down at the barricade deliberately. As much as I appreciate the sentiment, it's not necessary. "I've got it."

His attention drifts to the coconuts and the fish I cooked earlier this morning.

I don't want to gloat, but goddamn, the surprised look on his face has me wanting to break out into a victory dance. "I fished. I finished the SOS signal. I looked after you. That's what the past five days have consisted of."

He's at a loss for words because he's not used to being helpless and not in control. I'm expecting a thank you, or even a pat on the back, but I don't get anything warm and fuzzy. "I need to wash."

I can't hide my disappointment.

He methodically removes my arm and comes to a slow stand. He's unsteady on his feet, but he uses the wall to keep upright. I peer up at him, anger rising. Nice to know me saving his life has softened him up—not.

"Do we have any soap or toothpaste left?"

I gesture with my head to where it sits, which just happens to be near his journal. His head snaps my way, but I smirk. "Don't worry, I didn't read it. I didn't have to," I reveal. "I already know what a heartless bastard you are."

I shoot up, needing to put some space between us. I don't know why I'm so angry. I guess I was expecting at least some form of acknowledgment for not leaving him to die. But even skating with death doesn't seem to trouble the calloused Saint.

He doesn't bite back, but instead, he hobbles toward the exit.

I refuse to stay holed up in here, so I push past him and take three deep breaths as I step outside. My temper is raging because I am angry with myself for giving two shits about him. I think about the sorrow I felt at the thought of losing him because he doesn't seem to care either way.

The sun scorches me, adding to the heat coursing through me. I decide to go for a swim as there isn't anything else to do on this fucking island. As I'm halfway down the hill, I hear a pained grunt.

Do not turn around, I repeat over and over, but it falls on deaf ears when I peer over my shoulder to see Saint bent in half, clutching his side.

Good. The sight of him in pain should give me satisfaction. It doesn't.

"Goddammit," I curse to myself as I turn around and march the way I came.

The closer I get to him, the more evident it is that he's in severe pain. His breathing is labored, and he looks a ghastly shade of white. When he sees me pacing toward him, he attempts to stand upright but only manages a stooped stance.

I don't bother talking. Instead, I wrap my arm around his waist, hinting for him to lean on me. When he struggles, I tighten my hold on him with an annoyed sigh. "Stop being such a stubborn son of a bitch and let me help you."

My tone reveals this isn't negotiable. He finally caves and sags against me.

My knees almost buckle because he is so heavy, but I loop his arm around my shoulder so I have a better grip on him. We then commence our slow stagger down the hill. We both remain quiet. Even though I'm helping him, it doesn't mean I want to talk to him.

Once we arrive at the pond, I release my hold on him slowly. He is shaky on his feet, but he stays standing, leaning against the tree trunk, catching his breath. He drops his clean clothes on the ground and unfastens the button on his pants.

That's my cue to leave. "Don't drown," I quip, turning to leave. But I'm stopped in my tracks.

"Where are you going?"

I clear my throat, trying to mask my embarrassment. "You're dreaming if you think I'm going to scrub your back."

A smirk tugs at his lips. My insides do a little happy dance at the sight. "Just don't go too far away, okay?"

An eyebrow raises higher than the other. "Why not? I've survived just fine without you. I don't need you telling me what to do."

Saint groans in annoyance. The sound is music to my ears.

I don't bother waiting around for him to bark any more orders and turn around, leaving him to wash in private. I can't shake the winner's grin as I make my way toward the beach.

Stripping out of my shorts and tank, I venture into the water, sighing as the temperature is perfect. My anger simmers, and I enjoy the quiet as I swim into the depths.

Now that Saint is awake, I wonder what happens now.

We are days away from depleting the medical and toiletry supplies. Not to mention our diet needs something more than fish and coconuts. I wonder how long someone could survive stranded on an island.

Our fresh water is almost out, and I have no idea when we will get another downpour to replenish our supply. Not to mention Saint is still in a lot of pain. He's susceptible to other illnesses now that his immune system is so weak. And what about sepsis? Surely, he's at risk of this as well.

Getting off this island is even more imperative. But how?

My body, it appears, is in tune with Saint because when my skin prickles in awareness, I know that he's standing by the shore. I wish I could say I despise this awareness, but I don't. Being lost in the wilderness, it feels nice to be connected to someone, even if that someone is an irritating son of a bitch.

Swimming back, I don't bother concealing my near nakedness when I emerge from the water. My bra is barely modest, and my white underwear are completely transparent. But what do I have to hide? Saint has seen me bare. The thought has my cheeks flushing.

Wringing out my hair, I lock eyes with Saint who is still glistening wet. His tousled hair is tied back, and his ripped shorts sit low on his narrow waist. We both play the role of castaways perfectly.

"Did the hut survive the storm?" he asks, snapping me from gawking at his muscled chest.

"Yes. That thing was built to last."

"Did you sleep in it when I was out cold?"

I bite my lip, embarrassed. "No, I stayed with you." I know how ridiculous that sounds, but I was scared to leave him alone.

He thankfully doesn't touch on the topic. "Good, so you'll be okay with me tearing it down?"

"What?" I ask, surprised.

"We need to get off this fucking island. And I'm not going to sit around, dick in hand, waiting for that to happen."

"But the SOS—"

"Forget the SOS. We haven't seen anyone in almost two weeks. No one is coming." He doesn't seem too upset over that fact. I wonder why. "I want to make a raft. It's our best chance."

The unspoken lingers. And then what?

"I could use your help." He clutches at his side, hinting at the lingering pain.

Questions are long forgotten. I almost fall over my feet when I hear him asking for help. I playfully wiggle my finger in my ear while he rolls his eyes.

"Or you can stay here. I don't care either way."

All playfulness subsides.

Narrowing my eyes, I nod. "Fine. I'm in."

I'm presuming he wants to start immediately, so I step into my shorts and tank. When I'm dressed, I meet his eyes to see a deep desire in his. I remember the last time I saw it—when his mouth was coaxing me to the point of no return.

I swiftly put such thoughts out of my mind, but when Saint scans down my body quickly, I wonder if he remembers too. However, it doesn't matter either way because his admission of him leaving, with or without me, rings loudly.

"Ready?" he asks, snapping me from my thoughts.

"Yes," I reply. "Let's get the fuck off this hellhole."

The future remains unclear, but the present is certain—it's time to go home.

CHAPTER THIRTEEN

> We need to get off this island. The longer we stay, the greater risk she's in, the greater risk they're both in.

Day 25

The hut which I once called my sanctuary is no longer. But I suppose if what Saint proposes works, then it'll be a savior in a different sense. We've worked for the past four days solid, dismantling the hut and transporting the wood to the beach.

Saint is on the mend, but he's still sore. This has delayed our raft building because as strong as I'd like to think I am, we both need to carry one piece of wood at a time, which is taking forever.

He has thankfully allowed me to dress his wound, which definitely looks better. But I know it still hurts. He constantly needs to catch his breath, and I catch him every so often flinching when he twists the wrong way.

But he doesn't complain. He seems focused on getting off the island and sooner rather than later.

As I stand staring at our materials, I know that was the easy part. Now the hard part is finding something strong enough to tie the wood together with. It seems hopeless, but I'm trying to remain positive.

It's night, and although I'm gauging how many days have passed by counting the sunsets and sunrises, all days now merge into one. I'm roasting fish over the fire, waiting for Saint to return. He's adamant he will find something to bind the wood, but hope's dwindling.

He emerges from the trees empty-handed, looking more than infuriated. I don't say a word while I serve up our dinner in the coconut shells acting as our makeshift plates.

"Do you want some rum?" he asks.

We've been limiting how much we drink because god knows it's been our only saving grace at night. If we run out, I'm afraid to think of facing the nights here without a rum buzz. "Thanks."

We go about our usual routine, which is scary to think we've been forced into having one at all. When he passes me the coconut shell, I arch a brow. This is a little fuller than usual.

"I have searched high and low, and I can't find a fucking thing." This explains the binge drinking.

I lower my fatigued body onto the sand and am surprised

when he sits near me. He usually sits across from me. We eat in silence. After two mouthfuls of fish, I push the shell away from me, unable to stomach another bite.

"I'm so sick of fish," I confess, placing my hands against my gurgling belly.

"You have to eat. You're so skinny."

He's right. I've lost weight since this ordeal started. I have always been small framed with curves, but now, I just look gaunt. "I can't believe we haven't seen anyone. How is that even possible?"

"The world is a big place," he counters.

Usually, I sip my rum, but tonight, I just want to forget where I am. Whether I'm sipping or shooting, the rum tastes horrible, but when a comfortable buzz overtakes me, I want more.

Saint is in the middle of taking a sip when I steal his shell. I can't help but laugh at his speechless expression. When I finish his as well in one long gulp, I offer him both shells. "Next round's on me."

He doesn't argue and stands to refill our drinks.

The alcohol goes straight to my head, which is what I wanted. I watch the way his angel wings come to life under the moon. They really are beautiful. And when he turns back around, I can't deny that so is he.

"It means...angel."

Usually, I would avert my gaze, but the liquor gives me the confidence to lock eyes with him. Something crackles between us. I instantly feel faint, and it has nothing to do with the rum.

"How long do you think we'd survive out here?" I ask, needing to distract myself.

He raises his broad shoulders. "A human can last about three weeks without food." I blanch at that thought because surely, that can't be right. "But can only last about three to four days without water."

"Wow." I gasp, unable to mask my surprise. He passes me my rum, which I gratefully accept.

"We have enough water for the time being. But the coconuts will eventually run out. And we can't rely on the rain."

"How does a former math professor know all this?" I ask in awe of his knowledge. It's out before I can stop myself as we haven't discussed his former occupation since he mentioned it nights ago.

I'm expecting him to clam up, but he doesn't. He smiles and sits down beside me. "I learned quickly how to fend for myself."

"Did your new profession teach you that?" I question cautiously.

"Yes, ahreл."

"Oh." I sip my drink, unsure what to say as I was expecting him to tell me to mind my own business.

I haven't breached the Zoey topic. So many times, I wanted to share with him how he called out her name when he was sick, but I didn't. A part of me is scared to know who she is to him.

"Is Saint your real name?" This verbal diarrhea will get me into trouble, but I blame the rum as it's given me some Dutch courage.

Saint catches me off guard—again. He laughs. The deep, honeyed sound is toxic. "Yes, my real name is Saint. Why?"

I shrug, cheeks billowed as I swallow down my booze. "I dunno. For someone who sure as hell isn't saintly, it seems like a weird choice."

Oh, shit.

Did I say that aloud?

Saint leans back on his hands, a grin tugging at his full lips. "Fair enough."

"What's your last name? How old are you?" I can't help but fire questions at him.

"It's Hennessy. I'm thirty-three."

I can imagine all the college girls swooning over their young, attractive professor.

It's information overload, but the more he shares, the more I want to know. "When is your birthday?"

"November eighteenth."

"Ahh, Scorpio, that explains a lot," I reveal, swallowing down my rum. When he waits for me to elaborate, I say, "Part of your psyche resides in a very dark place. You also don't like people disagreeing with you because you need to be in control. Tick. Tick." I mimic a giant ticking motion in the air, making Saint smirk.

"But you're also brave, loyal." I decide to add because Scorpios are one of the most devoted star signs. "Scorpios are extremely passionate, and when they...fall in love..." I pause as I'm suddenly getting hot. "They are very dedicated and faithful."

Saint watches me closely, sipping his drink.

I have no idea why I feel the need to share this with him. He doesn't really seem like the horoscope type. But being able to share this with him is inadvertently telling him how I perceive him.

"And what star sign are you?" he asks, surprising me.

Licking my lips, I answer, "Cancer. My birthday is on June twenty-fourth."

"So I suppose Cancer and Scorpios are the two signs which constantly argue?" he quips.

I can't help but laugh. "Actually, no. We are two of the most compatible signs," I confess, averting my gaze. "It's been said Cancer can understand the needs of their Scorpio partner to help them express their deepest, darkest emotions in life. When a Scorpio falls in love, trust is the most important thing to them. Cancer just wants someone to share their life with, so they have no reason to lie or cheat."

"So Cancers are the light, and Scorpios are the darkness?" he questions, which has me lifting my chin slowly.

Locking eyes, I shake my head. "No. They both care too much. They just express that emotion in different ways." The air suddenly heats, and referring to the signs and not us makes this easier to confess. "They connect emotionally, intellectually, and…physically. Once a bond has been formed…the relationship tends to be long-term."

Saint seems to ponder everything I just shared.

I'm left dizzy and lightheaded, and it has nothing to do with the rum. Acknowledging this is like looking in the mirror at Saint's and my relationship. The attraction between us—well, from my end—was instant. He has never lied to me, and when he touched me...my skin blisters at the memory.

I'm drawn to his full lips. They glisten with rum under the moonlight. I wonder what they would taste like. I remember Saint voicing his no kissing rule to the woman he had no qualms fucking. I wonder if this rule would also apply to me?

"And what star sign was your husband?" The mention of Drew has my drunken brain scoffing instead of mourning our bullshit relationship.

"Gemini," I reply, curling my lip. "Ironically, one of the worst matches with a Cancer. I should have known not to trust him. The Gemini symbol depicts two entities—a perfect reflection of his two-faced nature."

Saint appears pleased by my response. "Then why did you marry him?"

There isn't judgment, only curiosity in his question. "Because I wanted to believe in fairy tales. But I should know by now they don't exist." I throw back my drink, relishing in the burn as the rum flows down my throat.

When thinking of what Drew did, an anger surfaces as my sadness has now taken a back seat. "That asshole," I say with a slight slur. I am way past drunk, but I don't care. "I can't believe he used me like that. You must think I'm a fucking idiot."

I have just admitted that I believe Saint. The facts all point to Drew selling me like livestock at a farmers' market. Covering my eyes, I'm suddenly embarrassed. I can't believe I fell for his bullshit.

But when Saint's fingers gently remove my hands so he can look into my eyes, a whimper escapes me. "I don't think that. Not at all."

"Then what do you think?" I'm crossing a dangerous line, but I don't care.

"I think..." He pauses, choosing his words wisely. "You're the most infuriating woman I have ever met." Well, I was expecting that response. "You're also the bravest," he adds, which has me gasping. This is the second time he's called me brave.

"I also think you like to see the good in everyone."

"Is that such a bad thing?" I ask softly, leaning closer to him.

He shakes his head. "Not at all. That takes strength not to give up."

His voice is smooth, and it's sensory overload as his signature fragrance lingers between us. Being this close to him, I admire the intensity in his eyes, and the magnetic pull, which bounces between us, lures me toward his supple lips.

I shouldn't want to kiss them, but...I do. This isn't the first time this has happened, but unlike then, I don't think I have the strength to pull away. "Whatever happens"—I close the small distance between us, so we're inches apart—"know that I will never stop trying to find my way back home."

The air between us is so thick, I almost can't breathe.

His gaze never wavers from mine as he murmurs, "I know."

A quiver rocks me low. Who knew two words could hold so much immoral promise? The world begins to spin, and I know it has nothing to do with the rum and everything to do with Saint—the most potent potion of all.

Everything hits me all at once, and no matter how badly I want him, I can't forget what he did. Who he is. I need to leave. Yanking backward, I attempt to stand, but thanks to my universe being tipped on its axis, I only end up tumbling forward. On instinct, I reach for the first solid thing within reach, which just happens to be Saint's bicep.

Memories smash into me of when we first met because just like then, I grabbed him, hoping he could anchor me. "Sorry," I pant, trying to pull away, but his hand snaps out and overlaps mine.

Peering down at our connection, I try to fight this wickedness within, but when a lopsided smirk tugs at his lips, I am helpless to the temptation. Letting go, I will deal with the self-hate and consequences later, and I surrender…to the darkness.

The moment I press my lips to Saint's, I know there is no turning back. He freezes, eyes wide, as he's just as surprised as I am, but he doesn't pull away. His mouth is warm, soft, and it instantly thaws out the chill to my soul.

I want more. I know he doesn't like kissing, but I am powerless to stop.

His lips part, and I know he's about to be the voice of reason, but I don't want to see reason—I just want to feel. With that roaring to the surface, I move my lips against his, hopeful he feels the magnetism too.

He does.

He groans into my mouth, surrendering, and kisses me so fiercely, I'm propelled backward with the force. Every fiber of my body is on fire, but the sensation only has me shuffling closer, pressing us chest to chest. His tongue fights for domination, but we duel for control because being locked this way unleashes a feral need within me.

I loop my arms around his nape, running my hands through his long hair. We both moan at the connection. He drags me onto his lap, and I wrap my legs around his waist, pressing my core against his enormous erection.

It pleases me to know I affect him just as he affects me.

He pulls away and bites my bottom lip. My eyes roll to the back of my head. He continues devouring my mouth, leaving me breathless as our kisses are soaked in utter passion. He controls the depth, the speed when he loops his fingers around the back of my neck.

I'm helpless and yield because his dominance leaves me slick and wanting more.

His tongue delves in deep, evoking a whimper from me with the slow, hypnotic dance. I can't get close enough and press my body into his. The barbell in his nipple is hard against me, and for some reason, it stirs my insatiable hunger.

I want to touch him, but I'm terrified. There is something deeper running between us. Something far more powerful than just a physical attraction as emotion drives my actions.

The kiss intensifies, and I tug at his hair, needing to grip onto something as I'm afraid I'll float away. He groans low as it seems he likes the aggression, which is no surprise. But so do I. His beard scrapes my skin, but the burn adds to the desire, and I angle my head to consume him whole.

With one hand fisted around my hair, he sweeps the other down my body, coming to rest at my waist. He works his way under my tank and begins to stroke along the small of my back. The gentle action combined with his kisses have me mewling and sagging into his touch.

My skin breaks out into tiny goose bumps, and my nipples instantly pebble. I am so turned on, but so is he. I can't help myself and begin to slowly rock my hips, his hard-on striking me in the most perfect way.

Unable to resist but with a wavering touch, I run my fingertips along his broad shoulders and down his firm arms. He is warm and strong, and being able to touch him so openly feels good. I continue my journey, leaving a heated trail across his chest before I circle his barbell softly.

He hums low, expressing his approval.

My lips are swollen, but I continue kissing him without apology as I make my way down his stomach. His abs feel like granite beneath my fingers, and I have the urge to run my tongue across each ridge.

He suckles my bottom lip and cups my ass, encouraging me to ride him harder. I do.

Things are getting out of hand, but the more I take, the more I want. I don't know where this is headed, but kissing is suddenly not enough. I make my intentions clear when I reach the top button of his shorts.

I am beyond nervous, but I quash that as I work to unfasten the button. My fingers are trembling, and my heart thrashes wildly against Saint's. When it finally comes undone, Saint does something which robs me of breath for an entirely different reason.

He pulls away.

"Wh-what are you doing?" I breathlessly pant, my eyes snapping open.

I'm unable to mask my disappointment when he says, "No, ангел, don't."

"Don't?" I repeat, confused.

He nods and gently untangles us.

I don't know what to say, so I timidly rearrange my clothes, wondering what I did wrong. He was into it. I know he was. And shamefully, so was I.

"Is it your n-no kissing rule?" I ask as I'm baffled to why he stopped. He arches a confused brow. So I explain. "On the boat, when you…slept with that woman, you told her no kissing."

He wipes his swollen, luscious lips, shaking his head. "I shouldn't have kissed you," he firmly states, not really giving me an answer.

"Oh."

Dread overcomes me when his words echo loudly out here in the emptiness. *Unlike everyone else, I don't want to fuck you.*

Have I misread the signs? I was the one who kissed him first. But who cares? The only thing that matters is that *I*… kissed him.

Oh, god, I feel sick.

What have I done? I could blame the rum, but I was in total control. I wanted to kiss him, and I thought he wanted to kiss me. Clearly, I was wrong.

I need to leave.

Standing abruptly, I ignore the headrush and turn to flee,

but Saint grips my arms and spins me around. "We can't do that again."

What a way to rub salt in the wounds.

Ripping from his hold, I squash down my embarrassment and focus on my anger. "I couldn't agree more. I'm drunk, sorry."

Lies, but it's easier than admitting the truth.

"Of course," Saint says, running his fingers through his snarled hair, the hair which I tugged at moments ago.

"I'm beat. I'm going to sleep." I'm about to make my way toward the hut, but there is no hut, thanks to Saint's harebrained idea to destroy it.

"Okay. I'll be in the cave if you need me."

We have been sleeping down here around the fire these past few days, but it seems that the kiss has reverted us to rivaling enemies. I don't fail to see the irony in that.

Saint rocks back on his heels as if he wants to say something, but he changes his mind at the last minute and storms off. I watch his menacing form disappear among the trees. When he's gone, I sag to my knees, covering my face in utter humiliation.

I don't know what just happened. The forbidden kiss was hot and intense; it was everything and so much more. But that had nothing to do with the actual kiss itself, and everything to do with the fact that behind each lash of his tongue and caress of his lips, there was something…more.

It wasn't just physical.

Groaning, I slowly curl myself into a ball by the fire. What the fuck have I done?

Day 26

My head is pounding, and my mouth is so dry, I wonder if I've eaten sand in my sleep.

Even though my eyes are squeezed shut, I know it's daytime. The blazing sunshine forces me to face what I did in the harsh light of day.

I kissed Saint, and I liked it. I was even tempted to take things further, but he was the one to slam on the brakes. I should be thankful that he did, but I'm not. I'm left with this cloud of confusion hanging over my head, and I hate it.

My feelings for him should be clear cut, but they're not. They never have been. And now that I've kissed him…I'm in way over my head.

And when his fragrance slams into me, sending my body into hyperdrive, I realize just how much so.

"Ahрел, wake up!" The urgency to his tone has me forgetting my woes.

Springing upward, I rub the sleep from my eyes and ignore the throbbing in my temple. "What's wrong?"

"Look what I found." He holds up long strands of thick vine while I cock my head to the side, confused. "It'll be strong enough to use as a rope for the raft." To emphasize his claims, he yanks at the strands. I'm expecting it to snap in half, but it doesn't.

"Oh, my god!" I jump up as this is good news. My first instinct is to hug him because I know how hard he's searched to find something, but I refrain from touching him.

He seems to be in sync with my thoughts as his excitement soon settles. "Sorry to wake you."

"No, it's okay. I was awake anyway. I was just prolonging the inevitable." When his Adam's apple bobs, I clarify, "Nasty hangover. Do we have any Tylenol left?"

His shoulders visibly depress. It seems he has no interest in discussing what happened last night. His aloofness angers me, but I can't force him to speak about what we did.

"Yes, I'll grab some." He goes to turn, but I stop him dead in his tracks.

"Don't worry," I quickly say. "I'll get it." I can't deal with his hot and cold behavior. I need to remember who he is to me, no matter how good a kisser he is.

He seems surprised, but soon recovers and he nods once. "Okay. I'll be back later. I'll bring back what I can carry."

I could offer to help, but I think we both need some alone time.

Making my way to the first-aid kit, I gulp down two painkillers, wishing it would help ease this pain in my heart. Saint's footsteps announce his departure, only adding to the heartache because he seems happy to pretend last night didn't happen, so I guess it's my turn to do the same.

Day 31

eing stranded on a desert island, you'd think one could enjoy the serenity of being left alone. But the quieter Saint became, the louder my furious thoughts raged.

It's been five days since we kissed, and although I wasn't expecting Saint to transform into a cuddly teddy bear, I was expecting we would at least discuss what happened. But it seems he's content to forget it ever occurred.

I should too, but I can't. Every time I get within five feet of him, the memory of his lips pressed to mine assaults me.

One thing is certain, however, and that is we're both eager to get off this island.

Saint was right. The vines he found were strong enough to use as a rope, so we busied ourselves with building our raft. It's a tough, laborious job, but we've got nothing but time. We are close to finishing it, which leaves me with the question yet again, what happens when we do?

We are sitting around the raft, putting our knot tying skills to good use. I'm at one end while Saint is at the other—a perfect analogy to how we co-exist.

"We are days away from finishing this," he says, interrupting my thoughts.

"Awesome." My reply lacks excitement, but he doesn't address my apathy because he'd rather ignore it, just like our kiss.

Why does it irk me so much? I shouldn't care, but I do. I've known him for thirty-one days. I knew Drew for roughly forty-two. Depending on how long we're stuck here, I'll probably have spent more time with my kidnapper than I did with my husband.

How messed up is that?

Saint senses my restlessness. "Go take a walk."

"Don't tell me what to do," I quickly snap, tying the rope firmly.

Saint sighs heavily. "Ангел—"

I can't stand hearing that name, and suddenly, taking a walk sounds like a great idea. "Fine." Jumping up, I brush the sand from my legs, refusing to make eye contact. "I'll go get dinner."

"I can do it," he presses, but I don't need him doing me any favors.

Ignoring him, I grab the spear we use for fishing and march away from him. Harriet Pot Pie follows but soon gives up when I quicken my pace.

I need to get over it, but I just can't. I'm not wired the way Saint is. I can't just pretend that a kiss didn't happen when it meant something to me. And that's the real issue here—it meant something to me.

I am frustrated with myself, for my foolishness when it comes to Saint because this ordeal has bonded me to him when it should have done the complete opposite. There must be something seriously wrong with me.

Tipping my face to the heavens, I beg the universe to stop being a torturous bitch and cut me some slack—for once. I don't expect her to listen, but she does.

The echo is faint at first as it's so foreign to hear a sound I was certain I would never hear again. But when it gets louder,

I shield the sun from my eyes with my hand to ensure I haven't succumbed to the madness.

I haven't.

It's a mere dot in the distance, but there is no mistaking what it is—it's a plane.

Life has been moving in slow motion, but now, everything whips around me, threatening to swallow me whole. "Hey!" I scream, jumping up and down and waving my hands in the air wildly.

My heart threatens to burst from my chest because I can't believe this is happening.

"Down here!" I bellow at the top of my lungs, waving like a madman.

The plane gets closer, bringing tears to my eyes.

"The SOS!" I frantically run along the shore, desperate to get it to before the plane flies overhead.

My muscles burn, but I persevere because this is my only chance. I don't know if I'll get this opportunity ever again. "Saint! A plane!" I cry, running rapidly. "Throw the rum on the fire!"

We need an accelerant to make that fire go boom! If they miss the SOS, then a bonfire, blazing into the heavens will definitely catch their attention. The sand kicks up as I pound along the shoreline, looking over my shoulder to ensure I keep the plane in my line of sight.

It's getting closer.

"Saint!" But when I reach the fire, he's nowhere to be seen. And neither is the rum. "No!"

I don't have time to search for it because the plane turns,

and the flight path is right above me. "Hey!" I jump up and down, waving and screaming like a madwoman.

I stand by the SOS, ensuring whoever is flying that plane can see that I need help. They're so high up, I can't be sure they can see me, but I continue trying to flag them down. The closer they get, the louder I scream.

When it flies overhead, the noise is my savior, and I wave madly. I'm expecting them to slow down, or at least acknowledge they can see me, but when the plane continues flying away from me, my stomach drops, and I run after it.

"No! Stop! Help me!" I roar, but I don't stand a chance of keeping up with it. "Please, no." Regardless of my pleas, it doesn't stop and flies away, taking my hope with it.

Breathless and running on nothing but fumes, I eventually cave and drop to the sand, sobbing. I slam my fists into the soft shore, tears of anger burning my cheeks. All I can do is watch the plane disappear into the distance. Before long, it's gone for good.

"Ангел?"

I yelp, my already frayed nerves on edge. "Where were you?" My tone is broken.

"I was picking more vines. Why?"

"Why?" I chuckle, but nothing is positive about the sound. "Because a fucking plane just flew over us. You didn't hear it?"

"No," he says in a rushed breath. "The density of the terrain blocks out any noise, you know that."

He's right. But how did he get there so quickly? The area where the vines grow is about two miles away. And it's rugged land.

"Where is the rum?"

"The rum?" he repeats.

I nod, unsure why he's choosing to be so evasive.

"It's under the tree, in the shade. Why?"

"Because I was going to use it to throw onto the fire," I explain, fatigue overwhelming me.

My back is still turned, so I can't see his face, but I can't shake the feeling that something is off.

"Let's hope they saw the SOS then," he reasons without any meaning. He couldn't care less. Our only lifeline has just flown away, and he doesn't even seem to care.

The fight in me has died, and all I want to do is cry myself to sleep. "I'm going to lie down." I come to a wobbly stand as this is the first time since this nightmare started that I've felt absolute defeat.

Saint doesn't say anything. And neither do I.

I stumble past him, unable to look at him as I'm fearful what I will see reflected in his eyes. Harriet Pot Pie follows me as we make our way through the trees. I travel on autopilot, a sense of doom shadowing us.

We trek the hill and enter the cave. I collapse onto the sleeping bag and tuck my knees to my chest. And here I stay, sobbing until oblivion comes.

Day 32

Something wakes me. Something ominous.

I gather my bearings and realize I'm still in the cave. For a split second, I believe the plane was a dream, but the hollowness in my chest reveals it wasn't.

I don't know how long I've slept, but as I rise slowly, my aching muscles hint it's been a long while. I guess it's well past midnight because when I look toward the entrance, it's pitch black outside.

Something about today troubles me. I don't know why, but I don't believe Saint. He claims he didn't hear the plane, but I think he did. I suppose my pent-up anger toward him could be clouding my judgment, but I guess there is only one way to find out.

Harriet Pot Pie stays where she is. She can sense the shitstorm moments away from erupting. I charge down the hill, adrenaline coursing through me. I can't get there quick enough because I need to get everything off my chest, and when I say everything, I mean everything.

We will have our long overdue talk whether he wants to or not. However, when I emerge from the trees and onto the shore, it seems we're way past talking.

"What the fuck are you doing?" I roar, coming to a sudden stop.

There must be some mistake. My eyes are surely deceiving me because there is no way I am seeing this—seeing Saint destroy the SOS. But when he turns over his shoulder, completely guilt-ridden, I know there is no mistake.

"I asked you a question," I cry, covering my mouth with a wavering hand. He's demolished endless hours of work because all that sits before me is rubble. "Saint! Why?"

He closes his eyes for the briefest of moments before tipping his head backward with a groan. "I had to," is his lame ass reply.

"You had to?" I repeat, anger exploding from me. I storm over to him and grip his bicep, forcing him to look at me. "Why?"

I am shaking in rage, and I cannot contain it.

"Because we will do it my way," he arrogantly replies, shaking free from my hold.

"What?" I stagger back, his pride almost winding me.

"I will get you off this island. I promise. The raft is almost finished—"

"Fuck the raft!" I bellow. "That SOS was the best way of being rescued. Now it's ruined!"

"Just trust me," he has the audacity to say.

"Trust you?" I spit, disgusted. "The only reason I'm here is because of you." An epiphany hits, and I snicker. "You can't stand that I'm the one who might save us, can you? You selfish asshole!"

"Don't be ridiculous," he snaps, folding his arms firmly.

"It's true," I press, refusing to back down. "You know, most people thank someone for saving their life, but not you. Your pride won't let you do that, will it?"

"You should have let me die," he professes, his jaw fixed. He isn't fishing for compliments. He truly stands by his admission.

"How do you do it?"

"Do what?" he asks, standing tall.

"How do you turn your emotions on and off like that?" I reply, suddenly feeling sorry for him.

But Saint reminds me just who he is as he advances forward and grips my biceps, dragging me toward him. "You forget...I don't have any."

Although every part of me trembles, I challenge, "Bullshit. You want to believe that, but it's not true."

But when I think about our kiss, and how he can treat me this way without feeling, I wonder if maybe I want to see something that isn't there.

He lets me go, and I sag forward, wrapping my arms around my middle. "I can feel it...every time you touch me. When you...kissed me."

He hisses, turning his cheek. "Do you know how many men I've killed?" he cries, startling me because I've never heard him so...emotional before.

"I-I don't care," I reply, surprising myself because I mean every word.

It appears I've surprised him as well when his lips part, but he soon recovers. "Well, you should," he spits with venom.

"What have I done to make you hate me so much?" My lower lip quivers, but I try my best not to cry.

"I don't hate you." He interlaces his hands behind his neck, inhaling deeply.

"Then why would you kiss me and then just disregard it like it didn't matter? It may not have mattered to you, but it did to me." I need to stop talking, but I can't. I'm done playing this cruel game. "I couldn't let you die," I confess, locking eyes with him, "because I didn't want you to. I should hate you, but you're right. I don't. You scare me"—he frowns—"but not because I'm afraid of you. I'm afraid of what you make me feel. I don't understand it, any of it, especially when I know you've lied to me. You heard the plane, didn't you?"

His silence is all the response I need.

"I just don't understand why you wouldn't want to be saved. Why did you destroy the SOS? Why did you touch me the way you have? Was it to humiliate me? And why would you kiss me the way you did and not mean it?" A sob escapes me because my questions are the ones that weigh heavily.

I know I sound desperate, but I am. I'm desperate to understand what any of this means.

The air suddenly whips around us and leaves me winded as Saint rushes forward and cups my cheeks between his palms. He frantically searches my face while I hold my breath. "It's because of that kiss"—he avidly pants, his touch wavering with emotion—"that I'm doing this. All of this."

A gasp leaves me. "Wh-what do you mean?"

"You're right; I did see the plane." His confession confirms what I already knew to be the truth. But I need to know why he didn't react.

"Why wouldn't you be happy about that? I thought you wanted to get off this island as much as I do."

"You don't get it," he spits, squeezing my cheeks gently. "That plane, it was most likely Popov's men."

My eyes widen.

"Which means he knows where we are. I destroyed the

SOS because, by some miracle, I'm hoping I'm wrong. I should have destroyed it days ago. I just didn't think he'd come for us. I thought he'd grow bored by now, but I should have known better."

"Maybe it wasn't them?" I try to reason. Saint's hollow expression reveals that's just wishful thinking.

"Maybe it wasn't, but if it was, that means he's found you and…he is coming," he pushes out in a rushed breath. "And that means I will have no other choice but to give you to him… no matter how badly I don't want to." Tears sting my eyes. "I don't have a choice, ahreл. But if we escaped, I wouldn't be forced to do the worst thing in my entire life."

"You'd let me go?" I whisper, not believing his admission.

A single word changes my life forever.

"Yes."

I have finally attained my freedom, but it's too late. What a cruel, cruel world.

"I never wanted this for you, and I'm sorry for everything I've done," he says while I begin to cry. "I've done some unspeakable things in my life, but this…" He brushes away my tears with his thumbs. "This is by far the worst thing I've ever done. He's already taken so much from me. Giving you to him…how can I do that when I—" He pauses, wrestling with his words as he stares me deep in the eyes.

"I shouldn't feel this for you…but I do," he concludes with sadness while my mouth parts in utter shock. "I don't even know what this is, but the thought of you and him…" His jaw clenches while a guttural growl gets trapped in his throat.

My mind swirls as his confession has left me a speechless mess.

Saint has just admitted that he too feels this inexplicable connection, and regardless of our current circumstances, I need him to know I feel the same way.

Placing my hand over his, I softly declare, "I feel it too."

A weight lifts off my shoulders because I suddenly feel free from my oppressive guilt. But Saint takes a step backward, running a hand through his hair. "Then we're both screwed."

"Why are you doing this?" I've asked him this before, but unlike those times, he's ready to tell me the truth now.

With hands threaded atop his head, he exhales deeply. "Remember when I told you I don't get paid in money for doing this?"

I nod once, too afraid to reply.

"Giving you to Popov, I get paid with my..." Everything slows down because all roads lead to this moment in time. "Freedom. Freedom for me and...Zoey. My sister."

Time comes to a standstill, and the noise quietens.

You'd give up everything for this whore? Zoey would be very disappointed to know that. I know now what Kazimir meant.

"Zoey is your *s-sister?*" I stumble over my words because I feel like I've just swallowed lead.

This is the final piece to the puzzle, the piece I've been missing this entire time.

"Yes."

I stagger backward, covering my gaping mouth with a wavering hand. "So you've done all of this for...her? You trade me for your freedom? And for Zoey's freedom?"

He tips his head back, staring into the heavens. "Yes."

Oh, god.

The truth has been presented to me. It's what I wanted all along. I thought once I knew it, I'd understand everything, but I was so wrong.

My legs threaten to buckle, but I wrap my arms around my middle and blink away my tears. "I feel sick," I whisper, my voice hollow, broken.

"Everything I did was to teach you a lesson because I couldn't give you to Popov the way you are. He would break you, ангел. Badly. I couldn't let him do that to you."

This cruelness is the only kindness I can show you. I can't deliver you to him with you behaving this way.

Saint's words play on a loop as I didn't understand them when I first heard them. But now, I do.

"All the things I did." He slowly lowers his chin, meeting my eyes. "All the horrible things I've done to you...Popov will do to you. But far worse. I wanted to be the one who broke you because I've seen what he can do."

"Why did you sleep with that woman?" I cry, emptily. It wasn't him needing to get off. And it stemmed far deeper than him simply needing to teach me a lesson.

"Because I was, *am* crazy in whatever this is with you... Willow. I needed an outlet. I needed to forget how much I wanted you. And I needed you to see what it will be like."

My name has never sounded sweeter than right now.

"You are so innocent but so brave. Underneath strength is a vulnerability Popov will thrive on. He will break your modesty any way that he can because you're a challenge for him. He is the fox while you are the rabbit. He will hunt you until you're his. He will force you to watch him do some deplorable things. And other times"—he inhales, closing his eyes—"he will force you to engage."

My stomach turns. I was right all along.

"He will be your tormentor, but he will also be the person who will make the pain go away. I was cruel because I needed you to submit...any way that I could. My ways are less painful than Popov's. He would destroy you. I've seen it. I've seen what he's done to my sister." He shakes his head slowly as if attempting to rid whatever memory plagues him.

"So that's why you treated me...touched me the way that you have?" My disappointment shines. "To prepare me for what Popov has in store for me?"

His chest rises and falls, and my heart sinks. But it kick-starts back to life.

"No, ангел. I touched you because I wanted to, and I hate myself for being so weak." He runs a hand down his face in exhaustion.

"Why?" I don't understand.

"Because my weakness is Zoey's demise," he explains, his tone pained. "You were supposed to be the solution I've been searching for, for over two and a half years. But this...pull I feel toward you, it will destroy so many lives."

And there's the kicker.

His feelings for me result in his sister being imprisoned forever. I am a trade for Zoey. For his freedom. I finally understand why he's done it. You sacrifice everything for the people you love.

"What happened to Zoey?" It feels alien to speak her name as for so long, it was forbidden.

He laughs, but nothing is humorous about the sound. "It happened so long ago, but this memory is one that will haunt me for the rest of my life."

I dare not speak and allow him the time he needs.

He stares off into the distance as if he's going back in time. "Zoey is my younger sister. She's always been the free-spirited one while I was happy to follow the norm. She would light up whatever room she walked into. My parents adored her. We all did." His Adam's apple bobs, and I hold my breath.

"Her dream was to backpack around the world. To most, it would stay a dream but not to Zoey. So one day, she packed up her stuff, bought a one-way ticket to London, and left. She sent the occasional email, but she wanted to backpack off the grid. To see the grittier side to life. She got a lot more than she bargained for.

"I was busy at work but living a good life. The last time we spoke, she had called and asked if she could borrow some money. For some reason, I snapped. I told her to stop wasting her life and to come home. To get a job and to be an adult. I was so stupid. So narrow-minded. I should have known something was wrong as she'd never asked for money before.

"When my mom called and told me she hadn't heard from Zoey in over two months, I knew something was wrong. We called the police, but without knowing where she was, they had nothing to go on.

"We had no idea what to do. At the time, I was dating a woman named Jessica."

I curl my fists, leaving crescent moon prints in my palms.

"She was an IT specialist and was able to trace the last

email Zoey sent. It was to her best friend, asking if she could wire her some cash. She was in Moscow, and she had run out of money. She asked Betty not to tell me or my parents because she didn't want to worry us. She had started working to earn some money. Her plans were to stay in Moscow for no longer than a month. All we had to go on was that she was working at a bar. No name. No address. Nothing.

"Something didn't sit right with me, but I didn't know what it was. My parents were sick with worry, so I decided to go look for her. I told work I would be back in a week, two weeks tops. But little did I know, I would never go back to America again."

I gasp, shaking my head in shock. "What? You stayed in Russia?"

"Yes," he replies, nodding once.

"What about your parents?"

He inhales sharply. "I broke their hearts all over again."

I chew the inside of my cheek to stop the tears because I don't want to cry. Besides, what right do I have? Here he stands, suffering the memories, only for me to understand. I owe him the respect of listening to his story without tears.

"I didn't know what I was in for. I searched every fucking bar, but no one wanted to talk to a privileged American boy. They pretended they didn't speak English. But they all knew what I was there for.

"I looked for Zoey for over two weeks but found nothing. My parents told me to come home, but I just couldn't shake that feeling that something wasn't right, and with every corner I turned, that feeling just got worse. I was desperate to find her, so desperate that I did something that changed both our lives forever."

One decision changed the course of Saint's life. It's unfair it was the wrong choice to make.

"I was getting nowhere it seems because I was asking the wrong people. Moscow can be beautiful. But mostly, it can be cruel. I stumbled across a group of men who were nothing but trouble. That was the night I met Kazimir. I asked if he had seen Zoey. They all looked at her photo, and I knew they had, so I wasn't leaving until they told me where she was.

"But that's not how it works. These people, they abide by a different set of rules. They told me they would give me information if I did something for them. I was to deliver a small parcel the next night to an address they gave me. I had no idea what it was, but I didn't care. I agreed."

This is where his tale turns.

"I was on my way the next night. The moment I turned the corner, four masked men jumped me. They took me to an abandoned building and tortured me for twelve hours," he calmly relays, and I gasp, horrified.

"They wanted to know where I got the parcel from. I didn't budge. I couldn't. I knew Zoey's life depended on me being strong. I had already failed her once before, and I wasn't going to do it again. They were very…creative with their torture methods." He absentmindedly rubs over his side—over one of the many scars he has.

"But I still didn't talk. When they were satisfied, they removed their masks, and I saw they were the men who gave me the parcel."

"It was a test?" I question although I know the answer. I know the game well as Saint had delivered his own tests when we first met.

Saint nods. "Yes. They wanted to make sure they could trust me. And they did. They took me to meet their boss, Popov...the bastard who had my sister." Waves of anger roll off him. "He told me Zoey was well. She was happy. But I didn't believe him. She would never do that to my parents. He showed me a picture of her, and it seems a picture doesn't lie.

"He would allow me to see her if I did a small job for him. I had no choice, so I said yes. The small job was, in fact, a two-million-dollar drug deal. The thing about the bad guys is that they don't like change, so when they saw me, they instantly thought they were being set up. All hell broke loose, but I was a quarterback. And I also know how to throw a punch.

"When I came back bloody and bruised but holding that bag of money, Popov saw more value in me alive than he did dead. No doubt, the drug drop was yet another test, one that I passed. So from that day on, Popov made me his personal... security." Nothing but sarcasm laces his statement as it's clear security is the code word for what he was forced to become.

"I agreed, thinking that when I finally saw Zoey, we would get the fuck out of Dodge. But when he finally allowed me to see her..." He pauses, needing a moment. "It was apparent that wasn't happening."

"Why not?" I'm almost afraid to ask.

"Because the person standing before me wasn't my Zoey. She had changed because Popov had broken her. He had broken her spirit, her soul." The moonlight accentuates the shine to his eyes. "She was hooked on whatever drugs he fed her. She was his slave and a slave to whatever she snorted or injected. She was his personal zombie to do whatever he pleased."

Nausea rises, and I cover my mouth to stop from being sick.

"Most days, she sat by his feet while he patted her head. And other times..." He squeezes his eyes shut, before opening them.

There is no need for him to elaborate. I can fill in the blanks.

"So I worked for Popov. I did his dirty work in hopes that one day, he would get sick of Zoey and let her go. The times when she was sober, small glimmers of the spirited sister I once knew would shine, but she's broken, Willow, and it's all my fault."

"It's not your fault, Saint," I press, storming forward, clutching his hand. But he rips from my hold, not wanting my sympathy.

"Yes, it is. I should have asked if she was all right when she called. I was so caught up in my life that I didn't even think to ask if she was okay. I could have stopped all of this from happening."

I can see why he would blame himself, but we don't have a crystal ball. No one can predict the future. We all make choices, and those choices come with consequences.

"She was Popov's любимый. His favorite. His pet," he explains. "And in her own warped way, I think she believes he loves her. So for two and a half years, I've watched my sister be treated like nothing but a dog. I've wanted to escape with her so many times, but he's brainwashed her. She believes she can't live without him. She keeps going back to him, no matter how many times I set her free because that's what he does. He is the most potent drug of all."

"What about your parents?"

Saint casts his gaze downward. "I've saved them as much heartache as I can. I've told them that we're okay and that we've made a new life in Russia. But we will be back. One day. I can't go back home. I can't look in my mom's eyes after everything I've done. And I won't go back home until Zoey is with me. I won't leave her. Not again."

My heart breaks for this family. One man has destroyed the lives of so many—the man who is set on shaping my future like Zoey's.

"Popov is growing bored with Zoey. I'm surprised he's kept her for as long as he has. But I'm not stupid. I know it's because of me. I'm good at what I do because I have so much pent-up anger within me." He makes a tight fist on his chest over his heart. "Each person I kill, they wear Popov's face, and they bring me one step closer to bringing my sister home."

A tear rolls down my cheek, but Saint steps forward and wipes it away.

"Your husband," he spits, curling his lip in disgust. "He was my out. When he made that deal with Popov, I knew it was because Popov wanted a new pet. Zoey knew it too. After two and a half years, I finally saw my sister. She begged to go home. She begged me to do what Popov wanted, and in return, Popov promised to set me and my sister free. The conditions were simple—you were to take the place of Zoey. You were to be Popov's new pet."

I always knew this was my fate, but now, it means something else.

"So I told Popov I would do it. I would bring you to him. My conditions were that this was the last thing I would ever do for him. And that he would send Zoey to rehab. He agreed. And I believed him because he knew that I was at the end of my tether, and it was only a matter of time before I snapped."

"How can you believe he'd let you go?" I ask as Popov hardly strikes me as an upstanding citizen.

"Popov does hold some honor among his men, and he will let me go. I have served him well, and in return, he will allow me to leave with my head intact."

"What about your soul?" I whisper because the things he's been forced to do change a man.

"That was sold long ago," he replies desolately.

This is too much. I need a minute.

"I understand if you want nothing to do with me. I never should have agreed. I was just so desperate to get Zoey home, and I was running out of options. I should have told your husband and Popov to both go to hell. I should have taken Zoey home years ago," he says, his words heavy with regret.

The mention of Drew has my finger suddenly feeling like it weighs a thousand pounds. Peering down at my ring, it cements my stupidity for wearing it for as long as I have. Without thought, I brush past Saint and make my way toward the water. There is something I have to do.

When I enter the water, the coolness sends a shiver down

my spine. Something about the water is cathartic. I suppose it's because it's our life source. It has the ability to baptize and cleanse, which is why I remove the ring from my finger and hurl it along with my regrets into the ocean.

The moment it leaves my hand, tears stream down my cheeks. There are so many players in this equation, all of which have played a part in my future. I don't know what comes next. Everything has changed.

If Saint lets me go, it will ensure his death, as well as Zoey's. But if he sticks to the plan, then it will ensure mine. This was never clear cut, but now, everything is a fucking mess.

Saint stands beside me, allowing me the space I need. But I don't want space. I want to forget. With a hesitant touch, I reach for his hand and am surprised when he links his fingers through mine. We don't speak. We stand in waist-deep water, peering up into the star-filled sky, wondering what tomorrow holds.

"I'm sorry, ahгел."

I now understand why he calls me angel. I was supposed to save him. An angel and her bad Saint.

"Make me forget," I whisper, turning toward him, not masking my tears.

His brow scrunches in uncertainty, but I clear up any confusion when I close the distance between us and press my lips to his.

He freezes as he still isn't comfortable with me touching him, but after a few seconds, he grows lax and allows me control.

The gesture unleashes everything bottled up within me, and I coax his mouth open with my tongue. He groans low and surrenders. We slam our bodies together, frantically pawing at each other. He lifts me up, and I wrap my legs around his waist.

We kiss like starved fiends, the passion between us setting every part of my body alight. I yank at his hair, and he bites my lip. Our tongues clash together, forgetting everything but this electric potency between us.

I want him all over me, and when I feel his delicious erection pressed against me, I know he wants that too. Tearing my mouth away, I kiss my way down his throat, inhaling deeply because he smells so good. His racing pulse hammers beneath me, and without thought, I bite down and suck—hard.

A raucous moan leaves him as he tilts his head backward, allowing me free rein. I lick and bite, latching onto him and feasting on his flesh. All bashfulness is gone when I rock against his hard-on, hinting at what I want. What I need.

He reads my body perfectly and walks us back toward the shore with me kissing and devouring him whole. He lowers us to the sand, our lips never missing a beat. Still kissing frantically, he thrusts his hand into my shorts and sinks a finger into my sex.

I gasp, breaking our kiss as I need to breathe before I pass out.

He finds me wet, and that has nothing to do with the water. "Oh, fuck," he hums, licking his bottom lip, his eyes slipping to half-mast. I shamefully arch into him, deepening the angle. We both hiss at the profound intrusion.

Everything is happening so fast, but I don't fight it. He

works my body into a frenzy until I'm panting, clawing at his slick shoulders, begging to come. He's all over me, his lips, hands, his bare chest pressed to mine. But I suddenly want more.

I've never felt such a strong desire before, and the need for him to be my first collides into me. But I don't know how to ask, so I decide to let my actions speak for me.

With his fingers buried deep within me and our lips locked urgently, I timidly brush over the bulge in the front of his shorts. When I feel how hard he is, my sex pulses. I am so turned on. I unsnap his button, and with fumbling fingers, I slip my hand into his shorts.

He isn't wearing any underwear, so I touch his hot, hard length instantly. He rips his lips away, pressing his forehead to my shoulder as he hums low. I'm all thumbs because I've never touched someone of his size before. I take my time feeling him because each stroke has us both moaning fervidly.

"Show me what to do?" I whisper, embarrassed.

"What you're doing right now feels incredible," he encourages, pumping into my grip.

He circles my clit. I mimic the action and trace around his thick tip. If possible, he grows bigger in my hand.

"I need you naked." He doesn't give me a chance to reply because he's yanking off my shorts and tank. My bra soon follows.

He caresses my breasts before lowering his head and suckling them with his lips and tongue. I am a soft mess, but a tight coil unravels inside. He circles my nipples, sucking them, before biting them softly. He sinks two fingers back inside me, all the while lapping at my breasts. I think I'm about to die.

"More," I pant, yanking his hair, my body undulating with his touch.

He attempts to slide down, but I clutch his cheeks, dragging his face to mine. His uncertainty isn't a sight I see too often, so it makes what I'm about to ask a little easier. "No, I want you…inside me."

His eyes widen before he gently brushes the hair from my cheeks. "Not here," he says, which leaves me speechless.

"You don't want to?" I can't help but feel a little rejected.

"Of course, I do." He grabs my hand and places it over the front of his shorts. The evidence doesn't lie. So what's the problem? "Just not here. Not now."

This is hardly the place where I'd choose to lose my virginity, but with Saint pressed to me, it feels perfect. "If what you said is true and Popov is coming, then I don't want my first time to be with someone like him. I want it to be with you," I confess shyly, stroking over his hard-on.

His eyes flutter, but he eventually shifts from my grip. "I'll get you off this island. I promise."

But I want him. Now. "But—"

He swoops forward, stealing the air from my lungs. "No more talking."

Openly kissing him has my mind turning to mush, so this will do—for now.

We kiss madly, unable to stop touching one another, and it feels so good. My sex pulses with every touch, and Saint knows it. I've never wanted to come more than I do right now. I am on the cusp of begging, but the air is ripped from my lungs when Saint flips us over so I'm straddling him. I have no idea what he wants me to do until he drags me up his body and coaxes me onto his face.

I try to resist, horrified, but I don't stand a chance when he positions me so my knees are on either side of his head. He anchors my hips so I'm slanted at an angle where he can latch onto my sex and drive his tongue into me.

I scream, instantly rolling my hips and working in sync with his mouth. He cups my waist while I lean backward, resting my hands against his hard abs. He begins to eat me out slowly, arching his neck and burying himself between my heat. Being suspended above him this way gives me the perfect bird's-eye view of him pleasuring me to the brink of ecstasy.

He doesn't rush. He pays attention to every inch of me, suckling and licking. His fingers dig into my hips as I unhurriedly arch into him. Being positioned this way is beyond intimate because our eyes are locked. We watch one another, and I know he's opted to devour me this way because I'm in control.

I control the depth, the rhythm. He's handed over the reins. And for a control freak, I can only imagine how difficult that must be. The thought has me moving faster.

He hums around my sex, the vibrations rocking me deeply, and I groan, bowing backward, running my hands over his stomach. He flicks his tongue over my clit before sucking gently. I see stars and increase the tempo, ensuring not to go too fast because I don't want to hurt him. But Saint's grip on my hips tightens, and he coaxes me to move faster.

I am powerless and surrender.

He eats me out while I ride his face, screaming in wanton desire. A surge whips through me, and I arch back, bucking forward. Anchoring one hand on his washboard abs, I snare his hair with the other and coerce his mouth to work faster, his tongue deeper, and he happily obliges.

All reservations are long gone as I chase my release. And when Saint bites my clit and slaps my ass hard, I come with a thunderous cry. My body undulates, and I ride the wave because nothing has ever felt this good.

Saint continues to suckle me, my arousal coating his face. The aftershocks rock me for minutes, but when I finally come back down, another hunger burns. I watch as he wipes his lips deliberately before sucking his fingers, licking my arousal clean.

The sight sucker-punches me, and I slide down his body, frantically pulling down his shorts.

When his enormous cock springs to life, I gasp. I'm suddenly afraid I've bitten off more than I can chew, figuratively speaking. He is impossibly masculine with soft dark curls highlighting his straight, thick, deliciously plump cock.

"You don't have to," he hoarsely says, peering down at me. But that's not the issue. I don't know where to start.

"Tell me what you like." I bite my lip nervously.

He groans and cups my flushed cheeks. "Just go slow. It's been a while."

I nod, understanding what he means. Yes, he had sex with some random woman, but this is different. This is more personal in some ways as he's allowing me control. And for someone who wouldn't allow me to touch him just days ago, this is a big step.

"Okay," I whisper.

He lifts his hips so I'm able to remove his shorts. Completely naked out here in the wilderness feels nothing but natural. I sit back on my heels, examining him from head to toe. From the rise of his chest to his well-defined abs, he is a true vision.

When my attention lands between his legs, I'm unable to conceal my hunger. And neither can Saint.

"Fuck," he hisses, tipping his chin upward.

His desire has me reaching out and gripping his cock gently. It twitches in my hand. We both need more.

I begin to stroke his shaft, the heat from his skin almost burning me alive, but I like it, and I increase the tempo. He is so thick; it takes me a while to find my groove, but when he reaches down and places his hand over mine, encouraging me to squeeze him harder, I'm quick to catch up to speed.

Saint likes pain, just as I like to be punished, a fact I wasn't even aware of until I met him. Him smacking my ass as I came on his tongue has me increasing my rhythm, whimpering when I see a drop of moisture glisten at his plump tip.

Groaning, I work on instinct and bend down to lick it off. Saint's hips jolt off the ground as a guttural moan leaves him. His taste is spicy and sweet, and I want more.

Brushing my hair to one shoulder, I wrap my lips around his cock and slip him into my mouth gradually. Tears sting my eyes as I try to take him all in, but it's impossible. I pause, savoring the feel of him.

"Ангел." He sighs, his trembling body evidence he's holding back.

His voice, his taste, the feel of him surrendering, everything about this explodes around me, and I relax my throat, taking more of him in. He hits the back of my throat, and I gag, but when he attempts to pull out, I hold him and encourage him to move with me.

Drawing back, I cover his root with my hand and begin to move my head up and down, using my tongue and mouth, just as he did to me. He grunts and begins to buck his hips, fisting my hair when I increase the tempo.

I sample him, stroking and sucking, the combination leaving me slick once again. Even though he uses my hair as reins, I know it's to control the speed so he doesn't go in too deep, too fast. He's holding back, but I don't want him to.

I intensify the movements of my lips and hand until he's groaning, thrusting into my mouth wildly. If possible, he seems to grow larger, and I whimper when a salty sweetness lingers on my tongue.

A string of Russian leaves him, which I can only assume are curse words because they are heavy with lust and a desperate need to come. I hollow my cheeks, squeezing him tightly, and he roars, his hips rocketing off the sand.

His response spurs me on.

I tongue the underside of his shaft while drawing back and suckling his round tip. "Fuck, ангел. I'm going to come." He attempts to push me away, but it's music to my ears.

I slide my lips back down over his shaft and bob madly,

breathing deeply through my nose as he thrusts his hips. With a piercing growl, he quickly brushes me aside, and I watch in awe as ribbons of come coat his stomach.

His breaths are labored, and his cheeks are flushed as his body ripples with the powerful orgasm I elicited from him. The vision will forever be singed onto my soul.

"Fuck," he pants, sagging into a well-sated mess, squeezing his eyes shut.

Unable to resist, I cautiously trace my finger through his arousal, mesmerized by its texture and what it's capable of doing—creating life. His eyes pop open as he watches me, breathlessly. I draw my finger to my mouth, and when my tongue darts out for a taste, Saint hums low.

I don't know why I just did that, but it's apparent I'm changing, but who am I changing into?

"Come here, ангел." Saint drags me down beside him, curling his naked body around mine. As we fall into a deep slumber, the question lingers—who are we *both* changing into?

CHAPTER FOURTEEN

Being with her erases the pain, and I will move heaven and hell to protect her. I will figure out another way to save Zoey, but I can't give her to Popov.

She is mine.

She always has been.

Day 34

"We leave tomorrow morning."

I never thought I'd hear the words, but Saint did what he promised—he made a raft capable of getting us off this island.

We worked for two solid days, day and night, as time was the enemy. We didn't know if that plane was Popov's, but we worked like it was. We didn't speak about what happened between us because we didn't need to.

The gentle touches, the longing stares, they all amounted to what we both felt. Getting off this island was even more imperative now because I need to know if what I feel for Saint is real.

When I watch him drag the raft from the water, his strength never more commanding than now, I know what this is. We have bonded over the most heinous circumstances, but somehow, under the horror, I'm stronger. I could have surrendered to the darkness, and I almost did. But I survived because I need to know what the next chapter of my life is.

"You okay?" Saint brushes the hair from my brow, interrupting my thoughts.

I shake my head to clear it. "Yes." I smile, leaning into his touch. "I can't believe you did it."

"We did it," he corrects, running his thumb along the apple of my cheek. "I wouldn't be alive if it wasn't for you. Thank you, by the way."

"It's only come about a week too late, but you're welcome," I tease while he smirks. "I might wash before dinner." We are running low on supplies and have been limiting our bathing. But now that we're finally leaving, I plan to depart this island with clean hair.

"Take your time. I'll have everything ready by the time you're done."

"The last supper," I say, a touch of sadness to my words because I don't know what's ahead of us.

Saint sighs, before bending forward and caressing the

cross at my throat. "The last supper where we eat fish," he quips, instantly easing the mood. "Go." He gives my lips a quick peck before turning me around and slapping my ass.

I yelp and hustle forward, desperate to get away before I ask for more.

I grab my things and make my way toward the pond. We've had some brief rain, which has been enough to keep the water fresh, but I will be glad when I can stand under a warm shower.

There are a lot of things I look forward to like socks, using a toilet, and eating a buttload of chocolate, but the most important is I wonder what's in store for Saint and me. He's told me he will let me go, but what does that mean for us?

He would never leave Zoey, which means I will return to America while he'll return to Russia. There is no way I am setting foot in that country, so I what? Wait for him to come home? This should be the least of my problems, but it seems to be the one weighing the heaviest. What awaits him? I gulp at the thought.

When I reach the pond, I take one last look around my sanctuary because no matter what, good and bad, I will never forget my time here. Things haven't been easy, but I can leave with the satisfaction of knowing I did everything to survive.

I take my time, floating on my back as I stare into the heavens. It's hard to remember the woman I once was because so much has changed. I still don't know what I will do about Drew, but I know he has to pay.

Going to the police would be the sensible thing to do, but a blood-thirsting voice inside me whispers he deserves something much worse. Shaking away that darkness, I wash before quickly getting dressed.

My choice of clothing is slim, but this green summer dress has proven to be my favorite. It's pretty, and it reminds me of my former life, a life which now feels alien on my skin.

I don't know where this doom and gloom has come from. You'd think I'd be happy to get off this island, but the unknown scares me. Here, things were simple, but out there, in the real world, I will have to face what I've done.

Zoey comes to mind. I was supposed to be the key to her freedom, but the only freedom I've granted is my own. Saint will still be a prisoner, and so will Zoey.

My stomach twists at the thought.

I can't help but feel sorry for her. She never wanted this, any of it. But she was forced into slavery, and in turn, she lost who she was. I can still hear Saint's anguish when retelling his story. He got his sister back, and she finally escaped from Popov's mind games, but now, thanks to me, they are back to square one.

How can I celebrate my freedom when I know it comes with a price?

There has to be some other way, a solution where we all win. But the only winner is Popov because a man like him doesn't lose.

Sighing, I brush my fingers through my hair, leaving it loose so it can dry.

I suddenly feel so disheartened. Saint will suffer because of me. How can I go back to my comfortable life knowing that? I can't. I need to talk to him. There has to be some other way where things aren't so bleak for him. I can't live with myself if there isn't. But the truth is, unless Saint delivers me to Popov, he will never be free.

Slipping into my tennis shoes, I quickly make my way through the terrain, the need to see Saint overwhelming me. I almost can't breathe. A shadow overcasts me, and when I peer into the sky, I hear a sound which tears my heart into two.

"Ангел!"

Something is gravely wrong.

Adrenaline soars through me as I run, frantic to get to Saint. When I hear my name again, panic overcomes me. "I'm coming! I'm here!"

The blood whooshes through my ears, and my heart is in my throat as I continue running faster than I ever have before. I duck and weave my way through the forest, knowing the route like the back of my hand. But when I see Saint storming toward me, I come to a screeching stop.

"You have to hide!" he screams, waving his hands for me to turn back around.

"Hide?" I question, panic strangling me. "Why?" When he reaches me, he grips my bicep and attempts to drag me away. I yank from his hold. "What's going on?"

His eyes are wild, his breaths labored. It can only mean one thing. "He's…here."

Two words shouldn't be able to change your world forever, but those two simple words have.

I stagger backward, my mind reeling as I shake my head. "No, that's impossible." But it's not. Thanks to my SOS, I led the bad guys straight to us.

"Please, ангел." He wraps his hand around the back of my neck and draws me into him. He kisses my forehead with a quiver. "Please hide. I'll tell them you're dead, and I will send someone to get you. I promise."

Everything is spinning out of control, but in the end, Saint stuck true to his word, confirming what I always knew—he's a good man. He has the opportunity to save himself and his sister, but he's chosen me.

Tears fall freely because no one, no one has ever done that for me before.

I throw my arms around him, hugging him tightly. I never want to let go. "Thank you," I whisper, nestling close and committing our connection to the deepest place in my heart.

I will never forget this…and it's because of this…that I can't.

"Go. Please." He lays frantic kisses all over me, and I close my eyes, relishing in his touch. I don't know when I will feel this again. Our seconds are precious, and I will savor every one. "I will come find you. I promise."

But I can't hide forever.

Pulling from his hold, I place my palm to his cheek. I will never forget him. "I now know why you're called Saint."

He blinks once, confused. I soon seal our fate.

"I can't."

"You can't?" he repeats, eyes wide.

"I won't allow you to sacrifice everything for me. How could I live with myself if I did?"

"Obey me!" he orders, but I've made up my mind.

"Forgive me." Before he has a chance to ask what I'm asking absolution for, I raise my leg and knee him in the balls, catching him unaware. This was the only way I could escape.

He grunts, clutching himself, his face turning red as he slumps forward. He reaches for me with one hand, but I dance out of his range and run like a woman possessed—I run toward what my fate always was.

"Ангел!" His pained cries only have me running faster because I won't be the cause of so many people's demise.

I think about Saint's parents, about Zoey, and about Saint. They now have a chance to live a normal life. I once thought I would never give up everything and sell my soul for another like Saint has done, but as I run toward the shore, I now know that I would.

A white yacht comes into view, preparing me for what I'm about to do. Just as I'm about to emerge from the trees, ready to face my destiny, I'm dragged backward and slammed into something warm, something which sings to my heart. "Don't be the hero. This is what you've always wanted. Your freedom."

I sag against him, crying the last of my tears. "I found something I want more."

The air is heavy, our hearts beating to a frantic staccato.

Closing my eyes, I confess something which cements who I am. "…You." Regardless of his crimes, I want him because he is mine.

A stunned gasp leaves him as his grip slackens, allowing me to take the last step, which, ironically, is the first step toward the end. The sun shines brightly, but it does nothing to thaw the chill to my bones.

I can hear Saint walking behind me, but I don't have the guts to face him. I pick up Harriet Pot Pie and wait with my head held high.

The huge yacht is one you'd expect to see a Hollywood starlet lazing on in the sun as the paparazzi have a field day taking her picture. It's definitely a lot nicer than the one I was on a lifetime ago. But I suppose being a Russian mobster does have its perks.

When the door slides open and a man in white chinos and a short-sleeved shirt emerges, I wonder if maybe Saint was wrong because this man doesn't look like a bad guy. He's wearing a pair of Ray-Bans, so I can't see his eyes, but I certainly am not getting the psychopath vibe.

However, when a slender woman with long dirty blonde hair in a red bikini saunters out, her arrogant nose tilted to the heavens, I can't say the same for her. She makes my skin crawl, and when her gaze narrows on me, I shrink backward.

Who are these people?

Saint answers my question for me.

"Zoey..."

What?

That's Zoey? I don't know what I was expecting, but I certainly wasn't expecting her to look like she was moments away from ripping out my eyeballs.

"Hello, brother."

What the fuck is going on?

The man removes his sunglasses, and the air is suddenly thick with supremacy. He instantly rouses a ball of nerves inside me. "Hello, Saint. I was so worried we had lost you. Luckily you had the good sense to leave me a way to find you with that SOS."

The anger rolling off Saint leaves me breathless. But eventually, he puts an end to my questions. "Hello...Aleksei."

The world crumbles around me, and my knees buckle. *This* is my kidnapper? This man isn't by any means the monster I envisioned him to be. I instantly let Harriet Pot Pie free. She doesn't need to bear witness to this.

Saint's fingers instantly wrap around my bicep, stopping me from falling into a messy heap. But regardless, I still feel seconds away from passing out.

I watch on in what feels like a hallucinating state as Aleksei and Zoey descend the ladder and make their way toward us. I'm impressed he can scale the narrow rungs in his brown Italian loafers.

Saint stands by my side, never letting me go. I'm thankful for this touch because I need it. They stop a few feet away.

Aleksei doesn't hide his appraisal of me. I instantly shuffle my feet. He makes me nervous. His astute blue eyes scan over me, as he no doubt wants to look at his prize.

He is younger than I thought he would be. In his late 40s, I'd guess, and in good shape. He's dressed sharply, and his cologne smells like sandalwood. His wavy dark brown hair is slicked back, exposing his strong features and full lips.

Some may call him attractive. Zoey certainly does.

She makes her stance clear as she huddles close to him, eyeballing the fuck out of me. I don't understand what I've done wrong.

Saint said she was ready to go home, but her body language does not display that. "So this is the bitch who is supposed to take my place?"

I blink once, my mouth agape.

"You definitely got screwed, darling." She loops her arm through Aleksei's, grinning victoriously when my cheeks flush. Aleksei seems to enjoy the possibility of a catfight.

"Zoey," Saint scolds, stunned. "What is wrong with you?" I can understand his confusion because his impression was evidently wrong. "You wanted me to do this. You told me you wanted to go home."

She rolls her eyes, eyes so much like her brothers. "Aleksei *is* my home."

The man in question grins, and I instantly have the urge to slap the smugness from his cheeks. "You must be Willow," he says with a slight accent, gently removing himself from Zoey's claws. He is well spoken.

If looks could kill, I would be a smoldering pile of ashes as Zoey glares.

I dare not breathe as he steps closer. He is tall, and his broad shoulders make him all the more intimidating. "It's lovely to meet you. I have been waiting for this moment for weeks." His attention snaps to Saint, hinting waiting isn't usually a word in his vocabulary.

"There were some setbacks," Saint says, drawing me into his side protectively. The action doesn't go unnoticed by Aleksei.

He eyeballs the connection, before slowly rivaling Saint's glower. "Yes, well you can tell me all about it when we get on the yacht."

That sounds like an awful idea. Saint agrees as we both stand our ground.

A sulking Zoey notices Saint shadowing me also, and a wicked grin tips at her red lips. She doesn't see me as a threat any longer.

"Is there a problem?" Aleksei asks; his icy voice filled with warning.

As much as I appreciate Saint's protection, we can't stay here. I gently shrug out of his hold, nodding subtly to hint I'm okay. He is seconds from exploding.

"No," I reply, deciding to keep my replies to a minimum.

"Good girl." Aleksei's piercing blue eyes reflect dominance and control, but when he looks at me, I don't see complete coldness. There seems to be some humanity lurking beneath the shadows.

He reaches out to brush the hair from my cheeks. I stand still, my chest rising and falling rapidly. "You're absolutely beautiful."

A growl slashes the air, and I know without looking it's come from Saint.

This moment is suffocating me, and what I see next has me yelping and raising my hands in surrender.

It happens so quickly.

One second, I'm facing a gun-toting Zoey, and the next, Saint is shielding me, holding a gun of his own, the gun he had hidden in his shorts in the small of his back. "Zoey!" he shouts, protecting me with his back as he shoves me behind him. "Put the gun down."

Aleksei turns to look at Zoey, clearly surprised she had

the balls to pull a gun on me. His attention then rivets on Saint. This world of madness is one he has created. And when he smirks, it appears he wouldn't have it any other way.

"Move, Saint. I don't want to hurt you," Zoey snarls.

"What is the matter with you? I did what you asked." Saint beseeches her to tell him what's going on.

I risk a glance around his body, and what I see, terrifies me. Zoey cackles, waving the gun like it's a toy. "Yes, I asked you to do this so I could fucking kill this bitch. Alek is mine. And any whore who thinks they can replace me will suffer the same fate as this bitch."

Aleksei couldn't look happier. His project has turned rouge. Saint was right—Popov is the most potent drug of all.

"So you never wanted to go home?" he asks, his voice filled with utter defeat.

She snickers, utterly amused at his gullibility. "No, brother. I lied."

And that's it.

No excuses to pardon her behavior. She is a desperate woman, and it appears no one, not even her brother, will stand in her way as she cocks her gun. "Now move. I'm done playing nice."

I huddle behind Saint, petrified because there is no way Zoey is of sound mind. Saint was right. She is broken, but I don't think she cared being carved into this twisted person. I can't believe I felt sorry for her. I can't even imagine how betrayed Saint feels because all of this was for nothing.

Saint steadies his arm, training his gun on his sister. "You're sick, Zoey. Let me help you."

"I don't want your help!" she screams. "I told you to go home, that I was happy with Alek, but you always have to be the good guy, don't you? But it's too late...you had your chance to help me, and you blew it. Alek saved me. Not you."

She has played on Saint's insecurities, ones which were the reason he chose this life in the first place. He did all of this for her...

"You ungrateful bitch." It's out before I can stop myself, but how dare she. This isn't Saint's fault, and I'll be damned if I allow her to make him think otherwise.

Aleksei turns to look at me, lips parted. He likes what he sees. Goose bumps, not of the good kind, coat my skin as I suddenly feel like prey.

"Enough," he says, appearing bored by the melodramatics. "Give me the gun, Zoey."

I can't hide my surprise, which seems to please Aleksei.

"What?" Zoey whines. "No, I want that whore dead!"

The air falls silent because Zoey has just done something which she shouldn't have—she disobeyed her master.

"Give me the gun," he repeats slowly. There is warning lacing every word.

When I don't hear her argue, I risk a glance around Saint, who stands rigid, transfixed by the sight of Zoey walking submissively toward Aleksei. Her eyes seem glazed over like someone in a trance, but I suppose she is—she's spellbound by this asshole.

She passes him the gun, then drops to her knees beside him.

The sight sickens me. He begins to pat her hair like a

beloved dog. She nuzzles into his leg, moaning. "Now, as entertaining as this all is, we have a deadline. So get on the yacht." He points the gun at Saint, who stands, unmoving, his own gun still raised.

Something is about to explode, and I'm afraid to see what the outcome is.

"You disappoint me, брат."

"I am *not* your brother," Saint spits, his aim directed on Popov.

"You're right..." The noise hits me before I realize that a shot has been fired. When a pained grunt leaves Saint, and his gun drops into the sand, I know he's the one who's been shot.

"No!" I scream, attempting to turn him around to see if he's okay. But he shrugs from my hold. He's still standing, but he's clutching his bloody shoulder.

"It's okay, ahreл. Just a flesh wound," he assures me with a firm nod.

Zoey's maniacal laughter reveals she and Aleksei are a perfect match—a match made in hell.

Aleksei appears unperplexed at the sight. "You're not my brother. You're my fucking employee! So do what I say and get on that goddamn boat before I make you choose who I kill. I only need one of them."

Saint is barely holding it together, and when Aleksei raises his gun, intent on shooting him again, I quickly run in front of Saint and drop to my knees. I've caught Aleksei off guard as he takes a small step backward. Saint stands behind me, placing his hand on my upper shoulder.

"Well, this is a pleasant surprise. Maybe I will spare your

life, after all, Saint. You've taught her well. And ангел…I like it. It suits her."

"Thank you…мастер." I now know why Saint asked me to call him this. He was preparing me for this moment in time, for the moment when I met my master.

Aleksei's mouth pops open before thunderous laughter erupts. "You never fail me, Saint. Sorry about shooting you. It's just a scratch," he flippantly says, waving his gun in the air. "Let's go. We have so much to discuss." It appears he wants to know everything there is to know about his new plaything.

He pockets the gun, before gripping Zoey by the back of her neck. He isn't gentle, but she moans deeply. "You must be punished for your behavior."

"Yes," Zoey whimpers in anticipation, standing when he yanks her up by the hair. Is this what I'm to become?

Saint's fingers squeeze my shoulder as he watches Aleksei abuse his sister, but he doesn't move to help her. Aleksei drags her toward the yacht by her hair.

"Oh, god," I cry, blinking back my tears.

"It's okay, ангел. I won't let him hurt you." I place my hand over his, needing the connection more than ever.

"What about you?" I whisper because who is going to protect him.

My question remains unanswered because when Aleksei gestures with his head that we're to follow, we have no other choice but obey. I'm about to pocket Saint's gun, but Aleksei tsks me. I raise my hands in surrender as he's shown what a good shot he is.

Saint helps me stand, but I suddenly remember Harriet

Pot Pie. She's better off here anyway because where we're going, I wouldn't wish upon my worst enemy. "Bye, Harriet Pot Pie," I whisper, a single tear scoring my cheek. I quickly brush it away with the back of my hand.

"She'll be okay," Saint assures me as we hobble to the yacht.

Turning, I take one last look at the place I once thought was hell on earth, but as Aleksei presents me his hand, offering me assistance as I board the yacht, I know this place wasn't so bad. Saint and I made it ours, but now, nothing will be ours ever again.

I slip my hand into Aleksei's, whose eyes flicker with excitement. When I make my way to the top, I quickly turn to help Saint as he's wounded. But he doesn't need my help. He was always the strong one.

Aleksei makes his way over to the control, humming happily while Zoey kneels by his feet. Saint's sharp eyes scan our surroundings, looking for an escape, but when six men appear from inside the galley, we know we don't have a fighting chance.

"Buckle up," Aleksei singsongs as the motor stirs to life.

One of the men holds up a length of rope. "Nice to see you, Saint." Saint lunges forward, but the man knocks him out cold, and he falls to the deck with a thud.

I scream, intent on killing this bastard with my bare hands, but he apparently has no qualms about hitting women and punches me in the nose. I stumble backward, cupping my face, but he shoves me down. My ass hits a chair, and he goes about tying me to it.

I glare at Aleksei, strategizing ways I'm going to kill him. He peers over his shoulder and has the gall to wink. My rebellion seems to rouse him, and he smirks. "You and I are going to have so much fun."

With Saint unconscious at my feet, I allow myself to be kidnapped yet again, and just how this tale began…I'm tied up, on a yacht, destination unknown.

FALLEN SAINT, Volume Two coming July 2019!

ACKNOWLEDGEMENTS

My wonderful husband, Daniel. I love you. Thank you for believing in me even when I didn't believe in myself.

My ever-supporting parents. You guys are the best. I am who I am because of you. I love you.

My agent, Kimberly Brower from Brower Literary & Management. Thank you for your patience and thank you for being an amazing human being.

My editor, Jenny Sims. What can I say other than I LOVE YOU! Thank you for everything.

My proofreaders—Lisa Edward—More Than Words Proofreading, and Virginia Tesi Carey. You guys are the best! Ps. Lisa, you are amazing!

Sommer Stein, you NAILED this cover! Thank you for being so patient and making the process so fun.

A special shout-out to: Christina and Lauren, Elle Kennedy, Lisa Edward, SC Stephens, Vi Keeland, Penelope Ward, Adriane Leigh, Pam Godwin, Natasha Preston, Beverly Preston, Natasha Madison, Len Webster, K. Bromberg, Tina Gephart, Rachel Brookes, Debra Anastasia, Stina Lindenblatt, Sylvain Reynard, J.L. Drake, Jay McLean, Heidi McLaughlin, Audrey Carlan, BJ Harvey, K.A. Tucker, Kylie Scott, Mia Sheridan, Helena Hunting, Tijan, Kimberly Whalen, Gemma, Louise, Heyne, Random House, Kinneret Zmora, Hugo & Cie, Planeta, Art Eternal, Carbaccio, Fischer, Harper Brazil, Bookouture, Egmont Bulgaria, Brilliance Publishing, Hope Editions, USA TODAY/ Happy Ever After, Buzzfeed, BookBub, PopSugar, Love Letters Convention—Berlin,

Aestas Book Blog, Natasha is a Book Junkie, Hugues De Saint Vincent, Nikki McCombe, Mary Matta, Romance Writers of Australia, Paris, New York, Danielle Sanchez, Sarah Sentz, Ria Alexander, Rosa Sharon, Amy Jennings, Gel Ytayz, Jennifer Spinninger, Vanessa Silva Martins, Cheri Grand Anderman, Lauren Rosa, Kristin Dwyer, and Nina Bocci.

To the endless blogs that have supported me since day one—You guys rock my world.

My reader group; My Sinners—sending you all a big kiss.

My beautiful family—Mum, Papa, my sister—Fran, Matt, Samantha, Amelia, Gayle, Peter, Luke, Leah, Jimmy, Jack, Shirley, Michael, Rob, Elisa, Evan, Alex, Francesca, and my aunties, uncles, and cousins—I am the luckiest person alive to know each and every one of you. You brighten up my world in ways I honestly cannot express.

Samantha and Amelia— I love you both so very much.

To my family in Holland and Italy, and abroad. Sending you guys much love and kisses.

Zia Rosetta and Zia Giuseppina—you are in our hearts. Always.

My fur babies— mamma loves you so much! Buckwheat, you are my best buddy. Dacca, I will always protect you from the big bad Bellie. Mitch, refer to Dacca's comment. Jag, you're a wombat in disguise. Bellie, you're a devil in disguise. And Ninja, thanks for watching over me.

To anyone I have missed, I'm sorry! It wasn't intentional!

Last but certainly not least, I want to thank YOU! Thank you for welcoming me into your hearts and homes. My readers are the BEST readers in this entire universe! Love you all!

CONNECT WITH MONICA JAMES

Facebook: www.facebook.com/authormonicajames
Twitter: twitter.com/monicajames81
Goodreads: www.goodreads.com/MonicaJames
Instagram: www.instagram.com/authormonicajames/
Website: monicajamesbooks.blogspot.com.au/
Pinterest: www.pinterest.com/monicajames81/
BookBub: bit.ly/2E3eCIw
Amazon: amzn.to/2EWZSyS
Join my Reader Group: bit.ly/2nUaRyi

ABOUT THE AUTHOR

Monica James spent her youth devouring the works of Anne Rice, William Shakespeare, and Emily Dickinson.

When she is not writing, Monica is busy running her own business, but she always finds a balance between the two. She enjoys writing honest, heartfelt, and turbulent stories, hoping to leave an imprint on her readers. She draws her inspiration from life.

She is a bestselling author in the U.S.A., Australia, Canada, France, Germany, Israel, and The U.K.

Monica James resides in Melbourne, Australia, with her wonderful family, and menagerie of animals. She is slightly obsessed with cats, chucks, and lip gloss, and secretly wishes she was a ninja on the weekends.

Printed in Great Britain
by Amazon